By Daryl Gregory

*Pandemonium*
*The Devil's Alphabet*

# the devil's alphabet

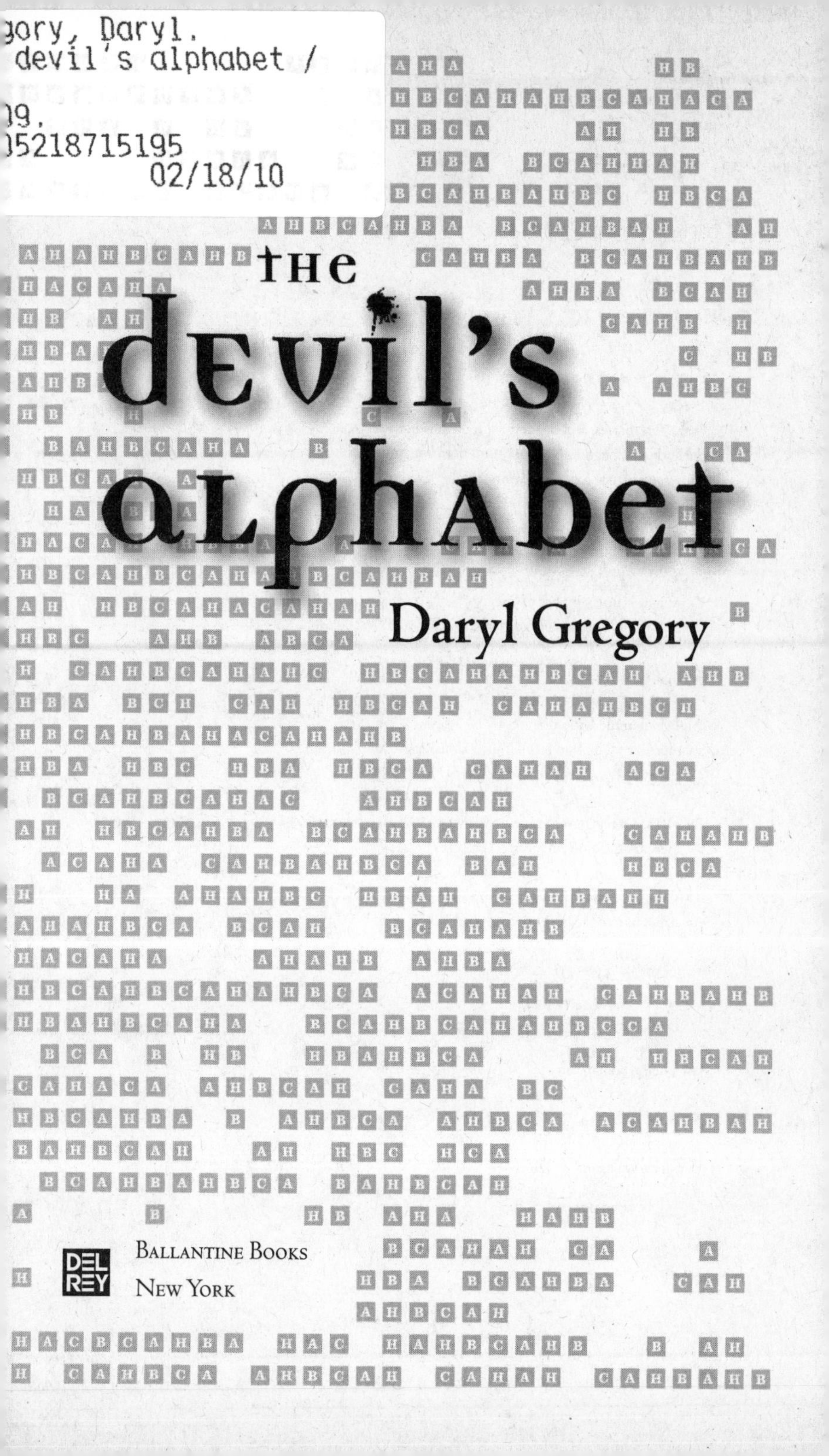

# The Devil's Alphabet

Daryl Gregory

DEL REY
Ballantine Books
New York

A Del Rey Trade Paperback Original



Published in the United States by Del Rey, an imprint of The Random House Publishing Group, a division of Random House, Inc., New York.



This book contains an excerpt from *Pandemonium* by Daryl Gregory. Available in trade paperback from Del Rey.

ISBN 978-0-345-50117-2

Printed in the United States of America

www.delreybooks.com

9 8 7 6 5 4 3 2 1

*Book design by Elizabeth A. D. Eno*

To Darrell and Thelma Gregory

# acknowledgments

Many people helped make the book you're holding (or viewing, or listening to) and I owe them my sincere thanks. Chris Schluep, with a deft hand on the editorial stick, guided this book the final miles over the chilly Hudson. Many more people at Del Rey worked to get these words in front of you, including some—Fleetwood Robbins (who acquired this book when its title was *Work to be Named Later*), and SueMoe! (one word, with exclamation mark)—who've moved on and are greatly missed. Deanna Hoak signed up for a second tour of copyediting. And David Bowie—well, he has no idea how much he helped me write this thing.

My gratitude goes as well to the early readers: Charles Coleman Finlay, Sarah Kelly, Cathrynne M. Valente, and the rest of the Blue Heaven workshop crew who critiqued the first draft; Heather Lindsley, who fine-tuned the second; and Kathy Bieschke, Gary Delafield, and Elizabeth Delafield, who marked up hundreds of pages in between. Emma and Ian Gregory read none of it, but informed all of it.

And to all the Gregorys, Barbaras, Meyers, Riddles, and

Heatons, the multitude of aunts, uncles, and cousins—so many cousins!—scattered over the Smokies: thanks for feeding your Yankee relation every time he came to town. Even more than the bizarre residents of Switchcreek, the lonely boy in this book is a creature of pure imagination.

A C B C A B A C A B
C B A C A C B C A C
A C B C A B A C A B
C B A C A H B C A C
A C B C A B A C A B

# chapter I

PAX KNEW HE was almost to Switchcreek when he saw his first argo.

The gray-skinned man was hunched over the engine of a decrepit, roofless pickup truck stalled hood-up at the side of the road. He straightened as Pax's car approached, unfolding like an extension ladder. Ten or eleven feet tall, angular as a dead tree, skin the mottled gray of weathered concrete. No shirt, just overalls that came down to his bony knees. He squinted at Pax's windshield.

Jesus, Pax thought. He'd forgotten how big they were.

He didn't recognize the argo, but that didn't mean much, for a lot of reasons. He might even be a cousin. The neighborly thing would be to pull over and ask the man if he needed help. But Pax was running late, so late. He fixed his eyes on the road outside his windshield, pretending not to see the man, and blew past without touching his brakes. The old Ford Tempo shuddered beneath him as he took the next curve.

The two-lane highway snaked through dense walls of green, the trees leaning into the road. He'd been gone for eleven years, almost twelve. After so long in the north everything seemed too lush, too overgrown. Subtropical. Turn your back and the plants and insects would overrun everything.

His stomach burned from too much coffee, too little food, and the queasy certainty that he was making a mistake. The call had come three days ago, Deke's rumbling voice on his cell phone's voice mail: Jo Lynn was dead. The funeral was on Saturday morning. Just thought you'd want to know.

Pax deleted the message but spent the rest of the week listening to it replay in his head. Dreading a follow-up call. Then 2 a.m. Saturday morning, when it was too late to make the service—too late unless he drove nonstop and the Ford's engine refrained from throwing a rod—he tossed some clothes into a suitcase and drove south out of Chicago at 85 mph.

His father used to yell at him, Paxton Abel Martin, you'd be late for your own funeral! It was Jo who told him not to worry about it, that everybody was late for their own funeral. Pax didn't get the joke until she explained it to him. Jo was the clever one, the verbal one.

At the old town line there was a freshly painted sign: WELCOME TO SWITCHCREEK, TN. POPULATION 815. The barbed wire fence that used to mark the border was gone. The cement barriers had been pushed to the roadside. But the little guard shack still stood beside the road like an outhouse, abandoned and drowning in kudzu.

The way ahead led into what passed for Switchcreek's downtown, but there was a shortcut to where he was going, if he could find it. He crested the hill, scanning the foliage to his right, and still almost missed it. He braked hard and turned in to a narrow gravel drive that vanished into the trees. The wheels jounced over potholes and ruts, forcing him to slow down.

The road forked and he turned left automatically, knowing

the way even though yesterday he wouldn't have been able to describe this road to anyone. He passed a half-burned barn, then a trailer that had been boarded up since he was kid, then the rusted carcass of a '63 Falcon he and Deke had used for target practice with their .22s. Each object seemed strange, then abruptly familiar, then hopelessly strange again—shifting and shifty.

The road came out of the trees at the top of a hill. He braked to a stop, put the car in park. The engine threatened to die, then fell into an unsteady idle.

A few hundred yards below lay the cemetery, the redbrick church, and the gravel parking lot half-full of cars. Satellite trucks from two different television stations were there. In the cemetery, the funeral was already in progress.

Pax leaned forward and folded his arms atop the steering wheel, letting the struggling air conditioner blow into his damp ribs. About fifty people sat or stood around a pearl-gray casket. Most were betas, bald, dark-red heads gleaming like river stones. The few men wore dark suits, the women long dresses. Some of the women had covered their heads with white scarves. A surprising number of them seemed to be pregnant.

An argo couple stood at the rear of the group, towering over the other mourners. The woman's broad shoulders and narrow hips made a V of her pale green dress. The man beside her was a head shorter and skinny as a ladder. He wore a plain blue shirt with the sleeves rolled up his chalky forearms. Deke looked exactly as Pax remembered him.

The people who were seated rose to their feet. They began to sing.

Pax turned off the car and rolled down the window. Some of the voices were high and flutelike, but the bass rumble, he knew, was provided by the booming chests of the two argos. The melody was difficult to catch at first, but then he recognized the hymn "Just As I Am." He knew the words by heart. It was an altar-call song, a slow weeper that struck especially hard for people who'd come through the Changes. Leading them through the song, her brickred face tilted to the sky, was a beta woman in a long skirt, a flowing white blouse, and a colorful vest. The pastor, Pax guessed, though it was odd to think of a woman pastor at this church. It was odd to think of anyone but his father in the pulpit.

When the song ended the woman said a few words that Pax couldn't catch, and then the group began to walk toward the back door of the church. As the rows cleared, two figures remained seated in front of the casket: two bald girls in dark dresses. Some of the mourners touched the girls' shoulders and moved on.

Those had to be the twins. Jo's daughters. He'd known he'd see them here, had braced for it, but even so he wasn't ready. He was grateful for this chance to see them first from a distance.

A bald beta man in a dark blue suit squatted down between the girls, and after a brief exchange took their hands in his. They stood and he led them to the church entrance. The argo couple hung back. They bent their heads together, and then the woman went inside alone, ducking to make it through the entrance. Deke glanced up to where Paxton's car sat on the hill.

Pax leaned away from the windshield. What he most wanted was to put the car in reverse, then head back through the trees to the highway. Back to Chicago. But he could feel Deke looking at him.

He stepped out of the car, and hot, moist air enveloped him. He reached back inside and pulled out his suit jacket—frayed at the cuffs, ten years out of style—but didn't put it on. If he was lucky he wouldn't have to wear it at all.

"Into the valley of death," he said to himself. He folded the jacket over his arm and walked down the hill to the cemetery's rusting fence.

The back gate squealed open at his push. He walked through the thick grass between the headstones. When he was a kid he'd used this place like a playground. They all had—Deke, Jo, the other church kids—playing hide and seek, sardines, and of course ghost in the graveyard. There weren't so many headstones then.

Deke squatted next to the grave, his knees higher than his head like an enormous grasshopper. He'd unhooked one of the chains that had connected the casket to the frame and was rolling it up around his hand. "Thought that was you," he said without looking up from his work. His voice rumbled like a diesel engine.

"How you doing, Deke."

The man stood up. Pax felt a spark of fear—the back-brain yip of a small mammal confronted with a much larger predator. Argos were skinny, but their bony bodies suggested scythes, siege engines. And Deke seemed to be at least a foot taller than the last time Pax had seen him. His curved spine made his head sit lower than his shoulders, but if he could stand up straight he'd be twice Paxton's height.

"You've grown," Pax said. If they'd been anywhere near the

same size they might have hugged—normal men did that all the time, didn't they? Then Deke held out a hand the size of a skillet, and Pax took it as best he good. Deke could have crushed him, but he kept his grip light. His palm felt rough and unyielding, like the face of a cinderblock. "Long time, P.K.," he said.

P.K. Preacher's Kid. Nobody had called him that since he was fifteen. Since the day he left Switchcreek.

Pax dropped his arm. He could still feel the heat of Deke's skin on his palm.

"I didn't get your message until last night," Pax lied. "I drove all night to get here. I must look like hell."

Deke tilted his head, not disagreeing with him. "The important thing's you got here. I told the reverend I'd take care of the casket, but if you want to go inside, they're setting out the food."

"No, that's—I'm not hungry." Another lie. But he hadn't come here for a hometown reunion. He needed to pay his respects and that was it. He was due back at the restaurant by Monday.

He looked at the casket, then at the glossy, polished gravestone. Someone had paid for a nice one.

JO LYNN WHITEHALL
BORN FEBRUARY 12, 1983
DIED AUGUST 17, 2010
LOVING MOTHER

"'Loving Mother.' That's nice," Pax said. But the epitaph struck him as entirely inadequate. After awhile he said, "It seems weird to boil everything down to two words like that."

"Especially for Jo," Deke said. A steel frame supported the casket on thick straps. Deke squatted again to turn a stainless steel handle next to the screw pipe. The casket began to lower into the hole. "It's the highest compliment the betas have, though. Pretty much the only one that counts."

The casket touched bottom. Paxton knelt and pulled up the straps on his side of the grave. Then the two of them lifted the metal frame out of the way.

Paxton brushed the red clay from his knees. They stood there looking into the hole.

The late Jo Lynn Whitehall, Paxton thought.

He tried to imagine her body inside the casket, but it was impossible. He couldn't picture either of the Jos he'd known—not the brown-haired girl from before the Changes, or the sleek creature she'd become after. He waited for tears, the physical rush of some emotion that would prove that he loved her. Nothing came. He felt like he was both here and not here, a double image hovering a few inches out of true.

Paxton breathed in, then blew out a long breath. "Do you know why she did it?" He couldn't say the word "suicide."

Deke shook his head. They were silent for a time and then Deke said, "Come on inside."

Deke didn't try to persuade him; he simply went in and Pax followed, down the narrow stairs—the dank, cinderblock walls smelling exactly as Pax remembered—and into the basement and the big open room they called the Fellowship Hall. The room was filled with rows of tables covered in white plastic tablecloths. There were at least twice as many people as he'd seen outside at the burial. About a dozen of them were "normal"—unchanged, skipped, passed over, whatever you wanted to call people like him—and none of them looked like reporters.

Deke went straight to the buffet, three tables laid end-to-end and crowded with food. No one seemed to notice that Pax had snuck in behind the tall man.

The spread was as impressive as the potlucks he remembered as a boy. Casseroles, sloppy joes, three types of fried chicken, huge bowls of mashed potatoes . . . One table held nothing but desserts. Enough food to feed three other congregations.

While they filled their plates Pax surreptitiously looked over the room, scanning for the twins through a crowd of alien faces. After so long away it was a shock to see so many of the changed in one room. TDS—Transcription Divergence Syndrome—had swept through Switchcreek the summer he was fourteen. The disease had divided the population, then divided it again and again, like a dealer cutting a deck of cards into smaller piles. By the end of the summer a quarter of the town was dead. The survivors were divided by symptoms into clades: the giant argos, the seal-skinned betas, the fat charlies. A few, a very few, weren't changed at all—at least in any way you could detect.

A toddler in a Sunday dress bumped into his legs and careened away, laughing in a high, piping voice. Two other bald girls—all beta children were girls, all were bald—chased after her into a forest of legs.

Most of the people in the room were betas. The women and the handful of men were hairless, skin the color of cabernet, raspberry, rose. The women wore dresses, and now that he was closer he could see that even more were pregnant than he'd supposed. The expectant mothers tended to be the younger, smaller women. They were also the ones who seemed to be wearing the head scarves.

He was surprised by how different the second-generation daughters were from their mothers. The mothers, though skinny and bald and oddly colored, could pass for normal women with some medical condition—as chemo patients, maybe. But their children's faces were flat, the noses reduced to a nub and two apostrophes, their mouths a long slit.

Someone grabbed his arm. "Paxton Martin!"

He put on an expectant smile before he turned.

"It *is* you," the woman said. She reached up and pulled him down into a hug. She was about five feet tall and extremely wide, carrying about three hundred pounds under a surprisingly well-tailored pink pantsuit.

She drew back and gazed at him approvingly, her over-inflated face taut and shiny. Lime green eyeshade and bright red rouge added to the beach ball effect.

"Aunt Rhonda," he said, smiling. She wasn't his aunt, but everyone in town called her that. He was surprised at how happy he was to see her.

"Just look at you," she said. "You're as handsome as I remember."

Pax felt the heat in his cheeks. He wasn't handsome, not in the ways recognized by the outside world. But in Switchcreek he was a skip, one of the few children who had come through the Changes unmarked and still breathing.

Rhonda didn't seem to notice his embarrassment. "This is a terrible thing, isn't it? People say the word 'tragic' too much, but that's what it is. I can't imagine how tough it must be on her girls."

He didn't know what to say except, "Yes."

"I remember your momma carrying Jo Lynn around the church in her little dresses when she was just a year old. She loved that girl like she was her own. So pretty, and so smart. Smart as a whip."

Pax waited for the slight, the veiled insult. Rhonda had been the church secretary while his father was pastor. She was a sharp-tongued woman with opinions about everyone and everything, including his mother's performance as a pastor's wife.

Rhonda shook her head. "And you two! You two were like brother and sister. Only three months between you, is that right?"

"Four," he said. A dozen feet behind Rhonda, a young charlie man, broad as a linebacker and not showing any of the fat that clung to the older people of his clade, watched them talk. His hair was shaved to a shadow. A diamond stud winked from one ear.

Pax spotted the twins at a nearby table. The girls didn't seem to be eating. The beta man who'd walked them into the church—a beta man in a dark suit—sat at the end of the table, the beta pastor beside him. The man seemed to be trying to talk to the twins, but they only stared at their plates.

Rhonda half turned to follow his gaze. "That's Tommy Shields, Jo's husband." There was the slightest pause before the word "husband."

"I'm sorry—what? Nobody told me she'd—"

Rhonda lowered her voice. "Oh, hon, not the way anyone but them calls a husband."

Pax didn't know what she meant. No betas had been getting married when he left town.

He knew Tommy, though. He'd been a junior in high school when Deke and Jo and Pax were freshmen. Complete asshole. That freshman year, Tommy had beaten up Deke, evidently for standing too close to Tommy's car, a red-and-white '76 Bronco that he'd restored himself. Pax didn't remember seeing Tommy after the Changes.

"Still," Rhonda said, almost sighing. "Tommy's a help to those girls. They've got a hard row to hoe—but I don't need to tell you that, do I?" She shook her head sadly. "It just breaks my heart. I let the sisters know that the town's going to help any way it can. And of course, they've got their church to help."

*Their* church. "You're not going here anymore?" Paxton asked. Rhonda's grandfather had been a founder, and Rhonda had held the office of church secretary for twenty years. Pastors came and went, she'd told his father more than once, but she wasn't going anywhere. Even during the Changes, when the church had closed and her own body was bloating, she'd refused to step down. Then again, Pax's father hadn't stepped down either, not until a year after Pax had left town. Pax had never tried to get the whole story—that was his father's life, nothing to do with him now.

"Oh, Paxton, it's not like it was before," Rhonda said, keeping her voice low. "This is Reverend Hooke's church now. I go to First Baptist, though I can't be as involved as I'd like."

Paxton's father had impressed upon him at a young age that attending First Baptist was almost as bad as converting to Roman Catholic. The First was where the rich people went—as rich as anyone got in Switchcreek—and everybody knew they didn't take their scripture seriously.

"Aunt Rhonda's the mayor now," Deke said, sounding

amused. He was bent under the ceiling, holding his plate and plastic cup of iced tea between big fingers. Waiting to see how Pax would react.

"Really?" Pax said, trying not to sound too shocked. "*Mayor* Rhonda."

"Six years now," Deke said.

"Well," Pax said. "I bet you keep everyone in line."

Rhonda chuckled, obviously pleased, and patted his arm again. Her mood kept changing, fast as switching TV channels. "You and I need to talk. Have you seen your father yet?"

He felt heat in his cheeks and shook his head. "I just got in."

"He's not in a good way, and he won't take my help." She pursed her lips. "After your visit, you give me a call."

"Sure, sure," he said lightly.

Her eyes, already small in her huge face, narrowed. "Don't *sure* me, Paxton Martin."

Pax blinked. She wasn't joking. He remembered a church picnic when he was nine or ten: Aunt Rhonda had found Pax and Jo misbehaving—he couldn't remember what they'd been doing—and she'd taken a switch to their backsides. She didn't care whose kids they were. Then she gave them both Moon-Pies and told them to stop crying.

"I'll call," he said. "I promise."

She smiled, all sweetness again. "Now you better go eat your meal before it's cold."

She turned away, and several people at the table nearest them resumed talking. The charlie man stepped away from the wall and followed Rhonda. He glanced back at Paxton, his expression serious.

Deke walked toward the other end of the room, where a

group of argos, including the woman in the green dress, ate standing up, bent under the drop-tile ceiling. Pax tried to follow, but he'd been recognized now, and people wanted to shake his hand and talk to him. Some of them seemed exactly as he remembered them. Mr. Sparks, already an old man when Pax knew him, had been one of the few of the elderly who'd survived, and in his own skin. He still looked trim and vigorous. Others had become distorted versions of their old selves, or else so changed that there was no recognizing them. Each of them greeted him warmly, without a hint of reservation or disapproval, as if he'd decided on his own to leave Switchcreek for greater things. After all, every other unchanged person under thirty seemed to have left town. After the quarantine lifted, after the Lambert riots and the Stonecipher murders, who the hell would stick around if they didn't have to? The skips skipped.

He squeezed past two tables of charlies, nodding back at those who said hello to him, even when he wasn't sure of their names. The people of Aunt Rhonda's clade were as wide as he remembered from the year and a half he'd lived among them: squat, moon-faced, engulfing their metal folding chairs. Finally he made it to the far side of the room where the argos had congregated. Most stood with their slouched backs touching the ceiling. A few perched on benches at the edges of the room, knees and elbows splayed, like adults at kindergarten desks. Each of them was a different shade of pale, from pencil lead to talcum.

Deke held out a long arm. "P.K., you remember Donna?"

Like all argos, the woman was tall and horse-faced. But while argo hair was usually stiff as straw and about the same color as their skin—troll hair, Deke had called it—hers was long and red, cinched tight close to her head and then blossoming behind, like the head of a broom.

The woman held out her hand. "Good to see you again, Paxton." Her voice was as deep as Deke's—deeper maybe—but the inflection was more feminine somehow.

"Oh! Donna, sure!" He put down his plate and grasped her big hand in both of his. Donna had been a year behind them at school. She was a McKinney, one of the poor folks who lived up on Two Hills Road. Poor black folk. And now, he thought, she was whiter than he was.

"You two have been married how long again?" Pax asked. As if it had just slipped his mind. He remembered a wedding invitation that had been forwarded to him from his cousins' house in Naperville. He'd meant to respond.

"Eight years at the end of the month," Donna said.

"You guys were kids!" Pax said. "*Tall* kids, but still. What were you, nineteen? That must have been some shotgun wedding."

"Not really," Deke said.

"Oh shit, I'm sorry," Pax said, then realized he'd said "shit" in church and felt doubly embarrassed. There was no such thing as a pregnant argo, no such thing as an argo baby. "I didn't mean—"

Deke held up a hand: Don't worry about it.

Donna said. "We want to feed you supper, then of course you have to stay at the house."

"No, really, that's okay—"

"We've got plenty of room. Unless you're staying with your father?"

"No." He said it too quickly. "I thought I'd just stay at the Motel Six in Lambert."

Deke said, "Have you talked to him lately?"

Pax started to say, *Twelve years, give or take*—but then the two argos looked over his head. Pax turned. Tommy Shields walked toward them, the twin girls trailing behind him.

Tommy had been tall before the Changes, but he'd lost several inches of his height. His face was hairless, without even eyebrows, and his skin had turned a light brown that was splotched with dark across his cheeks and forehead. But he was still first-generation beta, with a broad jaw and too much muscle in the shoulders, and the old Tommy was still recognizable under the new skin.

His voice, however, was utterly different. "You're Paxton," he said softly. His lips barely moved, and the sound seemed to start and stop a few inches from his thin lips. "Jo Lynn's friend." He extended a hand, and Pax shook it and released without squeezing.

Pax couldn't think what to say, and finally came up with, "I'm sorry for your loss."

"Girls," Tommy said, "this man was a good friend of your mother's."

The girls stepped forward. Heat flared in Paxton's chest, an ache of something like embarrassment or fear. They were the same height, their heads coming up to just past Tommy's elbow. They had to be almost twelve now.

Tommy didn't seem to notice Paxton's discomfort. "This is Sandra," Tommy said, indicating the girl on his left, "and this is Rainy." They were second-generation betas—the firstborn of that generation—and their wine-colored faces were expressionless as buttons.

"Hi," Pax said. He coughed to clear his throat. "It's a pleasure to meet you." He knew their names from decade-old letters. Jo had rejected twin-ish stunt-names. No alliteration, no groaners like Hope and Joy. The only thing notable was that Rainy—Lorraine—was named after his mother. "Your mom was—"

He blinked at them, trying to think of some anecdote, but suddenly his mind was empty. He couldn't even picture Jo Lynn's face.

No one spoke.

"She was a great person," Pax said finally. "I could tell you stories."

The girls stared at him.

"I bet they'd like to hear those," Tommy said. "Come by the Co-op and we can talk about her. Before you leave."

Pax hesitated. Co-op? "I'd like that," he said. "I'm not sure if I can, though—I have to see how my father's doing. But if I can get away . . ."

Tommy looked at him. "If you can spare the time," he said in that soft voice. He smiled tightly and turned away. The girls regarded Paxton for a long moment and then followed Tommy across the room.

Pax exhaled heavily. "Man," he said.

Donna said, "Are you okay?"

"Yeah, it's just those girls." He shook his head. "I know Jo loved them. She did, right?" Before they could answer he said, "Never mind, stupid question. It's just that I can't believe she'd leave them."

There was an awkward silence, and he looked up at the argos. Deke was frowning, and Donna wore a strangely fierce expression.

"She wouldn't," Donna said.

He looked from Donna to Deke, back again. He could see it in their faces. "You don't think she killed herself?"

Neither of them said anything for a moment. Deke shook his head. "It's just a feeling," he said.

"Show me," Pax said to him. "Show me where it happened."

# chapter 2

THEY WALKED INTO the midday heat, and Pax said, "My car or yours?"

Deke looked down at him.

"Oh. Right."

Deke led him across the gravel parking lot. One of the satellite trucks had left, and the other had its rear doors open. A young man in a blue suit jacket sat on the back fender, smoking a cigarette. He looked like he was going to ask them something, but a look from Deke made him put the cigarette back in his mouth and glance away.

"I wouldn't let 'em in the church," Deke said. For good reason, Pax thought. The media had been no friend to the town. The summer of the outbreak they'd been invaded, squads of masked reporters shoving cameras in their faces. The quarantine had forced the newspeople out, but the phone calls for interviews had kept coming, and the people of Switchcreek could see on TV what the world thought of them. Then came the Lambert riots, and the Stonecipher murders, and the feeding frenzy continued. A few betas had tried to go grocery shopping in Lambert, and the town went nuts. That's when the drive-bys started, rednecks roaring through Switchcreek to knock down mailboxes and shoot up the stop signs. A barn burned, and the state police finally started patrolling the streets. A few weeks after that, the Stonecipher brothers were found beside the road, shot dead. They were argos, big old boys and a little wild. The killers were never found.

The spotlight eventually moved on to the next hurricane or celebrity overdose, but Pax still saw Switchcreek popping up on TV every once in awhile, mostly for some science or health update. A couple times some website would run rumors about other outbreaks, in other countries, but they were never substantiated. Mostly Switchcreek was ignored. A normal death in the town probably wouldn't go further than a mention on local news, but a suicide or murder might be worth a few seconds on the cable news networks.

Deke opened the door of a green Jeep Cherokee with the canvas top rolled back. The back bench had been removed, and the front seats had been pushed back and raised. They climbed into the cab. Deke's long arms and legs easily reached the oversized steering wheel and foot pedals.

Paxton's legs dangled from the passenger seat. He felt like a kid in a car seat.

Deke followed Piney Road back to the highway, then turned south toward town, driving with one arm resting on the roll bar in front of him. His curved spine gave him the appearance of hunching over the wheel. The car speakers squawked with static, then went silent. Nestled into the dash was an elaborate black receiver.

"CB?" Pax asked.

"Police scanner."

Pax thought a moment. "You must have been one of the first to hear, then."

Deke sighed, a slow sound like a freight train coming to

rest. "I heard when the dispatcher called for the ambulance, but by then it was way too late."

"Jesus," Pax said. "I'm sorry, man."

They crossed the two-lane bridge and then slowed as they entered downtown. They passed the Gas-n-Go, the Power Rental, the Icee Freeze. Each building looked more run-down than Pax remembered, slope-shouldered and tired. Only the old one-room schoolhouse, which had been falling down when he was a kid, looked like it had been refurbished. The walls wore a fresh coat of red paint, and a new sign out front declared it to be the Switchcreek Welcome Center.

Right. Welcome to Monster Town.

Nobody had figured out what had turned the residents into freaks. Transcription Divergence Syndrome was just a fancy description of the damage, not an explanation. No strange microbe had been found skulking in their bloodstream. The water and air and dirt were radiation free, and no more poisoned with toxins than any other poor mountain town. The most common theory was that it was a new retrovirus, whatever that was, but if there'd been any kind of virus in the air it was gone now.

TDS wasn't contagious, either. No one who wasn't living within five miles of downtown that summer had ever caught it, even though during the outbreak victims had been parceled out to a dozen hospitals in Eastern Tennessee. After thirteen months with no new victims it became clear that the quarantine was a waste of money. The national guard pulled out. The government still kept tabs on them, and doctors and reporters still made their own drive-bys, but most of the rest of the country, satisfied that TDS couldn't happen to *them*, lost interest in the town.

Pax was surprised, then, to see so many cars in the parking

lot of Bugler's Grocery. A smoked-glass tour bus was disgorging middle-aged people in shorts and shirtsleeves. One of them saw the Jeep and lifted a camera to her face. Deke stared straight ahead as they passed.

Pax stared at Deke. "Oh my God, were those *tourists?*"

Deke looked at him, a half smile on his lips. "We get a bunch every weekend," he said. "Not so much since the anniversary." The ten-year anniversary of the Changes had been three years ago. Pax had avoided watching any of the specials.

Deke stopped at the traffic light, even though it was yellow and there were no other cars at the intersection. On the corner was a new building, a gray brick one-story with white columns holding up the entrance roof. It looked like a library.

*"Oh my God,"* Deke said with a weird nasal whine, and then laughed.

"What?"

Deke shook his head, laughing.

"What, damn it?"

"Listen to yourself. You sound like a Yankee now."

"Hey, get beat up a few times in a Yankee high school and you drop that southern accent pretty quick."

Deke's short laugh was like the beat of a bass drum. Pax flashed on an image of them lying on the floor of Jo's living room. God they'd spent so many hours hanging out there during the quarantine. The beery, happy SOS meetings.

The light turned green. Deke turned right on Bank Street. He nodded toward the new building. "The free clinic," he said. "And worth every penny. All you have to do is keep filling out their surveys."

"Sounds familiar." In the early days of the Changes, they'd all been poked, prodded, and interrogated on a daily basis.

Even after Pax left Switchcreek he'd get fat envelopes in the mail requesting him to be in this or that study. He never followed up. He moved out of his cousins' house in the Chicago suburbs when he was eighteen, then kept moving through a series of apartments around the seedier parts of downtown, and somewhere along the way the scientists lost his scent.

The clinic was the only evidence he could see of the disaster relief money that had been supposed to rain down on Switchcreek after the quarantine lifted. When Paxton left town they were talking about new schools, scholarships, compensation for every family that had lost someone in the Changes. But now the place looked more run-down than when he'd left.

Pax said, "So what do people do for a living around here?"

Deke laughed shortly. "Most of the town's on welfare. Not much work for anybody since the economy tanked, but for us . . ." He shook his head. "We've got a hell of a preexisting condition. Even the service jobs with no insurance, nobody wants us serving burgers or talking to the customers."

Deke drove back behind the elementary school, which looked about the same as when Pax and Deke and Jo had gone there. In the blacktop recess area one of the basketball hoops was bent almost straight down, and the other was missing. Argo kids had to be hell on hoops.

Deke said, "So what do *you* do for a living? You work in some restaurant?"

"Not some restaurant. *The* number three Mexican restaurant chain in Chicago, not counting Chi-Chi's and Taco Bell."

"Really."

"Really." Pax shrugged. "It's not a career or anything." No shit, he thought. There were two types of people in the restaurant biz: temps and lifers. The lifers were alcoholics with hefty pot habits. He'd always thought he was a temp—marking time until he figured out what he wanted to do with his life—until he woke up one morning with his fourth hangover of the week and realized he owed his dealer $300.

"You got a girlfriend up there? An ex-wife? I don't see a ring on your finger."

"I'm not exactly husband material," Pax said. "Or boyfriend material. Actually, I'm not even sure I'm material."

At Creek Road they turned left, taking them higher, up along the side of Mount Clyburn. The mountain marked the edge of the state. Walk up into those trees and you wouldn't start back down until you were in South Carolina.

"I like Donna," Pax said. "You two seem happy."

"I got lucky." Deke slowed the car, swung onto a gravel driveway. "Jo moved out this way a couple years ago." He followed the driveway up in a steep S. After two curves and a couple hundred yards the driveway leveled out at a patch of ground dug into the side of the mountain.

The house was a simple wood bungalow that could have been built at any time in the last seventy years. The front door of the house was closed, and drapes covered the windows.

When Pax was a boy, well before the Changes, the house had been a run-down rental inhabited by a succession of nearly identical poor white families: rarely seen except for their dogs forever trotting into traffic. Jo, however, had fixed the place up as well as could be expected. The canary paint and green trim looked only a couple years old. There were flowerbeds along the front and a pair of dogwood trees at each corner.

A huge oak rose up behind the house, its full limbs spread protectively over the roof.

"Coming?" Deke said.

Pax looked away from the tree. "Sure. Yeah."

They walked around the side of the house. The backyard was just a strip of land before the wave of the mountain. The oak stood sentry between the house and the start of the forest.

The branch where she'd hung herself was very high, about fifteen feet in the air. The rope had been there a long time, its loops deeply incised into the bark. The stub end was frayed where they'd cut her down.

"Jesus," Pax said. He tried to imagine the strength of will it would take to hang yourself.

"The girls found her that morning," Deke said. "They called nine-one-one."

"That's awful." Pax breathed deep and looked away. A dozen feet from the tree lay the truck tire that had been the swing. "Was she upset about something? Was she depressed?"

"She's had a tough couple years," Deke said.

"So tough *Jo* couldn't handle it?"

Deke worked his lips. "I don't know, P.K. She was taking some medication for depression, but that was months ago. She had an operation. Hysterectomy. Dr. Fraelich—she works at the clinic—said it's normal to experience mood shifts after something like that."

"Normal for who?"

Deke nodded, conceding the point. Who knew what was normal for a beta?

Pax stepped toward the tree. He ran his hand across the rough bark. After a time he said, "My last night in town, we had a big fight."

Behind him, Deke said nothing.

"She told me I didn't have to leave. She said I didn't have to listen to my dad, I could live with her."

"The Reverend Martin would have liked that," Deke said.

"She was never afraid of him like I was. She said I was being a coward. I was abandoning the baby."

"Well, they weren't yours. Or mine."

"But we didn't know that at the time."

"Pax . . ."

"It was a test. You stayed. I ran."

"Pax, come on. Look at me."

Pax turned. Deke had squatted down so that they were eye level. "You were a kid," he said. "We were all kids. None of us knew anything."

It was true they were ignorant. They didn't know that the baby she was carrying was actually two girls. They didn't know that betas didn't need anyone else to make a baby, that fetuses simply arrived, like new symptoms. The scientists wouldn't figure that out for a couple years after Pax left town.

But Pax knew one thing, even then. Jo was right. He was a coward.

Pax walked back toward the house, turned, and looked up at the branch, the rope. "You don't think she did this to herself," he said.

After a moment, Deke said, "No."

"Then who?"

Deke shook his head. "Nobody knows. Maybe it was outsiders. People from Lambert." He didn't sound like he believed it. The riots were over ten years ago.

"Outsiders who knew her well enough to hate her specifically?" Pax asked.

"They don't have to know us to hate us. They just have to look at us."

"What about Tommy?"

Deke looked back at him, frowning. "What about him?"

"What is he? Rhonda said he was a husband, but not a husband. Were they married?"

"They had an arrangement. For the kids." He breathed out. "It's a beta thing."

"Did they get along?"

"Tommy didn't live with them anymore," Deke said. He rose up to full height. "Not since Jo moved out here." He looked down and saw Paxton's look. "There was some trouble with the Co-op," he said. "With the other betas. You know how Jo could be. She was stubborn. So she left or they kicked her out, depending who you ask. Tommy stayed with the Co-op, and Jo moved here with the girls."

"Are they investigating him?"

"Jesus, Pax, they're not investigating anybody that I know of. Listen, I'm going to a meeting with the sheriff and the DA on Monday. If you're still here then I'll be sure to tell you what they say."

Ah. There it was. Deke finally taking a poke at him.

"I can't stay," Pax said. "I've got to be back to work by Monday. In fact, I should probably drive back tonight."

"Tonight."

"Tomorrow morning at the latest. If you could drive me back to my car—"

"You're not going to go see your dad?"

Pax opened his mouth, closed it. "Listen, my dad doesn't want to see me."

"You need to see him," Deke said. "He's not doing so well. The charlies—the old men anyway—things get worse as they get older."

He had no clue what Deke was talking about. There *weren't* any old charlie men when Pax left town; his father was one of the oldest who came through TDS-C alive, and he'd only been fifty.

Deke said, "I don't think your dad's leaving the house much."

"Deke, he hasn't called me or wrote me in twelve years." Pax didn't mention that he hadn't tried either.

Deke put his big hand on Paxton's shoulder. "Then you're about due."

They left Jo Lynn's house, heading west until the road angled north and crossed the creek at the single-lane bridge. Some of the graffiti on the cement walls had been there since Pax was a kid. Deke turned onto Piney Road. They'd almost made a complete circle since leaving the church.

The house where Paxton grew up was a little three-bedroom ranch surrounded by trees. Paxton's father's car, a Ford Crown Victoria that was fifteen years old before Pax even left town, was parked in front in its usual spot. It looked like it hadn't moved in years. The tires looked low, and leaves were shellacked to the body and windows by sap and dirt.

Deke pulled up behind the Crown Vic and stopped, shut off the engine.

Pax made no move to get out. His ears felt warm in the sudden lack of wind.

The picture window drapes were closed. The white siding had grayed, begun to flake. The screen door hung open, but the wooden front door was closed. The grass on the lawn stood a foot tall, the tips sprouting seed.

Deke said, "Some ladies from the church bring food by, but he throws them out before they can do anything else for him."

"Really?" Pax couldn't picture his father being rude to church folk, especially women.

"And Rhonda's got some chub boys who come by every once in awhile. Mow the lawn, check in on him."

"Chub boys?"

"Charlies. 'Chub' is just . . ." He shrugged.

"I get it," Pax said. And thought, I bet you don't call them that to their faces. "Anyway, it looks like they haven't been around for a while."

Pax climbed out of the Jeep. He stood there, holding on to the door, looking at the house.

"You want me to go in with you?" Deke said.

"No, no, you don't have to do that."

Pax walked across the lawn to the front porch and knocked. He was eye level with the small, diamond-shaped window set in the door. After a minute he cupped his eyes and peered through the smudged glass. He could make out a patch of familiar wall, then nothing but shadows. He tried the doorknob—locked—and knocked again, louder.

Something glinted in the grass beside the cement step. He crouched to pick it up: a syringe and needle, the tube empty. What the hell? He stood to show it to Deke. The man's head stuck up over the Jeep's roll bars like a giraffe's. He squinted to see what it was, then shrugged.

Pax had no idea what that shrug meant. He set the syringe on the porch where he could find it later.

He walked around the corner of the house, stepping carefully through the high grass, wary of hidden needles. The side window for his parents' bedroom was filled by a silent air conditioner; the glazed bathroom window next to it was closed and dark.

Behind the house, the backyard had shrunk from the advancement of the brush line. The rusting frame of his old swing set leaned out of the shrubs. Farther back, the low, cinderblock well house—made obsolete by the sewer and water lines added in the '80s—sat almost buried in the undergrowth like a Civil War fortification.

The door to the back porch was unlocked. Pax went through it, to the kitchen door. He knocked once and turned the knob. The door swung open with a squeak.

"Hello!" he called. "It's me, Dad." The air smelled sickly sweet and fungal, a jungle smell. "It's Paxton," he added stupidly. From somewhere in the house came the sound of a TV.

The kitchen was as he remembered it, though dirtier than his mother would ever have allowed. Dirtier even than his father had kept it when it was just him and Paxton living here during the year of the quarantine. The garbage can overflowed with paper and scraps. Dishes sat in the sink. In the center of the breakfast table was a white ceramic casserole dish, the aluminum foil peeled back. From somewhere near the front of the house came the low murmur of television voices.

Pax made his way through the dining room, dusty and preserved as an unvisited exhibit, to the living room, where he found his father.

The Reverend Harlan Martin had a firm idea of what a pastor should look like, and it began with the hair. Each morning after his shower, he'd carefully comb back the wet strands from his forehead and spray everything down with his wife's Alberto

VO5, clouding the bathroom. Sunday required extra coats, enough hairspray to preserve his appearance through a fire-and-brimstone sermon, a potluck dinner, a visitation or two, and an evening service. His Sunday hair was as shiny and durable as a Greek helmet.

As a child, Pax loved when the hair was down, as when his father slept late and came to the breakfast table unshowered, pushing the long bangs out of his face like a disheveled Elvis. Like now.

His father sat sprawled on the couch, head back and mouth open, eyes closed. His dark hair, longer than Pax had ever seen it, hung along the sides of his wide face to his jaw.

"Dad?" Pax said. The atmosphere in the room was hot and unbearably humid, despite the ceiling fan turning above, the air heavy with a strange odor like rotting fruit. He took a step forward. "Dad?"

His body spread across most of the three cushions. He wore a blue terrycloth bathrobe half closed over a white T-shirt, and black socks stretched over broad feet. His face was deeply cratered, the skin flaking and loose.

His father's chest moved. A whistling wheeze escaped his mouth.

Okay, Pax thought. Alive, then.

The coffee table and chairs had been pushed to the walls, leaving a wide space with a clear view of the television's flickering screen. The television abruptly became louder—an ad—and Pax flicked off the set.

His father suddenly lifted his head, turned to glare at Pax. His eyes were glassy, the lids crusted with sleep matter.

"Out," his father said, his voice garbled by phlegm. He coughed, and raised a wide hand to his mouth. The arm was as pockmarked as his face. He pointed past Paxton's shoulder. "Out of my house!" He still had it: the Preacher Voice.

"Dad, it's me, Paxton." He crouched down next to his father, and winced at the smell of him. He couldn't tell if the man was delirious or simply confused by sleep. Did charlie men grow demented early? "It's your son."

The huge man blinked at him. "Paxton?" he said warily. Then: "It's you."

Pax gripped his father's hand. "How you doing, Dad?"

"My prodigal son," his father said.

"The only kind you've got." Pax tried to let go, but his father squeezed harder.

"Who called you? Rhonda?"

"I came for the funeral, Dad. Jo Lynn's funeral." Pax extricated his hand and stood. He was surprised to feel something oily on his palm, and rubbed his hand dry on the back of his pants. "You mind if I open some windows?"

"She wants me. Wants to milk me like a cow. You can't be here."

Pax unlocked the front door and pulled it open. Deke stood by the Jeep, elbows resting on the roll bar, smoking a cigar that looked as small as a cigarette in his big fingers. He turned at the sound of the door, and Pax held up a hand to tell him everything was okay.

Though of course everything was *not* okay.

His father's body, huge as it was, looked like a bag to hold an even larger man. The skin hung loose at his neck and cheeks, and now beads of sweat appeared along his brow.

"You've got to leave," his father said, but his tone was no longer firm.

Pax wondered how long it had been since his father last ate.

Could he even move? Pax pulled open the big front drapes and fought down a wave of dizziness. The air in the room was too close, too fetid. The sickly sweet odor had blossomed, become suffocating.

His father's face shone with sweat, as if breaking a fever. A water blister had appeared on his cheek, as large as a walnut, the skin so tight it was almost translucent. Pax stared at it in horror.

"Oh," his father said softly. "Oh, Lord."

"Dad, what's going on?"

"You took me by surprise," he said. He looked up, smiled faintly. His eyes were wet. Two more blisters had appeared at his neck. They seemed to expand as Pax watched. "You better leave now."

Pax turned toward the door, lost his balance, and caught himself. At the front door he braced himself against the frame, and the wood seemed hot under his right hand.

"Deke!" Pax called. Deke and the Jeep swam in and out of focus. "Call Nine-one-one!"

Keeping a hand against the wall to steady himself, he made his way back to the couch. Stains the color of pink lemonade had appeared on his father's T-shirt.

His father looked up at him with half-closed eyes. "Paxton Abel Martin." He said the name with a slow drawl, almost singing it, in a voice Pax hadn't heard in a long time. He had a sudden memory of being carried up the church stairs in the dark—he must have been four or five—held close in his father's arms.

Pax kneeled in front of him. The rich, fruity smell enveloped him. Pax gently pushed the robe farther open and began to lift the T-shirt. Blisters had erupted over the skin of his belly: tiny pimples; white-capped pebbles; glossy, egg-sized sacs. The largest pouches wept pink-tinged serum.

"Oh Jesus, Dad." Pax bunched the edge of the T-shirt and tried to cover one of the open sores, but the oily liquid soaked through and slicked his fingers. "Dad, we've got to get you—get . . ."

His fingers burned, but not painfully. He looked at his hand, rubbed the substance between his fingers. Slowly his gaze turned to his father, and their eyes locked.

*There you are,* Pax thought. There, waiting underneath the sagging flesh, the mounds of pitted and pocked skin: the man who had carried him up the stairs. Relief flooded through him. What if they'd been lost forever? Pax and his bloated father were here, in this stinking room, and they were also Harlan Martin and his four-year-old son, climbing out of the church basement after a long Sunday-night service. He felt himself being carried, and at the same time felt the weight of the boy in his arms.

And then Pax was off his feet, an arm across his chest hauling him backward, heels dragging. Big hands carried him through the door and dumped him on the lawn.

"Don't touch your mouth," Deke said. "Or your eyes."

Pax raised his hands. "Don't worry, I'm not—" He tried to sit up, but the world slipped sideways, and he fell back again into the long grass. "Shit."

"Just lay there," Deke said.

Through half-lidded eyes he stared at a crack in the sky. He slowly fanned his arms and legs, making angels in the grass.

---

Sometime later he heard the crunch of tires on the gravel, the slam of car doors. Huge figures hove into his peripheral vision: two young men in tank tops, arms like cartoon body-builders. *Chub boys.* One of them looked at him and shook his head, frowning. Pax saw the little diamond in his ear and remembered him from the church basement. The other one, younger with blond spiky hair, snapped the wrist of his latex glove and said, "Gotta use protection, son." He laughed.

Deke's voice rumbled like distant thunder—Pax couldn't turn the sound into words—and one of the charlies answered respectfully, "Sorry, Chief."

A minute passed, maybe longer, and then a hand reached down out of the sky and hoisted Paxton upright. Deke. The big man helped him to the Jeep and set him down in the passenger seat. Pax just managed to stay upright as Deke turned the vehicle around and got them back on the highway. The air felt good on his face.

"Sorry, man," Deke said. "I thought he was dry. Rhonda told me he was dry."

Dry? Pax didn't know what he meant. He wanted to ask why the chub boys had come, and what they were doing to his father, what the *fuck* was happening—but the questions failed to arrive at his lips. His thoughts refused to stay in order. He bounced along silently as Deke drove back into town, past the Gas-n-Go and the First Baptist Church, onto High Street where a row of houses overlooked the creek. When he was a kid, the only people who'd lived down here were the rich folks.

Deke parked in front of a two-story house, brick on the

bottom and wood siding on top, a traditional ranch with the roof raised ten feet.

"Can you walk?" Deke said.

Pax slowly opened the door and thought, *Can* I walk? He put a foot down on the cement driveway. He hadn't noticed before how all the driveways up north were paved with asphalt, but down here they were all cement.

"P.K., you want me to help?"

Pax lifted a hand and stepped down. When the surface refrained from tilting beneath his feet he followed Deke up to a tall, narrow door. Inside, the living room was as airy as a church sanctuary. Light poured through the row of new, high windows that had been set above the old walls. The furniture was all polished oak, all argo-sized.

Donna came out of a back room and looked at Paxton. "What happened?"

"Is the guest room made up yet?" Deke asked. "He needs to lay down."

At the end of a hallway was a room painted bright orange and white—University of Tennessee colors. The bed filled up most of the space. Twelve feet long and eight feet wide, practically a playing field in its own right, covered by a UT Volunteers bedspread. He couldn't guess where they'd gotten a mattress for it.

"Go Vols," Pax said. It was the first thing he'd been able to say aloud since leaving his father's. "My dad . . . ," he said.

"Your dad's going to be fine. Just lay down, P.K. If you need to throw up, there's a bathroom next door."

Deke left the door ajar when he stepped out. Pax lay on his back and breathed deep. The ceiling fan hung high, high above him, the blades turning slowly.

The blades slowed, came to a stop. Then the room began to turn.

He gripped the bed and closed his eyes.

The day the Changes started, they were riding Pax's fire-engine red Yamaha four-wheeler, ripping up and down the gullies behind Deke's place. It was the second week of July, a few weeks after Paxton's fourteenth birthday, 90 or 95 degrees. They didn't hear the siren until Pax shut off the engine to give Deke a turn. It didn't sound like a cop car or a fire truck. Had to be an ambulance, though ambulances didn't come up to Switchcreek much. Deke, scrawnier and a head shorter than Paxton, hopped on the back of the ATV and put his arms around P.K.'s waist.

When they reached the road Deke hopped off to listen—that way!—and they drove a quarter mile until they saw the ambulance parked in the driveway and two EMTs walking up the steps to the house. Jo Lynn's house.

Pax didn't remember getting off the ATV, or walking into the house. He didn't remember seeing another car in the driveway, though his dad's Crown Vic must have been there, because his mother was in the living room, her arms around Jo Lynn's shoulders. Jo had called her right after she dialed 911.

The EMTs were in the back bedroom, where Jo's mother lay. Agatha Whitehall had run a fever for days, Pax learned later. Jo Lynn hadn't been home that week, hadn't even known her mother was sick; Agatha and Jo hadn't gotten along for years, and lately Jo lived mostly at Paxton's house. It was only because she'd gone home to retrieve more clothes that she found Agatha screaming. Her head was going to explode, Agatha said. Her bones were on fire.

When they wheeled her body into the living room, Paxton's mother turned Jo's face away and pressed the girl to her, smoothing her hair and shushing her. She was the only one who could hold Jo like that.

The sheet didn't quite cover Agatha. She lay on her side, legs bent, white knees poking out. As they wheeled her to the doorway one of the EMTs leaned across her body to lift her knees out of the way while his partner backed the gurney out. The wheels dropped onto the second step with a clank, and the sheet slipped from her face.

Agatha hadn't been a beautiful woman. Too much like a naked bird: wiry body, hawk nose, a pinched, smoker's mouth. Now her skin was salt white, the new skull and jaw stretched into a permanent scream. Blood soaked her nightgown where the growth of the new bones had outpaced her skin.

The first wave of transformations and near-transformations would follow the course Agatha had set. First fever, then the parched skin like dried clay. After a couple days the bones would begin to stretch and rearrange, the body churning all available fat and protein into new growth, sometimes two inches a day. They'd call it Argillaceous Osteoblastoma, but that designation would be made obsolete a couple weeks later when the beta transformations began. In late August the symptoms would morph again, and all the victims would be charlies.

Argos, betas, charlies. Those names hadn't been in use yet, of course. Only at the end of the summer, after the Changes halted as suddenly as they began, would the scientists and newspeople settle on Transcription Divergence Syndrome. TDS-A, then B and C.

The EMTs tugged the sheet back over Agatha's face and

carried her to the ambulance. Deke and Pax were too stunned to talk. "Shee-it," Deke whispered.

In a week the same change would be coming for him.

"I got hit by this wave of, of emotion," Pax said. He sat across from Deke at his kitchen table, elevated on a barstool they probably kept around just for visitors his size. "I looked at my father and I just felt . . ."

What? Love, or something like it. Connection. The eggshell had cracked open, and for a moment everything had run together; he'd forgotten who was Paxton and who was Harlan. The feeling was exhilarating and suffocating at once. A child's emotion: love indistinguishable from total immersion.

Pax shook his head, laughed to cover his embarrassment. "I don't know," he said. "It was very weird." He rolled a near-empty Coke bottle between his hands. He'd slept for nearly four hours and woken up thirsty. Even now he was still deeply freaked out.

"I'm so sorry," Deke said.

Pax smiled. "You can stop saying that now."

"Your daddy's stuff must be pretty strong," Donna said. She stood at the counter, chopping green onions and red peppers and scraping them into a huge stainless steel bowl. "It hit you pretty hard."

Pax laughed. He couldn't help it. She was chopping vegetables and talking about this . . . stuff that was oozing out of his father's body as if it were no stronger than an extra-strong shot of whiskey.

"So this has happened before, then?" Pax asked. "Not just with my dad?"

"It happens with all of the charlie men," Deke said. "The old ones, anyway. There's only about twelve of them in town. But your dad, I'd been told he was dry. He hadn't . . . produced like that before."

"Produced," Pax said flatly. *She wants to milk me like a cow.* "Produce what?"

Deke shrugged. "Nobody knows what it is," he said.

Donna said, "The charlies call it the vintage. Usually only the younger charlie boys handle the old men, they don't seem to be as affected."

"Though even they use gloves when they're siphoning," Deke said. "Good thing you didn't swallow any. Usually a touch doesn't do much. When I got some on me—"

"Wait a minute," Pax said.

"—I just got a little nauseous. But your daddy's stuff really knocked you on your ass."

"Wait—they're *sucking* this stuff *out* of him?" He didn't try to hide his disgust. He looked from Deke to Donna, then back to Deke. "You're shitting me."

Deke looked uncomfortable. "The old men can't carry the vintage around with them," he said. "Makes 'em crazy. You got to get it out of their bodies or they, I don't know, overdose on it."

Pax shook his head. "So the boys take it. And then what do they do with it?"

Deke looked at Donna. She shrugged.

"What, damn it?" Pax said.

Deke said, "It's some sex thing. Rhonda sells it to the chub boys. And the chub boys take it because they think the stuff has some effect on the girls."

"You're shitting me," Pax said again.

Deke started to smile, but then seemed to recognize that Pax was starting to panic. "I don't know. Rhonda's probably selling 'em a bill of goods. Does it matter? Let 'em do what they want—it doesn't have anything to do with us."

"Not you, maybe. Me, I got knocked on my ass. I could have overdosed. You didn't even call Nine-one-one, you called them, those chub boys."

"Come on, Pax," Deke said. "They know how to handle it. Call the paramedics, they'd try to check your dad into a hospital." He turned over one big palm. "It's clade business. A charlie thing."

"Like hell it is. This is a father thing."

"And you're his son, now?"

Pax sat back from the table. He thought about saying, "What the hell's that supposed to mean?" But he knew what he meant. Pax hadn't called his father in years. He hadn't planned to come back to Switchcreek until the old man's funeral. He just never planned on the wrong person dying.

Pax stood. "You know better than anyone, Deke. *He* sent *me* away."

"Where are you going?" Deke said.

"Just take me to my car." He turned toward the door. His head still felt light from the dose, but he could move fine. Mostly fine.

"Come on, P.K.," Deke said. "You can't just walk away every time you—"

"Cut this out, both of you!" Donna said.

Pax blinked at her. Deke started to open his mouth and she shushed him.

"We're all going to sit down and eat dinner," she said. "Whether you like it or not."

The two men sat back down. When she turned back to chopping the vegetables, Pax raised his eyebrows.

"Don't piss off an argo woman holding a knife," Deke said quietly, but of course his voice carried through the house.

Pax said, "We're not done talking about this chub thing."

"Didn't think so," Deke said.

# chapter 3

THE NEXT DAY, one of the chub boys was waiting for him at his father's house.

It was the blond one, spiked hair like a patch of dried straw. He sat behind the wheel of a new-looking Toyota Camry parked in the driveway. Metallic green paint job, shiny rims, everything gleaming in the morning sun. Pax pulled past the car and parked between it and the house.

The boy sat with his elbow propped on the window, heavy bass thumping from the stereo. He nodded at Pax through the windshield, and kept smiling as Pax walked over to him. The music was some kind of slowed-down hip-hop, old stuff that sounded like eighties rap.

"You mind turning that down?" Pax said. He had to shout to be heard over the music.

The fat boy grinned at him, but didn't reach for the stereo. His close, pink scalp showed between those carefully gelled and sprayed strands. Pax wanted to punch this guy in the mouth, a straight-arm right through the open window. It was a pleasure to know something so certainly, spoiled only by the equally certain knowledge that the chub could break him in half.

Pax leaned on the car and felt the vibration of the speakers through the sheet metal. He smiled and said quietly, "You're going to be bald by thirty, dough boy."

The chub's smile vanished. He punched a button to silence the music and said, "What was that?"

"Thank you," Pax said. "Much appreciated." He glanced back at the house. It looked the same as the other day: door shut, drapes closed. "Your buddies inside?"

The chub regained his grin. "Nosirree, Cuz. Just me. Hey, you feelin' any better today? Or a lot worse?"

"Fine, thanks." Pax looked back at the house. "So."

"Yeah?"

"You can leave now."

"Nah, that's okay."

Pax stared at him. "Listen, you can't just sit here in my dad's driveway."

"Well I been doing it all night. Where you been, anyway? I was here from eight o'clock on."

Pax straightened. This kid had been staking out the place all night? What must Harlan have thought? "Listen, I'm going inside and I'm calling the cops."

"Aw, come on now, you can't do that to family." He smiled. "Aunt Rhonda says we're cousins. Your momma was a Pritchard, and her granddaddy was my daddy's granddaddy's brother." He worked a stubby pinky into his ear. "Or great-granddaddy."

"What's your name?"

"Clete Pritchard."

Pax didn't remember any kid named Clete. He would have been six or seven years old when Pax left.

"Well listen, Cuz," Pax said. "You got about two minutes before the cops get here."

"Uh-huh. I'll be waiting for 'em right here, then."

Pax wheeled away from the kid before he really did punch him. He strode back to his car, and behind him the music started again. Pax retrieved the plastic grocery bags from the backseat and carried them up to the front porch.

The door was unlocked. Pax went inside without looking back and closed the door behind him. He could hear the *whump, whump, whump* of the Camry's bass. Clete wasn't going anywhere.

Pax walked into the living room. His father wasn't on the living room couch, but the ripe smell still filled the air.

"Dad?"

He walked down the hallway. His father's bedroom door was closed, but the bathroom door hung open. The room had been renovated: the old toilet had been replaced by one with a huge seat like a car tire; sturdy metal handrails had been fastened to the walls on each side of it.

Pax heard the clatter of something metal. He backtracked to the front door, then made his way to the kitchen.

His father sat wide-legged on a chair nearly swallowed by his huge body, a comb in one hand and scissors in the other. He wore the same robe as before, but his hair was wet. A hand mirror lay on the table, and there were long chunks of black hair scattered over the table and floor.

After seeing his father yesterday Pax would have thought he was too big to move on his own, much less walk to the kitchen and wash his hair. And now he seemed even larger. The skin of his face, baggy before, stretched tight over his cheeks and forehead. The blisters on his face were shiny and pink.

His father blinked at him. "I thought I made you up."

"No such luck," Pax said.

"Here," his father said. He worked the scissors from his fat fingers. "I can't see the back of my head."

"I don't know how to cut hair."

"It's just hair, Paxton," his father said. He shoved the scissors toward him. "Snip snip."

Pax set the grocery bags on the table. He took the scissors by the blades. "There's a guy"— he almost said chub— "sitting out front in his car, watching the house. He said his name is Clete Pritchard."

His father grunted.

"Did you call the police?" Pax asked.

"Paxton, that's one of Rhonda's boys. He *is* the police."

"What's he doing out there? He can't just . . . sit there."

"You going to cut my hair or not?"

Pax stepped behind him, and his father bent his head. Up close, the damp black hair was shot with gray. His father didn't have to do this. Surely he could find somebody in town or in Lambert who could come in and cut hair.

His father grunted impatiently.

Pax wiped the handle of the scissors on his jeans and picked up the black plastic Ace comb. He smoothed the hair over the rolls of fat at his father's neck, careful not to scrape the necklace of small white blisters just above the robe's collar, and began to cut.

"You were here the other day," his father said.

"Yesterday."

"That's what I meant. I woke up and you were gone."

A minute or so later his father said, "When are you going back to—back to where you live?"

"I'm still in Chicago." Did the old man not even know where he lived? "I've got to leave this afternoon. I've got to get back to work."

"Good."

Paxton felt his face flush in anger. That tone. He'd forgotten how fast, how effortlessly, his father could piss him off.

His father leaned away from him, turned his head to eye him. "Look at what happened when you showed up. Before yesterday it hardly ever came. You're only making things worse."

Pax pushed down the top of his father's head and the old man obediently faced forward and bent his head.

Pax said, "Deke told me about—about how the chub boys suck that stuff out of you."

"They came again last night," his father said. Pax could hear the accusation in his voice. "Big day, they said. A double-header."

"I was with Deke yesterday. I was, well, recovering." His father didn't say anything. The hair along the sides of his head had dried and tangled. Pax tugged and cut, tugged and cut.

Several minutes passed. "I remember Jo Lynn when she was small," his father said. "I remember both of you . . ."

Pax's hand was resting against his father's head, holding it steady; he felt his big body tremble. "I'm not feeling so good," his father said. He exhaled heavily. "Help me get back to the living room."

"Just a second, I'm almost done," Pax said.

His father pushed up against the tabletop, tried to rise, and fell back.

"Hold on, hold on," Pax said. He put down the comb and scissors and stepped in front of him. His father was just so damn big. Pulling him upright, Pax realized, would be an engineering problem—an exercise in mechanics and leverage.

He straddled one of his father's legs and got a hand under each arm. "Ready?" he said.

He braced his feet on the linoleum floor and leaned back. His father held on to him, then with a lurch rose from the chair. For a moment they held each others' arms like dance partners: London Bridge Is Falling Down.

His father was much shorter than he remembered. It wasn't just that Pax had grown. Maybe the weight had compressed Harlan's spine. Maybe charlies gradually became perfect spheres. This old man came rolling home.

His father looked up at him and laughed. "He arose!" Like that his mood had lightened. He moved slowly toward the living room, planting each huge foot a few inches in front of the other.

His father's shape had been embossed onto the couch. The big man turned, put one arm on the back of the couch, and dropped into the same spot.

Pax parted the drapes. The chub's car was still out there. "Do you know what they're doing with the stuff, Dad?" he said. "After they take it from you?"

"Oh, you can ask Rhonda about that. *Somebody* ought to ask her." He pointed at the TV. "Turn that on."

Pax turned on the set, handed his father the remote, and then went back into the kitchen to make a sandwich from the deli meat he'd bought. By the time he returned with the plate his father was asleep.

Pax opened the kitchen windows, turned on lights. The kitchen was filthy, but ten years in the restaurant business, working every position from dishwasher to line cook, had inured him to vile substances that bred in the dark. He'd just clean up a little, and then when his father woke up he'd say his good-byes and get the hell out of there.

He swept up the hair clippings, and when he couldn't find a garbage bag, tossed them into the grocery sack. There was Palmolive dish soap under the sink—his mother's brand. He washed the dishes and rinsed them in bleach water. Then on to the refrigerator. The racks held nothing but condiments and Tupperware and foil-wrapped bowls. After inspecting a few of the containers and finding their contents far gone, he began to toss everything. His father's snoring drowned out the sound of the TV.

He could have come back here and started cleaning last night after supper at Deke's. Instead he'd driven up to the Lambert Motel 6. Deke and Donna had tried to get him to stay with them, but the vintage was still in his system and the oversized bed in the giant house was a little too Alice in Wonderland. He felt like he was overdosing on strangeness.

That night he sat on the polyester bedspread in his underwear, eating CiCi's pizza and flipping through channels. For dessert he smoked a joint while he watched a *South Park* rerun. Around ten he called in to work and told the night manager he couldn't make it back to the restaurant by Monday. The manager started to be a dick about it, as usual, but quickly backed off when Pax told him his father was sick. Pax must have sounded genuinely upset.

He said he didn't know how long it would take to get someone to take care of his father. Which was true, as far as it went.

Nobody at work knew he was from Switchcreek. None of his friends either. They knew he was from down south, but so far he'd never felt the need to open up a conversation—or shut one down—with *Hey, you know that biological catastrophe thirteen years ago? That was my hometown!*

It helped that nobody he knew in Chicago talked about the Changes, or had even seen a Switchcreeker in person. All the years Pax lived in Chicago the only Changed he'd seen was an argo boy on a talk show. He'd heard there was a beta in L.A. who ran some kind of fetish website, but he'd never looked it up. His people stayed home, or they became professional freaks. Only the unchanged, like Pax, had the option of passing in the outside world. Pax could slip back to his life in the city any time he wanted to. Any time.

He heard a faint thump from outside—the chub's car door shutting? He hurried into the living room, and stopped short before reaching the door.

His father's body had swelled. His stomach had pushed open the robe, and his face and neck had ballooned. His snoring had stopped, but his eyes were still closed and his breathing was coming heavy.

"Dad?" He went to his side, touched his shoulder. "Dad!"

His father's eyes slowly opened. His pupils were dilated. "Lorraine. Lorraine was here."

"Mom's not here, Dad. You were dreaming."

His eyes seemed to focus on Pax's face, then his head fell back in surprise. "Paxton? Is that really you?" He smiled. "The prodigal returns."

*Shit,* Pax thought.

"You mother was just here," he said. "Or maybe that was yesterday."

The blisters had erupted again. They were everywhere on

his skin, all sizes, weeping and shiny. His father reached for him and Paxton stepped back. He remembered that electric rush of emotion that had struck him, left him lying stupid in the grass.

He heard voices and went to the door. Through the diamond-shaped window he saw another car in the driveway—one of those new Cadillacs with a snout like a bulldog—and Aunt Rhonda waddling toward the house in her blazing pink pantsuit. Close behind came three chub boys: Clete, who was carrying a Styrofoam cooler; the one with the diamond earring and a head like a bowling ball who seemed to be Aunt Rhonda's personal bodyguard; and another muscled boy he didn't recognize who swung a duffel bag in his hand.

Paxton locked the door and stepped to the side, out of the view of the window. Even though he was expecting it, the knock made him flinch.

"Reverend Martin?" Rhonda called. "Paxton?"

He backed away from the door—he didn't want his voice to sound too close—and called back, "This isn't a good time, Aunt Rhonda."

"Don't let her in!" his father bellowed.

One of the men laughed, but was quickly cut off. Rhonda said, "Paxton, honey, I'm here to help. Boys, go back to the cars and sit awhile. Paxton and I need to talk."

Pax risked a glance out the window; the chub boys were walking back to the driveway, talking among themselves.

In a lower voice Rhonda said, "Paxton, open the door and let me explain what all's going on."

Pax glanced at his father. He was staring at his knees, shaking his head back and forth. Pax unlocked the door and slowly opened it. "I think we should talk outside," he said, and pulled the door closed behind him. The chubs glanced back but kept walking.

"How's the reverend doing?" Rhonda said. She looked like the Man in the Moon in drag: tiny blue-shadowed eyes and tiny red lips in the middle of a huge round face.

"Not too good," Pax said.

"Is he bloated?" she asked. "Talking to himself, hallucinating?"

"Something like that. Well, all of that, actually." She pursed her lips understandingly, and he said, "I know that you've been, uh, siphoning him."

She nodded, waiting.

"He says you're milking him like a cow."

She smiled wryly. "That sounds like your daddy." She nodded toward the window. "Has he told you why we're doing it? Or is he too far gone to say?"

"He said I should ask you."

"Well, that's good advice, at least. Here's what's happening right now—he's got a drugstore-worth of chemicals running through his system. If we don't drain the vintage out of him he's going to be high as a kite, and who knows when he'll come down. Let my boys extract it now, Paxton. You can watch if you want. But then you and I need to have that talk you promised me. Now that your father's producing, you need to understand what your responsibilities are."

"Get off my property!" his father yelled.

"Is it painful?" Pax said. "The process, I mean."

She patted his arm. "Maybe to watch, honey. But it don't hurt them none." She gestured to the chubs, and they started walking back. "It'll be good for you to be here, though," she said. "Your dad can be kinda feisty."

---

Rhonda stood well back from the old man and issued instructions to the boys. Everett, the serious boy with the shaved head and earring, sat on one side of Harlan, then hooked a foot around his ankle to hold down his legs and grabbed an arm. Clete took the other side. The third chub, a younger kid named Travis who had thick black hair and Elvis sideburns, worked the needle. Pax crouched near his father's knees, talking in a low voice through the paper breathing mask Rhonda had given him. His father could not be soothed. He struggled and shouted, but Rhonda's boys couldn't be budged, and in a few minutes his father was exhausted.

"Like trying to shave a cat," Clete said, and Travis laughed.

"Shave a cat," Travis said.

Aunt Rhonda excused herself. "Best not for me to get too close," she said, and went outside.

The boys started with the insides of his father's forearms. Travis would swipe the surface of a sac with iodine, then slide in the needle. Pax winced every time, his stomach turning. But his father didn't seem to feel the needle; they might as well have been poking at Ziploc bags. After his arms they opened his robe and lifted his T-shirt to siphon the larger sacs on his belly and chest. They ignored the smaller blisters and pimples.

When the syringe filled, Travis placed it in the Styrofoam cooler, then picked up a new needle and syringe from a box on the floor.

The siphoning seemed to go on and on, but when Pax checked his watch only fifteen minutes had passed. A sour odor filled his nostrils. He felt queasy, and sweat painted his neck.

At some point his father passed out or simply fell asleep; his head lolled to the side and he began to breathe deeply. The robe had fallen open, and Pax was alarmed to see that an erection tented his boxer shorts.

Pax pushed the robe over it and Clete laughed. "Happens every time," he said. "This stuff's better than Viagra."

"Cut it out," Everett said sternly. It was the first time Pax had heard him speak. Now that Everett didn't need to restrain Harlan, he could help siphon. He started using a second needle, and the extraction proceeded faster. A few minutes later they had only his father's back to do. They tilted Harlan forward and sideways, then pushed up his robe to his shoulders. Pax held his father's head against him, patting with his gloved hand the black-and-gray hair he'd been cutting two hours ago. He could not get used to the size of his father, his helplessness, the zoological strangeness of his body.

The boys began to pack up their supplies. Pax pushed his father back into a sitting position and straightened his robe. Then he followed the boys outside.

"That wasn't so bad, was it?" Rhonda asked him.

Pax stared at her.

She laughed heartily. "You held it together better than I thought you would. Most skips couldn't do it—certainly not a man. It's women who change the diapers and take care of the old people in this world. Most men don't have the stomach for it." She held open a plastic garbage bag and he tossed in his mask and gloves. "Do this every day and you'll get used to it."

Pax exhaled heavily. "Every day this has to happen?"

"If you want to keep him healthy." She gave him an appraising look. "Now I didn't come out here just for your father's treatment, though I was glad I could help. I came to show you someplace where there's a different way of doing this."

"I don't know," Pax said, glancing back at the house. Everett stepped out carrying the cooler.

"Don't you worry," Rhonda said. "We'll have you back in no time. Your daddy's going to be sleeping for a while."

# chapter 4

THE INSIDE OF the Cadillac smelled like a tub full of lilac petals—Rhonda distilled.

Pax rode in the back alone, while Rhonda sat up front in the passenger seat next to Everett. "My next project is to build our own high school," Rhonda said. Only the top of her hair-sprayed head was visible. "You know they wouldn't let Everett play on the football team at the county school? Can't pass the physical, they said, because he's morbidly obese. Obese! Not for a charlie, I said. Not for one of our people. They won't let the argo boys play either, especially not basketball. Lord, they're deathly afraid of argos playing basketball. Not that they're any good at it—they got hands like concrete. And nobody wants to even shower with the beta boys. Tell me that's not discrimination."

"That's discrimination," Pax said.

"You bet it is. We're going to sue their hind ends off, then use it to pay for the stadium. Everett here can be our coach." Pax could see the side of his face. The man shook his head, smiling shyly. It was the first time Pax had seen him break his frown.

They skirted the edge of town, taking Roberts Road under the eastern face of Mount Clyburn. The fields of the Whitmer farm opened up to their right, and a new white fence sprang up and raced alongside the road, pickets blurring. As they approached the entrance to the farm, he saw that they'd turned the place into a trailer park. Fourteen or fifteen mobile homes surrounded what looked like a white-painted warehouse, a cheap sheet-metal building with a low, flat roof. The Whitmers' ancient barn still stood in the distance, but the old farmhouse was gone. Beta children played between the trailers, and a few of the taller girls wore those white scarves on their heads.

Aunt Rhonda rolled down the window and waved at two beta women inside the fence who were unloading bags of insulation from the bed of a pickup. They wore nothing on their smooth heads, and one of them carried a toddler in a pack on her back. The women returned the wave without smiling, but maybe that was a beta thing.

"Those blanks are breeding like rabbits," Rhonda said, and rolled up the window.

*Blanks.* Another slang term. Every clade had to be put in their place, he thought. "Was that the Co-op?" he said.

"Jo Lynn started that after you left," Rhonda said. "Not her best idea."

"Jo did? But she was living on her own," Pax said.

"Just the past couple years, hon. She started the farm back in, oh, a year after you left, I guess. Several families moved in with her. She tried to call it a commune at first, but people didn't like the sound of that. Anyway, more and more of them started moving out there. There's quite a few blanks still living around town in their old houses, trying to keep their old families together. But I think deep down the betas like living close, sharing the babies."

"But Jo, did she leave, or was she kicked out?"

Rhonda laughed. "A little of both."

"How so?"

"Jo was all for *planned* motherhood. That didn't sit too well with the younger girls. Every single one of them wants to be the Virgin Mary, even if they're fourteen. *Especially* if they're fourteen. And then when Jo—well, I don't need to talk about that."

"About what?"

"Oh, there's all kinds of rumors. Nobody needs to tell *you* how people talk."

Pax sat back, his face burning as if he'd been slapped. Nobody forgets anything in your hometown, he thought. Ten years wasn't enough. Twenty. He'd die an old man and they'd still say, *You heard why his daddy ran him out of town, didn't you?*

Rhonda leaned over and looked between the seats at him, raising her eyebrows. "Paxton, you're a grown man now. You know how small-minded people can be. Jo Lynn never was shy about sharing her opinion, and what's more, she was ready to do more than just talk about it—she was going to take action. A lot of the sisters, especially the young ones—well, they thought she was the devil herself."

Roberts Road ended at the highway, and Everett turned the car south, away from town. A half mile after the south gate, one of the boundaries during the quarantine, he turned off onto a newly paved road that wound up into the hills. When Pax was a kid there'd been nothing out here but trees and scrub brush.

Near the top of the hill the driveway was blocked by a black iron gate set into a high stone wall. Everett stopped and spoke into an intercom set on a post a few feet from the gate. "Aunt Rhonda's here," the chub boy said.

"What's with the high security, Aunt Rhonda?" Pax said.

His tone was light, but the fortress set dressing had put him on edge.

"Can't be too careful, hon," Rhonda said.

The gate swung open. Everett drove up the hill and around a curve, where the drive ended in front of a one-story brick building like an elementary school. White cement columns supported a broad porch and entranceway. The bottoms of the columns were smudged with red clay, but otherwise the place looked almost brand-new.

They got out of the car, and Everett retrieved the Styrofoam cooler from the Cadillac's trunk. Pax knew there'd come a point when he'd have to ask Aunt Rhonda what she was going to do with those vials—and then all this polite chitchat would be over.

A charlie man in a brown security uniform came out of the building to meet them. He was in his forties, looking more fat than muscular. His hairline had retreated to high ground. "How you doing today, Aunt Rhonda?" he said.

"Just fine, Barron. This is Paxton Martin, the Reverend Martin's boy."

They shook hands and Barron said, "Welcome to the Home."

The guard led them up the ramps to the building and opened the door for them. The foyer was tiled in pale green slate, the air glowing with sunlight pouring through a row of high windows. A man older and more immense than Pax's father napped on a huge, sturdy couch.

"We have thirteen men living here now," Rhonda said. "We

take care of them because their families just can't. You've seen how hard it is. Come on, I'll show you around the place."

Rhonda led Pax toward a set of double doors. Barron started to follow, but at a look from Rhonda he stopped at the edge of the lobby. Everett had already disappeared in the other direction, carrying the cooler.

Rhonda pressed a button on the wall, and the doors glided open to reveal a small space before another set of doors. She gestured Pax inside, and when the doors closed behind him, a vent in the ceiling jetted warm air at them. Five seconds later the next set of doors swung open. Pax thought, Air lock?

The area beyond was a hallway and a row of serious-looking doors. She opened the first of them and showed him an empty apartment: bedroom, sitting room, bathroom, and kitchenette, all laid out wide for charlie bodies. The tubs and toilets were enormous.

"You certainly seem to be well equipped," Pax said. "I suppose that was you who set my father up with that big new toilet?"

"Hon, fixing up that bathroom was the least we could do. He didn't want to come live here at the Home, but there are certain needs for people our size. Our old houses just aren't built for our new bodies." She laughed and patted one of her big hips.

She took him to the next apartment. A man sat propped up in a queen-sized hospital bed, watching a game show on a huge flat-screen TV. The room seemed to be at least partly furnished with his own belongings: homemade quilts, lamps that didn't match, picture frames and knickknacks on the shelves. The man watched the screen intently, his mouth moving as if he was chewing on the inside of his cheek. His exposed skin was splotched with a white substance like dried sunblock.

"How you doing today, Elwyn?" Aunt Rhonda said, raising her voice over the sound of the TV. Elwyn's jaw hung slack for a moment, and then he resumed his chewing. He never looked away from the screen.

"Every room has a big-screen TV and five hundred satellite channels," Rhonda said. "Our boys like the TV."

She showed him two more rooms. Both occupants were about the age of Pax's father, and they looked much more alert than Elwyn. The men made small talk, and seemed happy enough to see Rhonda. Both were patched by white ointment—jalopies primed for a new paint job.

Rhonda said, "We've got three women who do all the cooking down at a kitchen I set up downtown, and we bring it in fresh every day. Nothing fancy—most of our men like their food home-style. We go through five pans of cornbread every meal." She glanced up at Pax. "So how's your father eating these days?"

"I don't know for sure, but I think it's kind of, uh, hit-and-miss."

She nodded understandingly. She was trying to score points, and she knew that he knew it.

"Who's paying for all this?" he asked.

"The whole clade," Rhonda said. "Every charlie pitches in."

"Really?"

"Oh, sometimes family members donate, the skips or people from other clades whose daddy starts producing. But mostly it comes from our own people. That's because we all know that we have to take care of our own. The blanks won't help; the argos won't help. And we aren't getting a thing from the government." She patted Paxton to point him back toward the double doors. She kept touching him, Pax noticed, but hadn't touched any of the residents. In fact, she hadn't gotten within five feet of them.

"Deke told me my father was dry," Pax said.

"Not completely," Rhonda said. "We checked on him every so often, but he wasn't producing more than a trickle, not like the other men his age."

"Why's that?"

"Well that's an interesting question, isn't it? Oh, hon, nobody knows for sure how all this is supposed to work—it's not like there's a lot of medical history on our people! Some of our older men are as regular as, well, it just comes flowing out of them. But your dad, he was like a rusty faucet. Dribs and drabs."

"Until yesterday."

She patted his arm. "That's right. Isn't that something?"

He smiled, feeling nervous. "Those vials you took from my father. Where'd Everett take them?"

"Why, down to the freezer," she said, as if that were obvious.

Pax rubbed at the back of his neck. "Okay, and then what?"

Rhonda didn't answer. She waited until the air had washed over them again and they were out into the lobby, and then she said, "Everett told me he found you laying in the grass at your father's, waving your arms."

Paxton felt his face heat. "All I did was get some on me. That stuff hit me like a Mack truck."

Rhonda shook her head. "I'm sorry about that, Paxton. Nobody ever thought it would have that kind of effect on you. Even so, I would have warned you if I thought your father was producing even a little bit." The guard, Barron, glanced in their direction, then looked away. The old charlie man on the couch snored heavily. "But in a way it's a good thing it happened." She gestured toward a door marked OFFICE. "Sit down, let me tell you a story."

Rhonda situated herself behind a big desk piled with paper, a PC on the oak return behind her. Her seat was raised; she was as tall sitting as standing. Pax took one of the leather guest chairs.

"Willie Flint was the first," Rhonda said. "He started producing a couple years after you left. His son, Donald—he was a bit older than you?—he turned charlie too." Pax remembered Donny Flint. Dumb as a box of rocks. "Well, Donald found out what it could do. It didn't take long for the vintage parties to start. He started selling the stuff to other charlies. Boys were using too much, girls were going crazy, boys and girls alike were starting fights. A couple kids ended up in the hospital. Donald had it too strong, and it was going to kill someone."

Pax nodded, even though he didn't understand most of what she was talking about. Going crazy how?

"Well," Rhonda said. "Nobody knew at first what this stuff was, or how he was getting it. They thought he was cooking it up at home, like that crystal meth? But Donald, he couldn't stop himself from talking about it. Word got around. The next thing we knew, Donald's disappeared, probably killed, and his so-called friends have decided to set up business for themselves."

"What do you mean—they started selling it?"

"Not just selling it. They were doing their own extractions. I wasn't mayor then, but I was with the group that found old Willie." Her voice had grown hard. "They'd made him a prisoner in his own house. They'd barely been feeding him, poking at him with the same needle over and over. His skin was all infected . . ." She took a breath. "He was already dead when we found him, Paxton. They'd killed him. You wouldn't of treated a dog like that."

Rhonda opened a file drawer in the desk, drew out a manila folder. "A couple weeks later one of our other men started blistering, then another. I knew if we didn't do something, it was going to happen all over again. Some stupid charlie boy with more muscles than sense would grab the next one, and the next one.

"You're involved now, Paxton. Your father's producing, so you should know what we're doing with the vintage. First and foremost, we're keeping it away from people who would abuse it. If we have it locked up here, then it's not on the streets."

"Then why not just destroy it?"

"Paxton, you don't understand how much the young charlies want the vintage. If we cut off the supply completely, they'd just get desperate, and desperate people do stupid, dangerous things. Better to let it out in dribs and drabs, to the people I trust. Then they're invested in keeping the system going."

"You're making a deal with the devil," Pax said. "You can't wave this in front of them and not expect them to come take it."

"Don't you worry about that. No place is safer than the Home." She opened the folder and slid it across the desk to him. There looked to be more than fifty pages of forms tagged with yellow SIGN HERE stickies. "This is everything we need to enroll your father in the program and start treating him. HIPAA forms, requests for records—"

"Wait," he said. "You said, 'First and Foremost.' What else—"

She waved a hand. "This packet here, these are the Medicaid forms and paperwork you'd have to sign for any extended care facility."

"What else are you doing with the vintage, Rhonda?"

Rhonda sat back in her chair. She sighed. "I'd like to tell you. I would. But at this point it's too early to get people's hopes up."

Pax let go of the pages and put his hands on his lap. "Forget it, then. I'm not signing."

"Now, Paxton, don't be difficult."

He stood. "I'm sorry, Aunt Rhonda. Now if you could tell Everett to drive me home . . ."

He stood holding the doorknob. She pinned him with a steady look, then seemed to come to a decision. "Okay, then." She nodded at the chair, then waited until he'd resumed his seat. "This has to remain strictly confidential, you understand? It cannot leave this room."

"It depends on what you tell me. If it's illegal—"

"No, it's not illegal! Paxton Martin . . ." She shook her head in exasperation. "This is about the men of my clade. I am not content to condemn every charlie boy to what's happened to your father, or God help me die locked up in some shack like Willie Flint. I am determined to end this."

"End this? How? You're not talking about euthanizing them, or—"

"Paxton, if you keep saying stupid things I will reach across the desk and slap you."

"I just don't know what you're talking about."

"I'm talking about research, Paxton. Scientific research. Getting the medical community to pay a little attention to the problems of this clade before another generation of men have to suffer. Every two weeks I send another shipment to Stanford University in California. There's a man there with a team of eight graduate students working on figuring out what the vintage is, what it does, and how we can turn it off."

"Why in the world would you keep that secret?"

"You're not from here anymore, Paxton. And you're not a charlie or you wouldn't ask that question. Do you think Clete or Travis or any of the young charlies want to give up the vintage? Do you think they want this to be cut off forever? Before you open your mouth, the answer is no, they would not."

She patted the stack of papers. "Now. I know this looks like a lot of papers, but they're already filled out except for the dates and signatures, and I can walk you through them so you understand everything that you're signing. After you do that, we can start taking care of your father. Today."

"I don't know," Pax said.

She looked at him. "Talk to me, hon."

"It's just . . ." The top page in the stack was some kind of confidentiality form, with his own name typed at the bottom. He was almost embarrassed at how relieved he felt. Each of the forms—fifty, sixty of them, it didn't matter—was like a rung on a ladder that would let him climb out of this pit. What else could he do, quit his job and move down here? Siphon the old man every day himself? He couldn't do that. He wasn't strong enough for that kind of work.

"I need to talk to my father," he said. It didn't sound convincing, even to himself. He'd already decided he would sign. All he needed was some time to explain to himself how this wasn't a betrayal.

"I know you feel that way. But remember, Paxton, your daddy's not in his right mind just now. The reverend's been my friend for thirty years, but charlie men can't function like they used to, not when the vintage is running in them. Whether you like it or not, you're his guardian now."

"I understand that," he said. "I do." He closed the folder

and pulled it onto his lap. "Let me just take this home, look it over, and I'll sign it tonight."

"Tonight," Rhonda said. She got up from her chair and came around the desk, opened her arms. "Don't look so worried, honey. You're doing the right thing. Now give Aunt Rhonda a hug."

His father was still sleeping when Rhonda and Everett dropped him off at the house. Pax stood beside the couch for a long time, watching Harlan's huge chest rise and fall, jowls shuddering with each snore.

Just below his father's collarbone a patch of skin glistened in the lamplight. A small white blister, too small for the earlier siphoning, had split.

It would be a simple thing, Pax thought. Just dip a fingertip in the wet from the blister. He wouldn't even have to wake the old man.

Paxton turned out the lamp. He made his way through the dark to the guest bedroom, put Rhonda's folder under the bed, and lay down. His father snored like a misfiring engine. In the dark, with the door open between them, it sounded as if Harlan were lying beside him.

# chapter 5

DEKE STOOD OUTSIDE the bathroom door, not listening. After several minutes, he said, "Honey?"

Donna didn't answer.

"Want me to hold the cup?" He made the same joke every time.

He had to be in Masonville in forty minutes, and he didn't want to be the last one into the courthouse. The last one to walk past all those cops.

Finally the sound of the toilet flushing and water running in the sink. Another minute passed.

"Donna . . ."

She opened the door. "Standing there don't speed things up," she said, and handed him an orange plastic cup with a white lid. It was uncomfortably warm.

"Uh, don't we have a bag or something?"

She shook her head, pretending exasperation, and led him into the kitchen. She found a plastic bag, tucked the cup into it, and cinched the bag tight. "There you go. Nobody'll suspect you're smuggling pee."

"On the street they call it Troll Gold."

That got her to laugh. "Too bad you can't sell it," she said.

Then, "They're probably not going to ask about the money, but if they do—"

"They're not going to ask about the money. That's all done through administration. We're only a few weeks late. The bank's supposed to call me soon."

They'd already run through the second mortgage on the house. He'd applied for a loan through Alpha Furniture, his business, but the bank hadn't gotten back to them yet on whether it had been approved.

"Okay, then. You've got your envelope?"

He patted his front breast pocket. "Right here next to my heart."

"If you leave those somewhere—"

"Have I ever lost them?"

"You do, don't bother to come back," she said.

"I'll guard them with my life." She followed him to the front door. The hall clock showed that it was a little past 8:20—he'd have to haul ass. "Hey, I may stop by and see Paxton afterward if I get done early at the shop."

"Okay . . ."

He heard the skepticism in her voice and turned. "What?"

"Are you sure you two were best friends?" Donna said. "You and Jo, that makes sense. But Paxton . . . I just don't see it."

"He's different than he was," Deke said.

"He's skittish is what he is. All the time you're talking to him he's got one foot out the door."

"That's not like him. Back then . . ." He shrugged. Before the Changes, Paxton had been sure of himself. Cocky. He had the money, the toys, the big house—what Deke used to think was a big house, anyway. And Deke had been happy just to be his friend. "I don't know. He's a little lost, maybe. It can't be easy to come back here."

"Maybe he's in the closet."

"What? No."

"Why not? Have you asked him?"

"No." Then: "I don't know. I don't know if Paxton would know himself." He shook his head. "Listen, I better get going or I'm going to miss the meeting."

"Hey," she said. She turned him around, then bent her head and kissed him hard on the lips. Her expression had gone serious. "Are you going to be okay hearing all those details?"

"I doubt they're going to tell us anything new," he said.

"Still," she said. "Call me at work when it's over." Four days after Jo Lynn's death and they were still being careful with each other.

Once he left Switchcreek he had to watch his speed. He'd been stopped dozens of times over the years. Sometimes the cops said they were checking if his car was street-legal (he had the handicap permits for the modifications, the special plates, the note from his insurance—every damn thing), and sometimes they said he was speeding. Sometimes they didn't give him any reason at all. The first time he complained about getting profiled—this was when they'd just started dating—Donna had laughed and laughed.

He got onto 411 and joined the line of cars heading into Masonville. The area had outgrown the two-lane highway years ago, but nobody had come up with the money to expand the road. He listened to the intermittent squawks of the police scanner and tried not to think of the time. He ignored the other drivers. It helped that they were all below eye level.

When he finally reached the center of town he parked in a metered lot behind a row of police cars. He loped toward the entrance to the Mason County courthouse. A woman and a boy about five years old walked toward him, the kid jabbering away, and when the woman looked up and saw Deke she put an arm around the boy, who gaped up at him. Deke didn't mind kids. Their stares were honest.

Going into the courthouse he had to crouch to make it through the revolving door, baby-stepping to keep his knees from banging the glass. The lobby was mostly empty. He walked through the unattended metal detector—no beeps—and approached the woman sitting behind the counter. Behind her a cop came out of a rear office, glanced up from a paper in his hand, and stopped cold. His right hand moved to the top of his holster.

Deke raised his hands. "Hey," he said, keeping his voice friendly. "I'm just here for an appointment with the DA."

The cop stared at him like he was a goddamn T. rex. He didn't move his hand from his gun.

"It's okay, Kyle," the woman said to the cop. Then to Deke she said, "I'll take you back."

Jesus Christ, Deke thought.

She buzzed him into a back hallway, then led him down to a conference room. Aunt Rhonda and the Reverend Hooke were already sitting at the table. The DA and the sheriff hadn't arrived yet.

"Morning," he said to the women. He felt underdressed. He wore a work shirt and jeans that had been stitched together at Donna's shop—it took three pairs of XXL jeans to make a pair that would fit an argo. Rhonda was dressed in a pale green business suit, with shoes and eye shadow to match. (Thanks to Standard American Obesity, chubs didn't have to make their own clothes.) The reverend wore a white peasant blouse hanging over a long dark skirt, and a colorful vest like the kind she wore on Sundays, this one appliquéd with rose petals. Her smooth head was uncovered—no scarf for her.

None of the chairs would hold him, so he squatted with his back against the wall.

"You haven't missed anything yet," Rhonda said. She sounded annoyed.

He wondered if making them wait was some kind of political statement. Rhonda had forced the meeting, but maybe the DA wanted to show he couldn't be pushed around.

Three years ago, right around the tenth anniversary of the Changes, a beta girl named Sherilyn Manus was beaten up and raped outside a bar in Sevierville. Despite Sherilyn giving descriptions and first names of the men who'd assaulted her, the police didn't arrest anyone for weeks. Rhonda started calling newspapers and TV stations, telling every reporter she could find about the prejudice the people of Switchcreek faced. The district attorney, Roy Downer, spent almost as much time holding press conferences. The police eventually arrested two men, and only then did Rhonda take her foot off Downer's throat.

The DA came in a few minutes later with the sheriff right behind. Downer carried a stack of files under one arm and a laptop under the other. He set them on the table, and then both men went around the table shaking hands, making somber noises. The DA paid most of his attention to Rhonda. He looked like a bobble-head doll, a little man with an enormous, wobbly noggin. Then again, a lot of the normals had started to look like that to Deke.

Downer sat across from Rhonda and the reverend and turned on the laptop. "We're going to release a statement to the press very soon," he said. "Tomorrow morning, hopefully. Normally we'd never share details about an open case like this—you don't want to hinder the investigation, or expose the office to criticism until we've checked all the facts. You have to get your ducks in a row . . ."

"We appreciate the immense risk you're taking, Roy," Rhonda said dryly.

"Well, I think we all agree that in cases like these, the county has to reach out to the local community. Though you all understand this has to remain confidential until we make a more public announcement."

"Yes, of course," the reverend said. Blanks were hard to read, but Deke had spent enough time around the clade to know the pastor was on edge. The woman sat straight in her chair, barely moving, like a squirrel catching the scent of a hound dog. "What have you found out?"

"Not a thing," the sheriff said. He was a white-haired, broad-faced man with a complexion like a permanent sunburn. Deke had worked with him a couple times before when Deke had stepped in to keep the peace between Switchcreek folks and the county police. He was quiet and competent.

"Uh, what the sheriff means," Downer put in, "is that we've found nothing that changes what we already thought. The coroner's report said that she died of strangulation, not a broken neck, which is typical in suicides. People don't usually manage to break their necks."

"Jesus," Deke said under his breath. Rhonda shook her head, but the reverend seemed to be holding herself in check.

"As for the house," Downer said, "there were no signs of a struggle, or forced entry. The materials she used were all on hand—the rope was already hanging from the tree for the tire swing, the patio chair was nearby. The two girls didn't hear anything. They didn't even know their mom was outside until that morning, when they called Nine-one-one. That was at 6:10 a.m."

"How long was she up there, then?" Rhonda asked.

Downer looked to the sheriff, and the cop said, "She died at least several hours before the call. The blood had time to pool in her feet before we found her. Besides that . . ." He shrugged. "It ain't like on TV. That's about all we know."

"And nobody saw her just hanging out there in the open?" Rhonda said.

"The tree isn't visible from the road," Deke said. He didn't add that even if someone from Switchcreek had managed to see something, he doubted they'd have called the police—any one of the clades would have called Deke or Rhonda or the reverend, one of their own.

"Which of the girls made the call?" the Reverend asked.

Downer stared blankly at her. "I don't see how that matters, but . . . well, let me see." He opened a manila folder, started flipping through papers.

"Rainy," the sheriff said. "Though she doesn't say so on the tape. Later she told us that she was the one who called. Sandra agreed."

"What *did* she say on the tape?" the reverend asked.

Downer opened a folder and started flipping through the pages. "I have the transcript somewhere . . ."

"You can just summarize, Roy," Rhonda said.

"The girl gave her address," the sheriff said. "Then she said that her mother had killed herself. Very calm, very composed."

"Our girls can sound calm to outsiders, even when they're upset," the reverend said.

Rhonda said, "She said that? 'Killed herself'?"

The cop shrugged. "Near as I recall. We also talked to Dr. Fraelich, the doctor who was treating her. She confirmed that Jo Lynn had been prescribed antidepressants since her operation two years ago."

"Oh! Here we go," the district attorney said. "Yes, 'killed herself.' Exact words." He pushed the sheet across the table.

"What kind of operation did she have?" Rhonda asked the sheriff.

Deke looked at the mayor. She wore a concerned expression that was very convincing.

"Uh, female problems," Roy said. "A hysterectomy."

"I see," Rhonda said.

Deke glanced at the reverend, then back to Rhonda. Both these women knew that Jo had had an abortion a month before the hysterectomy, and Dr. Fraelich had helped with both procedures. Rhonda was fishing to find out what Fraelich had told the police.

The sheriff said, "Hormonal adjustment is how the doctor put it. She said it was perfectly normal in women to experience periods of depression after the operation."

Deke said, "She'd stopped taking those pills months ago."

"You know this for a fact?" the sheriff said.

"Maybe that was the problem: She'd stopped taking them," Downer said. "Anyway, we'll have the drug report this week and we'll know if there was anything in her system."

The sheriff said, "We know she was distraught. Her daughters said she'd been upset that night. Crying and whatnot."

"Upset about what?" the reverend asked.

"They didn't know."

Downer said, "I got the impression it was just general weeping. Something she did a lot, evidently. If these kinds of hormonal problems affect menopausal women, who knows what affect it would have on a, a woman in Ms. Whitehall's condition?"

The reverend leaned back in her chair. "What condition would that be?"

"I think he means the beta condition," Rhonda said.

"No!" Downer said. "I didn't mean to imply anything of the sort. It's just, I mean, even normal women—"

Rhonda raised her black-penciled eyebrows. "Yes, Roy?"

The DA stopped himself before he began sputtering. He'd learned at least one thing since the Sherilyn Manus case, then.

"I think we're done here," he said. "If we learn anything new, of course we'll call you." He started closing down the laptop. The sheriff stood, hands at his sides.

The reverend said, "The ruling, then, is that this was a suicide?"

"That's what the coroner's report says," Downer said. "I can't see any reason to overrule it."

"What about the note?" Deke asked.

"Pardon?" Downer said.

"If it was a suicide, you'd think there'd be a note."

"Not always," the sheriff said. "Sometimes it's impulsive."

"Did you check her laptop?" Deke asked.

Downer looked up. "The laptop . . . yes." He looked at the sheriff.

"We don't have a computer listed on the report," the cop said. "And I didn't see one."

"It was a Mac," Deke said. "A little white one with a fish bumper sticker on it. She used it all the time."

"It's probably in the house, then. Of course we'll look at it."

As they left the conference room Rhonda took his arm and let the reverend walk out ahead of them.

"What's that look about?" she asked. "You've got your Chief face on."

"I don't know," Deke said. "The laptop. Plus Dr. Fraelich didn't tell them—"

"Shush. Your voice carries like a foghorn. Tell you what: Why don't we stop back at my office. I'd like to talk to you about some things."

"I've got some errands to run," he said. "Up in Knoxville."

"Oh, of course," she said, as if she knew exactly where he was going. Maybe she did. It was near impossible to keep a secret from Rhonda. And if she knew a secret, she never let you forget it. "I'll just nab you when you get back, then."

They passed the cop Deke had seen on the way in. The man watched them as they crossed the lobby. Deke ignored him.

When they were outside Deke said, "Nab me about what?"

"Paxton's going to sign the papers for his daddy."

She looked at him, waiting. She wanted to know if Deke was going to fight her on this.

"P.K. has to make up his own mind," he said.

"I was hoping you'd say that," she said. "Once I showed him the Home—"

"Either way," Deke said firmly. "Either way, it's his own decision. If he backs out, he backs out."

"Well of course, honey." She patted his arm. Her lipstick smile was unwavering. "You enjoy yourself in Knoxville, now."

University Hospital was a maze of hallways like one of those haunted houses thrown together by the Jaycees every Halloween. Except he was the monster. When people caught sight of him they jerked in surprise and looked away. Deke resisted the urge to yell, *Boo!*

He followed the signs to the elevators. Not that he was going to take one. The carriage might be able to take his weight, but he'd have to squat on the floor to fit. He found the stairwell door next to the elevators and ducked inside.

The fertility clinic was on the eighth floor. The two women at the front desk greeted him by name. How was traffic? How's Donna doing? Deke and Donna had been coming here twice a month for two years, and the staff was still trying hard to be as pleasant as could be.

"Sorry I'm late," Deke said. "I had to ask three different women to get a sample."

The youngest woman blinked at him, not sure if he was joking, then decided that he must be. "Oh, you," she said. She whisked the bag off to the back of the lab. The other woman took a key ring from the wall and said, "I think the room is free."

"Sure hope so," Deke said. "Hate to walk in on somebody."

She led him down the hall and unlocked a room. At the door she handed him a cup and lid that was a lot like the one Donna had filled, as well as a plastic, insulated sack to put it in. "Okay then!" she said, and closed the door behind her.

Well, he thought. Here we are again. Ready for romance?

The room contained a stand-alone wardrobe on wheels, a brown plaid couch, a coffee table, and a reading lamp. A door led to a small room with a toilet and shower. The drapes were closed, but bright sunlight peeled the edges.

He turned on the lamp, opened the wardrobe. Three of the shelves were piled high with magazines. He knew from past explorations that most of them were Playboys, some of them nearly a decade old. The kind of porn women would buy. A few Hustlers hid in the mix, probably left behind by clients who couldn't get inspired by the vanilla stuff.

On previous visits he'd tried looking through the magazines. All the girls looked like marshmallow-and-toothpick manikins: bulbous heads on spindly necks, massive doughy breasts, claw-hands tipped with red fingernails. And those mouths, Jesus Christ. Lips like red rubber suction cups, and tiny pink tongues lapping over sharp white teeth. The girl-on-girl pictorials were almost too much to bear.

On the floor of the wardrobe were a stack of hand towels and an industrial-sized bottle of sanitary gel, the same stuff they rubbed on Donna's belly during sonograms. He took the bottle and one of the towels back to the couch, set it on the coffee table. Then he reached into his breast pocket and took out a folded envelope.

Like everything else in the argo world, what didn't exist you had to make yourself. Donna had been happy to do her part. She'd even gone to buy the digital camera and the printer that made little Polaroid-sized pictures. He removed the pictures from the envelope and laid them out like he was dealing solitaire.

He laughed to himself. Solitaire. That was the game, all right.

---

When he delivered his cup the nurses thanked him as if he'd brought them donuts. "Don't use it all at once," he said.

"Pardon?" the young woman asked.

"Never mind." He waved good-bye and left his boys in their care. The UT doctors would count and evaluate them—were their heads properly bulbous, their tails sufficiently whiplike? did they swim like salmon, or laze about like carp at a dock?—and then ship them off to Boston and Barcelona. Once a month Donna came in for a date with a long needle, and the extracted eggs would be mailed off too. Sperm and eggs would rendezvous at a swank petri dish in a foreign city, where the close quarters and forced intimacy would hopefully lead to wanton permeability and penetration. So far the orgies had been a bust. Either his boys lost their nerve or Donna's girls rebuffed their advances, or something went wrong down the line. The few times when fertilization had taken hold, the subdivision had ground to a halt a few hours later. No one could tell them why.

He clumped downstairs, crouched to make it under the exit door, and walked out into sunlight. He should be thankful that anybody at all was taking an interest in their problem. Two different research teams were working on argo fertility. The geneticists had figured out ten years ago that while none of the clades could cross-fertilize with unchanged people, the clades could breed with their own kind. So chubs made more chubs and blanks pumped out two or three bald girls at a time—but argos remained as barren as winter trees.

It was becoming clearer and clearer that nobody had the slightest clue about how to fix the problem. TDS had rewritten their genes, and nobody knew how to read the new language. Deke and Donna were considered "mature onset"—the Changes had caught them after they'd gone through puberty—so maybe the problem wasn't that they'd been changed, but that they hadn't changed enough. The younger argos had grown taller, stronger, more "purely" argo. Maybe their odds of reproducing would be better. But so far only two other argo couples had volunteered for the fertility study. The costs were tremendous, and the young couples either couldn't afford it or weren't desperate enough yet. The old ones, the people over forty who'd spent most of their lives as normals, had no desire to make more freaks.

He paid the parking lot attendant, a black kid about twenty years old who didn't look too happy either. Deke thought about saying, *So, this troll walks into a bar and the bartender says, Hey buddy, why the long face?* And then the kid could tell him a nigger joke, and they'd share a big oppressed-minority laugh.

Sure, it would go just like that.

The argos weren't a minority—you had to be human to be part of that pie. Down deep the normals understood that they were a separate species altogether, a race of predators, and any one of them could slaughter a human with a swipe of an arm. The humans knew it, and no argo could afford to forget it either.

He drove fast, anxious to get home. He was happy to have the wind beat him around the head.

Not long ago he couldn't understand why Donna wanted to go through all this fertility nonsense. They didn't need children to be *fulfilled*, did they? Couldn't he and Donna be happy on their own? Lots of normals went their whole lives without making babies. So why the hell were they pining for a person who didn't exist? Might never exist.

But he came to share the ache. Maybe it was the species thing. Something in his cells that demanded to go on, to not let the humans win.

Jo Lynn had given him a picture once, something she'd found on the web and printed out for him. She'd given it to him and said, *This is your future.* And even though the picture was a fake, one of those Photoshop jobs people liked to put on the web, he'd folded it up and kept it with him, tucked away like—

"Shit!"

The photographs of Donna.

He slapped his shirt pocket, dug into his pants pockets as best he could while keeping the Jeep on the road, but of course the pictures weren't there. They were laid out on the donation room coffee table. He swung into the left lane and braked hard. He dropped the Jeep into the wide, shallow ditch dividing the interstate, turned around, and accelerated hard to rejoin the traffic heading back into town. Maybe the nurses hadn't gone into the room yet. Maybe they'd gone to lunch.

Twenty seconds later he saw the lights flashing in his rearview mirror and he swore again.

# chapter 6

THE MOSQUITO, INVISIBLE in the dark, tiptoed across the skin of his biceps.

Pax sat on the front stoop, all the house's lights turned off, and stared at the moonlit tops of the trees, waiting. When the bite came he didn't flinch. It was a kind of pleasure to keep his arm perfectly still, to let the little thing insert its needle snout and drink from him. He could almost feel its tiny body fill up with blood.

Behind him his father's snores augered through the walls. Last night the sound had gnawed at him, keeping him awake until the early morning. Pax didn't fall asleep so much as lie still until sleep fell on him. Now the snoring seemed less like a personal attack. Not quite background noise yet, but getting there. A couple more nights, Pax thought, and he wouldn't be able to sleep without it, like those people in Chicago with their bedrooms next to the El.

A couple more nights. He hadn't called his manager to tell him he wasn't coming back soon. He knew he should call in, negotiate for more time. But fuck it, his father was sick, and if they didn't give him his shitty job back when he got back to town, well, there were plenty of shitty jobs.

So instead of thinking about his nonlife in Chicago he'd

spent the day doing everything required of a dutiful son. He made Harlan breakfast, helped him to the toilet, even finished cutting his hair. His father's size complicated everything. The quarter ton of flesh didn't seem to be part of his father at all, but some great cargo he was forced to carry, a penitential weight. Pax knew that his body was an effect of the Changes, a symptom as inarguable as Deke's powdered skin, but he couldn't stop himself from thinking, Jesus, Dad, how did you let yourself get like this?

Pax helped him navigate back to the living room. Every movement had to be strategized, paced, evaluated. What would happen if he fell? There was no way Pax could get him up on his own. Finally he settled onto and into the creaking couch. Another task accomplished, another checkmark in Paxton's column. When I leave, Pax thought, he won't be able to say I didn't help him. He won't be able to say I didn't try.

Harlan napped, and then in the afternoon Pax sat beside him and they watched TV together the way they always had, talking only during the commercials and saying nothing of consequence. His father liked the Discovery Channel. Animals killing animals and being killed, having sex, raising animal babies.

Paxton's thoughts kept returning to the stack of legal papers he'd hidden under the bed. If his father sensed that Pax was distracted he didn't mention it. He didn't ask where Pax had been with Rhonda the day before, or when Pax was going back to the city. Both of them seemed determined to prove that they needed nothing of each other.

For dinner Pax made spaghetti and they ate on the couch together. His father fell asleep watching the news. Pax got a blanket from the hall closet and tucked it around his father's shoulders. Harlan's skin had started to swell and blister. Liquid gleamed on the backs of his hands.

When the snoring reached full production, Pax went into the kitchen and tore off a square of paper towel from the roll. He went back to the living room and crouched next to his father. A blister near his father's knuckles had already split, weeping vintage. Pax touched a corner of the towel to the spot, let it soak up the substance. Then holding the darkened tip away from his fingers as if it were a lit match, he walked out to the front porch. It was evening but not yet fully dark.

He held the paper towel for a long time, not looking at it. He felt like he was readying himself to jump into a cold pool. He laughed at himself, then quickly opened his mouth and touched the tip of paper to his tongue—a quick, light tap. He felt nothing. After thirty seconds he touched it to his tongue again. Then he sat and waited for something to happen.

His arm itched, but he let the mosquito finish its meal. He felt its happy fullness as it lifted off from his skin. He could picture the world through its gemstone eyes, feel the weight in his thorax as he weaved drunkenly toward the trees, humming like a clarinet, winging mightily to keep his bloated body in the air. . . .

He slipped back into his body with a lurch. Something was watching him from the trees.

He sat very still. Not out of fear—though he realized that any other time he might have been afraid—but out of curiosity. About twenty feet up one of the big pines, he could just make out a dark mass that clung to the trunk. It had stopped moving as soon as he'd looked directly at it, or else it was about to move. He slowly tilted his head, trying to tease out its outline—but then headlights sliced through the trees and the spell was broken.

A car came down the drive. More chubs? Pax thought tiredly. He'd just about had it with the fat boys.

He pushed the paper towel into his pocket.

The vehicle parked behind his father's car. It was a classic Ford Bronco from the seventies with a white hood and red body, big tires, shiny rims. It still looked good.

The cab lit up as the door opened, and a figure in a baseball cap climbed out of the truck and came around the hood. It was a beta man, dressed in a loose button shirt and jeans.

"How you doing, Tommy?" Pax said.

The man stopped abruptly. "I didn't see you there," Tommy Shields said in that soft voice. "I hope I—I know I'm coming awfully late. I just came to drop something off."

"It's fine. I was just getting some fresh air." Pax decided that his own voice sounded perfectly normal. "My dad's asleep, though, if you came to see him."

Tommy gave no indication of hearing the old man's snoring. "No, no," he said. "It's for you. I'm glad I caught you before you left town. I found something in Jo Lynn's things, and I thought . . . well, I thought you might like it."

"Just a second," Pax said. He stood quickly and had to pause for a moment, lightheaded. He opened the front door and reached in to flick on the porch light. Gnats immediately converged on the light, fizzing. He blinked up at them.

"Are you okay?" Tommy said. "You don't look so good."

Pax turned back to him, shaking his head. "I'm fine. I was just . . . What you got there?"

Tommy lifted the thing in his hand. "Jo Lynn kept this on her dresser," he said. "When we used to live together."

It was a framed picture. Pax took it from him and tilted the glass face to catch the light. Pax, Jo, and Deke, twelve or thirteen years old, a couple summers before the Changes. They stood in bright sunlight, sheer gray rock behind them. The boys were skinny and shirtless, Deke in cutoff jeans and Pax in real swimming trunks. Jo wore a one-piece suit, her brown hair hanging to her shoulders, wet and straggly. The three of them beamed at the camera.

He didn't remember the day the picture was taken—not exactly—but he felt the overlay of dozens of days like it: skin and sunlight and cold mountain water. "My parents used to take us all swimming," Pax said. "This looks like it was up at the Little River."

"She talked to me about you," Tommy said. "You were important to her."

"Well, Jo was—" He wanted to say, She was important to me too. But his life had made a lie of that. After leaving Switchcreek he'd never talked to Jo again, and never talked to anyone about her. Then he'd moved into the city and set about making his old life into fog, too indistinct for anyone to ask about or remember. Erasing the past was easy, like walking in a snowstorm. The footprints filled in by themselves.

Tommy said, "You don't understand, she talked to me about what happened." The beta looked at him, that flat dark face intending something that Pax couldn't interpret. "She told me what you did together. You and Jo and Deke."

Pax stood very still, a slight smile on his face. "We did a lot of stuff together. She was like a sister to us. My mother practically adopted her."

"She *told* me, Paxton," Tommy said. "You don't have to pretend with me. I was her husband. When you raise children together, you share a trust. A bond."

"A bond."

"I know it's hard for someone like you to understand, but Jo Lynn and I—"

*Someone like me?* "Jo Lynn left you, Tommy. She moved out on her own. So what kind of bond was that, exactly?"

"Jo Lynn made a bad decision. And the past couple years . . . well, she hadn't been herself. If you were around, if you had talked to her, you would know that. She wasn't the same person anymore."

"Maybe she just figured out she didn't need you—hell, didn't need any of you. This husband thing . . ." He tried to remember what Aunt Rhonda had said about betas and husbands. "How's that work exactly? You're not the girls' father, you're not—"

"Maybe not their biological father, but I *am* their parent," he said. "That's the only way that counts."

Pax almost laughed. He suddenly saw himself as Tommy saw him: a cocky skip, untouched by the Changes and untouchable, riding back into town to claim old rights he'd long abandoned. It was ludicrous, but a dozen other emotions jostled for Pax's attention—anger, amusement, disgust, jealousy—and he felt them all at once. He couldn't decide which of the emotions were his own and which were Tommy's.

Pax said, "And now you've got the girls back, you're keeping 'em, huh?"

Tommy closed his eyes, opened them. "Rainy and Sandra are my daughters. That's not a secret, Paxton. Everyone in the Co-op knows that they mean everything to me."

"And you're the sole owner now."

"Stop making it sound like that! This isn't about—" Tommy shook his head and stepped forward. "I know what you're thinking, Paxton. You're remembering the old me. It's true, I wasn't the nicest guy. But the Changes woke me up, shook out all that bullshit. For the first time in my life I started thinking clear."

"Born again," Pax said.

Tommy stared at him. "You don't understand anything, do you?"

"Why don't you explain it to me."

Tommy turned and began to walk back toward the Bronco.

"Did you kill her, Tommy?" Pax said. "Come on, you can tell me, we're buddies." He realized that he was equally ready to strangle the little bald man or hug him. "Maybe you got angry that she took the kids away from you. That makes total sense. Anybody would sympathize with that."

Tommy put a hand on the fender and looked over his shoulder at him. "I came to tell you that Jo forgave you, Paxton. For running out on her, for never calling, never asking about the girls."

Pax blinked.

Tommy shook his head. "Me, I couldn't let that pass. But Jo's a better person than I am."

Pax watched Tommy turn the four-wheel drive around and drive away. Then he rubbed his face with one hand, holding the picture to himself. Damn, he thought. This is mighty shit. He'd barely tasted the vintage. A dab. For a minute there he felt like he was halfway out of his skin and into Tommy's.

He turned toward the house, the glass of the picture frame smooth under his thumb. Inside, his father was waiting for him, snores rattling the walls, his robe open like a medicine cabinet.

"Show us," Pax said. It began as simply as that.

Jo tilted her head and said nothing. She sat in the armchair, one smooth leg draped over the arm. It had become so hard to read her new body that he couldn't tell if she was angry, embarrassed, or amused.

"Oh! You Pretty Things" played on the boom box. Jo was into old Bowie, Ziggy Stardust and earlier. She'd declared *Hunky Dory* to be the official soundtrack of the Switchcreek Orphan Society. From "Changes" to "Kooks" to "The Bewlay Brothers"—their whole story was there.

"No," she said finally. "All of us. Right now."

Deke laughed, a thump like a drum. He lay sprawled across the floor, surrounded by crushed Budweiser cans. Six months after the Changes he was almost eight feet tall and still growing; during a growth spurt his back would sometimes seize up, paralyzing him. Growing pains, the argos called them, even though nobody knew if they were temporary, or if they'd be part of their lives forever. Deke's preferred treatment was to lie flat on the floor and try to get drunk, which because of his giant body required the openmouthed throughput of a storm drain. Pax and Jo drank with him, less in solidarity than because the quarantine and curfew left them few other entertainment options.

"Y'all knock yourselves out," Deke said.

Jo slipped out of her chair and stood with her hands on her hips. She wore gym shorts and a cropped tank top that showed her smooth, flat belly. Her skin gleamed in the light of the single floor lamp. "As chairperson of the SOS," she said, looking down at Deke, "I'd like to make a motion." Jo was chair, Deke president. Pax, as a half orphan, could not hold office, but he could vote.

"I second," Pax said.

Pax fell on Deke, pinning him across his wide chest while Jo unsnapped his jean shorts and began to tug them down. Deke grunted and laughed, halfheartedly pushed Pax aside. Even buzzed and immobilized by back pain he could have thrown them across the room if he wanted.

Deke wasn't wearing underwear. Pax had seen him naked dozens of times before the Changes, but this was the first time since.

"Well would you look at that," Jo said. "You'd think you argo boys would be bigger."

Deke roared, laughing, and reached for his pants. Jo pushed his hands away. "Come on now," she said. "This is for science."

Deke stopped struggling, and Pax, sprawled across his chest, looked down the length of his friend's body. The sunken stomach, the hip bones like shovel blades, a patch of gray pubic hair like a tuft of straw. His penis seemed too short for his giant body, though it was wide as Paxton's fist. Pax had no idea if all argos were shaped like this. Probably Deke didn't know himself.

Jo pulled Deke's shorts down his thighs. He raised his knees and she slid them the rest of the way off.

The atmosphere in the room had changed.

Jo touched her red-brown hand to Deke's white thigh, only a few inches from his dick. She looked up and said, "You next, Paxton."

Jo, as always, was in charge. Even changed, she was the referee, the intermediary. Later she'd tell him, What choice did they have? There were no books for their people. No skin mags, no soft-core movies on Cinemax to show them what their bodies were supposed to look like. It was no crime to be curious.

Paxton leaned back on his knees and pulled off his shirt. Then he stood and without looking at them slid down his shorts, stepped out of them. He was naked except for his white Hanes underwear.

"Everything," Jo said.

He didn't want to take off his underwear. He was already hard.

Jo stood and walked to him. She slipped off her tank top. She wore a dainty bra, startling white against her wine-dark skin. She reached behind her, performed tiny magic with her fingers, and the bra fell away.

Her chest was almost as flat as Paxton's. Her nipples, dark red and small as dimes, were set a couple inches lower than he expected. She grasped Pax's arms and guided him down to the floor so that he was lying shoulder to shoulder with Deke. Deke's skin was cool and dry, and Paxton felt feverish.

Jo squatted over his legs and with both hands peeled the waistband over his rigid cock. "There we go," she said.

Pax felt flushed with embarrassment and excitement. If she touched him he would explode.

"Your turn, Jo," Deke said.

She seemed not to hear him. She was looking at their bodies, but seemed not to see them.

"Jo?" Pax said.

"You got nothing to worry about from us," Deke said.

She pushed her thumbs into the waistband of her shorts and stepped out of them. Her crotch was a smooth mound, her cleft like the jot of a pencil. Everywhere she was hairless as clay, her skin dark as raspberry syrup.

"Nothing to see here, people," she said. Her tone was light, but her voice trembled.

"Shush," Deke said, and held up a hand. Pax shifted over, and Jo lowered herself to lie between them.

---

He woke to his father calling his name. Pax's eyes opened to slits against the light. His father was looming over him, his shadowed face haloed by the overhead light. It was his father as he was before the Changes: the white shirt, the black pompadour.

"Wake up, now," his father said sternly, in that voice that could rattle the back pews. He leaned down, abruptly becoming a fat old man in a robe. A chub. "We don't have much time."

Pax pulled himself upright, and the picture frame fell from his chest to his lap. It was deep in the night, 3:00 or 4:00 a.m. He'd passed out on the bed fully dressed, still wearing his shoes. "What's wrong?" he asked. "What's going on?"

"I've only got a little while 'til I'm mad as a hatter again," his father said. Then, "Why aren't you in your bedroom?"

Pax ignored the question, and his father turned and shuffled through the guest room door.

Pax rubbed a hand across his face. He felt shaky, unbalanced. He picked up the picture Tommy had given him and put it on the bookshelf next to the bed. This guest room had doubled as his mother's library. She'd been a voracious reader: mysteries, romances, true crime, anything she could get her hands on. During the Changes, when she was burning up from fever, she'd made him read to her.

Pax got to his feet. The vintage still fizzed in his bloodstream. The room quivered with a strangeness that coyly refused to reveal itself, as if each book and article of furniture had been replaced by a subtly imperfect copy.

He found his father in the kitchen, trying to open a can of Campbell's soup, the manual can opener almost lost in his huge hands.

"Here . . . ," Pax said, and reached to take the can from him.

"I got it," his father said. Pax sat at the table. Eventually his father did manage to peel the lid away. He dumped the soup into a pot on the stove and stood there stirring with his back to the room.

"I suppose Rhonda took you to see her place yesterday," his father said.

Pax was surprised he remembered her visit. "It was nice. Homey. Very clean."

His father grunted. "You don't think I can take care of myself."

"I never said that," Pax said, unable to keep the annoyance from his voice. He didn't know if it was fatigue or the vintage, but his emotions kept teeter-tottering between anger and grief.

His father said, "I do things the way I want, when I want. I'm not going to go to her little . . . *pet shop*. All this—" He made a gesture that could have meant anything. "All this bother, I'm not usually like this. I manage just fine. God always provides a way."

"If this is providing, then you must have really pissed him off."

His father half turned. "Watch it, boy."

"Not just you, the whole town," Pax went on. "The Changes? Now that was Old Testament–quality smiting."

"Not everything's a punishment, Paxton. There are trials in life. Tests that teach us something."

"Oh, got it," Pax said. "The Job thing. God makes you into a monster, takes away your church, kills your wife—"

His father swung toward him. "Shut your mouth!"

Pax remained stock-still. He and his father locked eyes, but only for a moment. Pax looked away first, shook his head.

His father turned back to the stove.

Pax quickly pressed tears from his eyes. What the hell was the matter with him? He breathed deep, trying to master his emotions.

After a couple minutes his father brought the pot to the table. He set it on a hot pad and picked up a spoon. Pax raised an eyebrow.

His father looked up. "I can do this because it's my house."

"Yeah. If Mom could see you she'd kill you."

"Trust me, she's watching."

Pax couldn't watch, though—Harlan was practically inhaling the soup. He looked away, but still had to listen to him. After a few minutes, Paxton said, "You remember your first sermon after they reopened the church?" Even though the town was in quarantine, the churches and schools had been shut down for several months for fear of spreading TDS to the remaining townspeople who were unaffected. When his father was finally allowed to hold a service, the pews were almost empty and the cemetery almost full. "You preached on the plagues of Egypt."

"Exodus twelve thirty," his father said. "'For there was not a house where there was not one dead.'"

"Jo said you had it wrong," Pax said. "It wasn't the plague story we were in, it was the Tower of Babel."

His father wiped at his mouth, made a questioning sound.

"I don't remember exactly how she put it," Pax said. "Something about humans growing too proud again. If a multitude of languages didn't teach us anything, then maybe a multitude of bodies would."

His father grunted, then scraped the last of the soup from the pot. Pax rose and carried it to the sink.

"So what's it going to be, then?" his father said. "Are you going to fight me on this?"

"I can't take care of you," Pax said tiredly. "I have my job, my—"

"I'm not asking you to take care of me!"

"You can't do it yourself, Dad. And at Rhonda's place you'd have your own room, home-cooked meals. They have big-screen TVs even. It's chub paradise."

"Don't be funny with me. You're doing this out of spite, Paxton. You're still angry."

"What are you talking about? I'm not angry about anything. I'm trying to help you."

His father made a derisive sound. "I raised you. I know when you're lying."

"I'm going back to bed," Pax said.

He stalked back to the guest bedroom. In the morning he'd talk to Rhonda, and by noon he'd be gone. He pulled back the bedclothes, unlidding the dank odor of mildew, and started unbuttoning his shirt.

His father's shape filled the doorway and Pax dropped his hands.

"She's selling the stuff," his father said. "To the young chubs, and anybody else they can sell it to. They get high off it."

"No she's not." Then: "How would you know anyway?"

"People talk. They come visit, say things. What else could she be doing with it?"

"Research," Pax said. "Scientists are using it to search for a cure for . . . what happened to you. What's happening to you."

His father snorted. "What scientists? Where?"

"It's a full research program, Dad. The government's involved." Actually, she hadn't mentioned the government, but they'd have to get involved if the academics found a cure. No pharmaceutical company would bother to manufacture a drug good for only a few hundred hillbillies in east Tennessee.

"She told you that?" his father asked.

"You can ask her yourself in the morning—she's coming by to get the papers. Try to be decent."

Pax lay on the bed, trying to ignore the noise from the living room. His father had turned the TV on again. Finally Pax sat up, pulled out the stack of papers from beneath the bed, and found a pen on one of the shelves.

He turned to the first yellow sticky, and signed. He sat there on the bed until he'd signed and initialed every blank. Then he rolled onto his side, pulled the pillow over his ears, and tried to sleep.

His father had discovered them a year and a half after the Changes, on an April day drowning in cold rain. Jo and Deke had already dropped out of school, and Pax had skipped that morning to join them at Jo's house for an impromptu meeting of the Switchcreek Orphan Society. He knocked at her door and Jo called out, What's the password? She'd insisted that their society adopt a password, and a Morse code knock to go with it: three short, three long, three short.

Deke and Jo were already lying in a nest of blankets in the living room, and he'd felt a stab of jealousy. Then they stripped off his clothes and pulled him into their warmth. Although the three of them had stopped having intercourse weeks before, they still fooled around in other ways. Much of the time, however, they did nothing but lie together in a warm bundle. They talked about stopping even this, but the damage had already been done, and they'd been unable or unwilling to break this cocooning habit.

That morning Jo lay between them, Deke with his arm under both their shoulders, Pax with his head and hand against her round, smooth belly. She'd told them that she could feel the child—they didn't yet know that there were two—rolling and moving. Pax had pressed gently down with his palm, afraid to hurt her or the baby, but so far had felt nothing but yielding flesh and a steady warmth.

Jo was terrified and excited—keyed up in a way she'd never felt before, she said. Paxton was merely terrified. It wasn't just that she was pregnant; it was that she was the first person with TDS—argo, beta, or charlie—to carry a child. No one could tell them what the child inside Jo would look like, or even whether Jo's new body could survive a pregnancy. Only Deke seemed calm.

The rain must have masked the sound of Harlan's car. Pax found out later the school had called home to report his absence, but he never learned how his father knew to come directly to Jo's house. He walked straight in—no coded knocks, no "S-O-S"—and froze in the doorway. For a moment his expression was quizzical. Only a moment. Harlan Martin was not the behemoth he would become, but the eighteen months since the Changes had doubled him: his weight, his strength, his anger. His father had developed a hair-trigger temper. And why not: His wife was dead, his church was falling apart, and his only son had insisted on defying him, disappointing him, disgracing him.

Pax scrambled to his feet. Harlan strode across the room and grabbed Paxton by both arms, spun and slammed him into the wall, shaking a framed photograph loose from its hook, and pinned him there. Jo screamed and perhaps Deke spoke, but Pax couldn't remember anything that was said. He only remembered his father's face, pressed close to his own, twisted by shock, fury, loathing—too many emotions to name.

"My God, Paxton," his father said, his voice filled with disgust. "What in heaven's name have you done?"

Paxton had fallen asleep to the sound of the television blaring in the next room, and when he jerked awake sunlight was pouring through the window and the TV still babbled from the living room. It felt like less than a minute had passed, but it must have been hours.

Behind the noise of the TV he heard the telephone ringing. A few seconds more and the ringing stopped. He didn't think his father owned an answering machine. He closed his eyes, lay there for a time, and then opened his eyes again. He couldn't hear his father snoring.

He sat up, found his watch where he'd put it on the floor. Eight-thirty. He pulled on his pants and shirt, walked barefoot out to the living room. The couch was empty. He went to the kitchen, then opened the door to his father's bedroom, then checked the bathroom.

"Shit," Pax said aloud. His father was gone.

He went out into the backyard and circled around the house, calling his father's name. The wet grass washed his feet. Both Pax's Tempo and his father's Crown Victoria were still parked in the driveway. The Crown Vic's driver's-side door was ajar.

He walked toward the car, a sick feeling in his stomach. He came around the back bumper to see through the open door—

and there was no one inside. He started to shut the door, and then saw a set of keys hanging from the ignition.

Pax leaned in, turned the key. The engine didn't even click. Stone dead. The dome light was off too.

He put the keys in his pocket and slammed the door. He was walking into the house when his cell phone began to vibrate.

It was Deke's number. Pax flipped open the phone. "Tell me you know where my father is," Pax said.

"He's at the church," Deke answered in that sub-basement voice. "You better hurry."

"The church? What's he doing at the church?"

"By the looks of it, getting ready to baptize somebody."

Pax went into the bathroom, peed. At the sink he splashed his face with tepid water, ran his wet hands through his hair. In the mirror he looked like a wild man. His father's son, all right.

It almost took him longer to get the Tempo started than to get to the church. It was just two and a half miles away down a twisty and hilly stretch of Piney Road. But his father must have walked there. How could a man who weighed six or seven hundred pounds walk it? Two days ago he could barely get off the couch.

Deke's open-topped Jeep was in the parking lot, as well as a dark blue Buick. Pax parked, tiredly climbed the steps, and paused with his hand on the door. From inside someone called out, and even without being able to make out the words he recognized his father's voice—his preaching voice.

The Reverend Harlan Martin was bringing the Word.

Pax pulled open the creaking door and went inside. The vestibule was dim and empty, but the double doors to the sanctuary were propped open. Inside, light shimmered from the yellow-paned windows on the eastern wall, making the tops of the pews gleam.

A broad aisle led down the center of the church to the raised pulpit. Set into the wall behind the pulpit was a recessed archway that contained the baptistry, a cement pool sunk below the floor.

His father stood in the pool, water up to his waist, praying or preaching or both at the same time.

His cheeks shone with tears. One hand gripped the panel of glass that acted as a kind of splash guard for the pool, and the other was raised above his head, fingers spread. He wore a white dress shirt, too tight to be buttoned over his stained T-shirt. His hair had been combed back from his head.

"Forgive us, Lord!" he called, his voice echoing. His eyes were tightly closed, his face anguished. Blisters stretched across his forehead and cheeks, larger than Pax had ever seen them. What he'd taken to be tears could have been oil from ruptured sacs.

His father clenched his raised hand into a fist, opened it again. "Let your mercy come down on us. Forgive us now, our weak flesh, our corruptible hearts . . ."

Deke and a beta woman in a skirt and loose shirt stood off to the side of the sanctuary, next to the organ, talking in low voices. They saw Pax and waved him forward.

As Pax drew closer to the pulpit he could smell the spicy-sour tang of vintage. His father was still praying—*We ask you, Lord, hear us, Lord*—eyes shut, hand up like a drowning man. For as long as Pax could remember his father prayed for "we" and "us." Pleading on behalf of the entire church, or the world.

Deke said, "Paxton, have you met the Reverend Hooke?"

Pax recognized the woman's clothing, if not her face. She'd

worn a shirt and vest like that when she'd led the singing at the funeral. They shook hands, and Pax said, "I'm sorry about this, Reverend. How long has he been in there?"

"I got here a half hour ago," Hooke said. "Who knows how long he was here before that—long enough to overflow the baptistry. I turned off the water as soon as I realized what was going on. I don't even know how he got in."

"Probably still got his keys," Deke said. He was keeping his volume low, as if reluctant to disturb Harlan's praying.

"Probably," Pax said. "Or he could just come in the side door—you just have to yank on it to get it to unlatch. They ever fix that?"

Hooke did not seem amused. "He won't listen to us at all, and of course we can't go in after him—look at him."

The blisters. They were afraid of touching him.

"Okay," Pax said, "why don't we let him finish? Whatever he's doing."

The reverend shook her head. "We can't let him stay in there all day. Now Paxton, you may have heard that your father and I had our differences, but that's got nothing to do with this. I respect him as a man of God. But it just isn't safe to have him in there, not with . . . not in his condition. I told Deke we ought to call Aunt Rhonda, and have her boys—"

"But I said that was your call to make," Deke said to Pax.

"No, you're right," Pax said. "My dad didn't want to go with her, but . . . look at him." He should have brought the papers with him. Rhonda had guards, gates, medical equipment—everything to stop this kind of thing from happening. "I don't think I can handle this."

"Well, today you're gonna have to," Deke said.

Pax felt his face flush. He didn't look at Deke, instead

turned to the reverend and said, "Call Aunt Rhonda. I'll try to get him out of there. You have any rubber gloves? Or some plastic I can put over my hands?"

The Reverend Hooke said she had some garbage bags in her office, and Pax followed her up the steps of the pulpit and through the narrow door behind the podium, to the hallway that led back to the offices and Sunday school rooms. To their right was a door, left ajar, that opened onto the baptistry.

"I'll be right back," Hooke said, and headed down the hall.

Pax opened the baptistry door. Steps led down into the pool, and the water was as high as the top step. His father was within arm's reach. His huge body almost filled the pool, and every movement sent water lapping over the edge.

This close, the smell of the vintage was strong, made heavier by the moisture in the air.

"Dad," Pax said. Then, louder, "It's me, Paxton. It's time to go home."

His father's eyes remained closed. "—to die in the flesh, Lord," he prayed. His voice bounced around the enclosed space, but it seemed both quieter and more desperate. "And yet to be resurrected in the spirit. We ask these things in your name, amen."

"Dad, you're hallucinating."

The Reverend Harlan Martin opened his eyes, turned. His face looked like it had been pummeled, a mass of protuberances and swelling flesh. It took him a moment to focus on Pax through eyes closed almost to slits.

He smiled and extended an arm to him. "Don't be afraid, Son," he said, his voice low, as if to keep a congregation from hearing. "Take my arm and I'll help you down."

The surface of the water seemed oily, reflective.

"I'm not coming in there, Dad." Pax breathed in through his mouth, tasting the vintage. "Step out now, okay? Can you climb out?"

His father glanced toward the front of the church. Who was he seeing, out there—and when? Pax remembered standing in this spot when he was twelve, his father reaching out to him exactly like this. Paxton's mother had bought him a new white dress shirt and had told him to wear an undershirt so he wouldn't look naked when the water soaked through.

His father chuckled, shook his head. "All righty then." He turned toward Pax, sloshing water over the sides of the pool, and moved toward the steps.

"That's it. Come on out and we'll get you dried off," Pax said.

His father grasped Paxton's forearm, his fingers surprisingly strong.

It's okay, Pax thought. His arm was covered by his sleeve, no skin contact. "Easy does it," he said.

"That's the spirit," his father said. He backed up, pulling Pax down to the second step. Pax yelped and grabbed the door frame with his free hand. The water splashed cold against his shins.

"Dad! Stop it!"

"In the name of the Father," his father said. He looped an arm around Pax's waist. "And of the Son—"

He yanked Pax toward him. Pax lost his grip on the door frame and fell onto his father's chest. The big man overbalanced and tipped backward and they plunged under the water.

Cold water surged into Pax's ears, his mouth.

Pax's left arm was smashed between his father's body and the side of the pool, his right arm trapped at his side. Pax arched his back, trying to get his head up above the surface. His father's arm cinched tighter, hugging him close.

Someone else was in the water with them. Pax felt something grip the back of his neck, slide down to tug at his elbow, freeing it. Pax reached up, found the top of the glass panel, and held on.

Pax got his legs under him, pushed. The arm around his waist loosened and his head broke the surface. He gasped, and immediately coughed up water.

From the sanctuary, murmurs of "amen."

Deke stood in front of the baptistry, reaching down, his arm covered to the elbow by a black plastic bag. Behind him the room was full of light, the pews crowded. The women wore colorful summer dresses. The men, in white shirtsleeves because of the heat, draped their arms across the pew backs. All of them were unchanged—not an argo or chub or blank among them. The organ played "Rock of Ages."

My church, Pax thought, but it was his father's voice saying it. My church, my church. Pax felt the tightening in his chest, love and gratefulness and sorrow blossoming like heat.

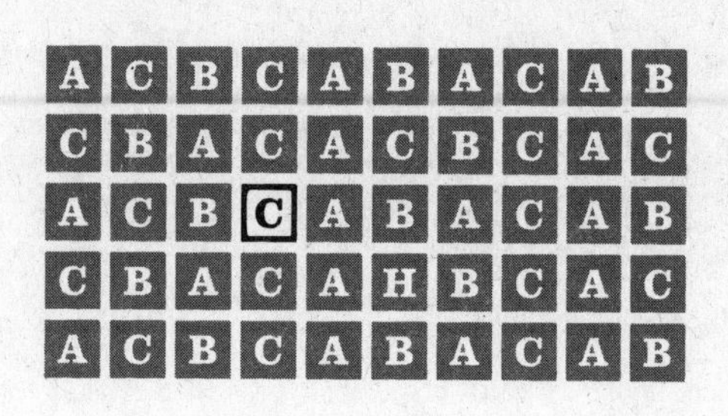
A C B C A B A C A B
C B A C A C B C A C
A C B C A B A C A B
C B A C A H B C A C
A C B C A B A C A B

# chapter 7

EVERY PAYDAY A gang of charlie men gathered in the lobby of the Home like eager pups. Rhonda Mapes could hear them outside her door, talking and joking, eager and impatient. Every week they came earlier and earlier. Well they could keep waiting. Rules were rules.

At fifteen before the hour, Everett knocked on her door, then leaned in apologetically.

Rhonda looked up from the accounts book. "It's not eleven yet," she said. "Tell the boys—"

"It's not about that," Everett said. He glanced to his side, and a young charlie poked his face around the side of the door. Travis was seventeen, hired as an orderly last year. Where Everett was bald, Travis wore a thick wave of black hair and long sideburns.

"He's doing it again, ma'am," Travis said.

Rhonda sighed, took off her reading glasses. "Is he producing?"

"No ma'am. But he's pretty worked up, and it looks like he's having trouble breathing. I was wondering if you wanted to do the sedative thing again, or—"

"No! I told you, he's got to come through this." She closed the accounts book. "Go back to the room, I'll be there in a minute."

Travis' face disappeared. Everett stepped into the office and closed the door behind him. "You want me to do payday?" he asked. "The boys have been out there a half hour, we can get rid of them early."

"Certainly not!" She got to her feet and walked to the floor safe, a squat black thing about the height of a two-drawer filing cabinet, and bent to squint at the dial. "Give it to 'em a half hour early, pretty soon they'll take an hour, and the next thing you know they'll be showing up on Mondays." She opened the safe with a few practiced spins, withdrew the key ring for the coolers downstairs, and tossed it to Everett. "You can get the bonus out, but don't give them a drop until I get there. I'm going to find out what Travis needs. Then after we pay the boys, we've got some errands to run."

The charlies in the lobby all stood when she walked out of her office. Twelve well-built men, the strongest in the clade, from boys not much older than sixteen to a couple of elders who were only a step or two from becoming Home residents themselves. She employed them all, but most didn't work at the Home; they were distributors and messengers, her hands, the means by which she touched every member of the clade.

Clete said, "Hey, Aunt Rhonda."

"Y'all here a bit early this morning," she said.

"You always say, on time is late, early is on time," Clete said, smiling.

"Too bad you only remember that on payday," Rhonda said. "Y'all sit down and wait your turn."

Rhonda plucked a paper surgical mask from the dispenser on the wall and walked toward the men's wing. She could faintly hear Harlan's caterwauling, and as she pushed through the second set of doors he let loose with a particularly full-throated shout.

"Goodness gracious," she said to herself. She had no use for crying and tears, not anymore. She'd buried her husband when she was forty-six, and oh, she'd bawled for weeks. But then came the Changes, and by the time her body finished blowing up like a Macy's Thanksgiving Day balloon all those tears dried up.

(Almost all. Ten years ago she'd walked into Willie Flint's cabin and the sight of the man had hit her like a punch to the stomach. She'd burst into tears, but only for a moment—the final spurt before that faucet sealed shut for good.)

The charlie men—the old ones, anyway—were just the opposite. Tough old coots, who before the Changes wouldn't have yelped if they'd grabbed the wrong end of a chainsaw, suddenly got as touchy as babies. You couldn't even frown without them taking offense. And when the vintage was flowing they just went out of their heads, laughing, crying, seeing things—and trying to hump anything that moved.

As she reached Harlan's door she heard the reverend shouting something about "bread and stone." More preaching, then. He'd been at it nearly nonstop.

Old chub men went crazy when the vintage hit them hard, but Harlan had it worse than she'd ever seen. He was crying out and talking to people when they'd picked him up at the church last night—it had taken Everett and Travis and Clete to pull the old man out of the water and get him into the van—and he'd kept making noise all night and into the morning. Rhonda kept her distance from him and let the boys handle him, of course. Harlan was throwing off vintage like a water sprinkler, and while the boys had a natural tolerance, charlie women had to be careful. A couple years ago she'd embarrassed herself terribly when she caught a splash off of Mr. Lukens. Everett had stopped her before she climbed on top of the man, thank the Lord, but she'd already started rubbing against the old chub's legs and—well, she wouldn't let that happen again.

Rhonda pushed open the door, and the smell of the stale vintage hit her through the mask. She didn't step any closer.

Travis put down some electronic gadget he'd been thumbing and popped to his feet.

"It don't sound like he's having any trouble breathing," Aunt Rhonda said.

"He was gasping," the boy said. "Now he's doing the preaching thing again."

Harlan lay on the queen-sized hospital bed, straining against the wide black Velcro bands they'd put across his chest, waist, and legs. He was sweating and red faced, his eyes wide and roaming the room. "Every good tree," he said. "Every good tree brings forth good fruit. And every corrupt tree . . ."

"I told you, you have to talk to him. Have you been talking to him?"

"I tried," the boy said. "It just seems to make him madder. He sure don't like those straps."

The boy looked like he could handle Harlan if the old man broke free—Travis was built like a clenched fist, all muscle and bone. He'd been a preschooler during the Changes, and at seventeen he was already broader and more muscular than Everett. That's how it went with the charlie boys; the younger they were when they caught TDS, the bigger those muscles. The second-generation charlies—the natural-born boys who were under twelve and looked like butterballs now—would probably be five-foot Schwarzeneggers by puberty.

And when they got old as Harlan? Maybe they'd go fat again and start producing. Or maybe they'd turn into something different altogether. Nobody knew what the course of life would be for a natural-born charlie. They were in uncharted territory.

Rhonda put her hands on her hips. "Is he making any more sense? Does he know where he is?"

"I don't think so," Travis said. "It's all Bible stuff, mostly. Sometimes he calls me Paxton." He laughed. "Or Lorraine. Which I guess is his wife?"

"She died in the Changes," Rhonda said, and her tone snapped the smile off the boy's face. "As for Paxton, well . . ." The last time she'd seen him, he was pale, wet, and unconscious, and Deke was carrying him off to Dr. Fraelich's clinic.

Rhonda risked coming another foot into the room. "Harlan!" she said sternly. "Pastor Martin!"

Harlan gave no indication that he heard her. "Is not the life more than meat?" he said. "Is the body more than raiment?" His voice was scratchy, but still strong. These backwoods preachers didn't tire easily; she'd seen Harlan do week-long revivals, bringing the fire and brimstone two hours a night.

"Time for you to wake up now, Pastor. You can't be carrying on like this all day." He kept babbling, his eyes focused on nothing. Rhonda stepped back and said to Travis, "Are you sure he's not producing?"

"I don't think so."

"What do you mean, you don't *think* so?"

"I mean, no ma'am. I check him every hour, but I haven't found any new blisters, and there's nothing coming through the cream." After they'd gotten him into the Home last night the boys had plastered his blisters with antibiotic cream—standard procedure. "I guess he's still drunk on the dose from last night."

"I suppose," Rhonda said. Harlan had produced more vintage in a burst than any charlie she'd ever seen. A regular Texas gusher. It made sense that he'd need time to recover and recharge. She had to admit she wanted him back online and producing steadily.

"Just keep talking to him," Rhonda said. "I want someone here when he comes to. He ain't going to be happy."

"Uh, when's that going to be, you think?"

Rhonda let her voice go sweet. "You getting tired sitting here, honey? You need to go home for a while, maybe stretch out on the couch?"

The boy brightened. "That'd be great, Aunt Rhonda. I could sure—"

"Sit down, Travis." God Almighty the boy was dim.

She went to the door and the boy said, "Uh, ma'am? It's payday, right? I was wondering . . ."

She turned to face him, raised an eyebrow.

The boy said. "I was just wondering about the bonus . . ."

"Not until you're eighteen," Rhonda said. "Until then, no bonus. You just sit here and call me when he starts producing. Oh, and hon? If I see that game thing in your hand again while you're on the clock, I'll have Everett break it over your big chub head."

She threw the mask in the garbage and stalked back to the lobby. More of her employees had arrived. They were all looking at her, eyes like hungry orphans. "All right," she said. "Line up."

They queued up outside her office. She sat at her desk,

signing and tearing out the checks one by one. Everett stood beside her, handing out the bonus, the small black plastic baggies from the cooler.

Clete tucked his check into his back pocket without looking at it, but he opened his bag right there and took out the little plastic vial. The frozen vintage occupied only the bottom two centimeters of the container. "Is that it?" he said.

Rhonda's hand froze in midsignature. "Excuse me?"

Clete said, "This is less than last time. At least tell me it's from Harlan. I saw what that stuff did to Paxton."

"Watch your mouth," Rhonda said. "That's the Reverend Martin to you."

"Come on, Aunt Rhonda." He looked at Everett. "You were there. Am I right?"

Everett said nothing.

"I'm just saying," Clete said. "If this is all we're getting, at least share the good stuff while it's fresh. Another few drops of Elwyn or Old Bob ain't going to do me much good."

Everett placed a hand on Clete's shoulder. "Say one more word," Everett said quietly. "Go ahead. One more."

Clete pushed his hand away and backed up. "I was just asking, Everett. Jesus, relax already."

"Take your bonus and get out of here," Rhonda said. She looked around at the other men. "This ain't Hardee's drive-thru. There are no choices, no specials, no family value packs, and nobody gets more than their fair share. Any of you have a problem with that?"

Clete looked sour but didn't speak. The others behind him in the line studied their hands or looked away.

When the last of the men had taken his check and bag and

made his way out to the parking lot, Everett shook his head, smiling, and said, "Hardee's. Heh."

"Can you believe that?" Rhonda said, but she was smiling too, now. She pushed back in her chair and stood. "All righty. After you get the cooler away, let's go see the Reverend Hooke. Maybe we'll be able to settle our bet."

"You think so?" Everett asked.

"You never know," Rhonda said.

Everett asked her if she wanted to take the long way through town. Rhonda said that sounded like a good idea and rolled down her window. He always knew when she was in a mood to greet her people.

He drove like a skilled accompanist. Without her saying a word he knew when to slow down so she could wave and say hello, when to roll past the people she wanted to avoid, and when to pull over. They saw the Robinson twins—one sister an argo and the other a charlie, walking down the sidewalk in matching yellow dresses like two sides of a funhouse mirror—and rolled on by. (You didn't start a conversation with the twins unless you had nowhere to go and packed a lunch.) A few charlie teenagers were hanging around the Icee Freeze, and Rhonda called them by name, letting them know that she was watching them even if nobody else was. She couldn't do the same for the beta children, though; when she passed a covey of young blank girls coming out of the Bugler's she just said, "How you doing, girls?" and moved on. Blanks all looked alike to her, but the young ones had even started dressing alike with those long skirts and white scarves.

At the north end of town Everett circled back south by going down Main, gliding past the old wooden houses that used to be at the center of town before the highway went through in the fifties. She exchanged greetings with half a dozen people, the car moving slower than a parade float.

Rhonda looked over at Everett and said, "What are you grinning at?"

"This always cheers you up," he said.

"It's just part of the job," she said. But it was true; she got a lift from being with her people. And she had a knack for working with folks, a gift she hadn't fully employed until after the Changes. "Now pull over at Mr. Sparks'. We need to chat."

Mr. Sparks, wearing a long-sleeved shirt and dress pants despite the heat, slowly pushed a wheelbarrow heaped with mulch across his lawn. Everett stopped the car and the old man came over, smiling. The Changes had skipped him, and at eighty-two he looked as fit as ever. "Goodness gracious, Mr. Sparks," Rhonda said. "You make me tired the way you work."

"Oh, it's not working that makes me tired."

"Well, you better keep your shirt on, or you'll have young girls swooning around you."

He laughed, a dry chuckle. The talk turned to clips of Roy Downer's press conference that had been shown on the local news last night. "It's a relief to hear that there was no evidence of foul play," he said. "Not to say suicide isn't a terrible thing . . ."

"I know just what you mean," Rhonda said. "You don't have to explain to me." They talked for a few more minutes, Mr. Sparks trying repeatedly to get them to come inside for some coffee cake, but Rhonda begged off. "I better not keep you. I'll see you at the next council meeting, all right?"

"I've already drawn up the agenda," he said. "We've got to take care of the sewer issue first thing. I don't see why we need brand-new sewers. We need *thoughtful*—"

"Thoughtful progress," Rhonda said, nodding. "I agree one hundred percent, Mr. Sparks. Let's get all that straightened out, and I've got a couple other things to bring up, too."

He frowned. "I've already printed up the agenda."

"Oh, it's nothing big! Just brainstorming. Not agenda-worthy at all. I'll see you next week then?"

Everett eased the car away from the curb. "I thought we needed the new sewers for the school," he said.

"We do," Rhonda said. "So I'll give up on digging up Main Street, which I never wanted anyway."

Everett laughed. "That's thoughtful, all right."

"Come on now. Let's go see the Reverend Hooke."

So many details, Rhonda thought. Nobody would believe how much work it was just to keep everything in this town running. But *somebody* had to take charge, and it might as well be her. Nobody else understood how vulnerable they were. They'd been lucky so far. Even with the riots, the killing of the Stonecipher boys, the Manus rape, the prejudice—they'd gotten off lightly. In those early days of the Changes, everyone thought TDS was just an awful disease that turned out to not be contagious. Fear gradually turned to pity, then indifference.

It would all have been different if the quarantine had still been on when Jo Lynn had her girls and the other clades started to breed. With the birth of those children—natural-borns who so clearly were healthy and more purely of their clade—the people of Switchcreek were transformed from mere victims to competitors. They could make their own kind. They could multiply. The quarantine might still be in place.

Rhonda knew that the government was still watching them, and the scientists were still trying to figure out if TDS was a danger. As for the rest of the world, the multitude of unchanged civilians, their apathy about Switchcreek could turn the moment they felt threatened.

It took only a few minutes to get to the Co-op. As they drove through the gates of the old Whitmer farm, beta children scattered out of their way like chickens. "Good Lord, there's more of 'em every time we visit," Rhonda said, and Everett grunted in agreement. Two hundred or so betas lived in the Co-op. Half of them were under the age of thirteen, and the other half were pregnant—at least that's what it seemed like.

The white nursery building sat at the center of the field with almost twenty mobile homes huddled around it. The trailers had been bought used, and looked it. The oldest ones were peeling paint, but even the newer, vinyl-covered homes were dented and scuffed with red clay, like shoes that had been worn hard.

Rhonda got out of the car and frowned as the muggy air enveloped her. She said to a group of girls, "Anybody seen Pastor Elsa?"

A pair of them—twins, probably, since so many beta kids came in sets, but who could tell?—ran off toward the nursery. Rhonda told Everett to wait at the car and started walking in that direction. Slowly. She wore a Talbot's silk sleeveless blouse and a $300 Liberty Jacquard linen jacket she'd ordered special from Ann Taylor, and she'd be damned if she sweated moons into the pits of that beautiful suit.

The spaces between the trailers were littered with bicycles, toys faded by the sun, and plastic Little Tykes furniture. The muggy air was made hotter by the back-blast of rumbling air conditioners poking out of the trailer windows. Most of the adults seemed to be inside, but a pair of white-scarf girls sat in the shade of an awning, snapping beans. Their bellies under their light cotton dresses looked equally round, as if they were racing each other to the first contraction. Rhonda didn't recognize them, so she nodded at them and they said hello.

When Rhonda was still a dozen yards from the nursery the building door opened and the reverend came out, wiping her hands on her skirt. She quickly hugged Rhonda. A stranger would be unable to see it, but Rhonda could tell the woman was flustered.

"Everything all right, Elsa?"

"As right as we can expect," the reverend said. "Better than we hoped. Come on down to my place; I've got some sweet tea." She led Rhonda past the nursery toward the outer circle of mobile homes, walking with that uneven gait of hers, as if she carried a stone in her shoe.

In the open space beyond the trailers was a makeshift playground wilting in the sun: a couple of knock-kneed swing sets, a trampoline listing on uneven legs, an aboveground pool sagging around the rim. It was too hot to touch metal, though; the dozen kids in the playground were all in the pool or running around the edge of it, through the water-slicked grass, naked as dolphins.

The gardens started out past the barn. The patches of tomatoes and corn and green beans were big enough to feed a few families but small enough to be tended by hand. A male beta wearing a baseball cap was bent over a row of beans, a blue plastic bucket over one arm. Tommy? Impossible to tell at this distance.

"I saw a bunch of your girls down at the Bugler's today," Rhonda said.

"Which ones?" the Reverend asked.

"Can *you* tell them apart?"

"Of course I can. What kind of question is that?"

"Well it would sure help the rest of us if you had them wear name tags or something. Maybe numbers on their backs—you could sell scorecards as a fundraiser."

The reverend was standing on her front step, and she gave Rhonda a look as she opened the door. "Mayor, that's the kind of redneck talk I expect out of your boys."

Rhonda huffed up the stairs and followed her into the trailer. The air was chilly but stale; perspiration prickled the wispy hairs of her neck. The half-sized living room was as spare and tidy as a ship's cabin: one couch, one chair, and between them a glass-topped coffee table like a display coffin. The only loose item in the room was a red leather family Bible set on a white doily at the center of the table.

"Girls?" the reverend called. To Rhonda she said, "Rest your feet a minute," and then she left the room through a curtained doorway. "Girls, I need you to go play somewhere else for a while."

Rhonda eyed the skinny legs of the chair and chose the couch.

Once Elsa had been married, to a man who had a good job at the Alcoa plant, and she'd lived in a handsome brick ranch up above the highway. When she first moved to the Co-op she jammed the contents of that house into the trailer, turning the living room into something between a furniture showroom and a self-storage unit. But then the babies started to arrive, crowding out her old life. Elsa gave away her extra sofa and armchairs to needier beta families, sold her cherry entertainment center and the upright piano at the flea market in Lambert. She put a Sheetrock wall down the middle of the room to make an extra bedroom.

A minute later two small bald-headed girls—the middle two of the reverend's five daughters—ran past Rhonda and out the door. Elsa reappeared, dusting her hands. "You want that tea?" she asked, then disappeared in the other direction toward the kitchen.

Rhonda had never been invited past the living room. She'd bet good money the rest of the trailer looked like a hurricane hit it. Kids were kids, no matter what clade they came from. "Those girls downtown," Rhonda called. "They were all wearing those white scarves. Two more pregnant girls I just passed were wearing them too. Seems like I'm seeing more and more of those."

"The younger sisters like them."

"*Like* them? It's starting to look like a cult, Elsa. It started with that effigy of the doctor, and now all the girls want to be like them." Three girls had burned an effigy of Dr. Fraelich and tossed it onto her lawn. The girls had been caught and punished, but they were still heroes to their sisters. "Next thing you know they'll be dressed in robes, passing out tracts at the airport."

Elsa came back carrying two tumblers full of iced tea. "A few of them got carried away. They're not pagans, Rhonda. All my girls are good Christians."

"Of course they are—they're *super* Christians." Rhonda drank from the glass with relish, and sat back. "Law, that's good." She sipped again and said, "Those teenagers, the ones that came through the Changes before puberty? I get the impression they think they're a little more *pure* than everybody else—even the older sisters in their own clade."

The reverend sat on the chair and sighed as if conceding the point. "They're growing up in a different world than we did, Rhonda."

"You don't say."

"The facts of life have changed. Those girls coming up now are sure they're never going to be 'defiled.' They get to have their babies without going through any of that . . . business that other women have to go through."

"They get to have their cake without having to eat it," Rhonda said, and cackled.

The reverend allowed a wisp of a smile, and then her frown returned. "All they talk about is babies." She pitched her voice to keep it within the thin walls of the trailer. "They don't want to do anything but play with their dolls and talk about how wonderful it will be when they finally get their own children. And the only ones they admire more than themselves are the natural-borns."

"I've noticed that, too," Rhonda said.

"I've got NB girls having their periods at eight, nine years old. The oldest ones are nearly twelve. It won't be long 'til I have babies raising babies, and the third generation will be upon us. And the white-scarf girls couldn't be happier. You'd think angels were coming."

"Hon, that's a cult."

"It's not a cult, it's just . . ." She shrugged.

"At the very least you've got another schism brewing."

The reverend's expression didn't change, but she hadn't missed that "another" slipped in like a knife. After the Changes,

Harlan Martin had been determined to keep his church together, and he'd succeeded for a couple years. But he wasn't about to alter his preaching to make it easier on all the people getting divorced, or moving in with people of the same clade. God doesn't change, Harlan said, even if he changes us. Then Harlan tried to excommunicate two blank women who'd moved in together, and that was it—the fuse was lit. Rhonda admired Harlan for sticking to his scripture, but she'd already felt the political winds changing and knew he couldn't win this fight. The blanks outnumbered the other clades in the church, and Elsa had led the charge to force him out. Her new church ordained her a week after Harlan cleaned out his office.

"They're just children," the reverend said. "They're being rebellious."

"Oh, listen to yourself. You already said they were growing up in a different world. You're just an immigrant here, and you don't understand the language. They think they're the real thing. They probably don't even think you're a real beta."

The reverend looked up, eyes slightly narrowed. In the limited vocabulary of beta expressions, that was outright anger.

So, Rhonda thought. The reverend had heard the girls talking about her.

"Listen to me, Elsa," Rhonda said. "You've got to get hold of this before it spins out of control. Before they spin *you* out. You're going to have to crack down on those teenagers. Make them throw out those scarves, for one."

"I can't just say, 'No scarves.' That would just make them more secretive, and I'd become the enemy."

"You're already the enemy," Rhonda said. "You just have to make sure they know they need you."

The reverend rubbed a finger over her smooth forehead. She went to the window and pushed aside the gauzy curtain. "Help me build the school, then."

Ah. Every conversation with the reverend eventually came around to the beta school.

"We haven't even broke ground on the high school yet," Rhonda said. "The town can't afford two new school buildings. Now if you wanted to start a private school . . ."

"You know the Co-op can't do that," the reverend said. "Most of us are on social assistance. We just don't have the kind of *resources* you do."

Rhonda almost laughed. The reverend also never failed to get a dig in about the vintage, thinking that her thinly veiled references would put Rhonda on the defensive. "I wish I could help you, Elsa."

"What about the grants?" the reverend asked. "Do you honestly need all thirty million? Some of that money, just two or three million, could be used for a beta school—it would still be for education, after all. And say my girls don't ever go to the high school, they go to this Co-op school instead. Then we don't need as big a building."

Rhonda pretended to consider it. "I hear what you're saying. I do. And I'd like to help you, especially if it would make your people happy." She shook her head. "But hon, that money's been preallocated—the plans are submitted to the state. The federal and state grants are for building Switchcreek High School. Nothing else. The government don't just let you spend it on whatever you want."

The reverend paced the small room. Rhonda let her stew about it, think it was as unfeasible as all the other times they'd talked. Then when she didn't say anything for a minute, Rhonda said, "Well, we could propose . . . No, Deke would never go for it."

"What?"

"A branch campus."

The reverend blinked at her. "High schools don't have branch campuses."

"Let's just say it's part of the high school that's not connected to the main building," Rhonda said. "We amend the plans to put a separate wing on the high school. Then after construction starts, we put the wing over here instead of over there—we don't even have to change the blueprints."

"You can't do something like that and not have anybody notice, Mayor."

"Oh, we wouldn't hide it from anyone. We just make sure the whole council approves it." The whole council being Mr. Sparks, the reverend, and Deke. Rhonda, as mayor, was a nonvoting member. "Then we make sure that none of our people make a fuss, or complain to the state. As long as we keep our paperwork straight and sell it to the town we'll be all right."

"That's one tough sell," the reverend said. "Mr. Sparks doesn't want to change anything. The argos went along with the school last time because of their young ones, but those kids will graduate in a few years, and there aren't any to replace them."

"Not yet," Rhonda said.

"Maybe not ever." A few of the younger argos still hope to have their own babies some day, and so the high school plans made a concession to optimism: fifteen foot ceilings and double-wide doors.

"I'll talk to Deke," Rhonda said. "Maybe if we promise to throw some of the construction work his way . . ."

"He won't take anything that looks like a payoff, Rhonda."

"Any work his company gets is money in the pockets of his workers. It's good for his people." She shrugged. "But it won't feel like a payoff if I convince him that the beta school is for the good of all of us."

"And what's *your* reason, Rhonda? That high school's been your pet project. I find it hard to believe you'd risk that."

"Oh hon, I'm not risking the school. I'll still get my football field. But I'm willing to cut out a few classrooms to help you build your school because I can do the math." She smiled sweetly. "You betas are breeding twice as fast as my clade. The argos aren't breeding at all, and the skips are dying off. In a few years the majority of voters are going to be little bald girls." She shrugged. "I'm just preparing for the world to come."

The reverend offered to walk Rhonda back to her car. The heat seemed worse when they stepped out of the air-conditioning.

They passed a group of natural-born girls, some of them only four or five years old, spread out on the patch of grass between two trailers playing Mother-may-I. They were being watched by some teenagers in white scarves. "Are any of these yours?" Rhonda asked.

The reverend pointed out a girl of about three or four, in matching green shorts and top. She held hands with one of the older white-scarf girls. "That's my youngest."

"Ah! The one that almost killed you." The reverend had

been on bed rest for the last five months of the pregnancy, her blood pressure through the roof. Two minutes after giving birth, she suffered a minor stroke. The right side of her face was briefly paralyzed, and she'd slurred her words for months. Even now her right arm was still weak, and she walked with a limp.

"A beautiful girl," Rhonda said. "Now is that one of Jo Lynn's daughters she's holding hands with?"

"No, that one's Marsha's daughter. I'm sure Rainy and Sandra are around here somewhere."

"I hope they're fitting in all right. It must be hard, coming back into the fold. Especially with what those white-scarf girls think of their mother."

"That's all history."

"Oh, hon, that kinda hate don't go out of style. When those girls found out about Jo Lynn's operations"—that was the politest word Rhonda could think of—"you'd have thought she'd been caught eating newborns for supper. And then when she tried to introduce birth control—"

"I'm not going to talk about this with you."

"Jo committed the unforgivable sin," Rhonda said, lowering her voice. "Maybe those white-scarves think that expelling Jo wasn't punishment enough. People are saying, who knows what those girls are thinking?"

The reverend turned to face her. Her red face was smooth, almost unreadable. "People?" she said.

"It's just rumors, Elsa. You know how people talk."

"The DA said it was a suicide. They don't believe the DA?"

"Of course they do! Some of them. Probably most of the town. Now you and me know that Roy Downer couldn't find his butt cheeks with both hands, but the public, what they don't know . . . Well, I'm just saying. If one of your girls, or God help us, Tommy Shields, had anything to do with this . . ."

"That's enough," the reverend said coldly. "Tommy loved Jo, and you know it. And these girls wouldn't hurt a fly—it's not in their nature."

They'd almost reached the entrance to the farm. Everett stood next to the Caddy, talking on his cell phone, but he was looking at them. "Get the air-conditioning on," Rhonda called. "I'm about to die of stroke."

The reverend touched Rhonda's arm, and Rhonda turned to face her. The reverend said, "I hope you aren't riling people up, Mayor. It's irresponsible and hurtful. If you go around accusing people—"

"Oh, I'm not accusing," Rhonda said, her voice calm. "I'm advising."

"What advice is that, exactly?"

"If your people had anything to do with Jo's death, Elsa, then you better take care of it." Rhonda patted her arm. "But I'm sure none of them did, did they?"

Everett drove slowly over the rutted drive. He waited while she dabbed the sweat from her forehead, but when they reached the gate he said, "So?"

"I didn't see any laptop sitting out," Rhonda said. "And I didn't really have a chance to poke around." She was sure that the reverend had grabbed Jo Lynn's computer. Rhonda had had Everett search the church, to no avail. It was really too much to hope for that Elsa would leave the thing sitting out in plain view. "She's got it somewhere," Rhonda said. "Or Tommy has it. They were first into the house after the paramedics."

"And what about our little bet?"

She allowed a little smile and put away her handkerchief. "Oh, most definitely."

"Huh! She tell you that?"

"I gave her plenty of openings, but she wasn't having any of it. Still, there's no hiding it. The reverend is pregnant again."

Everett shook his head admiringly. "You win," he said. He accelerated away from the Co-op. "So now that I'm paying for lunch, where do you want to go?"

"Just drive out to Lambert," Rhonda said. "And stop at the first place with a buffet."

# chapter 8

HIS FIRST SENSATION was of his own mass, the vast bulk of his body stretched out across the dark like an unsteerable barge. It took him some time to realize that he'd been awakened by the noise of someone moving about the room.

He tried to open his eyes. The light was very bright. He squinted and began to make out shapes.

A woman stood on the other side of the room, her back to him. She seemed vaguely familiar, but then again, so did everything in the room.

"Heh," he said. He'd been trying for "hello," but his voice had snapped off like a rotted board. His throat ached, and he was terribly thirsty.

She glanced at him, and didn't seem surprised that he'd spoken. She was in her midthirties, a thin, pale woman with blotched cheeks and forehead, as if she'd scrubbed her face with lye soap. She wore khaki pants, a plain collared shirt. Definitely an outsider.

"Good morning, Mr. Martin."

Mr. Martin? For a moment he was confused—the name seemed to fit and not fit at the same time.

"I can't believe you're at a loss for words," the woman said.

He tried to lift his arm and discovered it was tied down. Both arms were restrained. "Wah," he said. He swallowed painfully and made a tipping motion with his captive hand. "Water."

"I think we can do that."

He blacked out before she returned.

He came awake a second time with someone bending over him. At first he thought it was Aunt Rhonda, and he grunted in surprise.

The chub girl—not Aunt Rhonda, a young girl maybe only twenty years old with bright red hair—put a hand on his forehead and said, "Shush, Paxton." Her voice was a whisper.

That's right. His name was Paxton. And he was—where was he?

The girl slowly moved a warm washcloth across his chest, and as she leaned over him the neck of her blouse gaped to reveal a large pair of breasts straining at a white bra, threatening avalanche.

"Doreen!"

The girl jerked away from him. "Doctor F, I was just—"

"I think he's clean enough now," a woman said. It was the pale woman from before.

"I'll just dry him off and—"

"Doreen."

The red-haired girl left the room. The doctor pulled down his smock from where it was bunched around his neck and covered him with the bedclothes. "Sorry about that," the doctor said. "She's not herself. It won't happen again."

"Okay," he said. Wondering what exactly had happened.

"I've brought you some lunch," the doctor said. She pulled a sliding table up to his bed.

"Lunch," he said. "Right. Thanks." He thought he sounded reasonably sane. In control.

The doctor moved aside a plastic water pitcher and cup, then set out items she pulled from a white sack: a plastic-wrapped sandwich with the Bugler's Grocery tag still on it, a fruit cup, and a chocolate chip cookie. Supplies for a sixth-grade field trip.

He wasn't at all hungry. His throat still felt raw. It felt like hours had passed since he'd asked for water, but it could have been days.

Pax realized his arms were now untied. He started to push himself up, and Dr. Fraelich put a hand on his shoulder, then worked the bed's remote until he was sitting upright. How long had he been in this bed? Someone, this woman or the chub girl, must have changed him, emptied his bedpan, wiped his ass.

"I'm sorry if I was . . ." Embarrassment made it hard to find the words. He shook his head. "You're who?"

"I'm Dr. Fraelich," she said. "You're at my clinic, Mr. Martin."

"Please, call me Pax." A hazy memory came to him: Deke carrying him into a waiting room, setting him down in a plastic chair. At some point—the next hour? the next day?—he'd been put in a bed. Everything else was a blank.

He opened the metal lid of the fruit cup. His fingers felt clumsy. "I'm sorry if I caused you any trouble."

"No trouble. The first twenty-four hours you did nothing but rant, with brief pauses to vomit," the doctor said. "You eventually passed out, but then a couple hours later you went right back to the preaching and the yelling."

Preaching? Pax thought. "So how long have I . . . ?"

"You've been here three days."

"Ouch," he said. He tried to think of what day that made it. Thursday?

She put a hand on the door handle. "Any other questions?"

He had dozens of questions. He remembered the medical interrogations when he was a kid, the stream of men in masks who asked endless questions but never answered any. By September of that year the waves of transformations had stopped, but no one in town knew why, or if they'd stopped for good, or why some people like Paxton had been passed over. He eventually understood that the doctors weren't hiding information—they were as clueless as he was. Their uncertainty scared him more than the Changes.

He poked at the contents of the fruit cocktail can with his plastic fork and said, "Do you—" He cleared his throat. "Excuse me. Do you know what happened to my father?"

"He's fine. He's at the Home, the mayor's facility."

"Did he come out of it? Does he know what happened?"

"Rhonda hasn't reported back to me."

Pax looked up. Was that sarcasm? Her tone hadn't shifted from dry and impatient. "I guess you've had this, uh, kind of thing before," Pax said. "Accidents like this."

She raised her eyebrows. She couldn't have been much older than thirty-five, but she made him feel like he was twelve.

"I mean, the vintage," he said. "You know about it, right? You must have met others who . . . you know—"

"Took a swim in it? No." She glanced at the watch on her wrist, a transparent doctor gesture. "Be thankful that you can sit up and talk. You ingested an enormous amount of a substance that is both psychedelic and narcotic, though mildly so for most people. You seem to be particularly susceptible to the effects. Your limbic system and frontal lobe were slammed simultaneously, and right now you're recovering from probably the biggest dopamine hit of your life, which means you're going to be experiencing an emotional crash for the next few days. On the plus side, if you haven't developed schizophrenia by now you're probably not going to this week."

"That's good news."

"Enjoy your lunch."

"Wait! When do I get out of here?" She looked back at him. He said, "Not that I'm not enjoying the service."

"One step at a time, Mr. Martin."

Finishing the fruit cup exhausted him. He drank a few sips of water, then pushed aside the table, leaving the rest of the food untouched. He carefully turned on his side, pulled up the covers. He remembered from this morning the sensation that his body had become massive, immovable. Now it felt like a bag of fragile parts, nominally under his control, but ready at any moment to disarticulate.

He was tired but not sleepy. He lay in the bed listening to the air-conditioning and the muffled noises coming from outside the room. He should call his father. No, see him in person. It had been a mistake to call Rhonda so quickly. Paxton would clean up the house, bring his father home, make a go of it. He'd call the restaurant, and if he hadn't been fired yet he'd ask for more time off—family medical leave or something.

Outside the room someone laughed. He listened to the burble of voices and thought of water, his father pulling him into the baptistry, the rush of homecoming he'd felt when he looked out over the congregation.

The next time he opened his eyes he was surprised that the room was dark.

He blinked to make sure his eyes were working. Something about the silence, the coolness of the air, made it feel like the middle of the night. He didn't know why he'd popped awake, then realized he needed to pee, that in fact he'd been dreaming of water all night: swimming with Deke and Jo in the river, his baptism when he was twelve, the sound of rain thundering against the tin roof of his mamaw's house.

He sat up—too fast. After a minute the dizziness passed and he put his feet down on cool linoleum. He shuffled to the wall and flipped on the light. The sandwich and cookie were nowhere to be seen. It was disconcerting to think that people had been coming in and out of the room as he slept.

He opened the door, and the hallway was dark except for a faraway wedge of light—a room with a light on, the door ajar. "Hello?" he called. "Is there a doctor in the house?"

No one answered. He turned back to his room and started looking through the cabinets. Finally he found his clothes, neatly folded on a shelf. His shirt and underwear smelled faintly of bleach. He slowly pulled on his jeans, using a hand against the counter to keep his balance. He left the smock thing on, deciding that the dork poncho look was acceptable under the circumstances.

He padded back into the hallway. Halfway to the lit room he noticed that the dark space to his left was a bathroom. He went in, closed the door behind him. The sound of his piss hitting the bowl seemed obnoxiously loud. On the wall was a poster, "Four Facts on Transcription Divergence Syndrome." The target audience seemed to be frightened people who didn't live in Switchcreek. The four facts amounted to: You can't catch it, It only happened once, You can't catch it, and it won't happen again . . . probably.

Did we mention that you can't catch it?

Except that was a lie—you *could* catch it, but only from your parents. TDS permanently rewrote your DNA, and children born to the changed were as fucked up as their parents. More, evidently—those second-generation beta children looked more alien than Jo ever had. The world was only going to get stranger.

He switched off the bathroom light and went into the hallway. Instead of returning to his room he walked toward the wedge of light. "Hel-loo," he said again.

He knocked once on the door, pushing it open farther, and stepped inside. There was no one in the room. The desk nearest him was stacked high with multicolored paper and brown accordion folders. Opposite was another desk with an open laptop upon it, the screen showing some kind of application.

He picked up one of the packets lying on the desk. The top page was titled "IRB Human Subjects Consent Form," with a much-photocopied logo of the University of Tennessee in the corner. Under "Project Description" it said, "The effects of diet upon blood glucose and protein production in subjects with TDS-C." He flipped through the pages in the packet. They were all identical except for the names of the participants and their signatures. He saw a name he recognized: Cletus Pritchard, the young *cuz* who'd been watching his father's house. Was this the research project Rhonda was using the vintage for? He looked at pages on the tops of the other piles, but he didn't start going through stacks. He didn't want to make it obvious he'd been rummaging around. He set the packet down where he'd found it. The walls were lined with filing cabinets. The drawers were all closed, but there were short stacks of files on top of each of them. The office of an organized person whose control had begun to slip.

He sat on one of the cheap task chairs, strangely winded. He should probably go back to his room and try to sleep again.

The laptop screen showed an overcrowded data-entry form, full of tabs and drop-down lists. It looked like some kind of billing or insurance program. The currently selected patient was "Hooke, Elsa L." Reverend Hooke, he wondered, or a relative? Before he could lean closer the screen blanked; a moment later a blue cube appeared and began to bounce around the edges.

That's weird, he thought. Why would the screen saver come on in the middle of the night? He tapped the space bar and the form came back.

Somewhere in the building a door clanked open. Pax jerked upright, turned toward the door. Well shit, he thought. Hard clacking steps came down the hallway. Pax moved toward the door, stepped back. He put his hands by his sides. Act natural, he thought.

Dr. Fraelich walked into the room, her eyes down as she tucked something into her pants pocket.

"Hi there," Pax said.

The woman seemed to leap without leaving her feet. Her hands went up and she grunted like she'd been punched. "What the *hell* are you doing?" she yelled.

"I'm sorry! I'm sorry! I was just, I had to pee—"

"What are you doing in my office?"

"I saw the light on. I called out; I didn't think anybody was here."

She looked around at the papers on the desk, the screen of

the laptop. "Have you been looking at my files? These are confidential."

"No! I mean, yes, I saw them, but I wasn't *reading* them."

She pushed past him and snapped down the lid of the laptop. "You need to go back to your room, Mr. Martin. Obviously you're feeling better."

"Hey, have you been smoking?" he asked.

She stared at him. Her hair was down around her shoulders, and she seemed younger, less imposing. It was that Sexy Librarian trick women could do. He wasn't attracted to her—he wasn't attracted to most women, or most men either—but he could see now how someone could be. Theoretical sex appeal.

He said, "I haven't smoked in eighteen months, but I could really use one right now."

"I'm not giving a patient under my care a cigarette."

"I won't tell anyone."

"Out, Mr. Martin."

"Wait, what are you doing here so late? It's like, what, two in the morning?"

She looked at her watch. "Three-thirty. I'm working."

"You're here to watch me?"

"That's part of it. But I often do paperwork at night. I don't need much sleep."

"I guess not." He was conscious of his dork smock, his bare feet, his greasy hair. He nodded at the stacks on top of the cabinets. "You want me to help? I could file those. No, probably not. Confidentiality."

"Why are you still here?"

"I don't think the dopamine crash has happened yet. I'm achy, but mentally I'm kind of wired. Maybe this is what it feels like right before you slide off the cliff."

"I should have left you tied up," Dr. Fraelich said. She sat at the desk and began moving stacks of paper to the side of the desk farthest from him.

He sat down on a chair. "So all these forms, you're kind of in charge of these research studies?"

"I'm just the field administrator. I help them collect their data."

"I kind of expected more scientists to be living in town," he said. "When I was a kid, right after the Changes, there were doctors and scientists all over the place."

"You don't need to live in Chernobyl to study radiation poisoning," she said.

"Is that what you think? It was radiation?"

"That was a metaphor, Mr. Martin."

"Please stop calling me that. It's Pax. And you are?"

"Dr. Fraelich."

He laughed, hurting his throat. "You know, you're not very warm for a doctor."

"Have you *met* any doctors?"

He laughed again, and she looked away. Had he gotten her to smile? Not quite. But he'd come close.

"Okay, so what caused it?" Pax asked. "The Changes. I'm a little out of touch with the latest theories."

"You all are," she said. In the newly cleared space in front of her she rolled a pen under her palm. "The people in Switchcreek seem so incurious about what happened. I just don't understand it. You're in the middle of one of the great scientific mysteries of the century and all of you act as if the Changes were, I don't know, a hurricane or something. Bad weather. An act of God."

"What are we supposed to do? We're not scientists," he

said. "And they couldn't tell us how it happened anyway. Sure looked like an act of God. So we just went on with our lives."

"You don't have to be scientists to show some interest," she said. "TDS is a completely new class of disease—a cancer that's not just trying to replicate its own cells, but hijack the transcription process to rewrite an entire genome, while keeping the host alive. Not just alive, but healthy. Hox genes start spitting out new instructions, adult stem cells start acting like embryonic stem cells—it's unprecedented. Yet none of you even seem to wonder how this happened to you. The only one of you who seemed at all curious is—" He felt sure she was about to say "dead." She waved a hand. "Never mind."

"Are you talking about Jo Lynn? Did you know her?"

"Of course I did. I was her doctor." There was something too casual in her voice.

"You were friends."

Dr. Fraelich said nothing.

"I didn't see you at the funeral," he said.

"And I didn't see you."

"I came in—" He didn't want to say "late." "Well, there were a lot of people. All those betas. I met her daughters, and their father."

The doctor frowned. "Tommy's not their father. The betas reproduce through parthenogenesis."

"Yeah, I know that." Though he'd never understood exactly what the word meant: sex without sex, he supposed. "I just thought that the beta women—some of them, right?—had already had sex before the Changes, and that they'd stored up the sperm. Or the eggs. Later they released them when—what?"

The doctor was shaking her head. "Nobody's thought that for years. They had to toss out that theory with the first guaranteed virgin birth. There was a girl who was eight when she changed, with no evidence of previous sexual activity. She had twins when she was thirteen. Definitely no sperm involved."

"But there are male betas," Pax said.

"There are no 'male' betas, not really. Only men who contracted TDS-B during the Changes. Males who caught the B strain died at much higher rates than females. The men who survived, chemically and hormonally are practically female. TDS didn't make them grow ovaries, but it halted their sperm production completely. Penises shriveled, testicles receded. They're sterile and impotent."

"Jesus," Pax said. He felt a twinge of sympathy for Tommy Shields. "Okay, no male betas, but there's sex with other people—"

"What other people?"

"The other clades," he said. "Or, uh, skipped people."

He felt his face flush. The doctor looked at him oddly. "Clades can't breed with the unchanged, Pax. And they can't interbreed either. We've known this for a decade. Charlies breed with charlies, and argos—well, we're not sure what's happening there."

"But if there's no sperm at all, then how are they—how does it work? And don't say, 'When a beta loves herself very, very much . . .' "

The doctor didn't laugh. "No one knows. All women are born with all the eggs they're ever going to have. The Changes allowed beta women to fertilize those eggs somehow. Or maybe they're like aphids, born pregnant. Parthenogenesis happens in sharks and lizards and who knows how many other species, but nobody knows how it works exactly. It's just a Greek word for 'We don't know what the hell is happening.' "

Paxton sat back, rubbed a hand across his face.

She said, "You look . . . lost."

"Nothing. It's nothing." He stood, thinking of Jo's daughters. For some reason he was disappointed. When he was sent away from Switchcreek, Pax had thought that the girls were his, or maybe Deke's, or maybe both of theirs. And later, when people on the news started talking about parthenogenesis, he'd held on to the theory that maybe, just maybe, he was still the father. It was stupid, he knew.

He said, "I better get back to bed."

Dr. Fraelich tapped the pen against the desk. "We'll do one final checkup in the morning, but I think you're good enough to go home. I'll call the Chief and tell him you're ready for pick-up."

"Wait a minute—Chief?"

"Deke. I'll call Deke."

"Oh, right." He had a dim memory of someone else calling Deke the Chief. "Try to get some sleep, Doc."

The next morning Pax heard a deep argo voice vibrating through the walls, and thought, Deke. He sat up quickly, and his eyes blurred with tears. Jesus, tears? What was that about?

He quickly got dressed and made his way to the reception area. He felt stronger than yesterday but still shaky. He'd finally eaten, finishing off a granola bar and a bottle of orange juice that Dr. Fraelich had brought him.

In the reception area Deke leaned on the counter talking to the doctor, a collection of orange prescription bottles on the surface between them. Doreen, the charlie girl who'd bathed him, sat at a desk behind the doctor, staring down at an open magazine, pretending to ignore the conversation. She looked up as Pax entered and quickly looked down again, embarrassed.

Deke abruptly stopped whatever he was saying to the doctor and said to Pax, "Hey there, sleepyhead."

Pax smiled faintly. "Howdy, Chief."

Dr. Fraelich seemed upset, the blotches on her face angrier. She picked up the bottles and put them into a plastic bag.

Pax said, "Do you need my insurance or something? I remember signing a lot of papers."

Deke looked at Dr. Fraelich, and she said, "You're covered. Courtesy of Aunt Rhonda."

"Really?" Pax said.

"Just drink plenty of water," Dr. Fraelich said to him. Whatever familiarity they'd developed last night had been packed away.

"That's it?" Pax said. "Three days of drug-induced coma and all I get is water?"

"A coma would have been a lot quieter and a lot easier on all of us," she said. "You're detoxing. Eat some fruit if you want. Just stay away from male charlies of a certain age." She took the plastic bag of medicine and walked away before he could respond. Doreen kept her head down.

"That was . . . weird," Pax said. He felt like everyone was moving at double speed, flashing signals he couldn't detect.

"Come on, man," Deke said. "Let's get you home."

Home. Which was where, exactly? Sure as hell not Chicago. He knew now that it had never been his home. He'd spent ten years marking time.

Pax followed Deke outside. It was midmorning and humid as a greenhouse. Gray clouds hid the top of Mount Clyburn, promising rain.

"You look whupped," Deke said. "You need help getting in? You're walking like an old man."

"I got it. I've just been smacked upside the limbic system." Pax pulled open the door and after a false start managed to hoist himself into the cab. He fell back in the high bucket seat and gazed up through the roll bars at the gray clouds.

"Thank you, man," Pax said. "For coming to get me. For everything."

"Don't worry about it."

"No, seriously. Thank you. You've always been—you and Jo—you were the only people I . . ." His voice trailed off.

"It's okay," Deke said. "I'm just glad you're okay."

"I was inside his head, Deke."

"Whose head?"

"At the church. I was next to him in the water, and I saw what he saw. He was hallucinating about the church, the way it used to be. I could see it."

"You were doing some hallucinating yourself, P.K."

"I don't regret it happening, though. Okay, the hangover is hell, but I'm glad it happened." He rolled his neck to look up at the man. "My father loves me, Deke."

"Of course he does. He's your father." A strange thing for him to say, Pax thought, considering what an asshole Deke's father had been.

"You don't understand," Pax said. "I *know* he does. I could feel it. I felt what he felt."

"You're still high," Deke said. "Just a second." He reached into his shirt pocket and extracted a cell phone pinched between thumb and index finger. It was a bulky, old-fashioned thing that looked tiny in his hands. He held it in front of him, not even trying to fit it to his ear. "This is Deke."

A deep argo voice buzzed from the phone's speakers. "Deke, this is Amos. I think we've got some tourists over at the Whitehall place. I just saw someone pull in. Nobody from around here."

"You sure it's not the police?" Deke asked.

"It ain't that kind of car," the voice said.

Deke looked over at Pax. "You got a minute for a detour?"

"My day is wide open," Pax said.

# chapter 9

DEKE DIDN'T TURN on a siren or flip on a light, but the drivers in town seemed to recognize that he was on business and stayed out of his way. Once Deke cleared the curve at the elementary school and turned onto Creek Road he hit the gas. Mount Clyburn rose up ahead, shrouded in mist. They seemed to be driving straight into it.

"So you're chief of what, exactly?" Pax said.

"Pardon?"

Pax raised his voice over the wind. "Police? Fire? The Cherokee tribe?"

Deke shrugged. "It's just a nickname."

"Right."

"I helped set up the VFD, the volunteer fire department. Plus I do other, uh, community stuff. Keeping the peace."

"You mean cop stuff."

"County cops don't like to patrol here. People don't like the cops much either. They need somebody local to step in and help out sometimes."

At least that explained the police scanner. "So do you get paid for this?"

Deke laughed. "It's more of a barter system."

"Sure. Chickens, goats, that kind of thing. Do you have a gun?"

"Hell no."

"Deke, it's Tennessee! Every hillbilly out here has a gun."

"That's a stereotype, man." Pax laughed, and after a few beats, Deke said, "But yeah, everybody's got a shotgun in the closet, and that's why I make sure everybody knows I don't carry. You see a twelve-foot mother walking up to your house it's bad enough, but carrying a shotgun to boot? Last thing I need is some drunk chub so shit-scared he *has* to shoot me. Any more questions?"

"Yeah," Pax said. "What do you do in this thing when it rains?"

"Rain is not allowed to enter this vehicle. I'm the fucking Chief."

They reached Jo's house and turned onto the steep, curved drive. Deke parked in front of the house. Tucked around the side of the house, as if trying to hide, was the back end of a light blue Prius.

"Amos was right," Pax said. As if he had any idea who Amos was besides a voice on the phone. "The cops would never drive a hybrid."

Deke stepped out of the Jeep and said, "Why don't you stay here a second while I talk to these folks."

He walked toward the car in the slumped stroll of the argos, long arms swinging slowly. He bent to look inside the back window of the vehicle, then stepped around the corner of the house and out of sight.

Pax looked up. The oak loomed over the house.

He unbuckled his seat belt and stepped down out of the Jeep, his knees a bit wobbly. Of course tourists would come here, he thought. In your tour of Monster Town, why not visit the place where the tragic blank girl lived, the tree where she died? He took a few steps toward the side of the house and then the front door banged open.

A white man in a T-shirt and cargo shorts burst through the doorway and leaped off the steps. He landed awkwardly, and a palm-sized chunk of silver flew out of his hand and landed in the grass. He looked up at Pax with a shocked expression, then sprang to his feet and ran pell-mell for the Toyota.

Pax looked back at the house, expecting Deke to come charging out the door, but the big man was nowhere to be seen. "Deke?" Pax called. "You okay?"

The Prius backed up, then swung around so that the nose was pointing at the Jeep. Pax thought about stepping into its path, then thought better of it. He moved to the driver's side of the Jeep, leaned over the door, and pressed on the horn.

The Prius lurched forward, passed the Jeep, and headed down to the driveway. Pax looked back at the house just as Deke rounded the corner. He was bent over, legs and long arms churning, running like a huge gorilla. The motion looked much more natural than his usual gait. Graceful. Right.

"Car!" Pax said, and pointed down the road. A stupid gesture; Deke could see the car as easily as he could. The Prius slid around the first curve, spitting gravel.

Deke jerked left and launched himself down the hill, into the trees, on a path that cut through the S of the road like the slash in a dollar sign.

Pax had never seen anyone move so fast.

He opened the Jeep door with some vague idea of following, but then looked down at the pedals six feet from the driver's seat and realized—or rather, remembered again—that he'd never be able to drive this thing. Plus, Deke had taken the keys. Maybe he should chase them down the gravel driveway? Before he could make up his mind he heard the shattering of glass and the scrape of tires locking up on loose gravel.

A minute later Deke appeared, walking upright back up the hill with the man slung over one shoulder like a deer carcass.

"He's not dead, is he?" Pax asked.

"You're hurting me!" the man said.

Deke strode up to the house, dropped the man onto his feet. "Inside," Deke ordered him, argo voice set to Full Rumble.

Pax started to follow, then turned back to the yard. He looked around for a minute, then found the thing the man had dropped—a camera. By the time Pax got into the house the man was sitting on a couch, looking sour. Deke sat across from him, crouching to fit under the low ceiling.

The atmosphere was close, hotter than outside. And even without Deke's huge body the room would have felt small. Bookshelves of varying heights lined the walls like battlements. Crowded into the center of the room were the couch and an easy chair in matching brown and blue plaid, worn but not worn out. Along one wall, a plank spanned two bookshelves, forming a long homemade desk. Three wooden chairs, a different colored pillow tied to each seat, were lined up along the desk. He pictured Jo and the two girls sitting in a row, doing homework.

"You smashed in my window," the man said. He was a little younger than Pax, with a head shaped like a candy corn: a brush of bleached hair, a broad forehead, and cheekbones that narrowed to an elfin chin, a dark soul patch under his lower lip like the dot in an exclamation mark. Something about the hair and the deliberate counter-culture look said that he came from money.

"Next time you'll stop," Deke said. "Now, empty your pockets."

"I didn't steal anything!" he said. "I'm a journalist."

"Really," Pax said. He swung the camera on its nylon lanyard. "For who?"

The man didn't answer. Deke grabbed him by the front of the shirt. Pax said, "I think you should answer our questions."

"Fuck you," the man said.

Deke grabbed him by his face, his fist completely engulfing his head, and the man screamed into it. Deke's face was rigid with anger. His white arm trembled, as if he were on the verge of cracking his skull like an egg.

"Deke! Shit, Deke!"

Deke held the man for several seconds. Then the trembling stopped, and Deke released him. He felt to the floor, gasping.

"Your pockets," Deke said.

According to his driver's license he was Andrew Weygand, twenty-three years old, from Wheeling, West Virginia, and an organ donor. He said he ran a website called TheOpenSwitch.com. "TOS does investigative articles, opinion pieces—"

"Jesus, he's a blogger," Pax said. "Arrest him, Deke."

"You're a cop?" the man said. Pax couldn't tell if he was alarmed or relieved.

"He's the fucking Chief," Pax said. Deke sighed.

The man said, "I didn't even break in, you know. The back door was open."

"Right."

Weygand said he was looking for someone called Brother

Bewlay. Pax glanced at Deke—he couldn't tell if Deke recognized the name.

"It's the screen name for a guy who posted to the blog a lot," Weygand said. "TOS is supposed to be just about the Switchcreek Event, but it gets pretty tangential—government conspiracies, fringe science, political activism, you name it—all the usual nut-job issues, right? I let anyone comment as long as they don't get abusive. Brother Bewlay, though, was one of the serious posters. He knew his facts. Personally, I suspected pretty early that he was from Switchcreek. He never said so, probably because no one would believe him. Anybody can say they went through the Changes, right? But Bewlay—sometimes he said stuff that seemed so insightful and weird that it had to be true." Pax looked up questioningly, and Weygand said, "Like how betas weren't really male or female, they were a new, third sex. He won a lot of converts. Of course, some people thought he was a total bullshitter, and there were plenty of flame wars, but—hey, careful with that?"

Pax looked up from the camera screen. He'd sat on one of the wooden chairs and started clicking backward through the recent shots in the machine's memory. The first thirty pictures were of the inside of the house, five or six per room, as if Weygand was going to make a virtual tour of the place.

"Never mind the camera," Deke said.

"Is he okay?" Weygand asked. "He looks like he's going to pass out."

"I've had a tough week," Pax said.

"Get to Switchcreek," Deke said to the man. "What you're doing here."

Weygand took a breath, his eyes still on the camera in Paxton's hands. "About a week and a half ago Bewlay went offline, no explanation. It's usually not a big deal, right? And we were all so busy talking about the suicide in Switchcreek that nobody noticed for a while. I finally emailed him—we'd had a lot of personal conversations outside the blog—and when I didn't get an answer after a few days I thought, oh shit. Now I never do this—I believe in privacy, right? But I pulled the server logs and did a lookup on his address. The IP was definitely coming from the Lambert area. I decided I had to find out if he—if she was him."

"How would you know?" Deke asked. "If Bewlay didn't tell you anything about himself—"

"Her computer," Weygand said. "If some of Bewlay's files are on there, then that's that, right? But even if I couldn't get onto the computer, I thought maybe there'd be something in the house that he mentioned in one of his messages. Like—okay, look at this book I found."

Weygand popped up and went to the bookshelf. "This Richard Dawkins' book, *The Ancestor's Tale*? Bewlay quoted from it, more than once."

Pax took the book from his hand. It was a thick, beige paperback with a heavily creased spine. The book flopped open in his hand to a chapter headed "The Gibbon's Tale." Under a complicated diagram Jo or someone had written in the margins, "Missing branches—clade tree unrooted?"

"Anybody could have read this," Pax said, though he'd never heard of the book. The others on the shelf were heavy on medicine—a *Physicians' Desk Reference, The Handbook for Genetic Diseases and Disorders, Modern Obstetrics*—but there were an equal number of books on physics, quantum mechanics, and evolution. The Dawkins guy had his own shelf.

Weygand reached for another book. "Okay, look! This

physics book by David Deutsch? Bewlay talked about it and I went out and read it myself. Bewlay was the first person on the boards to find scientists who were applying quantum computation and quantum evolution theories to explain the Changes. He even started posting articles from the physics journals."

Weygand looked from Pax to Deke, excited now. "See, Bewlay's big thing was that the Switchcreek clades weren't *diseased*, they weren't damaged humans—they were *alternate* humans, with genetic information ported in from a parallel universe. Quantum teleportation, man."

Deke stared at him. "*What?*"

"Look, it's not that crazy. Do you guys know about the intron mutation counts?"

Deke looked at Pax. "Paxton, what was I just saying about that in the car?"

"I think you said they were undersold and overhyped. Or the other way around."

Weygand's smile was half-lit—he couldn't tell if they were playing with him. "Okay, everybody knows that TDS screwed with the DNA of people who caught the disease, but nobody suspected that the number of changes would *increase* with second-generation children, the ones born with TDS. Introns are these parts of the DNA that change faster than other parts."

Deke said, "What does this have to do with the children?"

"Okay, with second-generation children there's, like, a *huge* difference in the introns—it's like the kids descended from a completely different species than their parents."

Pax looked at Deke. Deke shrugged. "So TDS scrambles the introns too."

Weygand only seemed exasperated by their ignorance. "Not *scrambled—different*. People with the same type of TDS show the same changes. Betas have intron sequences like other betas, argos look like argos. And betas are as different from argos and charlies as they are from normal—uh, people who don't have TDS. You see what this means?"

They didn't see.

Weygand said, "Look, imagine if evolution took a completely different course millions of years ago. Let's say our ancestors died out, and instead some slightly different cousins took over. Neanderthals, say. If today those cousins dug us up and sucked some of the marrow out of our bones and looked at the DNA, these are the differences they'd expect to find, right? It's like betas and argos and charlies are visitors from another world, a parallel universe—you're what humans would have turned into if our ancestors had taken a few left turns two million years ago."

Deke shifted his weight, leaned forward. Even crouching he loomed over Weygand.

"So," Pax said. "You're saying Deke isn't human."

Weygand looked up at the huge man, his mouth working. "No! I mean, well, he's a *kind* of human."

The man yelped as Deke placed a huge bony hand on his shoulder.

"You're going to do something for me," Deke said. "You're going to go get the shiny little laptop I saw in your car and you're going to send me every email that Brother Bewlay sent you."

"I can't forward you private email! I'm a journalist!"

"Don't make me break you," Deke said.

The rain came down hard, hammering steam from the ground. Pax sat by the front picture window with the side of his head resting against the glass so that he felt it shudder with each gust of wind. Deke looked over Weygand's shoulder as the man fussed with the silver Apple laptop. Weygand was constantly complaining in a small voice: Deke had no right to do this; the inside of Weygand's car was getting soaked; Jo Lynn wouldn't appreciate how Deke was treating him. But he did as he was told and answered the big man's questions. Pax kept being surprised by Deke's easy authority. When they were kids Deke was a follower, a pup, eager for Paxton's approval, ready to follow him or Jo wherever they went. Now he was a leader, a goddamn chief. Which one was the true Deke? Did his huge gray frame armor a timid boy, or had the boy always felt like an undiscovered giant?

Or maybe they were both true. Maybe there was nothing essential to a person that could be separated from the muscle and blood and chemicals that motored him around; maybe everything depended on the body, was dictated by it. He thought of Deke charging into the woods, moving like a freight train. Maybe it was the residue of the vintage in his bloodstream, but Pax could imagine himself inside that powerful body, long arms churning, lungs working easily in the humid air.

Pax was jerked awake by a touch. Deke stood over him. "I'm escorting Andrew here to his car and then right out of town."

"Okay," Pax said. He leaned back in the chair, his neck aching. Outside, the rain had slacked off. Weygand stood by the door looking petulant. "I'll wait for you here."

"I thought you might say that."

When they'd gone, Pax got up, opened a few of the books on the shelves, put them back. After awhile he went down the carpeted hallway, past the small functional bathroom to the pair of bedrooms. The door to his left was open. Most of the space in the room was taken up by a bunk bed. Two of the walls were painted pale yellow, the other two sea foam, matching the stripes on the comforters on the unmade beds. There were two identical dressers, cheap pine. The drawers were ajar, as if that morning the girls had hopped out of bed and dressed hurriedly, late for the school bus. He felt a vague sense of déjà vu, then realized it must be because he'd just seen all this in Weygand's camera.

The other bedroom was smaller, and more plain—a beige double bed in a simple wood frame, a low mirrored dresser, plain white walls—as if all the energy for decoration had been spent in the girls' room. The only color came from the covers of the books stacked up along one wall. A single, curtained window looked out over the backyard.

The bed was still made, unslept in since the night before she died. He pulled back the bedspread and lay down on his side. He pressed his face into the single white pillow and inhaled deeply.

The scent was too subtle for him to tease apart. A hint of flowers that could have been perfume or detergent, a faint muskiness that might have been Jo's scent or simply the effects of humidity in the closed house. With a stab of sadness he realized that he couldn't recall how she smelled. Once he'd known her body—and Deke's—as well as his own. No, better. After the Changes, *all* skin had become strange, and in that first year he and Jo and Deke mapped their bodies for each other.

And then he had left them. The only people who knew him.

Somewhere a door creaked open. He quickly rolled off the bed and wiped the tears from his cheeks. He listened for Deke's heavy steps, but nothing came. Still, the feeling persisted that he was not alone.

Jesus, he thought. I'm a fucking mess.

He tucked the covers back over the pillow, and tugged on the bedclothes to smooth out the creases. Then he heard a clink, like someone setting a glass into the kitchen sink.

He went to the door of the room, leaned out. Far down the hallway, opposite the open door to the kitchen, a lozenge of light lay upon the wall. A shadow flitted across it, slowly slid back, and then vanished. For a moment it had looked like the silhouette of a face. Jo's face.

He stood there for a full minute, staring at the light, waiting for the shadow to return. Because he was alone he didn't have to pretend that he wasn't freaked out. Finally he left the room and stepped quietly down the hall. When he reached the edge of the kitchen doorway he stopped and studied the light on the wall. He decided that even with his imagination straining at the leash he couldn't see anything moving in it. He turned quickly and entered the kitchen, fists clenched.

The kitchen door hung open. Outside, the trunk of the oak tree rose up out of his line of sight.

The rain had stopped. He stepped outside onto the wet, shining grass. He looked at the tire, then up at the rope. He still couldn't imagine Jo doing that to herself.

He walked over to the plastic patio set and righted a chair that had blown over. As he straightened he saw in his peripheral vision two small figures drop down out of the trees at the edge of the lawn. They hit the ground and almost instantly vanished into the woods.

Two children with wine-dark arms and legs, bare heads like marbles.

Pax whisked the water from the seat of the chair and sat. For a while he scanned the tree line, wondering if the girls would come back or if they'd been scared back to the Co-op.

The Whitmer farm was probably only a half mile away as the crow flies. There were paths all through these woods.

Deke's Jeep rumbled up the driveway. He heard the big man go in the front of the house and a minute later come out behind him.

"There you are. How you doing, man?"

"Just great," he said. What he needed, he thought, was to see his father. What he needed was a touch of vintage. Instead he said, "You remember 'The Bewlay Brothers'?"

"'Kings of oblivion,'" Deke said, quoting from the song. The final track on Bowie's *Hunky Dory*. They'd listened to the album dozens of times at Jo's old house.

"So he was definitely talking to Jo," Pax said. "We should still check her computer, though. Maybe she was talking to other people."

Deke shook his head. "It's not here. I've looked."

"When?"

He shrugged. "I broke in yesterday."

Pax looked up at him, smiling. "Really?"

"Searched everywhere. Somebody got here before me."

"Maybe the girls took it."

"I asked the reverend. She was there that morning—her and Tommy were called right after the police. She packed the girls' things and said she didn't see it."

"The twins are clever girls," Pax said. "I think they've been back since that night." He told him about the girls dropping out of the trees and scampering away like squirrels.

Deke didn't seem surprised. "At least Weygand didn't get a picture of them," he said. He snapped something between his thick fingers and flicked the pieces into the grass.

"Camera memory card?" Pax guessed.

"Not anymore."

Pax laughed. "You know, when I saw you charge out of the house, I thought you were going to kill him. And then when he told you to fuck off . . ."

Deke took a breath. "Yeah. Me too."

"You're serious," Pax said.

Deke squatted beside him, his forearms resting on his knees. "I have a temper problem."

"What? You're the calmest guy I know."

"I'm the carefullest guy you know," Deke said. "I slipped up once. Now I have to . . . Well. Let's just say I keep a close watch on this heart of mine."

Pax laughed, and then they lapsed into silence. They sat without talking for several minutes. In the north people didn't just sit, Pax realized. Not unless they were on the bus or trapped in a waiting room. You said what you needed to say, then you moved on. At some point in the past dozen years he'd stopped noticing the Yankee rush to fill the silence.

Pax said, "So did you know about this stuff? That she was online, talking to people about Switchcreek?"

Deke exhaled heavily. "I didn't know, but it didn't surprise me. Jo didn't have many people to talk to in this town—people who could keep up with her, anyway. You know how she was. Didn't suffer fools."

"Oh yeah." She had scholarship brains. Nobody had expected her to stay in Switchcreek—until the Changes. Until she got pregnant. "You think Jo believed all that crazy shit Weygand was saying? I mean, her own girls. She couldn't really think they were . . ." He gestured vaguely. "Alternate universe babies."

"Just because she was smart doesn't mean she was always

right," Deke said. "Look." He reached into his back pocket and pulled out a wallet the size of a bank bag. With his thick fingers he fished out a heavily creased piece of paper and handed it to Pax.

Pax unfolded it. It was a printout of a black-and-white photo, a long-range shot blown up to the point of blurriness. In the foreground were pine trees, a chain-link fence topped with barbed wire. Beyond the fence was a wide, snow-covered plain. Half a dozen low, barracks-like buildings sat in the distance. Three figures were moving between two buildings. Two of them were clearly argos, all long arms and sloped back. Running ahead of them was a much smaller figure moving on all fours. Scale was difficult to assess, but considering the size of the argos, the third figure could have been a pony or a large dog.

"Jo gave that to me a couple years ago," Deke said. "She found it on the web. Said it came from China."

"Wait—argos in China?"

Deke shrugged.

Pax said, "What's that other thing, in front of them?"

"Can't you tell? That's an argo child."

Pax stared at the picture. "No fucking way."

"There's all kinds of theories. People think there was another Change, before Switchcreek. Completely covered up. Or maybe more than one—China in the sixties, Russia in the eighties. Or in the States, the usual secret military base in the desert. All that Area Fifty-one shit."

Pax said, "So this picture—"

"Doesn't mean a damn thing."

"What?"

Deke held out a hand, and Pax gave the paper back to him.

"It's a hoax, P.K. Urban myth, like Sasquatch. There's dozens of pictures like these on the web. Hundreds maybe. It's all done with computers, people jackin' around." He folded it up and placed it back in his wallet. "Argos in Mexico, betas in the northwest, chubs hanging out with Elvis. This ain't even one of the convincing ones."

"But if Jo gave it to you she must have thought—"

"Jo wanted to be fooled as much as anyone, Paxton. No one wants to think we're alone out here. It's the town disease."

# chapter 10

THE SMELL OF the house was driving him crazy.

His father's scent seemed to have infused every surface: the carpets, the cloth of the furniture, the walls. The smell couldn't have been much different than a few days ago, but it seemed worse to him now that he knew the taste of fresh vintage. Now Pax could smell only the decay, the corruption of the pure product, like a fruit farmer attuned to the taint of rot.

He opened all the windows and set up fans in the front and back screen doors to start a cross-draft, but the humidity only seemed to give weight to the odor, turning it into something physical that shifted in strength and intensity, moving from room to room like an animal.

He tried to ignore it. He went through his father's pile of mail, sorting junk from bills and bank statements, with the idea that he should figure out if his father was in financial trouble, but he quickly lost concentration. He couldn't even watch TV; the scent of his father was strongest there by the couch. Finally he fell asleep in the guest room with an arm thrown over his face.

When he awoke the next morning he was damp and aching and the scent was still with him.

I should leave now, he thought. Get dressed and drive out of Switchcreek as fast as I drove in.

He went to the bathroom, stripped, and sat on the edge of the tub for a long time waiting for the water to get hot. Despite the hollowness in his stomach he had no appetite. Finally he stepped under the shower, steadying himself with one palm against the tile.

Leave or go, he thought. Back to Chicago, or sink back into the life he'd left when he was fifteen? There was hardly anything calling him back to the city. He'd probably been fired from the restaurant by now. And there was no one back there who'd miss him, not really. He had coworkers, and people he got drunk with, and coworkers he got drunk with. Had even one of them called him to see if he was okay? Okay, his cell phone was dead and he hadn't packed the charger, but even if they had called, was there one of them he would have felt compelled to call back? People around him fell in and out of love affairs—some of them even got married—and he had no more interest in their dramas than he did for his father's Discovery Channel documentaries. Fuck or don't fuck. Move in together or not. Don't dress it up in all this costume emotion to make it seem important. There'd been a few women and a couple of men who'd wanted more from him, who wanted a *relationship*. But Jesus, no. He'd never had to do much to drive them away. He didn't have to be mean, or push them away. He simply shut off whatever part of him he'd let slip, whatever glimmer of him that made them think they knew him. Once he sealed that crack, soon enough they went away on their own.

He dried off and walked naked down the hallway. He knew there weren't any clean clothes left in his suitcase; he'd only expected to stay a couple of days. He walked past the guest room to his father's room and pushed open the door.

The room looked much as it had a dozen years before: a long, mirrored bureau, wood veneer bedside tables, the long gauzy drapes his mother had liked. The bed was unmade, the bedclothes pushed against the wall. The box spring had been lifted off the frame and reinforced by a row of two-by-fours, but his father's weight had still pressed a hollow into the mattress.

A pile of clothes lay on the floor beside the bed. Pax picked up a huge white T-shirt. He rubbed it through his hands, then lifted it to his face. He inhaled, breathed out, and inhaled again. The smell of the vintage swam thickly into his nose, his lungs.

He dropped the shirt over his head. The wide neck hung lopsided on his shoulders, open to his collarbone; the hem reached to his knees. He held out his arms and looked down at himself. The shirt was as big as a tablecloth.

He imagined his father laid out on some bed at Rhonda's Home, staring down the expanse of his body. Waiting.

He took off the T-shirt, went to the closet. He pushed aside hangers until he found his father's old clothes, from before the Changes. He pulled on a striped button-down shirt—several sizes bigger than what he wore, but in the realm of the wearable—then went back to the guest room to find his jeans.

He realized he had his father's T-shirt in his hand again. He spread it across the bed like a blanket.

His father loved him. His father needed him. The terms were indistinguishable.

He went back to the guest room and looked under the bed for the stack of papers Rhonda had given him. They weren't there. He sat on the bed, looking around at the bookshelves. He'd signed them that night, then—what? He remembered falling asleep, but he couldn't recall putting the papers away.

It didn't matter. He'd find them later, and burn them.

The gate was closed, of course. He leaned out of the window of the Tempo and pressed the intercom's call button. "Hello?"

After a long pause a male voice came back. "Can I help you with something?"

"Hi, this is Paxton Martin. Is this—" He couldn't remember the name of the security guard he'd met. Barry? Brian? "I'm here to see my father."

"Oh, hi there, Paxton," the voice said. Genuinely friendly. "I thought that was you. We met the other day."

Pax looked at the gate, then spotted the camera sticking up above the wall. Paxton lifted a hand in a wave. Another five seconds passed. "So if you could open the gate?"

"Rhonda's not here right now," the guard said. "You want to leave a message?"

"No message. I'm just here to see my father. Harlan Martin."

"Rhonda always tells me if we're going to have visitors. Did you call ahead? Visitors need to call ahead."

"Well I didn't do that." Pax struggled to keep his voice level. "So if you could just let me in, I need to talk to my father. It's important. Family business."

"You really need to call ahead."

"Listen—what was your name again?"

"Barron." Cold now.

"Barron, open the gate. I never signed anything, so you're

holding my father illegally. I've come to take him home. You can't stop the next of kin from seeing him."

"You're going to have to talk to Aunt Rhonda about that. Now if you can give me your phone number, I'm ready to write it down."

"Open the fucking gate, Barron."

"Son, there's no call for cussing."

"Open the fucking gate!"

No answer. Pax pressed the call button, then pressed it again.

He switched off the car, got out, and marched up to the gate. He grabbed the iron bars with both hands and yanked, but they didn't move.

He stepped back, looked at the stone walls that adjoined the gate at each side. They were about ten feet high, made of big stones set into the mortar. Maybe climbable, if his legs didn't already feel like Jell-O. An argo could have pulled himself right over them.

He walked back to the car, slid between the side mirror and the intercom post, and got in. He thought about gunning the engine and ramming the gates, but the little Ford would probably bounce off.

He took a breath and pressed the button again. "Barron, I'm sorry I swore. I'm a little frustrated. All I want to do is see my father."

No answer.

He pressed the call button again. Pax said, "I need to talk to Aunt Rhonda in person. Could you tell me where she is? Barron?"

"Hold on," the guard said.

A minute passed. Pax leaned against the steering wheel. The back of his head was wet with sweat. Another blazing August day in Switchcreek, Tennessee.

Another minute passed, then Barron said, "Aunt Rhonda says she'll talk to you. It's Saturday, so she's working at the Welcome Center."

Jesus, Pax thought, he couldn't have just told him that?

"Okay, thanks," Pax said. He started the car and then leaned out to the box again. "Could you do me one favor? Could you tell my father that I was here?"

"Uh, I'd have to ask Rhonda about that," Barron said.

"Barron?"

"Yes?"

He was going to ask him, When you take a shit, do you ask Rhonda if it's okay to wipe your ass?

"Have a *super* day," Pax said.

Downtown seemed busier than when he'd arrived last Saturday. There were two buses at the Icee Freeze, and scores of cars lined the streets and filled the Bugler's parking lot. He finally found an empty parking spot on Main Street and walked a block to the Welcome Center.

Pax didn't know how old the building was—late 1800s? Over the years it had been a church, a post office, and a one-room schoolhouse. It had been boarded up years before he was born and no one had gotten around to tearing it down.

He walked up the wooden steps and through the open door. Inside it was cool and shadowy. The wide, uneven planks of the floor looked original, but the rest of the interior had been refurbished into a combination information center and gift shop; half a dozen tourists were browsing through racks of books and postcards and knickknacks. A charlie girl worked the cash register in the back. Aunt Rhonda was talking to an older couple and pointing to a topographical map of the area hanging on the wall. She noticed Pax and let him know with a nod that she'd get to him in a bit.

He looked over the merchandise: commemorative plates; novelty "argo-sized" pencils; stuffed black bears with "Welcome to Switchcreek" dog tags; bald beta dolls you could dress in male or female outfits. One wall was all T-shirts and sweatshirts. The book rack held several scientific books on the Changes, as well as a couple photo-heavy coffee-table books and a slim, cheaply printed book titled *The Families of Switchcreek.* He looked up "Martin" in the index and found that his father was given an entire page. His mother got two sentences—one about her life as the pastor's wife and one on her death of TDS-B. Paxton got one line: "His son, Paxton Martin, was one of the few who did not contract TDS." He was relieved there wasn't more. Something like, "He lives in Chicago, where he smokes dope, plays Halo, and continues to be an embarrassment to his father."

"How do you like our little store?" Aunt Rhonda said. She'd slipped up beside him.

"It's . . ." He put the book back in its spot. "People buy a lot of this stuff?"

"More than you think. It's only been open two summers and we've already earned back the setup costs. Why don't you come on back?"

She led him to the back of the center. "We're part of the Smoky Mountain Tourist Complex. We've got the most visited national park in the country just down the road, and that generates all kinds of spillover." She lifted up a section of the back counter and held it open for him. "Now, we're never going to be Pigeon Forge or Gatlinburg. The whole unsolved genetic catastrophe thing keeps our numbers down."

Rhonda told the girl behind the counter that she'd be out back, then led him out to a fenced yard behind the center. Everett, bald head gleaming in the sun, sat at a patio table talking quietly into a cell phone. Rhonda took a chair next to Everett and gestured for Pax to sit next to her. "This is just the start," she said. "I'm working with an eco-tourist company to develop an educational entertainment package. Meet with the residents, see how they live, that kind of thing. Have you ever been to Williamsburg? The colonial village? Something like that. But with all the clades. Shake hands with an argo! Cook dinner with a beta. That kind of thing."

"A freak show."

Rhonda poked him hard with a stubby finger. "It's only a freak show, Paxton Martin, if ignorant people talk about us that way. How do you think we're going to get people to understand us and not fear us? Education. Education and exposure. I'm trying to get the Learning Channel to do a reality show on us, like they did with that midget family."

"Yeah . . ." Pax said. He had no idea what to say to that. "Listen, why I wanted to talk with you—"

"Barron said you were pretty riled up."

"I was a little frustrated. Your hired help wasn't that helpful."

Everett glanced up, eyes narrowed.

"I've decided that my father needs to stay with me," Pax said. "At home."

Rhonda looked at Everett, who was still mumbling into his

phone. A ghost of a smile crossed her lips, and she took her time turning back to him. "Oh, hon." She patted his hand. "That's sweet. And very brave of you."

"My father doesn't want to be in your 'Home.' He told me that himself."

"But you called me anyway, didn't you?" Rhonda said. "Your father ran away at the break of dawn, half out of his mind. And you asked for me to come and take care of him."

"I know that, and I appreciate your help, but I may have—I overreacted. I've thought about it now. It's my job to take care of him."

"I don't think you've thought about this at all. You know you can't watch your daddy twenty-four hours a day—the other night proved that. You don't know the first thing about taking care of a man like your father."

"I'll figure it out."

"You're going to quit your job in Chicago? Move back to Switchcreek, back into this house—and spend the next twenty or thirty years playing nursemaid?" She shook her head. "No. I don't think so."

"I'm his son. I can take him out of there whenever I want. Legally, there's nothing—"

"Legally?"

"I haven't signed anything. Yes, I called you, but—"

"Oh, hon, you signed those papers days ago."

"What?" He shook his head. "No, I didn't."

"Don't pretend, Paxton. They were sitting there waiting for me."

"You broke into my house?"

"Of course not. The door was wide open, and they were

sitting right there by the door—it was a wonder they didn't blow away. I'll send over your copies as soon as I can."

"You walked into my house and took them. Just like that."

Rhonda leaned back in her chair—or rather, her head leaned back, since her spherical body had nowhere to go—and crossed her arms under her enormous bosom. "Settle down, now," she said in a firm voice. "You're shaking, Paxton, and your color's not good."

Everett said something final into his phone and snapped it shut.

"You can't do this," Pax said. "I'm going to get a lawyer."

"You're welcome to," Rhonda said. "But I don't think it's going to make you feel better. There's only one thing that'll do that right now."

"What are you talking about?"

"I'll be frank, Paxton. You've taken a large dose of the vintage—maybe bigger than anyone's ever taken, and you're not even a charlie! The doctor told me there'd be effects. Right now you're feeling the loss. It feels like something's dying, doesn't it?"

For a moment he couldn't speak. Something *was* dying. Or someone.

He pushed away from the table and stood. "You can't do this," he said.

"Now you're just repeating yourself," Everett said.

"Paxton," Rhonda said kindly. "I'll talk to you again when you're feeling more like yourself. Go back to Chicago. Take some time. You're going to see that I'm doing right by you *and* your daddy."

"I'm not going anywhere," Pax said. But then he was walking away, back into the dark of the building.

---

Deke's house was only a block from where he'd parked. Pax knocked hard on the double-height door and a low voice called him in.

Donna and two beta women looked up at him. They were sitting in the living room, the betas on the couch. They'd all been gazing at something Donna held in the palm of one hand. At first he thought it was a napkin or lump of cloth, but then he saw a tiny red arm reach up and he realized it was a baby.

"Paxton," Donna said. "Are you okay?"

"I'm fine." Jesus, he was tired of people asking him that. "It's just hot." He'd felt a little nauseous on the walk over, and as soon as he'd stepped into the air-conditioning he'd immediately broken into a sweat.

"Paxton, this is my cousin Jocelyn, and her friend April. And this is Celia." She turned her hand so that he could see the girl's face. She was perfectly bald, with mottled, red-orange skin. Her eyes were closed, and her little mouth hung open.

"She's beautiful," Pax said to the women on the couch. Both of them were the color of raspberry syrup. He had no idea which one was Jocelyn, and if Jocelyn was the mother. He also didn't know if the baby really was beautiful for a beta; he'd only recognized that she was cute in the way of babies from so many species, from meerkat pups to ducklings.

"She's only a month old," Donna said softly.

"One month old today," one of the beta women said.

They made small talk for a couple of minutes, all of it about babies, which Pax knew nothing about. Donna didn't offer to let him hold the child, thank God. She rocked it in her big hand and talked to it in that rumbling voice.

"So is Deke around?" Pax asked finally.

"He's at the shop," Donna said. When he looked blank she said, "Alpha Furniture. Just go up Main and take a left on High Street. Listen for power tools and stop when you get to the fire truck—can't miss it."

"Nice meeting you," Pax said to the betas. "Congratulations."

Outside, he untucked his shirt and used it to mop his face. The shop was only a few blocks away, but it was uphill. He decided to drive.

An old-fashioned fire truck was parked in front of a garage like an old dog napping in the sun. It was thirty or forty years old, shiny and red and braced with white ladders, and fronted by a chrome bumper like a fat lip. Like so many antique vehicles it seemed smaller than it ought to be, maybe seven-eighths actual size. The small, round-roofed cab was topped by a single red cylinder light like a Shriner's cap.

The garage was attached to another building the size of a barn. ALPHA FURNITURE was painted in big blue letters on the slanted roof. Through an open bay door came the high whine of a power saw. Deke's Jeep was parked out front alongside another Jeep and a Chevy pickup with a roof peeled off like the lid of a can.

Pax walked up to the open door. An old argo man was pushing with one hand an enormous plank down a table saw; another, younger argo was catching the split ends. The man doing the pushing was about seven feet tall, shorter than most of the argos. His right arm ended in a stump at the elbow. Maybe he'd lost it to a saw, but more likely something had gone wrong during the Changes; not all body parts took to the transformation. After the plank had cleared he noticed Pax standing in the doorway.

"I'm looking for Deke?" Pax called.

The young argo gestured toward the far end of the building, where space had been sectioned off by plastic sheets hanging from the ceiling. Pax picked his way across the room through projects in various states of completion. Everything was giant-sized: bed frames, tables, chairs. At the far end much of the space was taken up by church pews, a dozen huge oak slabs with high backs. Most were still raw wood, but two had been lacquered and polished to a buttery gleam.

He reached the plastic sheets and stepped through a part in the curtains. Deke sat at an enormous desk, staring grimly at a computer screen.

"Cool fire truck," Pax said.

"Oh, hey there, P.K." He leaned back from the screen. Pax caught a glimpse of a spreadsheet. "Yeah, that's Bart. A 1974 Pierce. A town in Kentucky donated it to us. It was worth more to them as a tax write-off."

Pax nodded at the screen. "If this is a bad time . . ."

"No, no. Just paying the bills. I'd been hoping for some bank stuff to come through, but—never mind. Sit down, P.K. I'm glad you found the place."

"Donna gave me directions." There was nothing in the room but a pair of paint-stained barstools the size of step ladders. Pax leaned over one with his elbows on the seat. "She was at the house with some beta women and their baby—she said it was her cousin?"

"Shit. How was she doing?"

"Donna? Fine, why?"

"Donna and babies . . . It's hard for her sometimes, to be around them."

"She looked fine," Pax said. "Happy." At least she didn't look *un*happy. "So, have you looked at the emails from Weygand yet?"

Deke looked back at the screen as if he couldn't remember what he'd been working on. "Last night. I'm pretty sure they're from Jo Lynn. She talked about things only a real beta would know about, and a couple things she mentioned . . ."

"What?"

"They were personal things. Stuff only Jo Lynn would know." He sat up, changing the subject. "The rest of it, well, Weygand wasn't kidding when he said that Bewlay talked a lot about this parallel evolution stuff. Pages and pages of it. Gets kind of freaky. If I didn't think it was Jo I wouldn't believe a word of it. Like the stuff about genetic engineering."

"Not that shit again," Pax said. After the Changes, one of the most popular of the conspiracy theories was that someone was experimenting with them. The Russians, their own government, aliens. Half the town probably still thought that.

"Yeah, I know," Deke said. "I just was hoping to find something that would tell me what happened. What was going on in her head."

"Like what?"

"A suicide note?" He tapped at the keyboard with the eraser end of a pencil and the spreadsheet window minimized. "No, not really. But maybe some clue that she was upset, suicidal." He shook his head. "I don't know, man. I'm just bangin' around in the dark." He looked at Pax. "So how you feeling today?"

"I need your help," Pax said. "I need you to help me get my father out of Rhonda's place."

"Wait a minute," Deke said. "Back up."

Pax told him about the visit to the Home, the conversation with Rhonda, the papers she'd taken from the house. He'd started pacing.

"And even if I did sign them," Pax said, "I didn't give them to her."

"Did you leave the door open behind you?"

"Fuck, I don't know! I was in kind of a hurry, if you remember. You called me."

Deke looked away. The muscles of his jaw worked beneath chalky skin. "It doesn't matter," he said. "The papers, how she got them, all of that. Rhonda isn't the problem."

"Then who the fuck *is* the problem?"

Deke swung his big head around and regarded him squarely. After a long moment he said, "It's not your father you're wanting, Paxton."

Pax stepped back, his face hot. "You don't know what the hell you're talking about."

"Listen, man. What you're feeling is chemical. A few days ago you couldn't wait to get out of here, and now you're going to move back? Now I'm not judging you. You had an accident. But you have to realize that you're not thinking straight. That's why your dad needs to stay at the Home right now."

"That's bullshit. First of all, *Rhonda* is the one that wants him for what he's producing. I'm his son. I can't just sell him off—"

"Calm down, P.K."

"Don't tell me to fucking calm down! Jesus, how the hell did she get you wrapped around her fat finger? Is this some kind of clade thing? Chubs and trolls versus the skips?"

"You're over the line, man."

"Just tell me. You're the Chief, right? Are you going to back me on this or not?"

"It's not about backing you. Why don't you take some time to—"

"Time? Time?" Pax looked down at his hands clutching the edges of the barstool. His knuckles were white. He released his grip—one hand, two, easy does it—and stood up. "Forget it. I can see you're too busy for this. You have yourself a wonderful day."

"P.K. . . ." Deke followed him across the shop, trying to talk to him the whole time.

Paxton sat in the dark at the side of the highway, engine and headlights off. No car had passed for ten minutes. The only light came from the light pole set next to the driveway to the Home.

He got out, jogged across the road, and started up the drive. He'd planned on going straight up the hill, avoiding the driveway—because what if they had cameras watching it?—but he saw now that that was impossible; he hadn't remembered how high the banks were, how thickly the brush covered the hill.

The driveway was also much steeper than he'd thought. Immediately he was sweating, his heart pounding in his throat. He jogged around the first curve and the light from the pole vanished, plunging him into darkness.

He slowed to a walk, panting, then stopped altogether, hands on his hips. He stared at the ground, but he could barely make out his shoes in the scant moonlight.

Fuck it.

He clumped back down to the car, cranked the engine. He aimed for the mouth of the driveway and pressed the accelerator as far as he dared. The Ford lurched up the hill, engine whining. He swung through the first curve a little too fast, overbraked as he entered the second, and then the car stuttered and he was losing momentum. He dropped into low and hunched over the wheel, willing his headlights up the slope. When he passed the third curve and he thought he was almost at the top he stopped the car, cut the lights, and set the emergency brake.

Five more minutes of walking got him within sight of the iron gate and the stone wall. There was a light pole here as well, casting a circle of light on the gate and the patch of pavement around the intercom. He skirted the light, moving off to the right until he was standing at the base of the wall.

The wall was set into the slope. He couldn't take a running start because he'd be running uphill. He ran a hand over the surface, but the big stones didn't project far from the mortar; there was no way he could pull himself all the way up by his fingers, and a fall would send him rolling down the hill.

He started moving along the wall to the right. The ground had to level out at some point. Or maybe he'd find a tree or something close to the wall that would let him drop over.

With every step away from the light it grew darker. By the time he reached the first corner he couldn't see his hands. He moved around the corner and his feet slid out from under him. He stifled a yell, but then his chest hit the ground and his elbow struck rock, sending fire shooting up his arm. He swore loudly. Then he started to slide. It felt like the hill was almost straight down on this side. He threw out his left arm, hands clutching at weeds and grass, and spread his legs.

He slid to a stop after ten or twelve feet. He pressed his face into the grass and lay there, breathing.

Then he saw the lights.

Fuck, he thought. Fuckity fuck fuck.

A pair of headlights snaked up the drive. The lights disappeared for a moment behind the bulk of the hill, then reappeared, higher and closer. The underside of the car glowed neon green, and he could hear the thump of bass from its stereo.

The car stopped not quite up the hill. A spotlight switched on from the passenger side, and the light illuminated his Ford Tempo. After a few seconds the glowing car rolled forward and he lost sight of it again.

Pax rose to hands and knees and started crawling to his left, toward the driveway. A minute later he could see the glowing car again, stopped in front of the gate. The stereo had switched off. The spotlight played over the grass near the wall. Pax dropped low and began crawling backward. If he could drop down about fifty yards he could cut across to his car and get the hell out of here.

The light suddenly hit him in the face. Voices burst out in laughter.

"Hey there, Cuz!" someone called.

The slope here was less extreme. He got to his feet, wincing into the light. He made his way back to the gate, supporting himself with one hand against the wall. His elbow still buzzed with pain.

Two chub boys stood in front of a metallic green Toyota Camry. Two chub girls in the backseat laughed nervously.

"Hi, Clete," Pax said. He couldn't remember the name of the younger boy, the one holding the spotlight. Something like "Elvis," or maybe he thought that just because of the sideburns.

"What the hell you doing out here?" Clete asked. "You're liable to get shot, sneaking around in the dark."

"People might think you're a pervert," the other one said. *Travis,* that was his name.

Pax reached the edge of the driveway. His hands were shaking, and he felt ready to throw up. The girls in the backseat stared at him. The red-haired one was Doreen, the nurse who'd washed him at the clinic.

"I'm just going to go home," Pax said. From this close, the boys smelled of vintage, but vintage with a strange tang to it—nothing like his father's scent.

Clete said, "That's good. That's why they called us, to take you home. Before they shot your ass."

Travis aimed that light into his face. "It's kind of a last-chance taxi service."

Pax said, "Look, my car's right down there. I'll drive home, and you can tell Rhonda that I'll—"

The punch seemed to come out of nowhere. Pax hit the ground. For a moment he wasn't sure where he'd been hit. His nose burned.

"I have to ask you," Clete said. He picked up Pax under his arms and lifted him easily. Pax's knees threatened to give out, but Clete steadied him. "What the hell was your plan? Carry your six-hundred-pound daddy down the hill by yourself?"

"Clete, listen . . ." Pax said.

"No, push him down the driveway in his hospital bed," Travis said, laughing. "Get up to like sixty mile an hour, until he hits that first curve, then *air*borne!"

"UFO!" Clete said. "Unidentified Fat Object."

Inside the car the chub girls whooped with laughter.

Pax gripped Clete's forearms. "I know people in Chicago.

This is an incredible drug. You help me get him out, and I can help you, help you sell it."

"Really?" Clete said. "This stuff really got to you, huh?"

"UFO," Travis said, still laughing. "You kill me, man."

Clete said, "I gotta admit, your daddy makes some of the finest vintage I ever smelled. I'd love to try some on Doreen."

"Rhonda doesn't have to keep all this to herself," Pax said. "You could sell it."

Clete nodded. "I hear you, Cuz, I hear you. But right now?" He shrugged. "Right now I got to beat the living shit out of you."

# chapter 11

DEKE KNOCKED ON the back door of the clinic, waited half a minute, knocked again. The door opened and he said, "Hey, Marla."

"We're closed on Sundays," Dr. Fraelich said.

"I saw your car," he said.

He stooped to get under the doorway, then followed Marla to her office. "So did you look at them?" he asked.

She sat at her desk and opened one of the drawers. She took out the plastic bag he'd given her when he picked up Paxton. "There's nothing here I didn't prescribe for her," she said. "None of them have been switched."

"I had to check," he said. He'd pulled the bottles from Jo Lynn's medicine cabinet the first day he'd searched her house. The dates on the bottles were months old, and most of them were more than half-full. "It didn't look like she was using them anyway."

"That's because they weren't working. She kept getting resistant to them. Betas have an amazing immune system."

"So if she wasn't taking antidepressants, was she still depressed?"

"I don't think so," Marla said. "She got over that too. She seemed fine whenever I talked to her."

Deke sighed. "Yeah. Me too." He reached into his breast pocket and handed her two folded pieces of paper. "I want you to read something." He sat down on the floor, which put him at eye level with her.

She unfolded the pages, then read the top of the first page. "Who are these people?"

"Brother Bewlay's a screen name Jo was using," he said. "Weygand is some guy she met online." Marla looked surprised. "They wrote to each other for almost a year."

"She never told me that," Marla said.

Deke frowned. "I was hoping she had."

TO: aweygand

Sorry, Andy, I don't think you understand at all the mindset required for an asexual baby-making machine. Whether they've been genetically engineered this way or evolved to it, the beta is built for one purpose--breed at all costs. Asex makes things simple, but it strips away all the behavioral baggage that goes along with sexual selection. The only thing left is getting pregnant and taking care of the children. It's monomania. It's leaping over the rocks to lay your eggs and die.

In that kind of brain, the eggs are everything. Beta women who even considered abortions would be considered deviants, the worst kind of criminal. Young beta girls who went through the Changes before puberty would be the most militant about this, I suspect. The beta body is the one they've grown into, the only sexual body they've known. I wouldn't be surprised if beta women who weren't "orthodox" enough would be killed to protect the purity of the race. Watch CNN for the first stoning in Switchcreek.

--bb

TO: brotherbewlay
> The beta body is the only one they've known.
You keep coming back to this biological determinism stuff. These are sweeping generalizations based on what hormones you THINK are brainwashing them. Based on what evidence? Opposition to abortion is a moral position, not a mood disorder.

--Andy

TO: brotherbewlay
One more thing. Aren't we ALL evolved to breed at all costs?

--Andy

TO: aweygand
> Opposition to abortion is a moral position.
It's a moral issue _because_ it's a biological issue. The intellect's riding bareback on a brain hardwired to ensure our survival on the planet, and the poor thing thinks that it's the one doing the steering. Think about it. The brain makes up its mind on moral issues immediately--It's the intellect that has to go through contortions to reconcile emotional certainty with a philosophical position.

Here's a morality test: which is more wrong, swatting an insect or clubbing a baby seal?

Human babies are the most successful manipulators of all—those big eyes, that layer of baby fat, that truckload of opiates they trigger in the lactating mother. You have to read Natalie Angier--it's vicious to force a woman to bear a baby she didn't choose, because evolution throws every trick at its disposal at the woman. Now think of those 13/14 year old beta girls, getting pregnant through no action of their own, raped by their own biology. What choice did they have? The only sane thing to do is put them on birth control automatically, age 10 on. Then let them choose to go OFF it--when they're 16 at least. Maybe make them pass a test. A license to breed.

> And say, aren't we ALL evolved to breed at all costs?

Exactly. If that doesn't keep you up at night, Andy, I don't know what will.

--bb

When Marla finished reading she said, "How did you get this?"

He told her about Weygand driving down and breaking into Jo's house. He left out the part about smashing Weygand's windshield and threatening the man. "Most of it's trading conspiracy theories about the Changes," he said. "But this stuff about the young beta women . . ."

"The white-scarf girls, obviously. She's making it sound all hypothetical, but it's them. Weygand seems clueless. Did he even know that *she* was a beta?"

"He said he suspected it," Deke said. "Though he didn't know until after the funeral."

"So they weren't *that* close," Marla said.

Deke almost smiled. "No, not that close." Donna had told him that Marla was in love with Jo Lynn, and he hadn't believed it, until now. He shouldn't have been surprised. Everyone fell in love with Jo.

Deke said, "So the white-scarf girls, the talk about stoning. I can't tell if Jo was really afraid of them, or—"

"Not afraid," Marla said. "She just knew what they were capable of."

"Are you talking about the effigy?" Deke asked. "Come on, Marla. A fire's one thing, but murder—"

"You don't think they wanted me dead?" Marla said. "They tried to torch my house while I was asleep."

He felt his phone vibrate in his pants pocket but ignored it. Had to be Rhonda again. She'd called him twice already this morning.

"They're kids," Deke said. "They got carried away. They weren't trying to burn down the house." A straw figure—dressed in a white doctor's coat with a wooden knife taped to its hand—had been lit and thrown against the wall of Marla's house. The flames had scorched the paint, little more, before Deke and some of the boys arrived to put the fire out. After Marla threatened to bring in the police, three teenage beta girls, white scarves in place, presented themselves to the reverend. The reverend promised to punish them, and Deke talked Marla into not pressing charges. She'd held that against him ever since.

"It's one step from bombing a clinic, Deke. You don't understand these girls. They're different."

"Because they don't have sex? Do you believe this separate species stuff too—the teleportation stuff, the parallel universes, all that?"

"It's one theory."

"Jo's theory," he said. "That she got from real scientists, right?"

"Yes, there are reputable people who think quantum calculation could explain what happened," Marla said. "Most of the evidence is circumstantial, though. Statistical. TDS changed the chromosome so completely that they say it's impossible to see how the new order could arise from the old. It's like running a dictionary through a leaf shredder and spraying out Hamlet on your front lawn."

"You're talking about introns."

She raised an eyebrow. "You've been reading up."

"I got it from Weygand. Didn't make any sense to me."

"Introns are the part of DNA that don't code for proteins. Because they're not needed, they can mutate faster than other parts of the DNA where a change in the protein could kill the creature. You can look at intron sequences within proteins to tell small differences between related species, like the differences between humans and chimps. Both may produce the same hemoglobin protein, and their DNA is mostly the same, but the introns are very different. Between the clades, we've found differences in every protein sequence we've looked at: hemoglobin chains, cytochromes, histones . . ."

"Really," Deke said. She wasn't looking at him, and hadn't heard the smile in his voice.

"So while the sequences are a mystery, there's no need to invoke quantum weirdness. Most people are looking for a more realistic, testable mechanism that would cause those changes—a retrovirus, maybe, something small we've overlooked. My bet is that it'll be a variant of something we already know about, maybe a bacterial plasmid we've been carrying around dormant for thousands of years—something that's been unable till now to inject its own set of genetic instructions. See, plasmids can't usually get out of the cell they're trapped in, so they require—why are you laughing?"

Deke shook his head, still smiling. "This is what I felt like when I talked to Jo. You guys are just—" He fanned the top of his head. "Whoosh." He got to his feet.

"You asked," she said.

Not for all that, he thought, but let it pass.

Marla handed back the bag of bottles and the papers. "How's Donna doing?" she asked. "Is she okay?"

"She's fine," he said. Then shrugged. "The waiting is hard."

"Jo Lynn was right about one thing," Marla said. "Asexual reproduction would be a lot simpler."

"Amen," he said.

Rhonda's Cadillac was parked in front of his shop. He sighed heavily, then pulled in beside the car.

Rhonda stepped out from the passenger side. Everett, behind the wheel, lifted a hand in hello. "I didn't see you in church," Rhonda said. "Donna said you were working. I called, but you didn't answer your phone."

"I was doing some errands," Deke said. He unlocked the bay door and pushed it open. "Come on inside."

He flipped on the main lights and led Rhonda across the

shop floor toward his plastic-draped office area. He planned to put up real walls, but he'd hadn't gotten around to it yet.

Rhonda stopped at the first row of pews. "When you get these done you'll have no excuse for backsliding," she said. She rubbed the glossy back of one of the finished pews. "You do beautiful work, Deke. All your boys do." She looked up at him. "Do you know who the Shakers were?"

"Like Shaker furniture?"

"Your work reminds me of theirs. Do you know why there aren't any Shakers anymore?"

He shrugged. "I didn't know they were gone."

"They didn't believe in sex," she said. "Not just premarital sex—any kind. That was kind of shortsighted, don't you think? And they weren't much good at evangelizing either. So when they started to get old and die off, that was it for the whole religion." She smiled. "Left behind some beautiful furniture, though."

"So. You think argos should evangelize."

"Ha! I wish you could. Just do some preaching and have people start growing. You remember Ernest Angley? TV healer. He'd slap people's foreheads—whap!—and they'd flop over, quivering like fish." She hooted in laughter. "I used to love watching him. It was like professional wrestling for Baptists." She wiped at an eye, still chuckling. "Oh law. Is this sturdy?" She touched a bookcase turned onto its side, one of the few things in the shop low enough for her to sit on.

"Go ahead," Deke said.

He thought they'd talk in his office, but if Rhonda wanted to talk out here, then fine. He took a seat opposite her on one of the unfinished pews. "You said you wanted to talk about the school?"

"The reverend's on me again about her Co-op school. She wants to use part of the loan for the high school for it. She called it a 'branch campus' of the high school, so it wouldn't be considered a separate expenditure."

"Is that legal? The grant's for one school: the loan's for one school . . ."

"Oh, it may be unusual, but I looked into it and it's legal. I found some other high schools that do it. Usually they're for tech-ed programs or special ed, but there are also these 'alternative schools'—for problem students, nontraditional learners. I think the betas would qualify as nontraditional."

"The whole town qualifies," Deke said.

"And if we think it will cause problems with the grant, we use the grant for the main school, and part of the loan for the Co-op school. Of course the town council would have to vote on it."

"Two separate schools," Deke said evenly. "One for charlies, one for betas."

"I know, I know," Rhonda said. "I told the reverend, it's like a slap in the face to the argos. We've been telling everybody that the school is for everyone, that someday the argos are going to have children. But this way it looks too much like two clades grabbing all the money and telling the argos to go hang—and that's *not* the way it's intended. Still, you know how people are. I don't like what that would do to the town. If I were you, I wouldn't vote for it."

Deke leaned back in the pew. Whenever Rhonda told him what he shouldn't do, he started checking the locks.

"What *would* make me vote for it, Aunt Rhonda?"

She smiled. "If I were you, I'd want some of that high school money to set up a fund, a fertility assistance fund. Just for argos."

"Really."

"If argos don't have children, why should they pay for a school? I don't blame them. That's why every argo couple who wants to ought to be able to go to the fertility clinic at the university."

"Some of us are already doing that," Deke said.

Rhonda didn't pretend ignorance. "And it's expensive, isn't it? I don't have all the numbers, but I figure you're spending twenty, thirty thousand every time you try to fertilize an egg, none of it covered by insurance. Is that right?"

"You're in the ballpark."

"We're a poor little town," Rhonda said. "That's a lot of money even for someone with their own business, and most of your people aren't even working. Tell them they have to pay thousands and thousands of dollars, you might as well tell them to build a rocket ship while they're at it. No, they need assistance."

"This fund. Now that *is* illegal."

"Well, it wouldn't hold up to an audit, that's for sure. It would have to be unofficial. When we build the school, we'd go through Alpha Furniture for part of the construction, on account of you're a local, minority-owned business, then we'd—"

"We're not minorities, Rhonda."

"Handicapped, then." She grinned. "Certainly a class of people oppressed by prejudice and bias—whatever the government wants to hear. Work with me, hon."

Deke laughed. "Jesus, Rhonda . . ."

"That money goes to Alpha, but a significant amount is for the fertility fund. I can show you how to set this up. The important thing is that you are the administrator of the fund.

People trust you, Deke. You're the Chief. They know you'll divide up the money fair and square."

"I know what embezzlement is, Rhonda. And fraud."

"Pah! We're talking about a higher law. I'm only suggesting this—and the only way the reverend would go along with it—because you're an honest man. That's the only way this would work. We trust you to do the right thing, especially for your people." She held out a hand. "Now, pull me up."

Deke helped her to her feet and walked her to the front door. "I'll come back around to hear your decision," she said.

"You can hear it now," Deke said, and Rhonda held up a hand.

"No," she said. "You go home and think about it. Talk to Donna." Everett hopped out to open the car door for her. "Oh, one more thing," Rhonda said. "Paxton tried to climb over the wall to the Home last night."

"Come again?"

"One of my boys almost shot him. They had to pull him down, and he went wild. Clete had to knock him down a peg."

"Jesus, Rhonda, Clete?" The boy was a moron and a thug. "What did he do to him?"

"Oh, don't worry, Paxton's a little roughed up, but he's fine."

"I told you last week," Deke said. "You can take care of Harlan, God knows he needs it, but Paxton is off limits."

"Paxton put himself *on* limits when he tried to break into the Home. I chewed Clete out when I heard what happened. But honestly, Paxton's acting like a drug addict. Next time he tries something like that they'll shoot him dead. Besides, there's no reason for him to break in." She opened the car door. "His daddy's gone dry again."

"Really."

"Hasn't produced a drop since we brought him home from the church."

"Maybe he's recharging. He was sure gushing that night."

"Maybe," she said. "I think it's something else. Something between fathers and sons. You know how ugly that can get."

His gut tightened as if she'd jabbed a two-by-four under his ribs. Goddamn her. She was talking about Willie and Donald Flint. As if he could ever forget what happened, what she held over him.

She tapped the top of the car. "You think about that fund, Deke. While you make your beautiful furniture."

There were four of them who found Willie that day, but it was Deke who'd led the way into the house, an ancient cabin that didn't even have an indoor toilet. He practically knocked down the door getting in. Rhonda came in behind him, followed by Barron Truckle and Jo Lynn.

It was Jo who'd come to Deke with the news of the charlie parties, the rumors of a new drug and bad things happening up in the woods. She'd convinced him they had to do something about it, and not only that, but since Willie and Donald were charlies, they had to bring Aunt Rhonda with them. Rhonda wasn't mayor then, but Jo said she was the leader of her clade. It was the first time he'd heard that word.

Donald Flint, Willie's youngest son, was in the front room, sitting on the couch with a half-naked charlie girl on his lap, facing him. Another charlie girl lay on a pile of blankets on the floor; she'd been jolted awake by the sudden noise. The place was a sty, beer cans everywhere.

Donald looked at them stupidly, then decided he should be offended. He pushed the girl off him and started to get up. Deke yelled something—he didn't remember what—but it made Donald stick to his spot on the couch.

Rhonda kicked the girl on the floor, told both of them to get home. She knew their families, and they knew she knew them. The girls scrambled for shirts and jeans and hustled out. Half a minute later they'd started up one of the six cars in the gravel driveway and peeled out.

Deke told Barron to watch Donald, and then he followed Jo down the hallway. She marched straight to Willie's bedroom as if she'd been there before. Or perhaps she was only following the smell. When that back bedroom door opened the stench rolled out in a wave: shit and rot and a strange sickly-sweet odor he didn't recognize. It would be months before Deke would be able to name it as the smell of stale vintage.

The old man's corpse lay sprawled sideways across a pair of double beds that had been pushed together. He was wider than any human being he'd seen to that point. Willie's body seemed to have collapsed in on itself like a rotted pumpkin, and his skin was pocked and cratered by infection and his son Donald's inept needlework.

Someone gasped, and Deke looked down and behind him. Rhonda had come into the room and burst into tears. He'd always thought that was just a phrase, but the tears were coming out of her like a cloudburst, a flood, making her cheeks gleam.

Then just as suddenly the tears stopped. Her face went rigid and somehow she willed herself to regain control of her body. Later, Deke thought that this was the moment she became mayor of Switchcreek.

I see now, Rhonda said. Or at least that's what he thought she said. I see now.

Rhonda turned and strode back down the hallway. Deke hurried after her, shoulders scraping the ceiling.

In the living room, Donald was off the couch and barking into Barron's face like a furious child. The boy was naked except for a pair of sweatpants hanging low on his hips. Two years before he'd been a skinny kid, and then the Changes had made him into a plump, round-faced charlie. Over the past few months, however, he'd transformed again, turning into a cartoonish mass of muscles: biceps too big for sleeves, shoulders swallowing his neck. A bodybuilder who'd been eating other bodybuilders.

Rhonda reached the boy in two strides and turned his head sideways with a slap.

Donald blinked, touched his cheek. Rhonda shouted something—Deke thought it was something dramatic like, *You killed him,* but perhaps it was only a string of curse words—and then she hit him again, this time with her closed fist.

Donald frowned, shook his head. Then he leaped on her.

Rhonda fell to the floor, Donald on top of her, his hands locked around her throat. Donald was fast, and strong. But still no argo.

Deke's memories of the next few minutes were disjointed, a collection of snapshots. He remembered his arm swinging down like a wrecking ball. He remembered Donald suddenly on the other side of the room, sprawled on the floor. An armchair and a lamp between them had been knocked over.

Then suddenly Donald threw himself toward the couch, reaching under it. Was there a gun? Deke couldn't remember if there was a gun.

The next moment Deke was across the room and Donald was tumbling through the open door like a rag doll. There was a sickening *whump* as he struck something outside—a car, as it turned out.

Deke wanted to destroy the man. It was that simple. And he got what he wanted.

Outside, Donald lay half sitting up against the crumpled front fender of Willie's Ford pickup, his head bent at a too-steep angle, as if he were trying to look inside his own chest.

Rhonda, Barron, and Jo came out sometime later. Maybe it was only a few seconds. "I fucked up," Deke remembered telling Jo. "I fucked up." Jo leaned over him and circled her arms around his gray neck.

A little later Jo and Rhonda would work out where Barron would take the body, who would call the authorities, what mix of manufactured and true facts they could agree upon—the standard bookkeeping of conspiracy. Rhonda would take care of the charlie girls who'd fled from the house. It would turn out to be almost comically easy to convince them that now that Donald had run off, and who knew if the police would ever find him, the only way they could avoid being charged with Willie's murder—accessories, at least—was to follow Rhonda's instructions to the letter. Rhonda told him that by the end they were thanking her, tears in their eyes, for protecting them.

But before all that, they waited for Deke. He took a long time to get to his feet. When he stood, Barron looked at him like he was a monster.

But not Jo, and not Aunt Rhonda. "You saved my life," Rhonda told him. "And this thing here?" She jerked her head toward Donald Flint's body. "You will not spend one second regretting the day you took this evil piece of shit out of the world. I'm only sorry you beat me to it."

Words.

He thought about Donald every day.

He walked downtown to Donna's Sewing Room—a too-quaint name for such a noisy workshop. He stepped through the back door and into a big room loud with the growls of industrial sewing machines, the blare of country radio, and the deep-voiced chatter of half a dozen argo women. Donna stood at the end of a row of machines, a huge bolt of cloth on her shoulder, explaining to her youngest employee how to clear a jam in her machine. The girl, Mandy Sparks, was only seventeen, and the bulky, secondhand JUKI sewing machine was older than she was. All the machines were secondhand and prone to breakdowns. Donna spent half her time playing mechanic.

She frowned to see him there—they usually didn't bother each other during the day. He said, "You got a second?"

Donna told the girl to cut the cloth and start over—"But slow down, for goodness' sake. Slow is steady and steady is fast"—and set the bolt of cloth down against one wall. She led him out to the smaller showroom, which was empty of customers.

"What is it?" she asked.

He slipped his arms around her waist and looked up at her. She was nearly a foot taller than him, but both of them were still growing. No one knew how long argos could live. Some days he felt in his bones that they had decades in them, maybe centuries. Years of slow growth, their bodies stretching up and out and into each other like trees. And some days he felt the future coming at them like an axe.

"Come on, Deke, I have to get back to work."

He wanted to make something better than him. Something as beautiful as she was.

"I've got some good news," he said.

# chapter 12

THEY'D COME TO him Sunday morning as he lay sprawled out on the grass. The voices crooned to him, making pitying, motherly sounds. Hands brushed the hair from his eyes, caressed the welts on his face.

Pax pushed himself onto his back, groaned. A voice like chocolate said, "There there. We got you."

Small hands slipped under thighs and waist—"One, two . . ."—and then he was off the ground and swaying. Bruised skin awoke. Nerves totaled up damages.

"Wait," he said. His voice cracked.

He forced open one eye. Two beta children cradled him between them, moving sideways toward the house. The girls were identical, with placid faces the color of wine.

"I can walk," he said.

"Are you sure?" the girl to his left said, and the other one said, "We got tired of waiting."

The sky vanished as they carried him inside the house. His father's house; even with his eyes closed he would have known it from the smell.

They lifted him easily onto the couch. They carefully peeled off his shirt, damp from dew, and tsked at his bruises.

They found washrags and dabbed at the crusts of blood on his face, then plastered him with Band-Aids. He asked for aspirin and they brought him two ancient powdery tablets and a water glass. The water pinked with his blood.

They tucked a blanket around Pax, then one of them sat next to him while the other attended to him. The girls traded places every ten or fifteen minutes. Sometime in the early afternoon they brought him Campbell's tomato soup and packets of Lance crackers they dug out of their backpacks.

The girls seemed most comfortable when Pax was asleep; several times he dozed, and he'd wake to hear them babbling to him and over him—about his injuries, or what was on TV, or some minor adventure they'd had in the woods—but when he spoke or asked them a question they would go silent, change the channel, or slip from the room to bring him Ziploc bags freshly packed with ice cubes.

He woke once to the phone ringing. He shouted for them not to answer it, and the girls obeyed: They looked at the phone as it rang seven, eight times before going silent. A few minutes later it rang again and he told them to unplug it.

Sometime before dusk they said that they had to leave, but they wouldn't stop fussing over him.

"Girls," he said. He still couldn't tell them apart. Was it Rainy in the jeans with the torn knee, and Sandra in the dress? "Thank you. I'm fine now." His lips were swollen and his jaw ached, so the words came out glued.

"We'll be back in the morning," one of them said, and the other said, "Don't you worry." They slung their packs onto their shoulders and slipped out the door.

---

The nightmares woke him, or else it was the pounding headache, or the stale scent of his father lingering in the air. He tried to sit up and his ribs scraped painfully. It took him many small movements to ease onto his side, then lever himself onto his feet. He shuffled to the bathroom, edged past the gigantic toilet, and flicked on the light above the sink. He opened the mirrored door to the medicine cabinet before he could look too closely at his reflection.

He turned on the faucet, splashed water onto his face and let it run down his neck. He pushed a handful of aspirin into his mouth and bent, wincing, to drink from the tap.

He'd been dreaming of fists, and elbows, and knees.

It had taken him only seconds to surrender everything, to submit. One punch, really. He was on the ground, his cheek scraping the pavement, before he registered the blur of the fist that struck him. He raised his hand as if signaling, Yes, that was a good one, you got me. Then Clete began the beating in earnest.

Pax didn't even try to fight back. When he was on the ground he tried to curl into a ball. When they held him against the car it was all he could do to raise his forearms to deflect some of the blows, but even that token of defiance seemed to anger Clete more. At first Pax had tried pleading with them—God knows what he tried to say—but soon he gave up trying to speak. He didn't disassociate. He didn't retreat to some safe place in his mind. He didn't *endure.* The pain seemed to turn him inside out like a reversible coat. All the nerves on the outside. Every thought was the same thought, over and over: I'm sorry, I'm sorry, I'm sorry.

He walked back past his old bedroom to the guest room. Without turning on the light he found the bed and gingerly lay down. Sleep seemed impossible now. Each strained muscle insisted on reporting in, each cut and bruise jostled to inscribe its name and serial number on his brain. His head throbbed. Incredibly, none of these sensations drowned out the ache he felt for his father. The craving was still there, skulking like a coyote outside the circle of a fire.

We don't live in our bodies, he thought. We are our bodies. A simple thing, but he kept forgetting it.

In the morning he heard someone rummaging through the kitchen, clinking dishes and closing cabinets. He managed to walk down the hallway and found them setting out bowls and pouring candy-colored cereal from a box he didn't recognize. A plastic gallon jug of milk sat on the counter.

"Don't you guys ever knock?"

One of the girls yelped in surprise; then both of them erupted into quacking laughter. It was the first time he'd seen either one of them laugh.

"You scared us!" one said, and the other said, "We're not ready! Go back!"

He raised his hands and stepped back around the corner. "I hope you're not using milk from the fridge," he said. "I can't vouch for anything in there." Come to think of it, there hadn't been anything in the refrigerator but condiment bottles. The girls must have brought their own milk and food.

After a few minutes they ushered him into the kitchen and sat him down at the table. One of them—the one in the yellow floppy dress—tucked a napkin into the neck of his T-shirt. The napkin dropped off a second later and he put it in his lap.

The cereal was generic, some kind of Froot Loops knockoff. "I hope you didn't steal this," he said.

"It's ours as much as anyone else's," the other girl said. She wore a red T-shirt and jeans torn at one knee.

"Tell me, which one are you?" he said to the girl in red. "Sandra?"

"I'm Rainy," she said.

"Okay, red shirt Rainy, yellow dress Sandra. Whatever you do, don't change clothes."

He chewed the cereal, the pain in his jaw and the alarming looseness of two of his teeth making him go slow.

"You know," Pax said to Rainy, "you're named after my mother."

"Lorraine," Rainy said. "She died in the Changes."

"That's right," Pax said. "You know, my mom loved your mom a lot. Like a daughter."

"We know," Sandra said breezily.

After perhaps a minute Rainy said, "You said you could tell us stories about her," she said. "At the funeral."

"Oh, right. Your mom." He started to beg off, but then he got an image of Jo Lynn at these girls' age, eleven or twelve years old.

"Once we were at the Bugler's," Pax said. "The checkout woman accused me of trying to shoplift a Chunky candy bar. Do you know about Chunky's? They stopped making them for a while." The girls looked at him. Quizzically? Patiently? He couldn't tell. "Anyway, I'm standing there petrified, but your mom got mad—*so* mad. She lit into the woman, whipping out words I couldn't even pronounce." He shook his head. "It was like watching Jesus in the Tabernacle. The clerk didn't know what to say back, she was just sputtering."

"What happened then?" Sandra asked.

"Jo slapped down a dollar and didn't even wait for the change. And then—" He shrugged, smiling. "Then we just strolled out of there."

Rainy said, "But you *were* trying to steal it."

"No! Well, okay, yes. But that was stupid; I shouldn't have tried to do that. The point is, no one was going to accuse one of *her friends* of a crime. Your mom would have defended me either way, because she'd already decided—"

He looked down at his cereal bowl, a sudden emotion closing his throat.

"Decided what?" Rainy asked.

He thought: She'd already decided he was a good person.

"Nothing," he said. He picked up his spoon, put it down again. "She just thought that that's what friends do."

Sandra said, "Your face looks worse today."

He laughed. "Thanks."

"Really, it's a lot more colors," she said.

Pax said, "Isn't anybody wondering where you are? Did you tell Tommy you were coming here?"

The girls exchanged a look. Pax had started to identify common facial expressions—the way their lips tightened and relaxed; the fractional droop of an eyelid, the slight downward jerk of a chin—but for most of those expressions he could no more interpret them than translate wind into words. But that look was easier—almost always it was Sandra checking in with Rainy, following her sister's lead.

Rainy said, "Where we go ain't anybody's business—"

"—especially Tommy," Sandra finished.

Something in their tone alarmed him. "Girls, is Tommy . . . Is he hurting you?"

Sandra looked at Rainy. Rainy said nothing.

Pax said, "Look, if something's happening—or if something happened that night your mother died? You can tell me."

Rainy said, "We were asleep."

"Maybe somebody came to the door. Did you hear anyone come in? Maybe in the morning—"

"We were asleep," Rainy said. She got up from her chair and began stacking the bowls.

"Did you ever hear her argue with Tommy?" Pax asked.

"Only all the time," Sandra said quietly to her cereal.

"Mom argued with lots of people," Rainy said. "They weren't as smart as her, and that got on her nerves sometimes." She carried the bowls to the counter and started running water in the sink.

Pax said, "What did she argue with them about?"

"Everything," Rainy said.

Sandra nodded. "Pretty much."

"It's hard to be smart," Rainy said. "Lots of people want things to be the same as they always were, but they can't. You can't do things the old way, not after the Changes. Life is different than it used to be." She sounded like she was quoting. "You have to take a stand. You have to follow your own moral compass."

"That's true," Pax said. "You have to do the right thing. Even if it's hard." He looked at Sandra and said, "If you're scared of someone, if you're afraid to speak, you can tell me, I can protect you."

Rainy turned around, looked at his face, his arms. "You?"

---

The girls packed up their things about 1:00 p.m. and vanished into the woods, promising to return with more food. Pax set himself the goal of walking down the driveway to the mailbox. He hadn't gone twenty yards before he'd broken into a sweat. He felt ancient, and something was wrong with one of his ribs; whenever he stepped a certain way pain shot up the right side of his chest, paralyzing him for a few seconds.

He heard a car pull into the drive and he stepped off the driveway, readying himself to—what? Fight? Run? He could barely walk. Then he saw it was Deke's Jeep, and he put a hand against a tree and waited, trying to catch his breath.

Deke stopped the car and climbed out. He looked distraught. "Sweet Jesus on a stick," he said.

Pax smiled tightly.

"I tried to call," Deke said. "You don't answer your phone."

"My cell phone's dead. I forgot to pack a charger."

"I mean both phones." Pax didn't say anything, and Deke said, "Anything broken?"

"My ribs hurt like hell."

"I'm so sorry, man." He sounded genuinely remorseful. "You should go see Dr. Fraelich."

Pax snapped a wedge of bark from the tree, tossed it into the underbrush. "What are you doing here, Deke? If you're trying to help me out you're a little late. Wait, maybe you're here to take my report? Track down the bad guys?"

"I'm not a real cop, Paxton."

"Then what good are you?"

"They said you tried to break into the Home. They were going to shoot you."

"Wait a minute—I'm supposed to be thankful?"

Deke looked at the ground. "They had no right to do what they did," he said slowly. "No right. But P.K., you can't just . . ." He took a breath. "Listen, this thing you're struggling with, this stuff from your father. I don't know why it's hitting you like this, but it must be pretty damn strong. But it's just a drug, man. You just need to clear your system. If you need some money to—"

"I don't need your money."

"You have a chance, here, man. Right now."

"A chance for what?"

"To get out of here. I'll drive you back to Chicago myself. Right now."

"I'm not going anywhere without my father."

Deke sighed. "Listen, I know you think that sounds all noble—"

"Saving my father sounds noble? *Noble?* Are you fucking kidding me?"

"This isn't you, Paxton."

"Fuck you."

Deke looked at him.

"Yes," Pax said. "Fuck. You."

Deke shook his head. Then he turned back to the Jeep. "Just call me, okay?"

The girls returned to him for every meal, and some days they spent hours with him. They refused to talk about their mother's death, or what enemies she might have made among the Co-op community; whenever he raised the topic, however obliquely, Rainy changed the subject, or Sandra discovered that he must need something, or else they simply announced that they had to leave.

Pax and the twins lived off the food that had arrived Monday noon. A trio of charlie ladies, all women of the church that he'd known growing up, had appeared at his doorstep like a clutch of enormous hens. They carried enough food to host a small party: a tray of deli meats and cheeses, a bag of Kaiser rolls, macaroni salad, two three-liter bottles of Diet Coke, a family-sized bag of Doritos, glazed doughnuts, and a glistening slab of pineapple upside-down cake as heavy as a radiator. They bustled into the kitchen and started unpacking boxes and bags, somehow managing not to bump into each other, and without once suggesting that he needed this stuff or even wanted it. He tried to thank them, but they wouldn't have it. Oh it's nothing, they said, nothing at all, and even apologized for disturbing him, as if the pounds of food were the result of some shipping accident and they were just grateful he could take them off their hands. They didn't mention his bruises or cuts, or even seem to see them. They didn't ask about his father. The women enforced a no-fly zone of southern politeness: Every unpleasant thing was known, or if not known then assumed, and therefore beneath comment.

They asked to say a short prayer before they left. Mrs. Jarpe, who'd been his piano teacher for three years before Paxton's mother finally admitted that her son had no talent for the instrument, took his hand in hers and asked for the Lord's strength, and for blessings on Paxton and the Reverend Martin. A-*men,* the ladies said, and then they were gone in a wash of perfume and hairspray.

TDS had changed everything and nothing, he thought. The three women were bloated by the disease, but they were still southern ladies, still Christians with a tradition of offering food like a sacrament, the same women who'd loved him and watched out for him when he was a boy. Who were watching out for him even now. That request for strength had stung and warmed him at the same time.

When he began to feel better he began to make the twins meals, though they didn't like it. "We can be the moms," Sandra said. But on Wednesday afternoon he set out three settings and served them all little sandwich triangles held together with toothpicks. The girls, judging from their voices if not their faces, seemed delighted.

After supper Sandra said, "Tell us another story about Mom."

"About when she got pregnant with us," Rainy said.

Pax looked up, measuring Rainy's gaze. "Girls," he said. "I'm glad you've been coming here. You've helped me a lot. But I think you've gotten the wrong idea. Your mom and I . . ."

They blinked at him. Did he want to do this? They weren't his daughters—he knew that now—but he couldn't help but think of them as his girls. Nieces, perhaps. But that was just fantasy. Playing house.

Finally he said, "You know I'm not your father, right?"

Sandra tilted her head, then looked at Rainy. Rainy said, "Betas don't have fathers, Paxton." Her voice patient.

"I know that. I was just afraid that maybe you girls were thinking . . . I don't know." He breathed out, smiled. "I'm glad we understand each other."

"Now tell us about Mom," Sandra said. "Was she happy when she found out she was pregnant?"

"Of course she was," Pax said. "She was . . . overjoyed."

"You can tell us the truth," Rainy said.

"She was scared, sure. No beta had had a child yet, so nobody knew what to expect. But she was excited."

"Really?" Sandra said.

"She didn't think we had ruined her life?" Rainy asked.

"What? Of course not," Pax said. "Listen, the first time I met you two, your mom put my hand on her belly, and one of you kicked back—thump. She was so happy to feel you moving."

"I bet that was Rainy," Sandra said. "She kicks in her sleep."

His walks in the afternoon grew longer. He went into the woods above the house, following the tracks he'd carved out with his ATV when he was a kid. Sometimes he'd burst into tears. Not from pain—though sometimes pain triggered it—but from a flash of memory, an image of fists or the sound of bone on flesh. Sudden fear would blindside him, leave him stumbling around bleary eyed and sobbing.

He tried to summon alternate images, counter-spells. A crowbar slamming into Clete's temple. Paxton's Ford mashing at ninety miles per hour into the driver-side door of the pimped-out Camry. Travis pleading for mercy; Aunt Rhonda on all fours, blood pouring from her mouth; the Home, burning . . .

The fantasies were thin soup. He'd had his chance to fight back, and he'd lain there. Dreaming of revenge was pointless.

He came out of the woods just as Aunt Rhonda's Cadillac pulled into the drive. Everett and Clete escorted the mayor to the door. Pax put his hands in his pockets to stop them from trembling.

"Oh, hon," Aunt Rhonda said. She surveyed his face, frowning in concern.

"It's not any worse than it looks," he said.

"Clete has something to say to you," Rhonda said. She turned to the boy.

Pax looked at the chub's face. His nose was the color and shape of an eggplant. Dark rings and swollen cheeks reduced his already small eyes to piggy slits.

Pax looked at Rhonda and she said, "The Chief took issue with Clete's behavior. As did I. Clete?"

"I'm sorry for hitting you," Clete said. He glanced at Aunt Rhonda. "Very sorry."

"What do you want?" Pax asked Rhonda.

"I came to ask you a favor," she said. His reaction must have showed in his face because she said reassuringly, "It's nothing big. In fact, it's kind of a favor to *you*."

# chapter 13

HIS FATHER ROLLED out in a wheelchair the size of a loveseat. The boy pushing him was Clete's sidekick, Travis. Everett trailed behind them with that bouncer-blank look on his face.

Travis steered Harlan toward the atrium windows, where Pax sat in the middle of an upholstered guest chair, also chub-sized. His father was slumped in the wheelchair, head back and eyes closed. He looked deflated, a man swimming in a giant's skin and clothes. Pax leaned forward, and Everett said, "Just keep your seat."

"I was just—never mind," Pax said. Rhonda had explained the rules: no touching, no leaving the room, and do whatever Everett says. "Otherwise," she'd told him, "just be yourself."

"Is he awake?" Pax asked.

Everett touched Harlan's shoulder. "Pastor Martin," he said. "Your son's here."

His father didn't move. Everett said, "Playing possum." He gently shook the man's shoulder. "Come on now," he said. "You've got company."

Harlan opened his eyes a fraction. "Get your hands off me," he said in a cracked voice.

"Ah," Everett said. "Grumpy." He nodded to Travis and they

walked to a desk and chairs about ten feet away, where Barron, the security guard, had spread out a newspaper.

Harlan turned his gaze to the windows, paying no attention to Paxton. The bright sunlight turned his father's skin to rice paper. His arms were stained with liver spots. He seemed decades older than he had two weeks ago.

"It's me," Pax said. "Your son."

His father didn't move.

Pax leaned back in his giant chair, scratched the side of his neck. The ache burned in him. Inside the Home, and this close to his father, Pax had expected to be engulfed by the scent of the vintage, and he hadn't been sure how he was going to stand it. But there was only a trace of it, and even that was almost masked by the smell of Pine-Sol.

"So," Pax said. He tried to make his voice sound relaxed. "How are they treating you?"

"Quit talking to me that way," his father said.

Pax glanced at the chub men across the room. They were pretending to study their sections of the paper. To his father, Pax said, "What way?"

"I'm not senile."

But you're not exactly sane, Pax thought. "Dad, I have to explain—"

"I asked you one thing, Paxton." Harlan turned his head to look at him, his eyes in that collapsed face bright and hard. "One thing."

"You didn't exactly make it easy on me," Pax said. He told him about the night at the church: the impromptu baptism, the way they had to drag both of them from the water. "You don't remember any of this?"

"You got what you wanted," his father said. "So why are you here?"

"This is not what I wanted!" Pax said. Everett looked over at them, and Pax lowered his voice. "I wanted you out of here. I wanted to take you home. I just . . . can't."

His father made a noise of disgust and looked away. Outside the window, a plastic fawn nestled in the grass beside an antique iron water pump. Someone had planted a row of flowers, but at the moment they were headless stalks.

Pax stared at his hands, then at his father.

Harlan reached up, scratched at a cheek, and white flakes of skin fluttered in the sunlight. Dry, dry, dry. Nothing there for him. He was dying of thirst and his father had become a desert.

After several minutes of silence, Pax got up and walked to the security desk. "This isn't working," Pax said quietly.

Everett looked up at him. "You saying you're backing out of the deal?"

"No, I'm *not* backing out. It's just not working right now." He looked back at his father, still staring out the window. "Look," he said to Everett. "Give me some now, just half, and tomorrow—"

"One more word," Everett said quietly. "Go ahead. Say one more word."

Barron and Travis froze, their eyes on Everett. Paxton closed his mouth.

"Now then," Everett said reasonably. "If you're done for today, that's fine. We'll take you back now. But you don't get paid unless he produces."

Pax turned away from the desk. He went back to the big chair opposite his father and sat, leaning over his knees.

They didn't speak. Pax studied his clasped hands, trying to get them to stop trembling. Jesus, he was a fucking wreck.

"You've got bruises," his father said.

Pax didn't reply.

"Are they making you do this?"

"No," Pax said. "They're not making me do anything."

His father nodded. Several minutes passed.

"So," Pax said. "How 'bout them Cubs?"

His father didn't answer. They spent the next two hours in silence.

The vintage refused to return.

Each night Pax decided that he wouldn't go forward with the deal. His craving seemed as strong as ever, but it wasn't getting worse. He could handle it. He'd go back to Chicago, get on with his life.

Yet each morning at 8:45 he was waiting in front of the house for Everett to pick him up.

The visits lasted until noon. Then Travis would wheel his father off to lunch, and either Everett or Barron would give him a ride back to the house.

Because his father declined to talk, and because Rhonda thought TV would interfere with the process, Pax had to find some way to get through the hours. Each morning before he arrived he and Everett would stop by the Gas-n-Go, say hello to Mr. DuChamp, and pick up three papers: the *Knoxville News-Sentinel, USA Today,* and the *Maryville Times.* In the atrium Pax and his father would thumb through them, and usually Everett and Barron would join them. Travis sat well away from Pax and surreptitiously played games on his handheld.

One morning in the second week of visits, Pax handed his father the *Sentinel* and his father said, "How's Mr. DuChamp's hair?"

Pax looked up. "What? Oh. Fine." He smiled. "Still looks as good as the day he bought it." Twelve years after the Changes, Mr. DuChamp still wore a coal black toupee, never acknowledging that he'd become a beta.

His father grunted. He was silent the rest of the morning. But the next day his father dropped the section of paper he was reading and Pax automatically stooped to pick it up. His father looked down at him, a half smile on his face, but he seemed to be seeing someone else.

"Dad?" Pax asked. Then he smelled it. The vintage.

He glanced toward the desk. Everett was on an errand with Aunt Rhonda, and Barron was out of the room. Travis was engrossed in his handheld.

Pax touched his father's hand. The skin seemed more moist than it had been. Quietly he said, "Dad, are you okay?"

"You said you wanted red, right?" his father said. "Fire-engine red." He didn't seem to be talking to Pax.

Travis still hadn't noticed the change. Pax returned to his seat but his eyes were on his father's face, his neck. He could see the skin of his cheek begin to swell, fast as a boxer's after a vicious punch.

"It's me, Paxton," he said.

"You have to promise me to be careful," his father said. "Don't ride it on the road. And if your mother ever catches you without your helmet on, it's going right back in the garage."

"I promise," Pax said. His parents had given him the Yamaha ATV when he was thirteen, seven months before the Changes. It was the best Christmas of his life.

The first blister formed just below his father's right eye. Pax leaned forward, reached up to his father's face.

Someone slapped his hand away. Pax lunged forward and Everett shoved him back in his chair. Pax hadn't heard him come back in the room. "Stay put," Everett said. "Travis, go get an extraction pack."

The smell of the vintage blossomed to fill the room. Aunt Rhonda came out of her office holding a handkerchief over her nose and mouth. She put one hand on Paxton's shoulder. "Good boy," she said.

Half the linen closet seemed to be flapping on lines strung across the front yard. The twins had been cleaning again.

They were waiting for him in the house. They saw his face and one of them said, "Did something happen?" That was Rainy. She seemed years older than her sister, a young woman deigning to act childlike on occasion for the sake of the smaller children.

"Listen, girls," he said. "I need you to go home tonight."

Sandra said, "But we're making supper! Spaghetti and garlic bread." She wore a billowing green dress. "Plus we need you to unlock the other bedroom. We couldn't clean it."

"Enough cleaning," Pax said. "And we can have the spaghetti tomorrow. Right now I just need some time alone, okay?"

"What's in the bag?" Rainy asked.

Pax looked down at the black plastic baggie. He hadn't realized he was carrying it in his hand. "Look," he said, "tomorrow before you come, why don't you go to the grocery store." He put the bag into his front pocket, then handed Sandra two of the twenties Rhonda had given him. "Buy us some food. Get whatever snacks you want."

"We need baby food," Sandra said.

Rainy glared at her. "We have to show you something first," she said, and then went into the kitchen.

"Oh, right," Sandra said. Then, "We don't really need baby food."

Pax said. "Rainy, I don't have time for games tonight, okay? You can show it to me tomorrow." The refrigerated bag felt cool against his thigh.

The girl came back into the room carrying a thin white laptop. She handed it to him. "We need you to open this," she said.

"Whose is this?" he asked, even though he was sure of the answer. Taped diagonally across the lid was a black-and-white bumper sticker of two fish: a Christian fish symbol, and right behind it, a larger Darwin fish with stick-figure legs, its mouth wide open to swallow the fish in front of it.

"It was Mom's," Rainy said. "It's ours now."

He sat on the couch and put the laptop on the coffee table. "Where did you get this? Your house?"

They didn't answer. He looked up, and Sandra was looking at Rainy. "Can you open it?" the girl said.

He thumbed the latch and lifted the lid. "Okay, what next?"

"No, un*lock* it," Rainy said. "It has a password." She sat next to him and pressed the power button. The computer started booting up.

"Why did you hide this?" he asked.

"*We* didn't hide it," Sandra said. "Reverend Hooke took it. Her and Tommy."

"What? When?" Pax asked.

"The morning after," Rainy said. "We saw her take it, and Tommy saw her too, but he didn't say anything."

"Why didn't you speak up? This is important. It could have Jo's—" He started to say "suicide letter," but thought better of it.

"Can you open it?" Rainy said. On the screen was a prompt for a password. "We can't get past this part."

"How would I know the password?"

"Just try," Sandra said.

He shook his head, put his fingers on the keyboard. He thought for a moment, then typed "BrotherBewlay" and pressed return.

"Incorrect password," he said.

Rainy was looking at him intently, but as usual he couldn't read her expression. "You're not even trying," she said.

"Okay, fine," he said. He tried "BewlayBrother," then several variations with different capitalization and spaces and plurals. Then "hunkydory" and "changes" and "prettythings."

Pax said, "If we keep putting in bad passwords we may lock it up permanently."

"But you could *hack* it, right?" Sandra asked. "You know about computers and everything."

"What? No. I mean, I've used computers, but I don't even own one right now. I use my roommate's."

"But you're from Chicago!" Sandra said.

"What does that have to do with anything?"

"Forget it," Rainy said, and slammed the lid down. Pax put a hand over hers.

"Wait. Leave it with me." He looked at both of them. "I can call some people who are good at this kind of thing. Maybe we can figure out how to boot it without the password."

"Really?" Sandra said, sounding relieved. Rainy seemed less sure.

"It's ours," Rainy said. "The laptop belongs to us now."

Pax said, "I know that. I promise you I won't let anyone else have it. Let me try some things, okay?" The twins didn't reply. "But right now I'm exhausted. How about you come back tomorrow."

He closed the door behind them and walked to the guest room. The vintage, frozen when he'd gotten it from Aunt Rhonda, had warmed to liquid again. He sat on the bed and swirled the plastic container, proving to himself that he didn't need to rush into this. He could wait even longer if he wanted to.

He pried off the rubber cap, then lay back on the bed and tilted the vial over his mouth. The serum seemed to take forever to slide to the lip of the container; the first drop reached the edge and hung there, swelling.

He didn't know what dose to use; most of his experience had been accidental, and at the extremes. Just a drop now, he thought. There was more in the vial if he needed it. Later he could even swab out the inside with a Q-tip if he needed to, or add water and rinse it into his mouth. And, he reminded himself, there was more where this came from.

He tapped the plastic with one finger and the drop broke loose, fell onto his tongue like a dollop of honey. He swallowed, and the warmth slid down the back of his throat. He put the cap back onto the vial and lay on the bed, waiting.

"And he returns," his father said each time Pax arrived for his visit. He sounded both sad and relieved.

Rhonda had decided that the optimal interval was every other day. Pax would arrive with his armful of newspapers and they would sit by the big atrium windows. Harlan was most lucid and in control in the first hour. As they shuffled through the pages one of them would try to make small talk. It didn't matter which one of them spoke first; it never went easily. One morning Pax said, "Did you know that some scientists think that the clades are an alternate strain of human evolution?" Harlan didn't look up from his paper. He didn't believe in evolution. "It's got to do with quantum mechanics," Pax went on. "These things called intron mutations prove that the disease is teleporting in from a parallel universe. They can prove it." He tried to sound like he hadn't learned this from an Internet weirdo a few weeks before. "People who went through the Changes are a whole different species. Technically, you and I may not even be related anymore."

His father chuckled without looking up. "You'd like that, wouldn't you?"

The conversation went better when Pax had specific questions—about the house, the car, the finances. Harlan could coach him through the bank statements and bills, tell him how to light the oven's pilot light, or how to jumpstart the Crown Vic and get it started without flooding the engine.

Harlan would grow more remote as the morning wore on. His gaze would shift to the middle distance, or else suddenly alight on Paxton's face as if seeing him for the first time. Sometimes Pax seemed to be a beloved child, sometimes a rebellious teenager. "I won't have this in my house!" he shouted during one extraction, and Travis had to put up a hand to stop Harlan from slapping the needle away. "Thank God your mother isn't alive to see this, it would kill her. I don't even know who you are anymore."

"I know, Dad," Pax said. He leaned forward but did not touch him. That was still against the rules.

When the extraction began Pax would watch the serum color the body of the syringe, and then he would catch himself watching and look away.

"Oh law," Rhonda would say when Travis delivered the syringes. "He's like Old Faithful."

Pax took his payment on Tuesday mornings with the rest of the employees. The chub boys started rolling in around 9:30, then sat around talking and looking at their hands until the clock struck 11:00 and Rhonda opened her office door.

Pax kept his distance, trying to hang back until the rest of them had been paid, but Clete went out of his way to get next to Pax, hugging him, slapping his back, punching his shoulder. "Looking a little rough this morning, Paxton," he'd say. "Can't wait to get that shot of ol' Grandad, huh?"

Each time Pax resolved not to flinch, to give nothing away. Weeks after the beating both men's bruises had faded, but Pax was still aching: the ribs along his right side still grated like a tire rubbing at a sharp fender; the headaches still woke him at night. So he smiled tightly and said nothing, waiting for Clete to become distracted by another conversation, or for Rhonda to tell them to line up.

The chubs were anxious to receive their checks and the little frozen vials they called the bonus, but their need seemed less immediate than Paxton's. To hear the younger chubs talk, it wasn't about getting high themselves, it was about impressing women and partying. "But you skips, man," Clete said, circling an arm around Paxton's neck. "You freak for it like the ladies, don't you?"

Pax smiled his fuck-you smile.

The twins had become disappointed in him. He hadn't been able to get past the computer's log-in screen, and hadn't even tried to find someone who could. "Never mind," Rainy said, and the laptop vanished from his house.

They didn't like how long he slept in the afternoons; they didn't like how little he ate. They disapproved of his long, stringy hair, the way he'd go days without shaving.

"You're starting to *stink*," Sandra said.

"It's September," Pax said. "Don't you have school?"

"They're not teaching anything that's important," Rainy said. "Our mother taught us biology, evolution, physics. *Quantum* physics."

"Little Miss Einstein," Pax said, but his tone was light.

"That's Rainy," Sandra said.

He lay on the couch, eyes half-closed, on the verge of bursting into tears or laughter. After a visit to his father he rewarded himself with a dab of the vintage, just enough to move himself a few inches out of his body, but even with that small amount it was all too easy to let his emotions run away with him. He knew Rainy and Sandra weren't his daughters—weren't related to him at all—but when they fussed over him and complained and told him their stories he saw right past their mask-like faces, right into their wounded hearts. He knew how they yearned for Jo Lynn, and he began to understand how Jo must have ached for them. When they ran their smooth hands over his rough cheeks, tut-tutting at his lack of hygiene, he felt himself losing track of where he ended and the world began. He was both a man stretched out on the couch and a little bald girl regarding him with narrowed eyes.

"So tell me," he said. "If the argos and betas and charlies are alternate forms of humanity, where are the Cro-Magnons and the Neanderthals?"

"Tals," Rainy said. "Not thals."

"Whatever." He scratched under his T-shirt. "My point is, if apes are our nearest cousins, where are the grunting, hairy clades? Where are the cavemen?"

The girls looked down at him, then burst into laughter.

The nights he took the vintage the house became alive with ghosts. He heard them clinking coffee cups, talking in low adult voices, assembling Christmas bicycles. He drifted asleep to the sound of "I'll Fly Away" sung slow in two-part harmony.

The headaches persisted. One night he woke curled up and shivering under the open window. Summer had ended while he'd slept, and chill autumn air had refrigerated the room. He shuffled in the dark to the bathroom, not willing to wake up completely. He peed, swallowed a few ibuprofen, went back into the hallway.

Light silvered the edge of the door to his old bedroom.

He watched the light for a long time, listening. Then he went to the door and touched it lightly. It glided silently away from his fingertips.

His mother lay on the big hospital bed the government people had delivered. The guest bedroom was too small for it, the master bedroom too full of furniture. Paxton's room was *just right.*

She looked tiny in it, a shrunken ancient or a newborn. Her skin, blotchy with stains like coffee, seemed too tight for her. Nothing remained of her hair but a few wispy patches.

"My son, my son," she said. The fingers of her right hand lifted from the bed, summoning him forward. She smiled up at him. "Still handsome."

She wore the lightest of nightgowns; anything heavier caused her terrible pain. He sat on the floor and carefully put his hand in hers. Her palm was velvety, but her fingers were rough and chapped, as if her body couldn't decide which direction it wanted to go.

"How is Jo?" she asked.

"Fine," he said. He didn't want to tell her. She loved Jo like a daughter.

"And Deke?"

"Still growing," Paxton said.

"Good."

A minute passed. Then she said, "When you were born the nurse put you in my arms and . . . oh my." She smiled through cracked lips. "The future just rolled open. Years and years. And I could *see* you, all grown up. Just like this. And I thought, I will know this little man the rest of my life."

"Yeah?" She'd told him this story before. He used to ask her to tell it.

"The first and only time in my life that happened. Don't tell your father." She smiled again and closed her eyes. Minutes passed, but he knew that she hadn't fallen asleep. He shifted his weight and she said apologetically, "You can go."

"No, I wasn't—"

"It's okay, Paxton." She opened her eyes again. "I don't mind that you don't like to come in here. I'm not too pretty. And you were just a boy. You'd already seen more than your share."

He shrugged. "Now that I'm here . . ."

"Off to bed," she said. "You need your sleep."

"In a little bit," he said.

He was still talking to her near dawn when a thick arm fastened around his neck and a voice spoke into his ear. "Hate to interrupt your conversation, Cuz." The arm yanked him to his feet and dragged him backward out of the room. A moment later he was dumped to the floor. Three chubs loomed over him like planets: Clete, Travis, and the redheaded chub girl from the clinic—Doreen. She wore a pink hoodie open over a black tank top that exposed sweeping vistas of cleavage.

Clete stood with his hands on his hips, a black pistol tucked ostentatiously into his waistband. Travis held a big roll of silver duct tape.

"Just in case you were wondering," Clete said. "This is not a hallucination."

# chapter 14

THE VINTAGE WORE off but the headache did not.

They'd taped his wrists and ankles and then tossed him onto a mattress in the back of a rusting, orange-brown Ford Econoline van with bare metal walls and no side windows. Clete hadn't driven far—ten miles at most—and as the sun came up he pulled into the woods, backed the van around, and then parked with the nose pointed downhill. Clete and Doreen sat up front with Travis squatting between them on a stack of three cases of aluminum cans, one Mountain Dew, two Bud Light. Along one side of the cabin were Wal-Mart bags and cardboard boxes full of supplies a teenager would buy for an all-night kegger: bags of Cheetos and Cool Ranch Doritos, a four-pack of Red Bull, a pack of Fig Newtons, paper plates, a box of plastic utensils. It was only when he realized that one of the bags held a jumbo pack of adult diapers that he guessed what the chubs were going to do.

They sat for what seemed like hours, Pax pretending to sleep. He wasn't sure of the time—7:00 a.m., 8:00? From his position on the floor of the van, watching through slit eyes, he could see nothing through the windshield but treetops and gray sky. He tried not to shiver. The van's heaters didn't reach past the driver's and passenger's seats. The air smelled like stale vintage—but not his father's.

"There's the Caddy!" Travis said.

The chubs said nothing for half a minute. Then Clete said, "It's *payday*." It sounded like he was quoting from a movie. He cranked the ignition, forgetting that the engine was already started.

Travis said, "Wait, I thought we were going to wait for a few minutes, let her get into the office."

"Not too long," Doreen said.

"I'm just getting ready," Clete said testily.

Doreen said, "When you get in there, don't let that bitch push you around."

"Don't worry about us," Travis said. "Just do your part."

"You know how she is," Doreen said. "And don't let Everett intimidate you."

"We got it, Doreen," Clete said.

The van jounced over ruts on its way downhill. They reached the highway, went along it perhaps a hundred yards, and then turned up the driveway to the Home. Travis glanced back at him, and Pax kept his eyes unmoving, his jaw slack.

"Playin' possum," Travis said. "Just like his daddy." Pax didn't move, and Travis laughed. "Have it your way, man."

The van stopped and Clete said, "Hey, Barron."

"You're here awful early," the tinny voice said from the intercom.

"We figure someday she'll pay us early just to get rid of us," Clete said.

"Not a chance," Barron said, laughing. A second later the gate buzzed and the van rolled forward a few dozen feet and stopped. Pax heard the gate squeal shut behind them.

"Y'all ready?" Clete said.

"You know I am," Doreen said, her voice low. "And I know

you are." A wet smack, and Pax risked opening his eyes a fraction. Clete and Doreen were attempting to inhale each other's tongues.

"Guys . . . ," Travis said.

"I love you, baby," Doreen said.

"Me too," Clete said.

Clete and Travis climbed out of the van, and Doreen scooted over to the driver's seat. "Three minutes, tops," she said.

"We know, we know," Clete said.

Doreen put the van in reverse and started backing up. Pax entertained a brief fantasy of jumping up, throwing his bound arms around the chub girl's neck, and choking her unconscious. But Jesus, he thought, he wasn't Bruce Willis. Doreen was twice his size and probably twice as strong. She'd just reach back and bash him in the head.

Pax said, "Doreen. You know this can't work."

"Look who's awake," Doreen said. She braked, then started turning the van around. "You don't know how well we've planned this, Paxton. This is just step two in our ten-step plan."

Pax pushed himself to a sitting position. "But this is kidnapping. You're going to have cops all over you. FBI, even. And you're not exactly going to be able to blend in with the population."

"Who's going to call the cops? Rhonda?" Doreen leaned to look in her side-view mirror and backed the van up to the Home's front door. "Uh-uh. Drug dealers can't call the cops. That's the beauty of stealing from a criminal."

"You're not serious," Pax said. "The only beauty is that instead of calling the cops they just kill you."

"Let 'er try," Doreen said.

Jesus Christ, Pax thought. They thought they were Bonnie and Clyde, but hadn't bothered to watch the end of the movie.

Doreen studied the side-view mirrors, her sausage fingers drumming the steering wheel. Pax turned sideways, which put him directly behind the driver's seat and a foot closer to the Wal-Mart bag holding the box of plastic utensils. Fifty spoons, forks, and knives.

Doreen must have noticed something in the mirrors. She leaned out the window and called, "What?"

Clete shouted something Pax couldn't catch. Doreen opened her door and hopped out.

Pax scooted closer to the bag and grabbed the box of utensils. It was glued shut. He tore at the lip of the lid, but the duct tape around his wrists restricted his leverage. Outside the van, Doreen and Clete argued about something.

Pax tucked the box under his knee and pulled back on the lid with both hands. The cardboard ripped open and utensils spilled onto the floor. He grabbed at a plastic knife—and then the rear doors unlocked. He tipped a Wal-Mart bag on top of the mess, then twisted around as the door swung open.

"Come out of there," Doreen said. Behind her Clete was already going back into the building.

"What's going on?" Pax asked.

"Can't leave you out here alone," she said. She grabbed him by the front of his shirt and dragged him toward her with ease. "We need to put you to work." She set him on his feet and gave him a little push that sent him hopping toward the building.

Rhonda, Everett, and Barron sat in chairs in the atrium. Only Barron looked upset: face beet red, patches of sweat darkening his brown uniform. Travis had duct taped the guard's arms to the chair and he'd started working on his legs.

"Morning, Paxton," Rhonda said.

"Morning," Pax said. He stood there with his bound wrists and ankles, feeling like a bowling pin. Everett, calm as ever, nodded at him.

Clete had acquired a second pistol—from Everett?—and waved both of them in the captives' direction. "This is taking too long," he said.

"We should have used tie wrap," Doreen said. "I said to buy tie wrap."

"I *told* you, they didn't have—never mind. Doreen, you go get the old man. He's in the first room on the right."

"Me? But he's huge. Have Travis do it."

"Travis is going to take Everett down to unlock the coolers."

"And what are you going to be doing?" Doreen asked.

"I'm going to be emptying the safe! You know that's part of the plan."

Rhonda said, "You have a *plan*?"

"A ten-point plan," Pax said.

"Everybody shut up!" Clete shouted. "Paxton, start wrapping Rhonda. Doreen, *please* go find Harlan? There's a wheelchair back there somewhere."

Pax lifted his wrists. "I'm kind of tied up here."

Travis got to his feet and slapped the big silver roll of duct tape into Paxton's hands. "Work it out." Then Travis withdrew his own pistol from his waistband and nodded at Everett. "Let's go downstairs," he said.

Everett looked at Rhonda. Rhonda said, "The key to the coolers is in the safe."

Clete stared at her. "You're lying."

Rhonda rolled her eyes. "Goodness gracious, Clete, where would *you* keep the keys?"

"Okay, fine," Clete said. "We were going to open the safe anyway." He pointed a gun at Rhonda. "It's *payday*."

"You said that when you came in," Rhonda said.

Pax started to mention how Clete had been practicing in the van, then thought better of it.

Doreen shook her head and walked toward the double doors that divided the atrium from the patient rooms. Her jeans rode low on her hips, exposing a pale freckled back and an angel wing tattoo over the crack of her ass. Clete herded Everett and Rhonda toward Rhonda's office, and Paxton followed, taking tiny penguin steps. He stumbled and Travis said, "Hold on a second." He took a pen knife from his pocket and sliced between Paxton's ankles. Pax worked his legs and the rest of the tape peeled apart.

"Thanks," Paxton said.

"Just move," Travis said. The boy was frowning deeply, as if this little adventure wasn't turning out to be as fun as he'd expected. Or maybe, Pax thought, he was figuring out that Clete and Doreen weren't the criminal masterminds he thought they were.

Inside the office, Everett leaned against one wall, arms crossed in front of him. Rhonda was stooped in front of the safe, working the dial. "So Clete, what was this plan of yours? I mean the other nine steps."

"Just open it," Clete said.

"You're going to, what? Drive to a motel somewhere, feed Harlan fast food and squeeze out vintage?"

"Something like that."

"Then what?"

Clete looked at Travis, his grin saying, Can you believe how stupid she is? "Uh, then we sell the stuff and get rich?" He laughed.

Rhonda pressed down on the safe's handle and pulled the door open.

"Don't you pull a gun out of there," Clete said. The pistol in his left hand was pointed at her temple.

Rhonda shook her head in annoyance. "Here," she said, and tossed him a key ring. Both Clete's hands were occupied, and the keys bounced off his stomach and hit the floor.

Travis stooped to pick them up. "Okay," he said to Everett. He didn't sound happy.

Everett shrugged and walked out of the room with Travis' gun at his back. "Hurry," Clete said.

Rhonda stood and straightened her suit jacket. "Let me understand this. You're going to take as much vintage as you can carry, and take Harlan with you, and take Paxton with you to keep Harlan producing."

"Wrap her up," Clete said to Paxton. He gestured with the gun for Rhonda to take a seat in her big leather desk chair. Rhonda sighed and sat, and Paxton kneeled next to her.

"After you sell off the vintage in the coolers, you've just got Harlan," Rhonda said. "Say you manage to keep him alive and producing. That gives you about four ounces of vintage to sell a day."

"At least four," Clete said.

"Okay, say five. Or ten! Why not?"

Pax pulled off a long stretch of tape with his teeth, then tore it off. He began to wrap it around her shins and the central post of the desk chair. Rhonda was wearing nylons, so at least the tape wouldn't pull her hair off when it was removed.

Rhonda said to Clete, "So how did you figure to make money with that? You can't sell it to charlies—after today you'll never be able to set foot in Switchcreek again. And I can't see much of a market anywhere else."

"Ha! Doreen said you'd say that. We're not idiots, Aunt Rhonda. We'll sell it to the outsiders, just like you do."

"Really."

"Don't play dumb. I've seen what the vintage does to them."

"Have you? Give an unchanged person the vintage and they get all weepy and sentimental, and then fall asleep. Not exactly a wonder drug. You'd be better off selling them Nyquil."

"That's the old weak shit," Clete said, and he squatted to look into the safe. "The stuff from Elwyn and Bob and the other old men. Harlan's vintage, though—that knocks skips on their asses. And the best thing is, it's addictive as all hell."

"So are cigarettes, hon, but even Marlboro has a marketing plan. Ooh, careful there, Paxton, I don't have the best circulation."

"Make it tight," Clete said.

A savage expression flickered across Rhonda's face, quick as the chop of a cleaver. Pax looked at Clete, but the chub boy had missed it—he was pulling out the account book and a stack of papers.

"All righty then," Rhonda said, her voice as calm as before. "Say that you did have the world's greatest narcotic—and you don't—you've still got major sales and distribution problems. First of all, how're you going to get people to try it? They never heard of this stuff, they don't know what it does. There's no demand. You'd spend the first year giving away free samples just to explain what your product was."

Clete looked up in annoyance. "No I wouldn't. Now where's the cash?"

"Then you've got to think about the competition," Rhonda said. She shifted her weight as Pax started to wrap her left arm. "How you going to outsell something as cheap as meth? Any hillbilly with a hotplate can make crystal meth. Or Oxycontin? Or cocaine? Tons of that stuff is crossing the border every day. You think you can meet those price points? It's like trying to compete with Wal-Mart. All you've got is a few dribs and drabs of vintage."

"But *you're* selling it to outsiders!" Clete said. "Everybody knows you're making a ton of money off the old men. Look at this place—you built this whole building, you've got that car, you run the whole town . . . Next you're going to tell me that bullshit that you're using it for research."

"Oh, hon, that's just what we tell the stupid people," Rhonda said.

Pax stopped his wrapping. "What?"

"The just-plain-ignorant—that would be you, Clete—think I'm a Colombian drug lord or something, selling vintage all over Tennessee. All I have to do is be vague and people let their imagination run away with them. And the smart people—"

"Yeah, what do you tell them?" Clete asked.

"Hon, the smart people figure it out on their own," Rhonda said, as if explaining it to a child. "That's how you know they're smart people."

Pax noticed movement and looked up. Everett stood just outside the doorway, his white polo shirt covered in a rooster tail of bright red blood. And then he stepped back out of Paxton's line of sight.

"You're lying," Clete said to Rhonda. A note of doubt had crept into his voice. "I know you're lying."

"Hon, you keep saying that, but I don't have to lie to you, because I know how screwed you are. You were screwed from step one. You jumped into this without doing some very basic research."

"You're just making this up," he said.

"Let me ask you, Clete. How many skips have you tried out the reverend's vintage on?"

"I didn't *have* the reverend's vintage, so I couldn't very well try it out, could I? Besides, I didn't have to. I saw what it did to Paxton. One drop and the boy starts tripping like a hippie. He told me he'd never felt any drug like Harlan's vintage. Ain't that right, Paxton?"

Pax said nothing. He knelt on the floor beside Aunt Rhonda, the nearly empty spool of tape in his hands. He'd finished securing her to the chair. He hadn't wrapped her too tightly, but he hoped it looked convincing.

"See, he's still half-stoned. This morning I caught him talking to the wallpaper. Doreen said Harlan's stuff sets off these mirror cells in your head—"

"Mirror neurons," Rhonda said.

"Yeah, the empathy thing," Clete said. "And the emotion stuff. Love Potion Number Nine."

Rhonda shook her head. "Clete, you do know that Doreen's not a real nurse? She's barely a candy striper. She only knows what Dr. Fraelich tells her, and I doubt she understands a tenth of that. And even then, the doctor's just guessing. The most data she's ever gotten was when she sat around watching Paxton rant and rave for a few days. And even *she* got it wrong."

"*What* wrong?" Clete said, frustrated.

"Hon, it's not Harlan that's different," Rhonda said. "It's Paxton."

Out in the hallway, a slam that sounded like a gunshot. Clete spun toward the doorway, one arm up—and then Doreen charged into the room. She saw the gun aimed at her and yelped.

"Jesus, Doreen, I nearly shot you!" Clete said.

"The TV," she said. "You got to see this."

"Where's Harlan?"

"I couldn't get him up! You have to see it. Some city in South America—"

"Shut the fuck up!" Clete swung back to Rhonda. "Now what the fuck do you mean, Paxton's different?"

"Just try Harlan's vintage on another skip, and you'll see it doesn't have anywhere near the same effect."

"Hey, who's bleeding?" Doreen asked. She was looking at the floor by her feet, where Everett had been standing a minute earlier.

Clete turned to snarl at her, but then he paused, frowned. Pax could see the bad thought forming in his brain. Travis should have been back by now, but Rhonda had kept talking and talking.

Pax looked up at Rhonda. Her expression was strangely sad.

"Travis?" Clete called in a strangled voice. He bolted for the door. "Travis!" He shouldered Doreen aside and ran through the doorway—and vanished.

Pax had seen nothing but a blur moving in from the right, and then Clete was knocked out of the frame, gone as if he'd been snipped from a film.

Doreen screamed and ran out of the room. Pax followed.

Clete was on his back, Everett on top of him, one hand braced against Clete's neck, the other clenched into a fist. He struck Clete once, twice. A white tooth shot out of the boy's mouth like a spitball.

"Paxton!" someone shouted. Barron, tied to his chair twenty feet away, nodded fiercely at the floor. Clete's pistol lay almost at the guard's feet. Pax ran for it, moving awkwardly with his arms tied in front of him. He bent to scoop it up and then suddenly he was knocked sideways. He crashed into an end table, fell onto his side. His ribs, still sore from the beating weeks ago, erupted into fresh fire.

Doreen had tackled him. She grabbed the pistol, jumped up, and swung it toward him.

Pax scrambled to his feet. He seemed to hear the gunshot a moment after he ducked. He didn't know where the bullet went, didn't know if he was hit.

There was nowhere to hide. Nothing in the lobby but two chairs, a couch, a few potted plants.

Doreen fired again. Pax ran pell-mell for the double doors that led to the patient rooms, wild with the need to escape. The thirty feet to the doors seemed to stretch to the length of a football field. Finally he banged through the doors, and then he was falling against the second set of doors and onto the floor beyond. He hit with his forearms in front of him and pain shot through his elbows.

His father's room was just ahead, the first door on the right. Pax tried to push himself to his feet, but his arms wouldn't work. He got his knees under him, then stood and stumbled forward. He dropped his bound arms like a club onto the door's handle and pushed it open with his shoulder.

His father was sitting up in bed, staring at the television.

Pax pushed the door closed and then leaned against it. "Dad." His father glanced at him, frowning, and then looked back at the TV. A female announcer said something about a state of emergency.

"*Dad.* We have to block the door."

Over the noise of the TV he thought he heard the sound of another gunshot, but from this distance, through so many doors, he couldn't be sure.

"Dad! I need you to listen to me."

His father slowly shook his head. "It's happening again," he said.

The handle rattled, and then the door opened a few inches and bumped against the back of the dresser drawer. "It's okay, Paxton," Aunt Rhonda said, sounding exasperated. "It's safe to come out now."

It took him a minute to shove the furniture out of the way. Rhonda came into the room with a paper mask held over her nose. The cuff of her sleeve was stained with dark blood. Her hair was in disarray.

"We aren't dead, in case you were wondering," she said, her voice muffled.

"Are *they*?" Pax asked.

"They ought to be."

"I think you should see what's on the news," he said.

He moved out of the way so Rhonda could see the screen. His father said, "It's bigger this time. A whole city."

"What's bigger?" Rhonda asked.

"The Changes," Pax said.

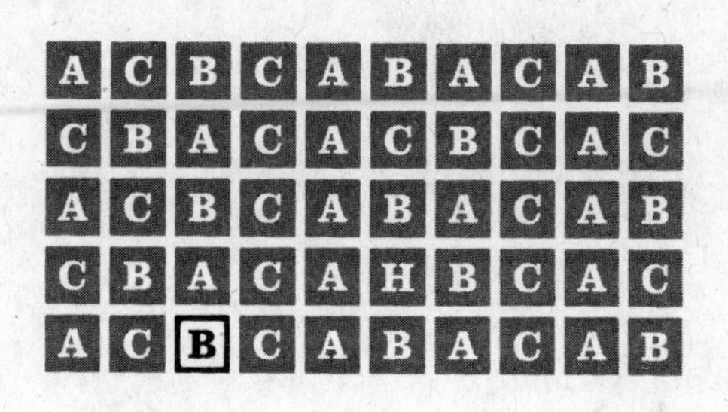
A C B C A B A C A B
C B A C A C B C A C
A C B C A B A C A B
C B A C A H B C A C
A C B C A B A C A B

# chapter 15

A TRIO OF beta girls stood awkwardly on the sidewalk, pinned in place by cameras and lights and microphones. One of them answered a question while the other two looked on. They didn't seem to want to speak to the reporters, but they didn't move away either. They may have been blanks, but they were also teenage Americans; they didn't know how to say no to television.

Pax stepped off the sidewalk to avoid the clump of media people surrounding them. He'd tried to drive to the clinic, but the downtown streets were packed. He'd been forced to park down on Bank Street, a quarter mile from the center of town. News vans, television trucks, and rental cars lined the street ahead of him; strange faces crowded the sidewalks. All this, just to cover the "local angle."

Before the Changes, the world had never heard of Switchcreek, Tennessee. And until yesterday, not many more had ever heard of Babahoyo, Ecuador. Now they were sister cities, united in disaster, death, and acts of God. Sodom and Gomorrah separated by two thousand miles and thirteen years.

At least a thousand were dead in Babahoyo, and who knew how many more were stricken. The exact numbers varied by news channel, but every hour the estimates climbed.

After Clete's botched kidnapping yesterday, Pax had sat in his father's room for most of the afternoon, watching the news. When he went home that night he kept the TV on, unable to look away: the cameras panning over rows of the sick laid out in hospital beds or across the floors of churches and schools; the close-ups of brown faces bleaching to chalk; the repetitive soundtrack of grunts and moans and cries in Spanish. And then, like a bizarre commercial break, a word from our previous victims, the people of Switchcreek. He saw Rhonda interviewed twice, and no one could have guessed that a few hours before she'd been duct taped to her chair and held at gunpoint. Back in the studios, scientists and special correspondents described the nature of TDS, charted its three variants, predicted that the current wave of TDS-A would give way to strains of B and C, and speculated baldly on the disease's causes and probable vectors of transmission. It was painfully clear that in thirteen years no one had made much progress in understanding the disease.

The cameras always returned as soon as possible to South America, to shots of Ecuadorians twisting in agony as bone and muscle frantically tried to outrace each other. He wondered if they'd call themselves argos or choose a Spanish name.

He reached the clinic, but the front door was locked. He pressed the doorbell, waited. A plaque next to the door declared the building to be THE PHILIP MAPES MEMORIAL MEDICAL CENTER. Philip had been Rhonda's husband, if he remembered correctly.

After half a minute he pressed the doorbell again just as a shadow moved behind the glass. He stepped back as Dr. Fraelich worked the keys in the lock and pushed the door open a few inches.

"Is this an emergency, Mr. Martin?"

"Why, are you closed?"

"I'm a little short on staff." She saw something in his face. "What?"

"Is it Doreen? I was hoping you'd heard from her. Or from Rhonda."

Dr. Fraelich glanced over his shoulder. "You better come in before the reporters notice. They keep asking for interviews."

She locked the door behind him, then led him down the hallway.

"I saw you on CNN," Pax said. "All two seconds."

"I was hoping no one had seen that."

"I've been watching too much TV," Pax said. "I couldn't stop watching. All those people . . ."

"I thought you looked a little shell-shocked." She pushed open the office door. The room looked as crowded and messy in daylight as it had that night. He sat on the same chair he'd used before. Dr. Fraelich turned off her computer monitor and sat opposite him, her legs crossed. She wore a wrinkled, French-blue shirt and charcoal slacks. Her black shoes were scuffed at the toe.

"It just seems so much worse than what I remember from the Changes," Pax said. "Our Changes."

"It's a lot more people," she said.

"Yeah, there's that. But it's just that this time I know what's coming, you know?" He'd seen Deke and Jo and his father transform. He'd watched his mother die. In the space of a few months he'd attended the funerals of dozens of friends and relatives.

"So this is bringing it all back to you. The trauma."

"What? No." He shook his head. "Look, I'm not saying it

wasn't terrible. People in Lambert screaming at us, and then when those boys were murdered . . . but it didn't wound me for life or anything. I moved on, even if other people couldn't let it go. A year after it all I'd still catch my cousins looking at me all misty-eyed—oh, the poor boy from Switchcreek."

"You sound awfully pissed for a guy who's over it."

"Well, yeah. It annoyed me. It wasn't me they should be sorry for—I came through fine. It was like *they* wanted to feel bad. Like all these reporters, glomming onto us. They want somebody to break down on camera."

"And clearly that won't be you," she said.

He looked up. He could never tell when she was being sarcastic.

"So," she said. "Doreen. She didn't make another pass at you, did she?"

"Not exactly," he said. He told her about Doreen and Clete and Travis grabbing him at home, then attempting to kidnap his father and rob Rhonda. When he got to their ten-point plan Dr. Fraelich stood and moved across the room. She crossed her arms, uncrossed them, then picked up a pen.

"Rhonda wouldn't let that happen," she said.

"Everett—her driver, bodyguard, whatever he is—stopped them," Pax said. "Then we were interrupted by the news about Ecuador."

"Where are they now?" she asked.

"Doreen and them? I don't know. I stayed in my father's room. Rhonda left to go downtown. When I finally went home, the lobby was cleaned up, there was nobody there but the security guard, Barron."

"You didn't ask him?"

"I was a little freaked out. I thought . . . I don't know what

I thought." Pax breathed in, then exhaled shakily. "I was hoping you'd heard from Doreen."

"Damn it." She went to her desk, took out a pack of cigarettes. "I'm going outside for a minute."

He followed her out and she didn't object. They walked around to the side of the building, where a plastic patio table and a couple of chairs were hidden from the highway by a row of bushes. She didn't sit down. She reached into her pocket and came up with a book of matches. He liked that she carried matches. The smokers he knew—and in the restaurant business, that was pretty much everybody—only used lighters.

"You think she killed them?" he said.

"No," she said. Then, "Probably not."

"Jesus," he said. "You think she could do it. Kill someone."

"We're all capable of killing, Paxton." She lit the cigarette, then waved out the match and flicked it into a small garbage can. "Did you tell the Chief about this?"

"No, I just . . ." Why hadn't he called Deke? He should have at least called him. But there was something shameful in having to run to him for protection yet again. *Deke, somebody hurt me! Beat them up now!*

Pax shook his head. "I don't know. Like I said, I was freaked out."

He tried to decide if he cared if Rhonda had murdered them. Didn't they deserve it? The three chubs had abducted him, tried to kidnap his father, and held them all at gunpoint. If they'd succeeded in getting Pax and his father to St. Louis it probably would have been only a matter of time until the idiots killed them both—through incompetence if nothing else.

"Explain something to me," Pax said. He sat on one of the chairs and looked up at her. "The male charlies are the ones who are tolerant of it. It's the women who go crazy for it, right? But Rhonda gives it to the males, like payment. She calls it the bonus. Why not just sell it to the girls?"

"It's complicated, Paxton."

"Humor me."

Dr. Fraelich inhaled, blew out a stream of smoke. "Have you ever been in love?"

He blinked. "Probably not."

"Not even with Jo?"

"I—I don't know. We were kids. What do you know about me and Jo?"

"How about your parents? You must have loved them when you were small. All children do."

"Sure."

"And they loved you. Why? They had no choice. Especially your mother. When she was in labor, a part of her brain was flooded with chemicals: dopamine, serotonin, oxytocin. The same flood occurred every time she nursed you. Other parts of her brain—the areas responsible for cravings, goal-oriented behavior, ecstasy—were also swamped in dopamine. Over time—"

"What does this have to do with the chubs?"

"*Chubs* is crude, Paxton. Pay attention. Over time, that association—baby equals pleasure—becomes burned into the brain. There are a couple of structures on each side of the brain called the caudate nuclei, each about the size of a cocktail shrimp. That's where behaviors get turned into habits, and skills become things that are second nature, not even conscious. With each little hit of baby-ecstasy the brain makes that bond a little more permanent. Your mother's brain rewired itself to love you—you, specifically. She became addicted. That's what bonding is, Paxton. Evolution's chemical cocktail to make mothers obsessively care for the bundle of next year's genes."

"All right, fine," he said. "So the vintage contains—what? Dopamine? The oxytocin stuff?"

"Not that we've found so far. Mostly it's water and blood and dead cells. But there are also long chains of amino acids we've never seen before, and some of those are probably psychotropic. Judging from the way charlie males act, I'd bet money on it." She shook her head. "We do know that the vintage does something to them. The serum triggers production of testosterone and adrenaline and all kinds of byproducts, including carrier compounds similar to MHC. It's those carriers the charlie women pick up on—and what triggers the bonding cascade. It's not a general aphrodisiac; they bond to that particular male. They feel empathy for him, like they're one person."

"Mirror neurons," Pax said. At her look he said, "Doreen mentioned them."

"When, during the kidnapping?"

"I didn't know what she was talking about, though."

"If you see someone laughing and you smile even though you don't know what's funny, those are mirror neurons firing. If someone yawns and you yawn, or you see someone get kicked in the balls and you wince—see, I just talked about it and you made a face."

"I'm not seeing what this has to do with my father or the other old men. If this stuff is such a love potion, why aren't the young, uh, charlie boys producing it themselves?"

She shrugged. "Maybe it's too expensive for young males to both create it and do everything else they have to do. Maybe it's a way for the older men to keep control of the tribe. In the animal kingdom this happens all the time—alpha males and alpha females control reproduction in the group, either through intimidation or chemical means. Elder bull elephants keep the young males in line by suppressing the youngster's musth."

*"Must?"*

"With an 'h' at the end. It's a period where the males go a bit crazy from horniness, rage. When older males are around, however, they don't go into it." She seemed to find the look on his face humorous. "Just watch the Discovery Channel for a couple days."

"I don't think I can buy the idea of my father as a bull elephant," he said. "Okay, maybe he's as big as one, but he's sure not in charge of the tribe."

"No, that would be Rhonda," Dr. Fraelich said.

"Heh." But the doctor wasn't joking. And then he realized that he wasn't joking either. Rhonda ran all the tribes. She'd jerked him around like a puppet.

"The point is," the doctor said, "nobody knows what's going on with the vintage. As they say in the journals, further research is required."

"Rhonda told me once that that's what they were doing with the vintage. Research. For a cure."

"Really," Dr. Fraelich said.

"Yeah. Only during the robbery, Rhonda said that only the stupid people believed that."

After a moment he looked up. "You could say, 'Oh no you're not stupid, Paxton.' "

"I could."

"Come on, what's so unbelievable about looking for a cure?"

"Nothing. Plenty of people are. But they're not using the vintage to do it."

"Why the hell not?"

She inhaled from the cigarette, blew smoke through her nose. "That's part of the deal, Paxton. We're keeping the vintage out of the literature, out of the media. Vintage chemicals show up in charlie bloodwork—no way to hide that—but no one but me is studying the vintage itself. And no one outside of Switchcreek even knows that men secrete the stuff, or that it's extracted."

"Why would you keep that secret?"

"Think about it, Paxton. Let's say it's a new narcotic. A wonder drug. How long do you think it would be before there was a bounty on every male charlie? If the government didn't grab the men, then it would be some pharmaceutical company. Or God help us, drug dealers."

"That's a little paranoid, isn't it?" he said.

"Tell me how I'm wrong."

After perhaps half a minute he said, "This deal. This is something between you and Rhonda?"

"By necessity," she said.

"Okay, you have the monopoly—you're the only one studying this stuff. So do you know what it does to non-charlies? Skips, argos, outsiders . . ."

"You?"

"Yeah, me too."

"Except for you, the vintage does hardly anything to non-charlies. A mild rush." She tapped ashes into the can. "But you took an extreme dose. When you swam in it you became sensitized."

"No, it happened earlier. The baptism may have sped me along, but even before that night the tiniest touch of the stuff got me high." He'd been primed for it, like a twelve-year-old with alcoholic genes waiting for his first sip of Southern Comfort.

*It's not Harlan that's different. It's Paxton.*

"I didn't know that," she said. "I can look at your bloodwork again, but I doubt I'd see anything. Trust me, the non-changed just don't react like you do."

"So how's she doing it, then?" Pax asked.

Dr. Fraelich cocked an eyebrow.

"Aunt Rhonda," he said. "If she's not making money from pharmaceutical companies, and if she's not selling the vintage to outsiders, and there aren't enough charlies to make a living off of, then where's she getting her money?"

Dr. Fraelich looked out over the bushes at the highway. Pax stepped closer. "Listen," he said. "I think Jo found out something about her. Figured out what she's up to. Something bad enough to make Rhonda stop her."

The doctor shook her head. "Watch yourself, Paxton."

"You're afraid of her," he said, surprised.

"You may have grown up here, Paxton, but you don't understand a thing."

"Can't argue with that."

"Forget about Rhonda. Jo made enemies more dangerous than her. There are fanatics in her own clade who'd—Jesus, what now?"

She was looking over his shoulder. He turned as a white sedan and a white SUV pulled into the parking lot. The vehicles stopped, blocking in a row of cars. A young man about Paxton's age popped out of the sedan.

"Oh, of course," Dr. Fraelich said. She dropped the cigarette and tamped it out with her shoe.

The man quickly strode toward them, smiling. He wore an

untucked linen shirt, khaki pants, and strappy, open-toed leather shoes that were a cross between sandals and slippers. "Marla," he said. "Good to see you again."

He gripped the doctor in a vigorous two-handed shake, then spun to face Paxton and offered his hand. "Eric Preisswerk, from the CDC down in Atlanta." His accent was standard TV American with a European vowel or two thrown in. Up close he didn't look quite so young; Pax put him at thirty-five, thirty-six. He was short and athletically trim, humming with positive energy. The kind of guy who'd kick your ass in racquetball and then insist you'd almost beaten him.

"Paxton Martin," Pax said, but the man's attention was already back on Dr. Fraelich.

"It looks like we get to work together sooner than we expected," Preisswerk said to her. The doctor frowned and the man said, "You got the message that we were coming, didn't you?"

"I got it," the doctor said. "I just didn't know why. Shouldn't you be in South America? There's nothing going on here."

"Another team is going into Ecuador, once it gets permission. Meanwhile, they want my team to search for any likely vectors." He glanced behind him. Five more people had exited the vehicles, and one of them was handing out laptop cases and small bags from the back of the SUV. Preisswerk turned back to them and dropped his voice. "Between you, me, and the lamppost, this is probably a waste of time."

Pax thought, And that would make me the lamppost.

Dr. Fraelich said, "You're still on the quantum teleportation theory, then."

"Is there any other vector that makes sense? But what can we do? We have to cover the bases."

"All right. I can set you up in one of the examination rooms." She walked to the back door and unlocked it. Pax stood back as Preisswerk and his crew filed in with their bags.

Dr. Fraelich started to close the door and Paxton put out a hand. "I have to ask you for a favor."

"I'm a little busy, Paxton."

"It's not about Jo and Rhonda, it's about—listen, it won't take ten minutes. Just a quick swab on the inside of my cheek—that's how they do it on TV, right? Then mail off my DNA to some lab."

"What? Why?"

"It's something Rhonda said. About me." The doctor looked at him impatiently. "See, when I was a kid I used to think about other clades. You know, more than just the three? That there could be other clades we didn't know about—because on the outside they looked completely normal, but on the inside they'd be different."

"Different."

"Not different organs or anything—physically they'd seem perfectly normal. But psychologically, I don't know, they'd have a different brain chemistry, maybe. A different way of thinking."

It explained everything, he thought. Why he felt like such an alien in his own skin. Why he'd gone his entire life without feeling connected to anyone but Jo and Deke.

"You're not a new clade, Paxton."

"Ten minutes," he said. "That's all it takes."

"And a thousand dollars and thirty days to get the results," she said. "All right, fine. Come back tomorrow, if I haven't been pushed out of my own clinic. And please, leave the police work to the Chief."

---

Pax knew it was past time to talk to Deke but didn't know what he would say, so he decided to walk to the man's house—slowly. He found himself cutting through Old Soldier Park and wondering how long it had been since he'd seen the place.

Old Soldier had been a giant elm that the original settlers of Switchcreek had somehow forgotten to chop down. The job fell to their descendants, who were forced into surgical action by the epidemic of Dutch elm disease that swept through the Smokies in the thirties. In apology they polished the stump and put up a plaque. Once when he and Jo were ten or eleven she'd hopped on the broad stump and said, Vote for me, citizens! Pax had smiled, not getting the joke. She'd rapped her knuckles against his forehead, one of her most annoying habits. Figure it out, knucklehead. When he told his parents what she'd said they both laughed, so he adopted the joke as his own even though it would be several years until he learned what a stump speech was.

He reached Deke's house on Creek Road, stepped up onto the front step, and rang the bell. It had been over a month since the last time he'd been here, sweating and desperate, yet the door seemed even taller now. He felt like a little kid asking if the big boy could come out and play.

He rang the bell again. He never would have walked up to Deke's front door when they were kids. Deke had lived with his father in a run-down trailer out near Two Hills. His father was a barker, a bully—a small man who liked to clomp out of his trailer with a baseball bat and yell at the black kids just to see them wet their pants. Mostly the kids just wanted to look at the bird-houses—a dozen or so hand-built boxes perched on poles around the yard. Deke had hammered together the first of them when he was in fifth grade, and each year the models were more elaborate, more detailed, more refined: log cabins, Gatlinburg-like chalets, multitier apartments . . . Paxton's favorite was the scarecrow that housed birds in its wooden head.

The disparity between the birds' accommodations and the humans' became a little embarrassing. Maybe that's why Deke's father kept scaring the kids off. He died in the Changes, but Pax couldn't recall whether it had been during the A, B, or C waves. Neither could he remember Deke ever talking about his father's death. Was Deke at his bedside when it happened? Off with Jo and him? Pax had never asked. And why was that? Was he that much of a self-absorbed asshole that he couldn't ask how Deke's father died?

No one answered the bell. He thought of leaving a note taped to the door: *Dear Deke, Rhonda may have killed some people. Call me.*

He decided to take a different route back to his car, walking along Creek Road to the highway to get an alternate angle on the media circus. The sidewalk in front of the Bugler's was completely blocked off; a row of TV reporters were lined up side by side, either talking into their own cameras or marking time until they went on. Half a block farther on at the salon, an argo woman and a chub woman in identical dresses had been cornered by what looked like at least two competing news crews. No one stopped Pax for an interview or even looked twice at him: the benefit of not looking like a local.

Pax turned the corner at Bank Street, stopped, and looked back at the car he'd just walked past. A light blue Prius. The windshield was unbroken, but that could easily have been replaced by now. The driver was inside, his head bent over something in his lap.

Pax walked around to the driver's side of the car. The window was down. "I thought Deke kicked you of town," he said.

Andrew Weygand jerked his head up, his fingers still on the laptop keyboard.

"Easy," Pax said. "I'm just messing with you."

"I have every right to be here," he said.

"That's right, you're a journalist." Pax thought he kept the sarcasm from his voice but wasn't sure if he succeeded entirely. "I'm Paxton, by the way. I don't think I introduced myself last time."

Weygand hesitated, then shook Paxton's hand. In the month since Pax had seen him the man's bleached hair had transformed to deep black with yellow tips, but the soul patch still clung to the underside of his lip like mold. The back of his car was a mess. Filling the seat was an unrolled sleeping bag, a pillow, and two blue plastic coolers. The floorboards were crowded with white plastic grocery bags.

"Are you living in this thing?" Pax asked.

"Temporarily," he said. "Turns out there's not a free hotel room between here to Knoxville."

"I'm surprised you're not in Ecuador."

"They're not issuing visas," Weygand said. "Total blackout except for a few of the mainstream press—typical old media hegemony." He glanced at the side-view mirror. "So, your friend Deke . . ."

"I'm looking for him, actually," Pax said.

"It's not, uh, totally necessary that you tell him you saw me, right?"

Pax shrugged and smiled. "Probably not."

"I'm just here for a night, maybe two. There's a town hall meeting at the elementary school tonight. I just want to interview some of the state and federal people who are coming, maybe get an interview with Mayor Mapes, then I'm gone again, I swear."

"Don't worry about it," Pax said. He hadn't heard of any town meeting. How many government agencies were rolling into town? "So what about the Brother Bewlay thing? Are you still hunting him down?"

"I didn't get much further after the last time I saw you," Weygand said. "Why don't you ask Deke? He's got all the emails. If Jo Whitehall was—what?"

"Nothing, I just . . ." Pax rubbed the back of his neck, thinking. "Listen, I've got a couple extra beds in my house, if you want to crash there after the meeting."

"I'm fine, dude, thanks," Weygand said.

"No, really. Jo Lynn was a good friend of mine, and you were her friend, too, even if you didn't know it was her." He smiled. "Besides, you'd be doing me a favor. I have a kind of tech support problem. You good at computers?"

Weygand looked down at the laptop screen. "I know my way around." He closed the lid and set the computer on the passenger seat. "What kind of problem?"

"I need to break into a password-protected laptop. A Mac."

Weygand laughed. "But not your Mac, right? No thanks, man, I don't—" Weygand stopped smiling, getting it.

"Yeah, we found it," Pax said. "But Jo locked it. I think it could tell us—" He almost said, *Tell us who killed her,* but he knew it would make him sound crazy. "—Well, a lot. Think you can do it?"

"How about right now?" Weygand said. "I just need to stop by the store and—"

"I don't have it with me," Pax said. "Tonight, after the meeting." He'd have to track down the twins, get them to retrieve the laptop from wherever they'd hidden it and bring it to his house.

"I'll get the supplies," Weygand said. He pushed the Power button on the dash and the Prius hummed awake. "Where can I get a couple big cans of compressed air?"

# chapter 16

RHONDA MAPES STOOD in the center of a bull's-eye. She looked around at the circle of people nearest her—politicians, bureaucrats, doctors, police, and military personnel (almost all of them men, twenty-first century be damned)—then lifted her head to take in the entire crowd.

The emergency meeting of the Switchcreek Town Council had swelled to include over twenty invited participants and more than two hundred spectators and media people. She'd expected a crowd, which is why she'd decided to hold the meeting in the elementary school gym. The folding chairs were set in concentric rings: leaders on the inside, flunkies behind them, and everyone else filling in back to the walls.

A more honest layout, Rhonda thought, would have placed the federal muckety-mucks in the outermost ring, all the better to corral the state functionaries, who were in turn trying to curb the county yokels, who only wanted to keep the freaks from Switchcreek in line. Rhonda, of course, would have been exactly where she stood now; smack dab in the center of everything. She wouldn't have wanted it any other way.

She smiled her grandmother smile. "Let me start," she said, "by thanking you all for coming out here tonight."

Tom Garvin, the regional director of the Tennessee Emergency Management Agency, opened his mouth to speak and Rhonda said, "Before we introduce our guests, we'd like to open this meeting with a word of prayer—for the people of Babahoyo. Reverend Hooke, would you lead us?"

Dr. Ellis Markle, from the Centers for Disease Control and Prevention, looked exasperated for a moment, then quickly assumed a pious expression. Rhonda thought of him as the man from COPTER. He led a division of the CDC called the Coordinating Office of Terrorism Preparedness and Emergency Response, but after watching him land his helicopter in the middle of town it was impossible to keep the correct acronym in her head.

Neither Garvin nor Ellis had wanted a joint meeting, let alone this public spectacle. The TEMA crew had wanted to talk privately with the CDC people, but Rhonda had arranged for a meeting between the town council and the CDC before Markle had touched down. The state officials had no choice but to insert themselves into the meeting. Then, somehow, half the town and all the news crews had learned of the summit and demanded to attend.

The Reverend Hooke prayed on in her loud, bell-like voice, earnest as all hell, and Rhonda surveyed the room under half-closed lids. All the clades were in attendance. A large contingent of blanks—most of them white-scarf girls—filled several rows on one side. A dozen argos loomed at the back of the room. And almost thirty charlies had scattered themselves around the room as she'd directed.

Only a few skips, though. Mr. Sparks sat in the first row, nervously paging through the minutes from the previous meeting. Paxton Martin was hunched over in the third row next to a couple of blank girls—they had to be Jo Lynn's twins—and an outsider she didn't recognize, a young man with a ridiculous hairdo like a black paintbrush.

Hooke ended her prayer with something in Spanish. That was a nice touch, Rhonda thought. She hadn't even known Elsa spoke Spanish. Then the reverend resumed her seat in the first row with her fellow council members, Mr. Sparks and Deke.

Rhonda reminded everyone that this was a council meeting and not a press conference; the media people would have to ask their questions later. Then she began to introduce their guests, starting with the lowliest of them, the county commissioner.

Nothing meaningful was said for the next hour. The officials took turns offering their support for the people of Switchcreek, without ever specifying why the people of Switchcreek needed any.

Rhonda noticed Deke leaning back to hear something Dr. Fraelich was whispering to him. The two of them had been talking earnestly before the meeting—and she had an idea what about. The doctor had nearly jumped out of her skin when Rhonda glided up and said hello. Rhonda had asked her if she could stay a little while after the meeting, and of course she'd agreed—as she'd better, after all the work Rhonda had done to keep her clinic funded.

The audience was bored, and even the newspeople were growing restless. It wasn't until the Man from COPTER said that a CDC field team would be going door-to-door with a survey that the crowd seemed to wake up. Someone from the crowd asked what kind of survey, and Markle then introduced the field team leader, a man named Eric Preisswerk who looked much too young to have both an MD and a PhD in molecular epidemiology. Nice shoes, though. They looked Italian.

"It will take only a few minutes to answer the questions," Preisswerk said. "But we hope it will help us determine if there's any relationship between what's happening in Babahoyo and what happened in Switchcreek." Copies of the survey were being passed through the room. Rhonda had already seen it. One of the first questions was, "Have you traveled to South America in the last ten years?"

A voice in the back of the room called out, "Are you saying TDS is contagious?"

Preisswerk held up his hands. "There's been no evidence of that. All we're trying to figure out—"

"What about quantum teleportation?"

This came from one of the Whitehall girls sitting next to Paxton. "Are you looking into how TDS could be transmitted that way?"

Preisswerk laughed in surprise. To an outsider the beta girl must have looked about nine years old. "Okay, that's . . . Wow. What is your name?"

The girl stood up, slipped off her large backpack, and handed it to Paxton. Paxton had an odd look on his face—surprised but somehow proud. "Lorraine Whitehall," the girl said.

Preisswerk said, "Well, Lorraine, you sound like a very intelligent girl. I know you may have heard people talking about quantum this or that on TV, but that's just a guess—we really don't have the evidence to say that. We're not sure if teleportation of quantum states is even possible on a molecular scale, but much less responsible for TDS."

Lorraine said, "The Oxford group did room-temperature teleportation with a complex molecule last year."

"Yes, but—are you reading physics journals, too?"

"The articles are on the Internet," she said.

Preisswerk laughed again. "Okay, that experiment was in laboratory conditions," he said. "Those fifty atoms were carefully isolated. That's a long way from showing that teleportation can occur inside an organic system."

Mr. Sparks said, "This is getting completely out of hand. We haven't even approved the minutes from the last meeting."

A low voice from the back said, "What are you talking about—Star Trek? Somebody teleported the disease to us?"

Lorraine stepped up onto her chair and turned to find the person who'd spoken, a young argo man. "Quantum teleportation doesn't teleport bodies or things, just information," she said. "But lots of stuff in our bodies happens at the subatomic level—breathing, thinking, making DNA. TDS could be like a computer virus that tells our bodies to replicate DNA differently." Somebody said something Rhonda didn't catch, and Lorraine said, "I'm not making it up—lots of scientists think so."

"So TDS *can be* contagious?" the argo asked.

"Of course it is," someone said in a loud voice. "We caught it, didn't we?"

Paxton held up a hand to Lorraine, but the girl jumped down on her own.

Rhonda caught the eye of Chelsea Wilson, a charlie woman in her forties who was sitting in the third row. Chelsea lifted her hand and said, "Is there going to be a quarantine?"

Preisswerk looked at his boss. The Man from COPTER stood, started to speak.

"Louder!" someone shouted.

"I said, there are no current plans for quarantine."

The room erupted in shouts and questions. Rhonda glanced

at Deke. He was staring at the floor, frowning. She'd told him what the government people would say.

Rhonda stood and called for quiet. When she had the room back under control she said, "Dr. Markle, almost everybody in this room lived through the quarantine, and in the end there turned out to be no reason for it. I think the question they're asking, what we're all asking, is not whether you have *plans* for a quarantine, but whether you will guarantee that there won't be one."

He seemed to flinch at the word "guarantee." "Mayor, I already said that there are no plans whatsoever for, for any kind of detention."

Rhonda touched his arm. "Just say, 'I promise, there will be no quarantine. Period.' "

He blinked at her.

"That's all you've got to say."

Markle addressed the crowd. "Let me assure you," he said. And then louder, "I promise, there are no plans that I know of for any—"

He never finished the sentence. The charlies in the audience had jumped to their feet, followed by a few betas, everyone shouting and talking. Markle didn't understand who he was talking to. These people had been quarantined before, and after the quarantine they saw their neighbors riot just because they wanted to go to the damn supermarket. They'd seen dead boys by the side of the road, and one of their girls raped, and the feds and the police hadn't done a damn thing for them. They could smell weasel words at a hundred yards. Now they were *sure* the government was coming for them.

Deke and the Reverend Hooke rose to stand next to

Rhonda. The reverend leaned close to her and said, "I hope you're happy."

Damn straight, she was happy. Her people were waking up.

It was nearly midnight before Rhonda shook the hand of the last visiting official, soothed the last constituent, begged off from the last reporter, and finally made her way down the hall to the teachers' lounge. Deke sat on the floor with his arms around his knees. The Reverend Hooke and Dr. Fraelich sat at the largest table, holding Styrofoam coffee cups. The reverend, despite her masklike face, exuded impatience. Dr. Fraelich, looking more flushed than usual, had picked apart the rim of her cup and made a tiny snowdrift beside it.

"I thought they'd never leave," Rhonda said by way of apology. She assessed the structural integrity of one of the thin plastic chairs, chose a marginally newer one next to it, and gingerly sat. "I suppose the doctor told y'all that I'd invited her to sit in on our conversation."

"Is Mr. Sparks not coming?" Dr. Fraelich asked.

"Oh, this isn't a town council meeting, hon," Rhonda said.

The doctor smiled tightly. "The inner circle, then? The Star Chamber?"

"Call it the executive board," the Reverend said.

The doctor glanced at Deke. "I didn't know the town had one," she said.

Rhonda chuckled. "Neither does Mr. Sparks. Don't tell him, it'll hurt his feelings." She folded her hands on the table. "So. You speak their language, Doctor, and you've already had a run-in with the field team. What do you think they're planning?"

"Run-in?" Deke asked.

"This morning, Eric Preisswerk and his team came to my office and started going through my records," Dr. Fraelich said. "Everything they could get their hands on, paper or electronic."

"That can't be legal," the reverend said. "Those are private medical records."

"I don't think they're worried about lawsuits at the moment," Rhonda said. To the doctor she said, "So will they find a link?"

The doctor shook her head. "I can't believe they'd find something new. For thirteen years we've looked at all the usual causes and vectors—viral, bacteriological, toxicological—and come up with nothing."

"So why is Preisswerk doing it?"

"I've known Eric for several years. He's got to look for a standard link because that's his job, but what he's really working on is the quantum transmission theory."

"This teleportation stuff?" Deke said. "But he was putting Rainy down about it."

"Eric was being cautious because he was in public."

"And because his boss was right there," Rhonda said.

The doctor picked up the coffee cup again and pinched off a bit of Styrofoam. "Eric told me the CDC is taking the theory more seriously now. Ecuador is making them take it seriously."

"So is TDS contagious or not?" the reverend asked. "If they think we can spread it, then they're going to crack down."

"It's not that simple," Dr. Fraelich said. "If the theory's correct, and I don't believe it is, then TDS is transmittable, but not in the way we normally think. Instead it's—well, it's too complicated to explain."

"I think you better try," Rhonda said.

"Tell them what you told me, Marla," Deke said. "About quantum calculation, parallel universes."

Dr. Fraelich exchanged a look with Deke—the doctor wasn't enjoying this. She exhaled heavily. "Imagine that next to our universe there are millions of other universes. Trillions. Now imagine that in just one of them, some bacteria or virus figures out how to transmit its genetic instructions to the universe next door."

"How?" the reverend asked.

"If a cell is isolated from measuring events, then—never mind, let's just say it's theoretically possible. The point is, the probability of that happening is very, very low, *almost* impossible, but not quite. Given enough alternate universes, it's practically inevitable that one of them learns the trick." Everyone regarded her blankly. The doctor smiled in frustration. "Okay, think of how land animals that evolved in one place end up on other continents, like new world monkeys migrating from Africa to South America. It's too far for them to swim, obviously. But say a hurricane picks up a tree on the shore where a couple of monkeys are hanging on, and the tree gets blown into the right current, and somehow the monkeys run aground on an island before they die of starvation or thirst. Then a thousand years later it happens again, to their descendants, and they get blown to the next island, and the next. Eventually we get marmosets in South America."

"Come on now," the reverend said. "A hurricane, a tree, and not one but *two* monkeys . . ."

"Adam and Eve," Deke said, a smile in his voice.

"Or just one pregnant female monkey," Rhonda said.

"And then it happens again and again?" the reverend said.

"But that chain of events only has to happen once," the doctor said. "Once in ten million years. We know it happened, or something equally improbable, because the monkeys weren't there forty million years ago, and then they were.

"Now imagine what you could do with trillions of universes and millions of years. Just once, one virus has to figure out how to get to the next universe. Once that happens, the viruses ripple across many universes. The way quantum mechanics works, you'll have a nearly infinite number of universes in which this has happened, and a nearly infinite number where this has never happened. We just happened to be in the haves."

"I don't believe this," the reverend said. "That all this could happen by chance."

The doctor bristled. "I'm not going to argue with you about whether this is an act of God."

"That's exactly what you're doing," the reverend said.

Rhonda rapped the table with the underside of one of her rings. "Ladies. It doesn't matter whether God did it, or a virus, or quantum Santa Claus."

"Of course it matters!" the reverend exclaimed.

"Elsa, hear me out. It doesn't matter what *we* think, it only matters what the government thinks, and what the public thinks. Because *that's* what's going to decide whether they quarantine us again." She looked around the table. "You saw what I saw. Doctor, your friend Preisswerk bailed out when he was asked about the quarantine. Obviously they've talked about it. And if public opinion turns, then sooner or later they'll *have* to isolate us. That's what I'd do in their shoes."

The reverend made a disgusted noise. "Of course you would."

"Yes I would. Elsa, the only reason they dropped the quarantine last time is because it stopped spreading, and because the babies hadn't started arriving. Now it's started again, and they know those people will start breeding too. We're not disease victims anymore, we're a race—three races—and from another universe, of all things."

"That's ridiculous," the reverend said. "We are not aliens."

"Of course not," Rhonda said, and thought, Of course we are. "But think of this from the government's point of view. Even if a quarantine won't protect a single citizen, the public will demand that we be locked up. They're already nervous—did you see that interview with those yahoos in Knoxville? They've already started talking about 'those people' in Switchcreek. Pretty soon they'll be running to Wal-Mart for pitchforks and torches."

"We've gone down this road before," the reverend said. "Putting a fence around us didn't make any difference last time, and it won't this time. The government has to make it clear that it's not contagious. We are not a risk."

Dr. Fraelich shook her head. "You're not listening to me. It may not be contagious in the usual sense, but it's still *transmittable*. Look, imagine all the universes lined up in parallel lines." She set out her hands, palms apart. "The virus travels from one universe to the next one. Nothing would stop the virus from crossing back into our universe from a different point. We have to assume that we are infecting nearby universes. The more of those we infect, the more likely that the infection spreads back to us."

"If this quantum theory is true," Deke said.

"It doesn't matter if it's true or not," Rhonda said again. "If the government thinks it's true, or if they feel they have to act like it's true, then they're going to try to fence us in. Our job is to figure out how to stop that from happening."

Neither the reverend nor Deke had an answer for that. After several moments passed in silence, Rhonda stood and addressed Dr. Fraelich. "Well, we've got a lot to ponder. Thank you for offering us your opinion, Doctor. If you get any more information out of those CDC folks, of course we'd want to know right away."

The doctor seemed surprised that she was being pushed out. Surely she didn't think she was being invited into the Executive Council? For one, she didn't have the genes for it.

"What are you going to do?" Dr. Fraelich asked.

Take out genocide insurance, Rhonda thought. She smiled and opened the door for the doctor. "I'm sure we'll think of something."

"Your problem," Rhonda told Deke after the meeting had adjourned and the reverend had left the building, "is that you don't believe in the future."

They were walking through the school, shutting doors and turning out lights behind them. Rhonda had asked him to give her a ride home because Everett had the Cadillac.

Deke looked perplexed, not sure if he should laugh. "Of course I do."

"You don't, not really. Without children, you've got nothing to pin your future to. You're practically sleepwalking through these meetings. You're disengaged, Deke, and we can't afford that. All the clades have to pull together if we're going to make this work."

It had taken another half hour after Dr. Fraelich had left the meeting for Rhonda to lay out her plans. She didn't mention that she'd already starting implementing them. The shell of the website had already been created, though it wasn't online yet; the toll-free numbers had been ordered; and her lawyer in Knoxville had set the 501(c)(3) paperwork in motion.

As she'd expected, the reverend quibbled with details, even though—no, *because*—she saw no other choices. She had the most people to consider, Elsa said, and so many of her clade were children. Deke had said very little, but when he finally said, "Okay," it was like the strike of a gavel. The reverend gave her consent and quickly left.

Rhonda opened her purse and handed him an envelope. He frowned, opened it with his thick fingers, and frowned again at the contents. The check was drawn against the school construction fund and made out to Alpha Furniture Company, for $83,522. Rhonda thought that $22 was a nice touch—specificity made it look less like a payoff.

Deke said, "I don't think this is the right time to be starting this, do you? The whole point of your plan—"

"Nonsense! We don't have time *not* to do it. My only requirement is that you and Donna have to use this money too. After that, start finding other argo couples. Like that boy who works for you, him and his new wife—they have to be thinking of a baby." They reached the front doors. Rhonda withdrew her big key ring from her purse, inserted the Allen wrench into the side of the door's push bar. "And by the way? It's *our* plan, hon."

Deke rubbed his thumb across the envelope but still didn't put it away. "I noticed a few of your people weren't here tonight," he said. "Everett, Clete, Travis."

Rhonda turned the wrench, winching down the bar so that the door would lock behind them when they left. "Everett's running some errands for me," she said.

"Really?"

Rhonda looked up, unable to keep a wry smile from her face. "You've got your chief face on, Chief."

"Marla told me what happened at the Home yesterday," he said. "She got it from Paxton."

"Don't you worry, that's all taken care of now."

"That," he said, "is what I'm afraid of."

She straightened, dropped the key ring back into her purse. "Don't tell me you're worried about Clete and Travis. You beat up those two boys yourself just a few weeks ago."

"Nobody's seen them for two days. Or Doreen either."

"*Doreen*, now that girl's a piece of work. Doesn't have the sense that God gave a hamster, and I do believe she was the brains of the outfit." Rhonda pushed through the door, and the big man stooped to follow.

Deke's Jeep, parked under a streetlamp, was the only car left in the lot. Not only would she have to somehow climb up into that thing, her hair would be blown to heck. Thank goodness it was the middle of the night.

*"Rhonda,"* Deke said. His voice had dropped into an Old Testament rumble. "What did you do with them?"

She breathed deep, exhaled. The night air was pleasantly cool and smelled of cut grass.

"Oh, all right," she said. "I'll show you on the way home."

Rather than just telling him where they were going she directed him by rights and lefts into the bottoms west of town. The Jeep rode rough, but she had to admit it was damn handy on these deeply rutted roads; the Caddy had had a much tougher time of it.

When they were a half mile from their destination Deke looked at her. "Willie Flint's place?"

"It was available," she said. "And it seemed appropriate."

"Jesus Christ, Rhonda."

Rhonda directed Deke to pull in beside her Cadillac, and when he shut off his headlights the night seemed to swoop in to surround them. Not quite pitch-black: Faint yellow light flickered in one of the cabin's small windows.

"Help me down," Rhonda said. Deke came around the Jeep—and froze. Rhonda followed his stare. The cabin door was open, and a figure stood in the shadowed doorway with his hand hanging at his side.

"Don't shoot," Rhonda said. "It's me."

"I was thinking of shooting myself, actually," Everett said. "Barron was supposed to be here a half hour ago." He stepped back to let them inside and nodded—warily, Rhonda thought—to the argo. "How you doing, Chief?"

The living room was dimly lit by a battery-run Coleman lantern and two old-fashioned kerosene lamps Rhonda had brought from her house. The old furniture had been pushed back to the walls, leaving the middle clear for a kind of campsite: a plastic cooler, three blue nylon camp chairs, a boom box, and the junk food and cases of beer and soda from Clete's van. A big plastic bag in the corner held the garbage.

Doreen Stillwater sat on the floor on a rolled-out sleeping bag looking as miserable as a wet dog, an image aided by the six feet of heavy-gauge chain that connected her left ankle to the frame of the old couch. The girl perked up when she saw Deke. "Chief! Thank God! You wouldn't believe what they're doing to us!"

"Give it a rest, Doreen," Everett said.

Deke squatted on his haunches to get a closer look at Doreen's face. Her cheeks were streaked with mascara, but the girl was unbruised.

"Fortunately for her," Rhonda said, "she gave up without a fight."

Doreen gripped Deke's hand. "They're keeping us prisoner, Chief, and they won't let me see Clete!" Her voice had risen into a whine. "He's right down the hallway, and they won't even let me talk to him! This is illegal, Chief."

"I swear," Everett said quietly. "I'm just gonna shoot myself."

Deke extracted his hand. He looked at Rhonda. "And Travis?"

"He's dead!" Doreen said. "Everett shot him!"

Deke grimaced. "Jesus, Rhonda—"

"It happened during the robbery," Rhonda said.

Deke turned to Everett. "Is this true? You shot him?"

Everett moved his fingers in a suggestion of an apology: What can you do?

"Pure self-defense," Rhonda said. "It was Travis' own gun."

For half a minute or more Deke didn't seem to know where to look. Then he said, "Show me Clete."

"Take me with you!" Doreen cried.

Rhonda led him back to the bedroom where they'd found Willie Flint. The room smelled dank and animal-like, though it was the merest echo of the stink of ten years ago.

Clete was laid out on one of the double beds, both wrists chained to the bed frame. The boy's head, which had always been large, seemed twice its normal size. Purple bruises had inflated his cheeks so that his eyes were almost shut. His bloody T-shirt was pasted to his chest. His mouth hung open, issuing a gargled wheeze with each breath.

"Most of that blood was from his nose and mouth," Rhonda explained.

Deke stared at her. "Oh, that's okay then," he said.

"And don't worry, he's not sleeping all the time. He can walk, when he's motivated. Everett wakes him to pee and drink. He's not too good with solids, right now, but he'll get there."

Deke was silent for a long moment. He was bent under the ceiling like an adult in a child's playhouse. Rhonda thought, for perhaps the thousandth time, that that had to be mighty tiring.

"Damn it, Rhonda, you should have just called the police." Deke had dropped his voice, but in this tiny house it would be impossible not to hear that low rumble. "Even with Travis, it's an open-and-shut case. They broke in, Everett defended you."

"I wasn't worried about winning a trial, for goodness' sake. I didn't want what a trial would bring—all the attention on our clade, what we were trying to do at the Home, and Clete talking about his wild theories. We can't have the whole world thinking our seniors are manufacturing some kind of supernarcotic. Harlan and the others would be marked men, Deke. Marked."

"But it's not a narcotic," Deke said, a question in his voice.

"Not for skips—except maybe for Paxton Martin. Who knows what's going on with that boy."

"Either way, you can't just—" His head bumped the ceiling. "Let's talk outside," he said.

As they passed through the front room Doreen got to her feet. "Chief? Chief?" She stepped around Everett and tried to grab the argo's arm; the chain drew taut and the couch scraped against the floor. "You're not going to leave us here? Is Clete all right? What are they doing to him?"

Rhonda shut the door behind them. Deke straightened slowly, like a bear rising up on its hind legs. Law, Rhonda thought, an argo would be a scary thing to meet in the dark. And for good reason. She considered herself lucky to have seen early on what one of them—even the most conscientious of them—could do when he lost control. She never forgot it for a second.

After that night at Willie Flint's, Deke had made self-control his religion, but he was struggling against the design of his own body, and he could never win every battle. Chub boys like Clete and Travis juiced themselves up and went barking after trouble. But for argos, violence was the natural result of their existence in the world. They were shaped for it, like an axe blade, or a jagged slope. Throw yourself against one and you could no more blame the argo for hurting you than blame a mountain.

"What are you going to do, Rhonda?" Deke asked. He loomed over her in the dark. "You can't just keep them here."

"Not forever," Rhonda said. "I just need a couple weeks."

"What, until the newspeople clear out?"

"It has nothing to do with the new Changes," she said. "I need to wean them. From each other."

There was a long pause. Rhonda was annoyed that she couldn't make out his face.

"How about you explain that," he said evenly.

"I'm cutting Clete off from the vintage. I'll tell him that if he stays on good behavior there's a chance for him to get back on the dole. But that ain't going to happen."

"That's it? That's your punishment?"

"Well, then we kill him." She held up a hand before he could respond. "A joke, Deke, just a joke." Only barely, she thought. She'd indulged a number of daydreams about burying the boy back in the woods next to Travis and Donald Flint. But it was just too risky. Travis' disappearance was going to be hard enough to explain, and that boy didn't have hardly any people left. Clete, though, was related to half the town. She still might have managed it if the relations had been all charlies, but a good number were argos and blanks. Too risky. Especially with every reporter in east Tennessee camped out on her doorstep thanks to the Ecuador outbreak.

"Trust me," she told Deke. "Clete's going to think that going cold turkey is worse than death. His muscles'll go soft, the girls will stop paying attention to him. He'll be neutered. Doreen'll be off-limits to him, though it won't be long before she won't *want* to have anything to do with him.

"She's going on probation, too. I haven't decided how long yet—our clade can't afford to have a girl out of commission forever—but I'm thinking a year. At least six months. Then I'll match her to a boy that *I* pick out."

A long stretch of silence. Deke finally said, "I didn't know it worked like that. That you got to just . . . pick. Decide who falls in love with whom."

"Well, somebody's got to," she said. She saw him frown; her eyes were adjusting to the dark. "What, you don't approve?"

"It don't seem right."

Rhonda almost laughed. "You want *them* to pick? Those teenagers? Think about when you were their age, Deke. How much control did you have over your hormones? Your *brain* wasn't picking out the best of all possible mates. You were taking orders from the lieutenant governor."

"Works out just fine most of the time," Deke said.

"*Most?* Hon, you have not been paying attention. It's a roll of the dice out there. You and Donna may have struck the vein, and God bless you, but for most of the sorry people in this world sex hits them like a blindside tackle when they're sixteen and the next thing they know they're pregnant, raising babies, and waking up to five thousand mornings of cold coffee. I'd sooner let a monkey pick my husband than the girl I was at sixteen. The Indians have the right idea—not the casino Indians, the call-center Indians—let the parents arrange things. You can always grow to love someone, or at least tolerate them, if they're a good match. And I make sure they're a good match. You wait a couple years then look at the charlie divorce rate and tell me if I wasn't right."

"You already matched Doreen and Clete," he said.

"That was *too* good. I thought she'd give him some ambition, I didn't know she was some low-rent Lady Macbeth."

Deke tilted his head.

"Shakespeare, hon. Read a book."

Deke lifted his hands in surrender. He stepped up into the Jeep and dropped down into the driver's seat; the car rocked on its suspension. "I'll be checking on them," he said.

"I'm sure Everett and Barron would appreciate the company."

"I'm serious, Rhonda. I won't sit by if there're any more disappearances." He put the Jeep in gear. "Good luck with the kickoff tomorrow."

She watched the taillights slide and wink through the trees until they disappeared.

Well, that went better than expected, Rhonda thought. He hadn't even given back the check.

# chapter 17

PAXTON WAS MET at the front gate by a shotgun and a scowl. The chub—a middle-aged man whom Paxton recognized from the Tuesday-morning payday crowd—told him to drop the newspapers, turn around, and put his hands on the hood.

Pax didn't argue. He leaned against his car, the sheet metal already hot from the morning sun, and tried not to think of the gun in the man's hand. God, he was sick of guns.

The gate squealed open behind him. "Pull up your shirt." Pax hitched up his T-shirt, and a rough hand quickly patted him down: armpits, waist, legs, and ankles. The chub was more fat than muscle, but still looked capable of pinching off Paxton's head with one hand.

"You don't have to worry about him," another voice said.

Pax turned around. Barron, the Home's regular security guard, stepped out and touched him on the shoulder. "How you doing, son?" he asked. The man's uniform was slept-in. His round face sagged from fatigue. It looked like he hadn't shaved since Clete had tied him up two days before.

"I'm just coming to check on my dad," Pax said.

"Best thing," Barron said. "Get back to normal as soon as you can."

"Right," Pax said. "Normal." He picked up the newspapers

and followed Barron to the front door. The chub with the shotgun stayed outside.

Barron shuffled toward his desk without saying another word. Two other chub men filled a couch in the lobby, looking somber. One of the men nodded at him, but Pax had never seen either of them around the Home; Rhonda had been calling in the reserves. They were older men, perhaps the same age as Harlan, both of them bald and huge, just sets of dark eyes and mouths embedded in massive round bodies like fleshy snowmen. One step from becoming producers themselves.

No one had brought Harlan out to the lobby, and it didn't look like anyone was about to. Pax walked back through the sets of double doors.

His father's door was open. Harlan lay on the bed, half sitting up, eyes on the TV. The size of him came as a shock, every time. The white sheet covering his body made him into a landscape, an arctic mountain range.

"He returns," his father said without looking away from the television.

"I'm sorry it took so long to get here," Pax said—an apology that covered both his late arrival this morning and his absence the day before. "It's still a madhouse downtown."

His father was uninterested in the papers and wanted nothing to do with the news channels—he'd seen enough of Ecuador, he said. He was watching mole rats instead. Green-tinged night-vision cameras somehow followed the whiskered, bucktoothed things through the tunnels. When the show ended, his father made no move to change the channel or look away from the screen. The next program was about the hunt for giant squids.

Pax glanced at the clock on the wall. Half past nine. Too

soon to rush off—he'd just gotten here. He'd give his father another half hour, then get back to the house, where Andrew Weygand and the twins would be waiting for him.

He flipped through the newspapers. *USA Today* and both of the local papers were full of the Changes. The government of Ecuador had declared a state of emergency and sealed the borders to the Los Rios province, even as it refused to admit that the epidemic was indeed TDS. The pictures, though, made it clear that the argo strain was at work. If the disease followed the same course, the B strain would strike in a week or two, and then the C. The estimated death toll had already reached 5,000. By contrast, Switchcreek had lost only 378 the entire summer of the Changes, but that was almost a third of the population. Babahoyo contained 90,000 people. If the ratio held . . .

"Dad." Harlan didn't move his eyes from the TV. *"Dad."*

Harlan's great head turned. Pax said, "Thirty thousand people could be dead before the end of the month."

"Tell me that isn't His judgment," his father said.

Pax thought, Judgment of what—being poor? Living on the equator? But then a voice said, "Dr. Fraelich says it's all just chance."

Aunt Rhonda stood in the doorway holding a paper mask to her face, somehow making the pose seem less like a woman warding off germs than a courtesan flirting at a masquerade. She wore a salmon-pink blouse, a tailored midnight-blue jacket, and a matching knee-length skirt. On her lapel were an American flag pin and a loop of green ribbon. "Haven't you heard? We're surrounded by bunches and bunches of other universes. She says it was inevitable that a virus eventually learned to jump over."

Harlan grunted. "Maybe somebody should ask the doctor who created those universes."

"I'm sure she'd have an answer," Rhonda said.

"Ask her this, then," Harlan said. "In an infinite number of universes, wouldn't one of them *have* to give rise to an all-knowing, all-powerful God? Once he exists anywhere, he exists everywhere—the alpha and the omega."

Rhonda laughed. "Reverend, you could save the devil if you could get him to visit."

"Getting him to stop by is never the problem, Rhonda—it's getting him to leave. But you know that."

Pax sat back, listening to them bat words back and forth. They'd known each other for how long, thirty-five years? Forty? Even enemies had to derive pleasure from such a long relationship.

"And how are you doing, Paxton?" Rhonda asked a few minutes later. Before he could answer she said, "What did you think of the council meeting last night?"

"I'm just glad they're not going to put us in quarantine."

A penciled eyebrow arched above the paper mask. "I'm not so sure about us, but you don't have to worry," Rhonda said. "I'm sure they'll declare all you nice normal people clean and free. You can leave any time you like."

Harlan grunted.

Pax didn't look at him. "I'm not going anywhere," he said.

"Oh, I know, hon," she said, and conspicuously checked a diamond-studded watch. "Well, I've got to run. I hope you'll be watching the news—I've got a major press conference this afternoon. Oh, I almost forgot . . ." She gestured to someone in the hall, then moved aside to let in one of the chubs from the lobby. "You know Lawrence Teestall, don't you?"

"Oh, sure," Pax said, trying to mask his shock. Mr. Teestall had been his junior-high shop teacher. Back then he'd been a short, skinny man with a Brillo pad of bright orange hair. Pax hadn't recognized him at all in the lobby; all resemblance to his old teacher had been buried under an avalanche of fat.

Rhonda said, "Could you just take a few minutes to teach him how to do an extraction? He's good with his hands, I'm sure he'll pick it up in a snap."

"But I don't—"

"Come now, how many times have you watched? Lawrence, just don't let Paxton get sloppy and work bare-handed—the vintage hits him harder than most folks. And don't forget to turn on the news at two. I'd pick channel ten—they've got that nice Asian girl."

Pax needn't have rushed home—the twins hadn't arrived yet. Weygand was pacing around the room with his shirt off and his cargo shorts hanging low on his hips, talking to himself. No, not to himself—he turned, and Pax saw that he wore a tiny earpiece and microphone.

Pax went into the bathroom and closed the door. He pulled the latex gloves from the pocket where he'd stuffed them after the extraction, then turned them in his hands until he found a discoloration in one of them, and touched his tongue to that spot. Just a taste, nothing to incapacitate him. He needed to stay awake today. Then he carefully folded the gloves and tucked them back into his pocket.

When Pax returned to the living room Weygand had stopped talking and sat bent over his laptop. He had the gaunt face and the thin arms of a runner, so that he looked skinnier the more clothes he wore; with his shirt off the muscles of his chest and back were more apparent, as clearly delineated as a Renaissance Jesus stretched on a cross.

Weygand looked up from the screen. "You okay?"

"Was that the twins on the phone?" Pax asked.

"No, that was a guy I know who blogs about DHS. Homeland Security. Besides, the girls don't have my number, do they?"

"Oh, right."

Last night after the town meeting Paxton had tried to get time alone with Rainy and Sandra, but Tommy had hovered a few feet from them the entire time. His smooth face betrayed nothing to Paxton, but his body language spoke volumes. The blank man was still jealous of Paxton, still nervous that his place as stepfather would be usurped. No wonder the girls kept their visits to Paxton's house secret from him. Fortunately Rainy understood that Pax wanted to tell them something; she engaged Tommy in a conversation and in the break Pax managed to tell Sandra to come to his house at 10:00 a.m. with the laptop.

It was already 10:30. Weygand paced, fiddled with his laptop, paced some more. He didn't want to miss Rhonda's press conference, which he somehow knew all about even though Pax hadn't mentioned it. Something about a charity, Weygand said.

Just before noon Pax offered to make Weygand a sandwich. When he brought it out to him Weygand took it one-handed and started to eat, still tapping at the laptop.

Pax said, "So what did your Homeland Security guy say?"

"Not much." Weygand wiped a dot of mayonnaise from his mouth with the back of his hand. "The big question is, what if—hey, is this *baloney*? I haven't eaten baloney in . . . ever."

"It's better fried," Paxton said.

"Wow. That's so authentic. Next you'll be feeding me possum."

"Nobody eats possum anymore," Pax said. "It's all possum substitute now. I Can't Believe It's Not Possum."

Weygand gave him a weird smile. "You know, you're kinda funny when you're high." He nodded toward the kitchen. "What did you do back there?"

"Aw, just a little white lightnin'," Pax said with a drawl. When he was out of sight of the living room he'd taken out the gloves again, but the vintage had dried out. He threw them in the garbage, then went to the freezer, where he kept three partly filled vials. He uncapped one of them, scraped a fingernail along the inside, and touched the icy residue to his tongue. The hit had been less than satisfying. Pax said, "You were talking about the big question."

Weygand smiled, took another bite of his sandwich. After a moment he said, "The thing they're all wondering about is, what if it's not a natural virus? What if it's been genetically engineered?"

"Ah. The massive government conspiracy I've heard so much about." It was by far the most popular explanation for the Changes, at least in the early days of the quarantine. Several people in his church had been certain that secular humanist scientists had experimented on them without their knowledge. Second most popular was the cover-up-of-high-tech-accident theory—Switchcreek as a genetic down-winder story.

"Not our government, man," Weygand said. "They can't even keep their top-secret torture prisons out of the news. I'm talking about those other universes. What if the Changes are a deliberate incursion?"

"The other universe is attacking us? Sure, that makes sense. Every fifteen years they take out some town in the boondocks. In 2030 they'll finally get the Eskimos."

"'Attack' is the wrong word. Think immigration. Colonization. They're trying to cross over."

Pax laughed. "My dad may be a bull elephant, but he's still my dad. I find it hard to believe that he's a colonist from Planet Fat Boy."

"Bull elephant?"

"I meant chub. Charlie. My dad is—" Pax inflated his cheeks, exhaled. "—big."

"Oh, shit. I didn't mean—"

"Don't worry about it," Pax said. "There's a lot of it going around in this town." Weygand didn't seem to know what to say to that. He seemed genuinely sorry. After a moment Pax said, "I think I know what you're getting at. It's not my dad, per se." *Per se.* This may have been the first time he'd said that aloud. "You mean his DNA."

"Exactly," Weygand said. "Any species that could learn to send its genes across the universes would go a long way to ensuring its own survival. The invaders would soon run into competition, though, because whatever species it colonized would *have* to figure out how to replicate too, because now it's competing not only with all the other species on its planet, but with all its alternate selves across the universes."

"Arms race," Pax said, suddenly getting it. Or maybe he wasn't understanding it on his own, he was . . . syncing up. Andrew's thoughts seemed to be spilling into his own. "Argos versus chubs versus blanks."

"Yes!" Andrew said. "And them versus *us*." He hopped up, excited now. "Think about how weird it is that three *distinct* species came out of the Changes. It's almost as if . . . Okay, say that the argos discovered the trick first. Maybe they even did it by accident. But anyway, they replicate into the universe of the betas. Then the betas figure it out—they engineer the virus to work for them. Now argos and betas are together in one universe, and together they invade the universe of the charlies. And so on and so on, across the universes, until they get to us. We're at the front wave of a three-part war."

"Wow," Pax said.

"Yeah, wow."

"So this is what your Homeland Security guy thinks? We're at war?"

"He's not *in* Homeland Security," Weygand said. "He's only nineteen. He writes about them."

"Oh. Sure."

For some reason they both laughed. Weygand sat down next to him. "This is the crappiest couch in the world," he said.

"I should throw it out," Pax said. Weygand's arm was a few inches from his own, radiating heat.

A minute passed, maybe two.

Weygand said, "So, Paxton. What are you thinking right now?"

"I . . . I don't know."

Weygand laughed kindly. "Fair enough." He leaned forward, knees on elbows. Pax regarded the architectural curve of his back, the frets of his spine. "I've been down this road before. Listen, why don't you sober up and we'll talk some more."

Pax lifted his hand, then set it down between Weygand's shoulder blades. Pax felt both his hand against his skin and the heat against his back; touched and toucher at the same time.

After a moment Weygand shook his head, laughing to himself. Or maybe laughing *at* himself. Then he started to get up, and as he rose Paxton's palm slid down his back, each knuckle of his spine delivering a gentle tap. And then the contact was broken.

"I've got to get downtown," Weygand said. "Maybe by the time I get back the twins will have shown up."

Pax nodded.

"And get something to eat, okay, Pax?"

The twins didn't come all that day, or the next.

They'd stayed away before, sometimes for days at a time, but this was the first time Paxton had waited for them, worried for them. The atmosphere in town had grown tense over the weekend. Friday afternoon a dozen beta women had driven to the Lambert Super Wal-Mart for their weekly Co-op shopping trip and walked into a line of pro-quarantine protesters. No one was hurt, but there'd been pushing and shoving; the betas had been forced to leave without their groceries. The store manager said that he'd arranged for the food to be delivered to the Co-op, but he'd made it clear to the reporters that he preferred that the Switchcreek people stayed at home until the protests died down.

Aunt Rhonda kept appearing on his TV screen, pushing for support of her new relief fund: Helping Hands to Babahoyo. She'd announced an 800 number; a software company in Memphis had already put up a supporting website. Three times Pax had seen her give what Weygand started calling the Azzamurkin speech: "As Americans, we've always been the first to reach out to those struck down by tragedy. As Americans, we must share the hard-won knowledge we've gained about TDS. As Americans . . ." The flag pin on her lapel and the green ribbon—for the victims in Ecuador, she said—had become permanent accessories.

Weygand said, "You see what she's doing?" Pax thought, Running for office? But Weygand didn't wait for an answer. "At the same time that she says she's supporting the Ecuadorians, she's saying, They aren't us. *We* are Americans, *we* are Christians. They're just brown people who live far away and happen to have the same disease. She might as well be raising money for earthquake victims."

"I bet they'd rather have had an earthquake," Pax said. The death toll had stalled at 6,500, but only because the Ecuadorian government had clamped down on reporters. Babahoyo had been quarantined "for their protection and ours." Rhonda announced that one of the first tasks of her charity would be to send volunteers to the city—and some of those volunteers would be Switchcreek citizens, led by the mayor herself.

"I'll say this," Weygand said. "She moves fast."

Nothing sexual had happened with Weygand; they never even touched each other after that moment Thursday afternoon. By the time Weygand came home from Rhonda's press conference Paxton was asleep on the couch, and when he awoke Weygand was in the kitchen burning soy burgers and the attraction Pax had felt had vanished. For perhaps an hour he'd been someone Pax desired, someone he *understood*—and then he wasn't.

The next day Weygand helped Pax work on the yard. Pax kept trying to apologize and Weygand repeatedly told him not to worry about it. Pax wanted to explain that he wasn't like one of those gay-for-a-day, frat-party lesbians—he'd slept with a couple of men. A few women too. And it wasn't the vintage that made him suddenly want Weygand—or not *just* the vintage. He'd been this way since leaving Switchcreek. Most of the time he wasn't attracted to anyone at all, and then he was—for a few hours. His desire for whatever body ended up next to him never seemed to last longer than it took him to put on his pants.

Women thought he was gay. Men thought he was straight but playing tourist. And Pax thought he was . . . waiting. The last time he'd felt anything real—the last time *he* felt real—was with Jo and Deke. The three of them had been perfect together, a completed circuit. Everything since had been pantomime.

On Sunday afternoon Weygand told him that he was driving back home in the morning—friends in Amnesty International were organizing a group to drive into Ecuador from Colombia and record what was happening inside the city. Pax thought he was crazy; he could end up in a South American jail. Weygand shrugged it off. "What about this laptop thing? Are we going to do this or not?"

Paxton had no phone number for the twins, and he didn't even know where they lived inside the sprawl of trailers at the Co-op. Nothing to do for it but go over there and ask. "How about you drive?" Pax said.

The gates to the Co-op—the Whitmer farm's old iron cattle gates—were closed. Two teenage girls in white scarves, perhaps a few years older than Rainy and Sandra, sat on the other side in lawn chairs.

"Everybody's getting paranoid in this town," Pax said to Weygand, and got out of the car.

The girls looked at him but didn't get up. A small black music player rested on one of their laps, and they were sharing a single red headphone cord, one earbud apiece.

"Hi, girls," he said. "I'm looking for Sandra and Lorraine—the Whitehall twins?" Stupid: of course they had to know who Sandra and Rainy were.

"Nobody told us you were coming," one of them said.

"I didn't know I needed reservations." He smiled. They watched him with small tight mouths. "So. Can I come in?"

The girls looked at each other. One of them pulled the bud from her ear and walked off toward the center of the compound. She could at least run, Pax thought. The remaining girl inserted the other earpiece and immediately lost interest in him.

Pax looked at Weygand through the windshield, shrugged.

He rested his forearms on the top of a gate and looked up at Mount Clyburn. It was the first week of October, but the afternoon sunlight was still summer-strong. It wouldn't be long until the leaves began to turn, crowning the mountain, then seeping down in a months-long wave until the valley was drenched in color. He'd forgotten how long spring and fall were in Tennessee—in Chicago those seasons went by in a blink, just a couple weeks to toggle the thermometer between Too Damn Cold and Too Damn Hot. Why in the world had he stayed up there? When he turned eighteen he could have moved south, could have moved anywhere. For some reason he'd made the choice binary—Chicago or Switchcreek.

The girl who'd walked off was returning with another beta, a man wearing a baseball cap. Tommy. Sandra and Rainy were nowhere in sight.

Pax ran a hand across the back of his neck. He and Weygand

could leave now, but that would look like they were doing something wrong. Pax waved hello and waited.

Tommy stopped a few feet from the gate. "What can we do for you, Paxton?"

"I was worried about Sandra and Rainy," Pax said.

Tommy tilted his head. "Why would you be worried?"

Pax couldn't read Tommy's tone. Did he know that the twins had been visiting him?

"I heard about the stuff in Lambert Friday, at the Wal-Mart. I thought maybe they'd be upset by what was happening." It sounded lame even to himself. "I can see you guys are taking precautions."

"There are hooligans on the road. Knocking down mailboxes, vandalizing. We thought it better to keep an eye out." Then: "The girls are fine."

"That's great," Pax said. "Do you think I could see them?"

"Who's your friend?"

Pax looked back at the Prius. "His name's Andrew. He was a friend of Jo's."

"No he wasn't," Tommy said.

"You didn't know all her friends, Tommy." He wasn't about to tell Tommy anything about Andrew, or about Brother Bewlay and Jo's online life. "So how about I talk to Rainy and Sandra for a while, and then leave you alone."

Tommy stepped forward and put his hands on the gate. The man was trembling—from rage? Something else?

"The girls are staying home, Paxton. You may be too distracted to notice, but there's a crisis going on. We're not going to have them—*I'm* not going to have them—running around unsupervised, not until it's safe. But even then, even when this blows over?" He glanced at the two girls sitting a few feet away and lowered his voice. "I can't believe you have to be told this. They're twelve-year-old girls, Paxton. You're a grown man. If you come around looking for them again, or if you ever bring them into your house, I'll call the police."

"What? I'm not—"

"I don't know how this works up in Chicago, but here in Tennessee the cops do *not* tolerate pedophiles."

Paxton stepped back, his face hot.

"Good-bye, Paxton." Tommy stood with his hands at his sides, unmoving. After a long moment, Paxton turned, got back into the car.

Tommy was still standing there when the car pulled away.

# chapter 18

"WE CAN*NOT* BE late for the appointment," Donna told him as they stepped down from the Jeep. "The egg-timer is going off."

Deke laughed and plucked the plastic sacks from behind the driver's seat. "They'll keep warm for a couple more minutes. We'll just drop this off and leave."

The only other cars in the Martin driveway were the Reverend's old Crown Vic and Paxton's Tempo—no Prius in sight. He'd heard that Andrew Weygand had left town again, and it looked like he hadn't come back—yet.

The house was looking better than it had in several years. The lawn had been cut sometime in the last week, and the tall growth that had been encroaching on the yard had been hacked back several feet. The old swing set had been dismantled and lay in a pile beside the driveway, next to the ancient plaid couch. Deke made a mental note to take care of those for him—Amos could haul them to the dump in the company truck.

The front door was open. Deke knocked on the frame and leaned in. "P.K.! You up?" It was 9:30 in the morning. He wasn't sure what kind of hours he was keeping.

Paxton walked into the living room, drying his hands on a kitchen towel. "Hey, Deke. Hey, Donna."

He'd lost more weight, and he hadn't been fat to begin with.

At the town meeting a couple weeks ago he'd looked too thin for a skip, but now he was gaunt, his head too big for his neck. If he'd been growing taller at the same time he was thinning out you'd have thought he was turning argo.

Pax motioned them in. He asked them how they were doing, if they'd like something to drink.

"We can't stay," Donna said. "We've got to run to a doctor's appointment."

"We just brought you some chicken and mashed potatoes, some greens," Deke said. "Donna made too much last night and we thought you might be able to take them off our hands."

Pax's smile looked a little forced. "You didn't have to do that. I've got plenty of food."

"Not my food," Donna said. "Why don't I just put it in the fridge, then?"

Deke started to hand her the sack and Paxton quickly said, "I'll do it." He took it from Deke's hand. "Are you sure I can't get you a Coke or something?" He walked back into the kitchen.

Donna looked at Deke, reminding him that the clock was running. She was ovulating, and the doctors at UT were waiting with syringes to suck the eggs out of her. They'd agreed to try an expensive procedure that did something to the egg walls before they introduced Deke's boys to the mix. The words "sperm" and "permeability" were used so often that Deke started calling the procedure "that spermability thing."

Pax said, "I'm out of Coke, but I've got, uh, water."

"No thanks," Deke called. He walked through the living room—it was surprisingly clean—and stooped to get through the kitchen door.

Paxton closed the freezer door, then the fridge door. "So. Nothing serious I hope," he said.

"The doctor?" Deke said. "Naw, just fertility stuff." He squatted and was still taller than Paxton. "So I heard that that Weygand guy was hanging around a couple weeks ago."

"He left to try to sneak into Ecuador." Pax shrugged. "I haven't heard from him since. He's either in by now or dead." Two weeks after the second outbreak, the Babahoyo quarantine was still in full effect. Nobody knew how many were dead in the country, how many had been transformed. Rhonda's Helping Hands campaign had raised close to two million dollars even though it wasn't the only relief fund going. No relief trip had been scheduled yet—she hadn't gotten permission from either government to send a group of volunteers to the city.

Donna made a sound from the living room. Deke glanced back, then said, "Listen, I wanted to apologize."

"For what?"

"I talked to Rhonda about what happened with Clete and them—what they did to you, how they tried to take your father."

"That didn't have anything to do with you."

"Yes, it did. I should have seen it coming. I was supposed to be watching out for you and I—"

"Watching out for me. Really." A tight smile. "Oh, but that's right, you're the Chief. That's your job."

"This is not about my job."

"You're the Chief, you're on the town council, all the argos look up to you . . . You and the Reverend and Rhonda run everything."

"Come on, P.K. . . ."

"Help me out here. How's Rhonda doing it, Deke? Where's she getting all this money? What is she doing with the vintage? Rhonda told me the smart people figure it out on their own. Now, I'm not that smart, but you're the Chief; you must have worked it out by now."

"Now you're just being an idiot," Deke said. He sighed. "Rhonda was talking about Jo, P.K. She was the smart one."

Pax waited. After a moment Deke said, "Rhonda's been skimming the accounts. The TEMA grants, the school funds, especially the medical grants. Jo told me about it. She said she had proof. Copies of the grant forms, bank statements, e-mails. After she died I looked in the house for documents like that but didn't find anything. I was hoping it was on her laptop."

"Jesus, man, you knew all this, and you kept working with Rhonda?"

"I told you, I didn't have the proof. But even if I did—listen, even Jo wasn't ready to take action against her. What Rhonda's doing is illegal, but it may not be bad for the town."

"That's crazy. If she's stealing—"

"Pax, Switchcreek's just a small town, and the clades could be wiped out at any time. Somebody's got to do what it takes to guard the future."

"You took her money," Pax said.

*"What?"*

"Hey, that one stung," Paxton said. "She paid you off, didn't she? You work for her. So how much is she paying you?"

Deke lifted his hand and Paxton flinched.

"Jesus Christ, I'm not going to hit you," Deke said. "I love you, man, but do you know how hard it is not to whack you upside the head when you say shit like that?"

"How you boys doing?" Donna said.

Deke hadn't realized she'd come to the kitchen door. He rose partway out of his crouch and put his hand against the ceiling. "We better get going," he said. "We'll talk about this later."

Donna waited until they'd left the Martin driveway before she said, "You don't work for her."

"I don't know about that," Deke said. "Who paid for this doctor appointment?"

"That money belongs to the clades—all the clades. You've always done the right thing by your people and by your friends. God knows Paxton should know that. And can I say one more time? I do not get you two."

"He's my friend, Donna."

"Even when he talks to you like that?"

"That's just the vintage. Or the lack of it." He shrugged. "What can I say? He's always going to be my friend. There's no choice in it." His friend was the P.K. he'd grown up with. That part of him still had to be in there somewhere—some essential piece that couldn't be changed by drugs or time. "He has a good soul," Deke said.

Donna made a sound and Deke said, "You don't believe in the soul?"

"Honey, I believe in you and me. Everything else—"

Her words were drowned out by the roar of a helicopter. For a few seconds he'd been hearing the chop of helicopter blades, but as they reached the intersection of Piney Road and the highway a dark green helicopter thundered out over the treetops from the northwest and passed over them, heading toward town. A second helicopter flying at the same low altitude followed a few seconds later.

The new curse of Switchcreek: air traffic. The FEMA people had flown in and out several times in the first days of the Ecuador outbreak, and the news choppers from Knoxville had been constantly doing flybys. But these helicopters looked military.

"Any lower I'd have a haircut," Donna said.

Deke turned north onto the highway, but a minute later he had to brake to a stop behind a blue station wagon he recognized. Ahead of the wagon, a green National Guard truck was parked astride both lanes of the highway, its rear wheels almost in the ditch. Maybe they were just trying to turn the thing around and had gotten hung up. Or maybe not.

Deke turned off the Jeep and got out. "Why don't you wait here," he told Donna. She didn't bother to reply; she stepped out and walked with him toward the truck. When they reached the station wagon Deke ducked down to see the woman behind the wheel.

"Howdy, Mrs. Jarpe."

"Oh, hello, Chief." She was a chub woman in her sixties. Before the Changes she'd been the best piano player in town and maybe still was; he hadn't heard her play in years. "They just pulled over in front of me and stopped. I've been sitting here and the truck hasn't moved."

Deke exchanged a look with Donna, then said to Mrs. Jarpe, "Maybe you should turn around and head back to town."

"What? I'll do no such thing. Just tell them to clear the road, Chief."

"I'll see what I can do."

He strolled toward the truck. In the cab were two soldiers masked like motocross riders in goggles and plastic breathers that covered their noses and mouths. From the other side of the truck came the sound of a man barking instructions.

Deke waved to the men in the truck. "Y'all need some help?"

The driver held up a hand. Deke and Donna stopped. Three other masked soldiers came around the hood of the truck with automatic rifles in their hands.

"Whoa now," Deke said, and put on a smile. "What's going on, gentlemen?"

"Go back to your car, sir," one of them said. He sounded young, like a teenager. He nodded at Donna. "Ma'am. Return to town and you'll be—"

"Excuse me?" Donna said.

"We have a doctor's appointment in Knoxville," Deke said.

"I'm sorry, sir," the kid said. "There's a quarantine for the Switchcreek area now in effect. If you go home and turn on your radio you'll hear complete information on the situation."

Donna stepped forward. "Quarantine? Why? We're not contagious."

"Ma'am, there's a quarantine in effect for—"

"Hell, we've been here for thirteen years as a *tourist* attraction," Donna said. "You're telling us that *now* we're contagious?"

Deke put a hand on Donna's shoulder and she knocked it away. "Explain to me," Donna said to the soldier. She stepped forward and the men's guns swung toward her like compass needles. "Come on, explain to me how it is that we're suddenly contagious. It's been two weeks since Babahoyo. We've had every news reporter on the planet walking around down here. *Telemundo* sent a reporter. Are they under quarantine, too?"

Deke could see over the top of the truck now. On the other side, twenty yards away, a dozen men were assembling a barrier made of plastic pylons connected to each other by metal pipes. One of the pylons was being filled with water from a hose running out the side of the truck. He'd never seen that before.

One of the soldiers noticed Deke and said something. The other men looked up, and froze. None of them were holding rifles. Then one of them reached for the sidearm on his hip. The rest of the men ran toward the truck. Toward their guns.

"Donna," he said. "Let's go."

"I'm not going anywhere except Knoxville, right now." She stepped toward the nearest soldier. "We're going down *this* damn road, or I will know the reason why!"

"Donna—" He stepped in front of her to turn her around and he felt something bite him in the shoulder. He wheeled toward the soldiers, thinking—nonsensically—that one of them had thrown a rock at him. One of the soldiers yelled. Before Deke could say anything he was struck twice more, in the chest and in the arm. Only then did he take in the sound of the gunshots.

Donna roared—an almost subsonic shout that concussed the air like a bomb—then bent and leaped forward. She slammed into one of the soldiers and sent him cartwheeling away.

Automatic gunfire erupted—seemingly from everywhere. Donna planted one hand on the ground and spun toward another soldier. She seized both his rifle and an arm in one huge fist and yanked. The man's arm popped from his torso. She tossed it away like a doll part and the man collapsed to the pavement.

Deke lost his balance and fell back on his butt. He looked down at his chest. Blood soaked his shirt.

No one understands what it's like, Deke thought. All the little people thought that being an argo made life easy. Of course you get your way, look how big you are! Of course people respect you, you can break them in half! They didn't understand how much discipline such a body required, how much restraint. His old human faults were still bubbling in his brain, riding his bloodstream. The Changes hadn't erased fear and rage—Deke's daddy had worked too hard pounding those into him for them to go away. Sometimes the urge to strike back, to kill, came on so fast it took everything he had to hold himself in check. Sometimes he didn't have enough.

But it wasn't just Deke—it was true for everyone in his clade. It was the secret they kept among themselves. Each of them knew that idiot strength waited like a boulder at the top of a steep hill. Every day, each of them had to decide not to nudge that rock.

Maybe the next generation of argos would be different. More peaceful souls. He hoped so.

He called Donna's name, but she was beyond thinking now, moving fast. Another soldier collapsed under her fists. Those stupid, sexist bastards—they'd shot him first, even though it was Donna who was the larger of the two, the stronger, the more dangerous. They didn't understand. She was a full-grown argo woman. And they had hurt her man.

More soldiers appeared around each end of the truck, and some under the truck, aiming their rifles up at them. Donna leaped to the nearest man. He screamed in fear, and the rifles burst into new applause.

God she was fierce, and so beautiful. But there were so many soldiers, and their weapons could shred metal. They would kill her. He pushed himself to all fours, grimacing. He hoped that she was wrong, that there really were such things as souls.

Then he heard her bellow in pain. A great weight inside him trembled, shifted, and suddenly tumbled down.

He ran to her side.

# chapter 19

FOR THE FIRST hour and a half of the service Paxton felt as if he were floating above the congregation: apart from the proceedings, immune, unmoved.

Reverend Hooke, dressed in a billowing dark dress that made her look strangely bulky, had started the service with a long prayer that expanded in a widening circle to take in all nouns. She prayed not only for Deke and Donna, but this church, this town, all the people of Switchcreek; she asked God to embrace the soldiers who surrounded them, the people in the nearby towns who feared them, and their fellow Americans across the country. She prayed for the victims in Ecuador and for people the world over who watched the suffering on their television screens.

She had no other sermon. There was no program, she said, no plan; the spirit would lead. Then she opened the pulpit to anyone who wanted to speak.

The first to come forward was an argo woman. She stood at the podium, between two huge caskets of dark gleaming wood. Like all argo necessities, they were custom creations. They'd been fashioned by Deke's employees in the same shop where they'd created the argo-sized pews that this morning had been carried in to fill the front of the sanctuary. For once, the argos were not going to sit in the back.

Paxton found it hard to focus on what the argo woman was saying, or on what was said by the others who came after her. Most were argos, but people from other clades also felt called to say something. Sometimes they spoke only about Deke, sometimes only about Donna, but usually it was about the two of them as a couple, a partnership.

Donna's beta cousin, the one who'd given birth only a few months ago, talked about Deke and Donna's dream of having children. By now everyone knew where they'd been heading when they met the roadblock. The people in the pews around Pax, even the stone-faced betas, sobbed or wept silently, heads held still as tears ran down cheeks and into their collars. Pax sat impassively, wondering at the intensity of the emotion and at his own detachment. He should have tasted a little vintage before the service. He felt as if he were sitting in the middle of a burning house, breathing smoke like it was fresh air, unable to feel the heat.

His father would have been crying by now, Paxton was sure. Harlan had been stunned by the news of Deke's and Donna's deaths; during Paxton's visits this morning and the day before he'd been incapable of saying more than a few words. Yet he wouldn't come to the service. Aunt Rhonda said she would have allowed it, that her employees could have transported him, wheeled him inside, and guarded him, but Harlan refused. Pax knew that he was intensely embarrassed by his size and must have been petrified that he'd humiliate himself if the vintage struck during the service. The fact that the funeral would be held in his own church only made it more unbearable. "You go," his father had told him, and it had been not so much a command as a plea.

The stories and testimonials went on and on. The church

was packed as full as he'd ever seen it, and the doors were propped open so that the scores of people standing outside could hear. There were no reporters inside or out, no nonresidents at all—those had been bussed to an alternate quarantine site near Louisville, Kentucky. Already some of those reporters had been examined and declared clear of TDS-causing plasmids—whatever those were. Neither were there soldiers; they'd pulled back to their improvised headquarters at the Cherokee Hotel and to the newly reopened and fortified checkpoints. No one except the National Guardsmen had entered the town in three days.

Pax knew that he should stand up and speak for his friend. Who else here could tell about the boy he'd been before the Changes, before he'd become the Chief? The baseball fanatic who so loved a good game that he'd once broken a finger in the third inning and didn't tell anyone until the next day. The shy daredevil who'd invented Hillbilly Bobsled. The artist who'd built a dozen birdhouses just because his crazy-ass father mentioned—once—that he liked to watch the blue jays squabble. Nobody who knew only the Chief would believe how scared Deke had been of his old man.

Reverend Hooke stood in silence, waiting for anyone else to step forward.

Pax gripped the pew in front of him and stared at his hand. He could pull himself up, walk to the front. But his hand would not unclench, and seemed to become something alien, a knuckled stump that did not belong to him. A foreign object attached to someone else's arm. His body felt heavy as river stone.

And then the reverend nodded to a back row, and the moment passed. His hand fell into his lap.

Aunt Rhonda came slowly forward, an immensity in pink

like a parade float: pale pink dress and jacket, a wide pink hat with a brim ringed with white flowers, pink eye shadow and lipstick. Her lilac perfume followed like a bridal train.

Rhonda stepped up on a hidden riser and regarded them over the podium. Her mouth was pursed, and her mascara had smeared darkening her eyes. It was the first evidence Pax had ever seen that the woman could cry.

He could no more concentrate on the words of her eulogy than he could anyone else's, but he took note that her voice often trembled and at times broke, and that what appeared to be actual moisture made her eyes gleam. Performance or true passion? He couldn't decide. Maybe a smart person could tell the difference. The people around him certainly seemed to be moved. Their tears flowed; they leaned toward her, rapt.

"They call us freaks," Rhonda said. "They call us mistakes. They call us *unnatural*. But everyone in this room was blessed to know two giants. I'm not talking about their size. I'm talking about their spirit, their goodness, their courage. And what was their reward? The world cut them down, cut them down like the Old Soldier. *That* is the unnatural act. And that is the great mistake our captors have made.

"They thought they could *contain* them," Rhonda said. "But Deke and Donna cannot be contained. *We* cannot be contained. We *shall not* be contained."

Someone shouted an amen. Around Paxton people began to stand; the entire congregation was getting to its feet. Paxton rose with them, but he kept his head down and gripped the pew in front of him. People murmured and shouted. He'd never suspected that Rhonda could deliver a fire-and-brimstone sermon. But of course she'd been watching his father all those years.

At some signal he didn't see, the argos in the front rows turned to face the congregation.

Pax recognized Amos, the one-armed man who worked in Deke's shop, and a few others he'd either known before the Changes or had seen around town over the past few months. Most were strangers, gray- and white-skinned giants, some dressed in good suits, others in overalls and short-sleeved shirts and long cotton dresses.

And then they began to sing.

The first blast of sound rocked him back. The pew vibrated under his hands, traveled into his chest, buzzed the bones of his jaw.

He'd never heard so many argos sing at once, and never on their own; he'd only heard them in mixed choirs, taking the bass line in songs with the other clades. But this, this was something new, purely argo. New music that required previously unimagined vocal parts: Sub Bass, Deep Bass, Nether Bass, Double Mineshaft. He knew there must be more registers below his hearing, sub-foghorn frequencies that propagated miles through the Earth's crust: Tectonic Bass.

The song went on for five minutes, ten, fifteen. The throb and thrum hammered him back into his body; he gripped the pew as waves of sound beat against his face and chest and thighs, chorus after chorus after chorus. He didn't know what song the choir sang, but he sang with them, head back and mouth wide. He sang and he waited for the tears to come. He waited, teetering on the edge of that release, rocking in the embrace of that deep sound.

But no. He was dry. Dry as ancient skin, and the singing beat him like a hollow drum.

---

On the fourth day of the quarantine, soldiers brought him coupons.

Six masked national guardsmen knocked hard on his door at eight in the morning. Paxton came out in the T-shirt and shorts he'd been sleeping in. He couldn't tell how old the men were, or if they were frightened to be knocking on doors that could be answered by testosterone-crazed sumo wrestlers or twelve-foot trolls or hairless women who didn't need men to breed.

"Trick or treat," Pax said. It was only ten days to Halloween.

If they were relieved that Paxton looked normal their masks hid it. A man at the front of the group held out his hand. "How do you do," he said, his voice muffled. "I'm Colonel Duveen."

Pax had heard of him. The Maximum Leader. Chief Jailer. "Are you sure you want to touch me?"

The man didn't drop his arm. Finally Pax shook his hand. His gloved hand.

The other soldiers were spread out along the front lawn, and one of them faced the driveway. They held their rifles a little too at-the-ready for Paxton's taste. He wondered if any of these men had been at the roadblock. If any of those rifles had fired at his friend.

"I'm personally visiting each resident," the colonel said. "I want you to know that my door's always open. The guard is here to help you all get through this." He nodded at one of the soldiers and he—she?—handed Pax several small sheets of blue paper.

"You can use these at Bugler's Grocery," Colonel Duveen said.

"Use them for what?" Paxton asked. The unevenly cut slips looked like they'd been made on a photocopier.

"Food, home products, and medical supplies," he said. "We'll be ensuring regular delivery every few days." The Bugler's had been largely emptied in the first two days of the quarantine, instantly spawning a black market.

"For how long?" Pax asked. The government said that atypical plasmids had been discovered in the blood of changed people in Switchcreek, and supposedly in the veins of Babahoyo residents. He didn't know what a typical plasmid was, much less an atypical one, and no one had been able to tell him how they would check for their absence.

"As long as it takes, son."

"You realize nobody believes you, right?" Pax said.

"Pardon?"

"This is bullshit. This 'epidemiological hot zone' business—there's nothing contagious, and you know it."

Colonel Duveen didn't move, but the soldiers behind him shifted their feet, adjusted the angle of their rifles. The tension escalated by several degrees.

"You're being used," Paxton said. He wanted to poke the man in his chest, dare him to fire. "How's it feel to be occupying the town of your fellow Americans? Like it better than Baghdad?"

"If you have any questions about the supply program," the colonel said smoothly, "just call the number on each slip of paper." Then: "Have a good day."

The squad backed away and climbed into a Humvee. The colonel climbed into the front passenger seat. As the vehicle pulled away, one of the soldiers near a side window took off his mask and wiped his forehead with his arm.

Hot zone my ass, Paxton thought.

At least the government hadn't cut the cable or phone lines—yet. Most people in town were convinced a blackout was coming any day now. First the landlines, then the satellite and cell phone signals. The prevailing opinion was that once the town was completely isolated, the National Guard would quietly ship them off in small groups to a secret prison.

In the meantime, Paxton had no need to call anyone or leave town. He planned to work on the house, finish cleaning up the yard, visit his father.

And oh yeah, cut down on the vintage.

When he arrived at the Home he found that his father hadn't left the bed since yesterday afternoon. He'd pissed himself hours before, and still needed to go. Pax worked the controls of the bed and helped him to his feet. Once he was upright Harlan could shuffle to the bathroom.

Pax was angry, but there was no one to complain to. Rhonda wasn't in the building, and most of the staff hadn't shown up for work. The two chub men who were on duty said that they hadn't been working the night before.

Pax helped his father shower—soaking Pax's shirtsleeves in the process—and then supported him as he dropped into the huge wheelchair. Pax put on one of Harlan's huge T-shirts, then pushed him into the atrium and parked him in front of the big windows where the sunlight poured in.

Pax draped his damp shirt across the back of the chair next to him and sat, exhausted. Together they waited for the vintage to flow in like the tide.

There were no newspapers to distract them—Mr. DuChamp

hadn't received any new issues since the start of the quarantine—so they sat before the windows and looked across the foothills to Mount Clyburn. During the first quarantine, the hill the Home sat on would have been beyond the southern checkpoint, but Rhonda had somehow negotiated a new border with the National Guard. She made sure everyone knew that she held daily meetings with Colonel Duveen and had won concessions. She said she'd gotten the curfew moved from dusk to 9:00 p.m. She'd probably take credit for the coupons unless they turned out to be unpopular.

"The leaves are turning," his father said. Pax nodded. Red and gold dotted the mountain and the tops of the highest hills, each tree a pixel.

After awhile Pax said, "Did I ever tell you about Hillbilly Bobsled?"

Harlan looked at him quizzically.

"It was something Deke thought of," Pax said. "In the fall, when the gullies were full of leaves, Deke and Jo and me would cut up cardboard boxes and make sleds. After awhile the leaves would get packed down and you could really fly."

"Like to scare me to death."

"You saw us? You never stopped us."

"Paxton, you may think my sole job as your father was to stamp out every joy in your life—"

"I never said that."

"You didn't have to."

Pax started to reply, then stopped himself. He wasn't here to fight. He took a breath, exhaled.

His right hand was trembling again. He moved his hands to his lap, left hand over the right. The tremor had shown up a couple days ago, coming and going at random. He felt as if he were losing ownership of his body. Nerves fired without permission, muscles twitched in response—a thousand conversations he wasn't privy to.

"So you went to the funeral," his father said. "A lot of people?"

"The whole town showed up," Pax said. "So many people didn't get in that they're going to have an additional viewing tonight. The burial's tomorrow morning. It was a good service, though. You would have liked it. A lot of people stood up to speak."

"Did Elsa Hooke do a good job? What did she preach on?"

"She didn't really preach." His father frowned. He couldn't understand why pastors would pass up the chance to bring the salvation message, especially at the golden opportunity of a funeral, where the unsaved were both in church and in a mood to contemplate the disposition of their souls. "Too many people wanted to speak," Pax explained. "It was really Rhonda that delivered the sermon. People got pretty worked up. Afterward, folks were talking about a protest."

"What kind of protest?" Harlan asked.

"I don't think they know yet. Something after the burial."

"Rhonda's going to get more people shot," he said.

"If we don't stay visible, Dad, they'll make us disappear."

Harlan peered at him. "Who came up with that one?"

Pax looked away, annoyed. Was it so impossible that he could have thought of that on his own? After a moment he said, "It was on Rhonda's blog."

"Her what?"

"Her videos? She posts one every day." With the cable and phone lines intact, Rhonda had been able to hold regular press conferences via phone, and she'd expanded her Helping Hands website to include a daily video message from Switchcreek. Harlan didn't say anything. "Her website, Dad. Have you ever gone on the web?"

"Yes, I've gone on the web," he said disdainfully.

Pax doubted if he had. "We should order high-speed Internet for the house—we already have cable."

"We don't need the Internet."

"And fix up the living room. I've already started pulling up the carpets."

"What?"

"Dad, they're thirty years old and they stink. The floors are hardwood, so since we can't get new carpets until after the quarantine I thought I'd refinish them."

"Paxton . . . ," Harlan said quietly.

"I've never done it before, but I can ask people. I bet some of the argos at Alpha Furniture would know how."

"Paxton, she's not going to let me go home, no matter how clean or fixed up the house is."

Pax glanced around. Rhonda's office door was closed—he knew she wasn't at the Home, but he still had to check—and no one else was in the atrium. "I'm going to force her," he said.

Harlan pursed his lips, somehow expressing both pity and frank disbelief.

"Deke knew it," Pax said, his voice low. "Jo knew it. She had proof Rhonda was ripping off the town. I'll find it, and then I can—"

"Stop it, Paxton."

"Are you telling me you don't want out of here? Look what happened this morning, Dad. They're not taking care of you. Things are falling apart."

"That's the first time that's happened. I'll get by."

"You hate it here. I've felt what it's like—" He almost said, *Felt what it's like to be you.* "I know you're dying to get out of here. I've been dreaming about it."

"Your dreams told you this," he said skeptically.

"You know what I mean," Pax said. "Not dreams, exactly." Some nights when he took the vintage, distances collapsed, the lines between self and not-self disappeared. He'd lie in the dark not knowing which bed, which body he inhabited. His father's despair became his own.

"Oh, Paxton," his father said. He looked disappointed—that particular frown that could wound Pax so effortlessly. "Every drunk thinks he's found truth in a bottle." He held up a big hand before Paxton could object. "Look at yourself, Son. You're half-starved."

"I'm fine. I admit I'm not eating all the fried crap I used to eat, but—"

"I want you to stop coming," his father said. "Starting now. And when the quarantine is over, or whenever you can, I want you to go back home to Chicago."

"You're not doing this to me again," Pax said.

"What are you talking about?"

"Come on." He couldn't stand it when Harlan played dumb. "You sent me away once. I'm not going to let you do it again."

"I did that for your own good—I'm doing *this* for your own good."

"You did it for yourself, Dad. You were petrified people would talk and you'd lose your church. You were ashamed."

Harlan's face reddened. "That didn't have a damn thing to do with it. Do you even remember what you were like? You were the one who was—where are you going?"

"This isn't happening," Pax said, meaning the day's vintage. He picked up his shirt that he'd laid over the chair back. "I'll come back in the morning."

"Sit your ass down."

His father never swore, and he'd done it twice in ten seconds. Paxton put his hands in pockets but didn't sit. He kept his face neutral and waited.

"Please," Harlan said.

Pax breathed for a moment, thinking, and then pulled the chair over a few feet so that they could sit opposite each other.

"You were special," his father said. The sun was in his face; he squinted and looked at the floor next to Paxton's feet. "You'd been passed over. God had plans for you beyond this town. Nobody knew if the Changes would start again, or if they'd quarantine us again. Either way, if you didn't leave here you'd be trapped.

"I was trying to save your life, Paxton. Your mother wanted you to go to college, get married to a nice girl, have children. You couldn't have any of that here. And if the Changes came back and killed you, or turned you into something . . ."

Harlan shook his head, and looked up. Tears glittered in his eyes. Paxton sighed.

Somehow his father had recast everything from that year. It wasn't his anger at Jo Lynn's pregnancy, or his fear that his only son might be some kind of triple pervert who was fucking both Jo and Deke, or his dread that the whole town would find out and drive him out of his church . . . No, it was purely for the love of his son.

"I was only trying to spare you," his father said. "All this . . . disease. This death."

Pax leaned back. "Well," he said quietly. "That didn't quite work, did it?"

Jo had died anyway. Deke had died anyway. It didn't matter if Pax was in Switchcreek or Chicago or halfway around the planet. His presence couldn't protect them, and distance couldn't protect him.

He was alone. The sole surviving member of the Switchcreek Orphan Society. Hell, he was the fucking president.

"You have to understand," his father said, the words slurring. "Nobody knew. I was only trying, trying to . . ." The smell of vintage charged the air.

"I know, Dad," Pax said. He stood and walked to retrieve the extraction kit.

When he finally heard the banging at the front door he thought the soldiers had returned. It was 9:30, a half hour past the official curfew. Pax put down the mallet and scraper and turned off the radio. The hallway was a mess; the carpet had come up cleanly enough, but the ancient rubber backing had disintegrated into something like tar and had glued itself to the wood. It had taken him hours to scrape the living room, chipping away at piece after piece. He'd slowed as he tired, and so the hallway was taking as long as the front room.

He walked to the living room, rubbing his palms on his jeans. The banging stopped, and suddenly the front door pushed open.

"Jesus Christ, Tommy," Pax said. The beta man stood in the doorway, holding the handle. "It's after curfew. You nearly gave me—"

"Where are they?" Tommy said.

"Where's who?" Pax said, though he knew perfectly well who he meant. "And what the hell are you doing barging into my house?"

Tommy walked across the room, put his head through the kitchen door. "Sandra! Rainy!"

He turned, marched toward Paxton. "Are they in the bedrooms? They better not be in the bedrooms."

"The girls aren't here," Pax said, and stepped aside as Tommy went past him. "I haven't seen them in weeks, not since the town meeting." He realized that he hadn't seen them at Deke's funeral either, though they might have been there. Much of the day had been a blur.

Tommy opened his father's bedroom door, then the guest room. When he reached for Paxton's childhood bedroom Pax grabbed his arm. "That's enough, Tommy."

Tommy spun and seized Pax by the throat. His grip was incredibly strong, much stronger than those thin beta arms suggested. His lips pulled back to reveal small white teeth. Then he began to march Pax backward down the hall.

Pax backpedaled, prying at the man's fingers, and then he stumbled over the radio and Tommy thrust him away, sent him sprawling to the floor.

"You have no idea what it's like," Tommy said, breathing hard. "To love them this much. To feel as *helpless* as this."

Pax sat up, coughing.

"I feel sorry for you," Tommy said. "When I was like you, I felt nothing for anybody else. I couldn't even see the *point* of feeling anything." He bent, picked up the mallet at his feet. It was a big chunk of metal on a wood handle that Paxton's grandfather had owned, a tool too primitive to wear out. "Becoming a beta saved me. Becoming a father saved me. Suddenly I could see the future—it became real. Generations of grandchildren stretching out in an unbroken line, clear as day. More real than you are."

"The girls aren't here," Pax said. "I don't know where they are."

"Tell the truth."

"Search the fucking house! I told you, I haven't seen them since the meeting."

"They weren't at Jo's house," Tommy said. "This is the only other place they'd go."

"Then maybe you don't know them as well as you think you do."

Tommy stared down at him. The mallet twitched in his hand. Then he crouched and leaned in so that their foreheads almost touched. Even this close, inches away, his eyes were empty, his face as indifferent as a wall.

"You won't be seeing them again, Paxton," he said quietly. "You won't be able to find them. You won't be allowed to even look for them. There's too much that depends on them. If you even got within the same state, I'd be forced to kill you. Without a second thought."

Tommy rose to his feet, the mallet still in his hand. "I wanted to warn you. I owe the twins that much."

He walked to the living room. Pax sat very still.

A moment later he heard a double clunk—the mallet dropping to the floor—and then a few seconds after that the sound of Tommy's Bronco starting.

He waited a short while longer, and then Paxton pushed himself to his feet. He went into the kitchen, opened the junk drawer, and found the flashlight. Dead, of course. He shook out the corroded batteries and replaced them with the D-cells from the radio; a few shakes and the light came on.

He grabbed his car keys, walked to the front door, then turned back to the kitchen. The bag Weygand had left for him was still on the kitchen table. He picked it up, then quickly added to it a couple cans of soup, a box of Saltines, and a small plastic jar of Peter Pan peanut butter.

He looked at the freezer door, then opened it. On the top rack were two old vials and the six fresh ones he'd extracted this morning—the most he'd ever had at one time. The father load.

Pax tucked one of the plastic tubes into his front pocket, and left the house before he decided to open it.

# chapter 20

IT WAS NOT yet ten, but the night was already pitch-black, the moon snuffed by clouds, and Piney Road was a ribbon of lesser black winding through the trees. Pax hoped the Guard didn't have curfew patrols out on the smaller, interior roads. Or if they did, that they were already busy chasing Tommy.

Pax turned south onto Sparks Hollow Road. A hundred yards before the T intersection with Creek Road he stopped and cut his headlights. He reached for the flashlight and turned it on.

He eased the car forward, driving with his head out the window, playing the feeble light of the flashlight across the road ahead of him. A few feet from the intersection he turned off the flashlight and nosed ahead. To his right was a dim glow that had to be the guard shack or the interior lights of some vehicle. Did Humvees have dome lights?

The western checkpoint was only a quarter mile down Creek Road to his right, a straight shot. The guards would see headlights as soon as he pulled out, and then as he drove away his taillights would be glowing like fox eyes.

But he had to go east only five hundred, six hundred yards before the road bent again and he'd be out of their sight. He could drive blind for a couple football fields, right? And if he drove into a ditch, so be it. It was only a fucking Ford Tempo.

He turned the wheel left and gently tapped the gas. He could see nothing; the windshield was a black canvas. At any moment he expected to bang into a tree or tilt off the road into the ditch. He leaned over the wheel, ears straining, eyes wide.

Thirty seconds passed and he couldn't stand it any longer. He touched the brake—and the red glow lit up behind him. Shit! He'd forgotten about the brake lights!

Fuck it, he thought. He switched on the parking lights and accelerated. The faint yellow glow barely illuminated the pavement in front of him, but he thought he could make out the edges of the road.

Thirty seconds later he almost drove into the side of the mountain as the road hooked a hard right. He cranked the wheel, then flicked on the headlights to full and gunned it. He rifled through the single-lane bridge at fifty miles per hour and swung through the next big curve with wheels squealing.

No headlights appeared in his rearview mirror, no small-arms fire shattered his back window.

Jo's mailbox appeared faster than he expected. He braked hard, swung onto the driveway, and snaked up the drive. The little house was dark, the patch of gravel out front empty of cars.

He shut off the Ford and got out, his heart still beating fast. He walked quickly to the edge of the slope, where he could look down on the stretch of shadow where the road lay. No headlights, no sirens. The only sound was the rattle of leaves in the chill breeze. His right hand shook along with the invisible leaves.

He patted the vial of vintage in his pocket but didn't take it out.

All right, then.

He walked back to the house, calling, "Sandra! Rainy!"

---

He went from room to room through the dark, using only the flashlight because the house lights might attract Tommy or the Guardsmen. The girls weren't inside, but he'd guessed that—known it—as soon as he'd entered.

He went out to the back door and flicked the light across the backyard. The tree seemed to jump out at him, gray bark materializing out of the night. He raised the beam of light until he saw the bit of frayed rope still dangling from the tree limb. It would take a strong man to hoist someone up into the tree. An iron grip to hold on while he slipped the rope around her neck.

Paxton walked to the edge of the lawn where the forest began. "Rainy! Sandra! It's me, Paxton." He walked into the trees. "Girls? You can come out now." He stumbled against a root, stumbled again, and aimed the light up into the canopy. "Tommy's gone—he's already checked the house. Come inside. I'll make you some soup.

"I have Sal-*tee-eens,*" he sang out.

He swung the light across the ground. A dirt path ran up into the trees, climbing the side of Mount Clyburn. He followed it with the light—and froze.

A small black figure hung from a tree branch, legs slowly twisting.

He shouted wordlessly, and the next moment the silhouette became a girl hanging by her arm. She let go and dropped to the ground, landing easily. She straightened and smiled into the glare of his light: a bald, dark-skinned girl dressed in jeans with a torn knee.

"Rainy?"

She ran down the path to him, her huge backpack bouncing, and threw her arms around him. "Paxton! We missed you!" Her hug nearly drove the breath from his lungs.

"You scared the hell out of me!" he said.

She laughed—he'd forgotten how she could laugh.

"Where's Sandra?" he asked.

"She's coming."

They walked up to meet her halfway. She looked like an old woman: she wore a blanket draped over her shoulders, and below that was a long dress and furry boots. The path was steep so that when they reached each other her head was above his. She leaned down to him from her hips, embracing him at the shoulders like a grown-up. She seemed years older.

"You look cold, Sandra. Come on, let's get you in the house. I brought food." Then quickly: "Don't worry, Tommy's not there. He's already checked the house and left."

The girls didn't answer. He'd have to decide how much to tell them, and how quickly. First, he thought, food.

They searched for another flashlight, and when they couldn't find one they decided that it would be safe enough if they pulled all the drapes and set one or two lamps on the floor—no overhead lights. He warmed up the cans of soup on the stove—Rainy said, "Of course it's soup, it's the only thing you know how to cook"—while Sandra, wearing the blanket like a poncho, sat at the table making hors d'oeuvres of Saltines and peanut butter. "I should have brought popcorn," Pax said. "This is like a sleepover."

"We've never had a sleepover," Sandra said.

"What, never?"

"When we lived here, nobody was allowed to come over," Rainy said. "And when we lived at the Co-op, everyone was already there."

Sandra kept apologizing for not bringing the laptop and for not coming to see him, even though it wasn't her fault or Rainy's: Tommy had grounded both of them the night of the town meeting. "We were watched all the time," Sandra said. "Either Tommy or the white-scarf girls."

"What's with those scarves?" Pax asked. "Do you get them when you reach thirteen or something?"

Sandra laughed. Rainy looked at him with those flat eyes. "No."

"How am I supposed to know?" he asked.

"That isn't a Co-op thing—not the Co-op Mom started," Rainy said. "Some girls just started wearing them."

"To show they're pure," Sandra said. She leaned across the table, gave Rainy a peanut butter–smeared cracker, and Rainy placed it in Paxton's mouth.

"You need to eat more than us," Rainy said. Then: "They're not *beta* enough. Older women, like Mom and the reverend, they're tainted."

He made a questioning noise and tried to swallow the cracker.

"You know . . ." Sandra said.

"You mean sex?" Pax asked.

"Sex with men," Sandra said.

Rainy shook her head. "The white-scarf girls think it's something special that they went through the Changes before they went through puberty," she said. "Like a hat'll make them closer to natural-born."

"Like us," Sandra said.

"Right," Pax said. "You don't need no stinkin' hat."

"We're the first natural-borns," Sandra said. "The white-scarf girls practically *worship* us."

"And hate us even more," Rainy said.

He found bowls in the cupboards and rinsed them out. At least the water was on. And the electricity. "Hey," he said. "Did your mom own this place or rent it?" Somebody had to be paying the utilities. The twins looked more blank than usual. "Never mind." He doled out the soup, and the girls made him clean and fill a bowl for himself.

After awhile he said, "So these scarf girls, why don't they like you?"

"I said hate," Rainy said. Then she shrugged. "They hated Mom, and we sort of inherited it."

"But why? What did she do to them?"

Sandra looked at Rainy. Rainy said nothing.

"Girls, come on," Pax said. "I know she left the Co-op for some reason. You told me that she argued with lots of people."

"Mom had an abortion," Rainy said.

"Rainy!" Sandra shouted.

"He should've already known that," Rainy said to her.

Pax looked at the table for a time. "You're right," he said. "I should have known that." Jesus, why hadn't he come back sooner? Why hadn't he reached out to Jo? He'd left her to raise the girls alone, but he'd told himself she was better off without him. She was the self-assured one, and she had Deke. Hell, she had an entire clade to help her raise the girls and look out for her. He hadn't suspected for a moment that pregnancies would keep coming, or that her people would turn on her.

"So," Pax said. "They exiled her."

"You don't know how our clade feels about . . . that," Rainy said. “The white-scarf girls were outraged. They threatened her. And the doctor too. They burned things on Dr. Fraelich’s lawn. We had to leave.”

“Without Tommy,” Pax pointed out. “Did he threaten her too?”

*Generations of grandchildren stretching out in an unbroken line,* Tommy had said. *More real than you are.*

“He would never hurt Mom,” Sandra said.

Pax said, “You told me they argued all the time. He must have been furious that she’d had an abortion.”

“Stop saying that word!” Sandra said. “Stop talking about it!” She pushed away from the table and stumbled as she got up. Rainy leaped up to catch her and Sandra shoved her away and ran from the room, blanket trailing like a cape.

Rainy looked at him, her face unreadable, then walked after her sister, calling softly, “Sandra, Sandra, come on now, sweetie . . .”

A half hour later he knocked softly and went inside the girls’ bedroom. The room was dark, but he made out Sandra’s nightgown-clad shape on the lower bunk, and Rainy sitting on the floor beside her, one hand on her sister’s back.

Pax crouched down. “Already asleep?” he whispered.

“She’s been tired lately,” Rainy said. “It’s the stress.” She sounded so adult.

He nodded. “Say, how would you like to help me with something?”

She followed him out of the room and closed the door carefully behind her. In the kitchen she saw the laptop open on the table, the bumper sticker on the lid upside down now. Christian Fish looked the same flipped or not, but poor Darwin Fish seemed to be on its back with its legs in the air.

"You looked in our backpacks," Rainy said angrily.

"I picked it up and it was heavy—"

"You looked in our backpacks!"

He opened his mouth, shut it. "You're right. I shouldn't have done that."

Rainy blinked at him. "Well, we did bring it for you."

"And you haven't gotten past the password yet," Pax said.

"No, but the hacker guy already left town, didn't he?"

"He left me instructions. And tools." He showed the things that Weygand had left for him: two cans of compressed air, a Phillips screwdriver, a four-gigabyte thumb drive, and a sheet of notebook paper with six numbered steps—and several asterisks.

Rainy looked at the laptop. "Show me."

Weygand had explained the procedure several times, and Pax was reasonably sure about the details. He handed Rainy the Phillips screwdriver, and she set about opening the bottom panel of the laptop that allowed access to the RAM cards.

Pax read over the instructions again. "Okay, stand by with the compressed air."

He took out the laptop's battery, plugged in the power cord, and turned on the laptop. At the log-in screen he typed a series of random characters—anything would do, Weygand had said, because regardless of what was typed the operating system would retrieve the encrypted password off the hard drive, unencrypt it, and hold it in memory so that it could be compared to the typed characters. The clear text password only existed in RAM, never on the hard drive where hacking software could get at it. If the log-in succeeded, or if the computer was turned off, the clear text would be instantly erased.

The key to the whole process, Weygand said, was redefining *instantly*.

The screen came back with an incorrect password warning. "Ready?" Pax asked. He tilted up the laptop to expose the open compartment on the bottom. "Go."

Rainy blasted the opening with the compressed air. After ten seconds she switched hands. "It's cold," she said.

"That's the point. Keep going." Weygand had said that information in RAM didn't disappear for twenty or thirty milliseconds—and if the RAM card was immediately chilled, the information could persist for up to a minute.

When the can started to sputter he yanked out the power cord and the screen went black. "Here we go," Pax said. He grabbed the thumb drive, fumbled it into one of the laptop's USB ports, and plugged in the machine.

The screen remained black.

"What's supposed to happen?" Rainy asked.

Pax picked up the instruction sheet. "It's supposed to boot from the USB drive. There's some kind of hacker operating system that's supposed to load and go looking through RAM for the password."

"It's not even blinking," Rainy said.

"I can see that."

How much time had passed, thirty seconds? Maybe the USB port was dead. He looked at the side of the laptop and saw there was another port next to the first.

Another ten seconds passed. Fifteen. He yanked out the thumb drive and unplugged the laptop. Then he put the drive into the second port and plugged it in again.

"Should you have done that?" Rainy said.

"I have no idea."

The screen flashed, and the Macintosh loading screen appeared. In a few seconds the log-in dialog box appeared.

"Shit."

"It's okay, Paxton," Rainy said, and patted his hand. Her fingers were cold.

"It was probably working in the first port! I should have tested this first. All right, we're going to try this again." He picked up the instruction sheet and started reading through the steps yet again.

"Tommy says you're a junkie," Rainy said.

He jerked his head up. "What?" He could feel the heat in his cheeks. "That's crazy, hon. Do you even know what a junkie is?"

"We know about the vintage. We've taken care of you while you were on it."

"I don't think you understand—"

"We're worried about you, Paxton. Both of us are. We want you to stop hurting yourself."

He put down the paper. "I'm working on it," he said. He smiled. "The problem is, I'm a better person when I take vintage than when I don't."

"I don't believe that."

"It's true, hon. I just, uh, *feel* more." He picked up the screwdriver, ran his thumb along the metal. "It's hard to explain, but I get this feeling of, I guess, connection." He laughed. "Honestly, sometimes I lose track of where I stop and other people begin. Even people I have trouble relating to, on the vintage I can talk to them." Even dead people, he thought. His conversation with his mother had been better than any he'd had with her while she was living. "I can just . . . love them."

Rainy took the screwdriver out of his hand and put it on the table. "Maybe you should try doing it without the vintage."

She regarded him with that preternatural blank calm. After a moment he said, "You know, you're pretty clever for a twelve-year-old."

"You don't know many twelve-year-olds."

"Seriously, you're the smartest kid I've ever met. You remind me so much of your mom."

"Don't say that," she said. "Tommy says that all the time."

"Okay . . ." he said. Who *wouldn't* want to be Jo Lynn Whitehall? Pax certainly did. Maybe they didn't like it because of the way Tommy said it. "You know," Pax said, "You haven't told me yet why you and Sandra ran away from him."

She wouldn't look at him. She went to the sink, picked up a cloth towel.

"Rainy, did he hurt you? Or Sandra?"

"Tommy wouldn't hurt us," she said. "Not like that." She rubbed the cloth along the edge of the counter. "He wants to take us away. Out of Switchcreek."

"Ah," Pax said.

She turned to face him. "You knew?"

"Tommy came looking for you tonight," Pax said. "He said some things."

"What are you going to do about it?"

"It's an empty threat, Rainy. Tommy can't leave Switchcreek—soldiers are guarding all the roads."

"No, there's a plan," she said. "A plan to sneak us out. A couple of the white-scarf girls told us. People in the Co-op are working on it."

"What? Why? Why would they let him take you?"

Rainy looked away. "We told you—we're special."

"Yeah, the natural-born thing. But there are other natural-borns, aren't there? Why you two?"

She shrugged. "Because we're the first, I guess."

"Rainy, this doesn't make any sense. If you're that special, they wouldn't just let Tommy run off with you, they'd protect you."

"They think that's what they're doing."

"This is bullshit," Pax said. He got up from the table. "When was this supposed to happen?"

"In the morning."

"What?"

"That's why we left tonight. We can't trust Tommy, or the reverend."

"Wait a minute. How are they going to get you out? There are checkpoints, helicopters—"

"I don't know, they didn't tell us that!"

Jesus, he thought. Tommy was going to get them killed like Deke and Donna.

"All right, listen," Pax said. "I'll go to the Co-op, I'll talk to the reverend—"

"No! You can't talk to her!"

"I'll tell her that if Tommy tries to kidnap you that I'll tell the Guard."

"But she's a part of this! You can't trust her, Paxton."

"I'm not talking about trusting her—I'll be *informing* her. She won't be able to do anything to you, and Tommy won't be able to do anything to you. I promise."

She regarded him warily—or what he took for wariness.

"I promise," he said again.

"Look, there's nothing we can do till morning. We'll worry about all that stuff tomorrow. Meanwhile . . ." He picked up the remaining can of compressed air and put it in front of her. "Why don't we take another crack at this?"

---

Rainy fell asleep at the table with her head resting on her forearm. They'd made no progress on getting past the log-in screen. Weygand's hacker scheme had given them nothing but cold hands. They'd spent an hour trying every password they could think of—"sandra," "rainy," "lorraine," "switchcreek," "bowie," "changes," then birthdays and favorite places—and then when Rainy put her head down he went on trying the names of flowers and the names of authors on her bookshelf. Uppercase, lowercase, title case. Nothing worked, but at least the laptop refrained from locking him out.

The tube of vintage, melted now, seemed to burn in his pocket.

"Let's go, Rainy." She startled when he touched her arm. He helped her to her feet, then ushered her through the dark to her bedroom. He circled his arms around her thighs and hoisted her to the top bunk.

"Paxton," she said from the dark.

"Yeah, hon?"

She was silent for a long time.

"Are you crying, Rainy?"

She sighed. "No. I have trouble crying."

"Me too."

"I sure want to, though."

Another long moment passed, and then she said, "My mom did some bad things."

Rainy couldn't use the A-word more than once, it seemed.

"I know it's hard to understand," Pax said. "Some things aren't black and white. Your mom wasn't against children—she wasn't against you. She just believed that a woman has a right to choose when—"

"She killed her baby, Paxton. My little sister."

"Oh, hon," he said sadly. Rainy was the stronger of the two sisters, but this had obviously been eating at her, too. "Your mom wasn't a bad person. It's just that some people believe that a fetus isn't . . ." Isn't what? He wasn't prepared to have this conversation. "Maybe when you're older you'll understand."

"She talked about giving all the girls pills. She said they ought to put it in the water."

"She didn't mean that."

"Mom didn't say anything she didn't mean. Everyone knew that."

"Okay, you may be right on that one." He put a hand through the rails and squeezed her calf. "But those girls at the Co-op, they're getting pregnant without *having* a choice. Your mom wanted to protect them."

"No, she wanted *her* choice. The white-scarf girls *want* their babies, Paxton."

"But they're just girls. They're not old enough to make that decision. And when they do get pregnant, of course they want to keep the babies. It's hormones, it's—"

"It's not just hormones!"

"Okay, I shouldn't have said that. But someday you'll understand that even good people can do things that seem wrong. Bad things. Sometimes they have to."

"She was going to *keep* doing them, Paxton. She was going to keep killing the children. Mom and the reverend."

"Rainy, no. I don't know what you heard, or thought you heard—"

"I can prove it." She started to climb out of the bed. "It's in my backpack."

"Hold on, what's in your backpack?"

"Just get it."

He went out of the room, found the big nylon bag in the kitchen, and brought it back to the room.

Rainy searched through it for a few moments, unzipping pockets, then said, "Here." She pressed something into his hand. "Reverend Hooke gave these to my mom."

It was a pill bottle. It was too dark to make out the label. "What is this, Rainy?"

"Mifeprex is what it says on the label," the girl said. "Mom called it something with a number. It's an abortion pill."

He blinked. "RU-486?"

"That's it."

He didn't know what to say to that. After a moment Rainy said, "I heard Mom talking to Hooke on the phone about it. She asked the reverend for them."

"Maybe you misunderstood what—"

"I'm not stupid, Paxton."

"But who were they for?" He still didn't believe that she'd heard correctly. "One of the white-scarf girls?" Or Jo, he thought, though he didn't say that aloud.

After a moment of silence Rainy said, "I didn't hear who it was for."

"Okay, when was this? How long ago?"

"Paxton, it was the night she died."

"What?"

"She called the reverend after we went to bed that night."

Pax pressed his forehead against the wooden frame. "Did you tell anyone this?" he asked. "The police, or Deke?"

"We were too scared. If Mom and the reverend were doing this, then who knows—"

"Jesus, Rainy!" He kept his volume down for Sandra's sake, but his anger was clear. "You should have told someone."

He immediately regretted yelling at her. Of course they'd been afraid. What trusted authority figure would turn out to be the next monster? *Baby-killer.* The most depraved criminal a beta girl could imagine. No wonder the only people the twins trusted were each other. And maybe—now—Pax.

"Don't worry," Pax said. "I promise to take care of everything. In the morning I'll . . . well, we'll think of something." He found her face in the dark and kissed her on the smooth top of her head. "The point is, you're not alone in this anymore. We're a team, right? A club."

Pax had belonged to only one club in his life. As the only remaining member, he granted himself the power to silently induct them on the spot—they'd already met the organization's membership requirements.

He closed the bedroom door, thinking, Welcome to the Switchcreek Orphan Society, girls.

He sat in the book-lined living room with the computer open on his lap, its screen washing his face with cold light. He thought of unwanted pregnancies and chemical abortions, secret passwords and suicide notes, corruption and embezzlement and blackmail. Deke had said Jo had figured out what Rhonda was doing. The proof might be right under his fingertips. He pecked at the keyboard, typing random words into the password box, watching the machine instantly reject each one.

The vintage sat heavy in his pocket like a tiny bomb.

Instead he picked up the bottle Rainy had given him. The label was muddy and the ink smudged, but he'd been able to decipher the important details: the patient was Elsa Hooke; the prescribing doctor was Dr. Fraelich, Marla; and the three tablets were for something called "Mifeprex (Mifepristone)"—neither of which he'd ever heard of. The tablets came in large 200-milligram doses, and all three were still in the bottle. The prescription had expired more than six months ago.

Jo had known that the reverend had the pills and hadn't used them. He thought of Jo sitting in this room when she realized that her body had betrayed her again, that it had once again manufactured a fertilized egg like a tumor—unwanted, unearned, and unasked-for. The idea of three such invasions in a dozen years horrified him.

He put the medicine bottle into his pocket—and look, here was the vial of vintage.

He held the tube in his hand, turning it. He decided to empty the vial into the toilet. Later he resolved to take one sip and then throw the rest away. Sometime after that he committed to a new life: In the morning he'd return to his house, empty the freezer, and call his father to tell him he'd never be able to visit in person again.

Then, as morning approached, he thought, One last drink. A toast to my new life.

He removed the cap and kissed the lip of the vial, small mouth to his larger one. He tipped the tube higher and held it until he could no longer feel the thick drops on his tongue.

Even after it was empty he couldn't let it go. He sat on the couch for a long time, turning the empty thing in one hand while he typed nonsense words and strings of numbers and every Bowie lyric he could think of.

The wind picked up, setting the back door to knock against the frame like a cranky child. Finally he set aside the laptop and walked to the kitchen. He started to close the door but instead opened it wider. The cold breeze felt good against his face. It was 6:00 a.m., still an hour before dawn, but the blanket of clouds had begun to thin. The huge tree, still bulky with leaves, held back a charcoal gray sky.

He sensed someone behind him and turned. She leaned in the kitchen doorway, her arms folded across her chest. She was dressed for warmer weather: a white wife-beater T-shirt, khaki shorts, bare feet. Her skin shone, a glaze of dark raspberry.

"Hey, Jo," he said.

She smiled, turned, and walked into the living room. She looked at the laptop.

"Yeah," he said. "I've been trying to violate your privacy. Haven't had much luck, though."

She tilted her head and smiled.

He said, "So what's the password, Jo?"

And then he knew. As surely as if she'd spoken it aloud.

He sat down and put the computer on his knees. He was such an idiot. There was only one possible password. And if it didn't open the laptop he'd chuck the thing out the window.

He typed three letters—SOS—and tapped return.

The password dialog box blinked away, and a screen full of icons replaced it.

"Switchcreek Orphan Society," he said. Jo pursed her lips, silently laughing.

He opened a folder on the hard drive just to see if he could. "You care to tell me where you left your suicide note?"

She shook her head. He didn't know whether that meant she hadn't left one or didn't want him to read it.

"I can look at this later," he said. "Right now I want to—"

He noticed a folder on the desktop named "RM" and forgot what he was going to say. He clicked on it and saw a long list of word processor documents, spreadsheets, scanned images, as well as a dozen subfolders. The names "Rhonda" and "Mapes" and "RM" were on most of them. He clicked on a folder at random—Tema2007—then opened an image named MedFund2007Page01.tiff. It was a scan of a complicated form from the Tennessee Emergency Management Agency—some kind of payment for medical services. Dr. Fraelich's name was near the top, and he wasn't surprised to see Rhonda's name right after it. The dollar amount was for over a million dollars—$1,100,022.00 to be exact. And there were a dozen more forms just in this one folder.

If he was going to understand what the form meant he'd have to go through all these documents, look for any notes from Jo herself. But he was pretty sure it wouldn't paint Rhonda in a positive light.

He shook his head, amazed. "How much did you have on her, Jo?" He looked up and she was walking away from him, toward the back door. He set aside the laptop and hurried after her.

She walked out into the backyard. Her hand trailed across the trunk of the huge oak, but she didn't glance up. He almost caught up to her as she entered the trees at the edge of the yard.

The faint light from the sky vanished. She was only a few feet ahead of him, but he could barely see her pale T-shirt against her dark shoulders. They went uphill, Jo moving quickly and noiselessly, Pax stumbling over roots and rocks, cursing, jogging to catch up with his hands held out in front of him to warn him of tree trunks.

After ten, fifteen minutes they stepped out into a clearing like a basin of moonlight.

Jo turned to look at him. Her eyes gleamed. Her shirt seemed to glow.

He looked around. The path continued on the other side of the clearing, heading back down into the valley, toward the Whitmer farm and the Co-op.

At the high edge of the clearing was a makeshift bench made from three logs. Jo sat down and held out a hand. He sat next to her and she warmed his hand in hers. They stared out at the silvery grass, the dark woods. He knew she was a figment of his imagination, a chemical dream like all the other vintage-prompted hallucinations. He didn't care.

"I'm sorry, Jo," he said. "I'm so sorry."

She said nothing. That was all right. The heat of her skin against his was enough.

Above them the gray sky took on indigo hues. Color seeped into the air, painted the grass with faint greens and yellows, rusted the leaves at the edge of the clearing.

Jo looked at him, then looked back at the bushes behind her. He followed her gaze but didn't see anything. He stood, stared up the slope into the trees. They were still a half hour's hike from the top of Mount Clyburn.

"I don't know what you want me to see," he said to her. He moved behind the bench, still peering into the woods, and his foot came down on something round and hard.

He reached down into the long grass and picked up a metal flashlight streaked with mud. Jo's flashlight, he decided. He clicked the button, and the light snapped on. After months in the woods, the batteries were still good.

She looked up at him over her shoulder, her gaze steady.

She'd come here that night, he realized. She'd left the house after the girls were in bed, then made her way up to this place, following the flashlight. She'd sat on this bench, waiting.

And this is where she died.

He clicked off the light and came around to the front of the bench and kneeled in front of her, instantly wetting his knees.

"Who was here, Jo? Who did you meet? Was it the reverend?"

She gazed down at him with oil-black eyes. Then she smiled—a very un-beta smile that summoned the girl she'd been—and then rapped her knuckles against his forehead: tock, tock. Figure it out, knucklehead.

He stood up, looked back the way they'd come, then at the path that led down to the farm, the Co-op. This clearing was the halfway point. He started down the slope, then realized that Jo wasn't following.

He looked back. She sat on the bench, her eyes on him. She was going no farther.

He lifted a hand. He knew that she wasn't really there, but he was nevertheless reluctant to leave her behind. Yet again.

She nodded toward the woods behind him. Finally he turned and started down.

# chapter 21

"MAYOR?" ESTHER SAID. "A couple of them stormtroopers to see you." The charlie woman looked nervous. Until a few days ago she'd been just the elementary school's cook, and then Rhonda had promoted her to administrative assistant to the mayor. Mostly that meant answering the phones.

"Just a second, Esther," Rhonda said. She loaded another ream of paper into the photocopier and slammed the door. Full circle, she thought. Here it was the crack o' dawn and she was working the copy machine like she'd never stopped being church secretary. Harlan never used to write his sermons until the last minute—couldn't even tell her the scripture he'd be using until Saturday night—so she used to have to come in early on Sundays to type up the programs and run them off.

Rhonda had commandeered the elementary school for her quarantine headquarters because it had the most phones, computers, and photocopiers—and because nobody was using it. School had been canceled because almost all the teachers lived outside of Switchcreek. She'd have to do something about that, eventually. Idle children equaled insane parents.

Rhonda picked up one of the finished copies and turned to Doctor Fraelich, who was tapping at a computer. "You're sure Dr. Preisswerk got this to the newspaper?" Rhonda asked.

"Eric met with them yesterday—it's definitely going out this morning." The doctor looked haggard from lack of sleep. Well, join the club, Rhonda thought.

"Let 'em in," Rhonda said to Esther. The woman moved aside and two National Guard soldiers in breathing masks stepped into the room. Rhonda thought she recognized the lead one as an assistant to Colonel Duveen, but she wasn't sure.

Rhonda said, "You know, it would really help us if y'all wore name tags."

"Likewise," the assistant said.

"Young man," Rhonda said sharply. "Do *not* mess with me."

"Yes, ma'am." He looked at the other soldier. "Colonel Duveen would like to see you—as soon as possible."

"I bet he would," Rhonda said. She took a few more copies of the document and tucked them into her bag. "Esther, keep running those. Make sure you hand one to whoever wants one, and make sure *everyone* has one of the blue sheets." She nodded to the light blue, half-size instruction sheets stacked on the table next to Dr. Fraelich. Rhonda took an inch off the top of one stack and put those in her bag too.

"Good luck," the doctor said.

Rhonda followed the Guardsmen outside. It was not yet full light, and the cold breeze teased at her fortress of hair. Everett stood beside the Cadillac, waiting. "I'll take my own car," she told the soldiers.

Evidently this was permissible. The soldiers got into the Humvee and Everett held open the Caddy's passenger door for her.

"Did you get any sleep?" Rhonda asked him. He'd been on duty nonstop since the quarantine began, and last night she'd sent him out to the car to take a nap.

"You're the one who should be resting, Aunt Rhonda," the boy said. "You can't keep burning the candle at both ends."

"I'll rest a little easier after today," she said.

Everett followed the Humvee the three blocks to the Cherokee Hotel, which the Guard had commandeered as *their* headquarters. He hopped out to open her door. "You want me inside?" he asked.

"I'll be fine," she said. "Just keep the phone on in case the newspeople call."

The soldiers were holding the door for her. Oh so polite. Rhonda walked up the front steps, patted the shiny, much-rubbed cheek of the wooden Indian by the door, and went inside.

The renovation project had been proceeding on and off for three years, whenever Rhonda had extra money to pour into it. When it was done it would be the world's first hotel that could accommodate all three clades—and skips in wheelchairs to boot. The new ceilings were high enough for argos, the doors broad enough for charlies. For the betas she'd specified that the women's restrooms outnumbered the men's four-to-one. Before Babahoyo, people thought it was a waste of money—everyone who could use the new features were already residents in Switchcreek. But she'd always intended it as a model for the outside world to follow, and if not that then a political statement. And now that there'd been a second outbreak Rhonda looked like a visionary. Someday Ecuadorian clades would visit.

Colonel Duveen had made his office in the banquet room. The walls had been stripped to the studs, but the wiring was all in place and bare bulbs lit the big room. His desk was at one end of the room, ten yards from the desk of any assistant. Duct-taped cables snaked across the bare wooden floor.

The colonel didn't look up from his papers until she was almost on top of him. Typical power gesture—she'd used it herself. She said, "It's awful early for a meeting, don't you think?"

He smiled and removed his glasses. "I appreciate you making time for me," he said. In defiance of his own regulations, he wore no breather mask. His voice was soft, and his boyish haircut and earnest eyes gave him the look of a Mormon missionary. She'd found it hard to believe he'd served two tours in Iraq and one in Afghanistan—until she started working with him. He permitted no bullshit. She respected his competence and liked him because he didn't underestimate her.

"Rumor has it," he said, "you have something planned for this morning."

"Oh, Colonel, I would have told you sooner, but it's all been decided in such a rush." She opened her bag and gave him one of the blue instruction sheets. "The march starts at eight-thirty a.m. Or oh-eight-thirty for you military types."

He frowned at the sheet. "You want to walk all the way down to the north gate?"

"We're putting in two little crosses there," Rhonda said. "It's a tradition around here—when someone dies in an accident, they put up a little white cross to mark the spot."

"Those are for car accidents, aren't they?"

"An accident is an accident," Rhonda said.

"That's it? Two crosses?"

"Two little crosses. As well as eight little flags—one for every fallen soldier."

"Interesting touch."

"It's the Christian thing to do."

He took a breath, then shook his head with a nicely calibrated display of regret. "I'm sorry, no."

"Excuse me?"

"It's too dangerous. Emotions are running too high."

"Among your soldiers or my people?"

"Both. I'm surprised at you, Mayor. We've talked about the need for calm."

"My people will have firm instructions." She nodded at the blue sheet. "They won't do anything to your men, not look at them, not talk to them. This is a silent march—no one will even speak until we get to the checkpoint, at which point Reverend Hooke will say a prayer. You're not against prayer, are you?"

"Mayor, it's already abundantly clear that the argos cannot be controlled."

"The same could be said for your soldiers." A moment passed, and then Rhonda changed tactics. "Colonel, my people need this." She let the weariness surface in her voice. "They need to express their grief. If you make it impossible for them to let off steam, this town will explode."

"Mobs don't let off steam, Mayor, they generate it."

"The anger's already there. My people know that this quarantine is a sham. And after today, the world will know it." She brought out the document she'd copied this morning. "This will be coming out in *The New York Times* today. It'll be on every news channel by the time we march."

He put on his glasses and peered at the first page. "Why don't you tell me what I'm looking at?"

"That's a leaked CDC report, Colonel. The report was suppressed, but a few scientists are blowing the whistle. The rationale for this quarantine is full of holes. Not only has no one found a transmission method that would let these plasmid thingies hop from body to body, but it turns out—and this may come as a surprise to you, it certainly did to me—that all those cases the president talked about on TV, those cases of TDS plasmids showing up in unaffected people? Not one has panned out."

"You don't say," the colonel said.

"No, sir, not a one. In fact, the only people who seem to have them, in Switchcreek or in Ecuador, are people who already have TDS." Rhonda shook her head as if marveling at the impossibility of it all. "Isn't that something? They're an effect, not a cause."

"The government's never said that plasmids definitely caused TDS," the colonel said. "Only that it couldn't be ruled out. Besides, this is just the opinion of a couple of scientists. Other scientists say differently."

"Yes, yes, the government managed to find their own scientists—and their own lawyers too—to give them a pretext for isolating us. But the jury can't be out forever."

"This won't change anything," the colonel said.

"Oh, I have no illusions that a couple of leaked reports are going to change the government's position. I fully expect this quarantine to go on for as long as the public is petrified of getting TDS. But sooner or later, as the evidence keeps coming out, the public will realize that this quarantine isn't protecting them, that it's never going to.

"Hell, even if you killed every last charlie, beta, and argo in Ecuador, Tennessee, and across the planet, TDS is going to spread. Someday, I'm betting soon, we'll turn on our TVs and there will be another outbreak. Then another one. And another. A new world is coming, Colonel Duveen. And then do you know where you're going to be?"

"In a war zone?"

"Worse than that." She leaned forward. "You're going to be on the wrong side of history."

He took off his glasses and set them on the desk. "That may be so," he said. "But that doesn't change this morning. No march, Rhonda, silent or otherwise. No service at the checkpoint."

"Oh, hon, there's going to be a march whether you want one or not. Your only decision is to figure out how you're going to respond to it." She glanced at her watch. "Well, I better get going. Oh, and afterward we're having a breakfast at the church. You like biscuits and gravy, don't you?"

"Are you inviting me?"

"You and as many of your men as you want."

He chuckled. "I don't think so. It's a little difficult to eat through those breathers."

"Well, we'll think of something else, then. Maybe a softball game? If we're going to keep our people from killing each other, I figure they should get to know each other."

# chapter 22

PAX CAME DOWN out of the trees at the western edge of a fog-wreathed field. In the distance, the orange, quavering sun struggled to rise over blue hills. The clouds glowed a score of shades between blue and violet.

A few hundred yards away were the first of the mobile homes that made up the improvised neighborhood of the Co-op. He'd come in behind them, their white backs and small windows all alike. No one moved between the buildings. He aimed for the nearest trailer and set off across the field.

The frost-rimed grasses burned silver; they wet his shins and crunched beneath his shoes. So beautiful. He wondered if he would have noticed any of this if he hadn't been riding a wave of chemicals.

He passed between two trailers on the outermost row and stopped. No one was outside. He thought about knocking at one of the trailers at random.

He walked on until he reached the innermost row of homes that faced the main drive. To his right was the big sheet-metal building at the center of the compound. As good a place to start as any.

Before he reached the building a door opened at a trailer in front of him and he heard the squall of a baby. A tall, older beta woman stepped out, holding a tiny child whose smooth, ruby head gleamed like a marble. The woman had taken two steps down from the front porch before she noticed him.

"Hi," he said. "I'm looking for Reverend Hooke."

She stared at him. He wondered if he'd known this woman before the Changes. Maybe she'd gone to his church. Maybe she'd been a friend of his mother's.

She nodded in the direction Pax had been walking. "Elsa is two down," she said.

"Thank you," Pax said. "Good luck calming her down." The baby's cry sounded no different from that of any human baby.

He climbed the short steps to the reverend's trailer and knocked. He put his hands in his pockets, huffed steam. The woman with the baby paced along the drive, not bothering to hide that she was studying him. He knocked again.

The door opened, and a beta woman dressed in a bathrobe looked down at him. The size of her belly, even through the robe, was apparent.

"Paxton?" the reverend said.

He looked up, embarrassed. "You know, I'd noticed at the town meeting and at the funeral that you were dressing differently, that you seemed . . . bigger. But I never took the next logical step."

"You're a man."

"I suppose that's why," he said. "Or maybe it's just me. I miss a lot of things."

"Why are you here, Paxton? It's awfully early."

"I came to tell you that you can't take the girls away. Sandra and Rainy."

"How did you—?" She stopped, looked around, and saw the woman with the baby staring at them.

Pax said, “And I also came to tell you I know where you were the night Jo died.” The reverend’s face was as still as any beta’s, but he could feel the woman’s alarm. He said, “Do you want to do this out here?”

She pushed the door wider. “Come inside,” she said. “It’s cold.”

She walked across the small living room with a slight hitch in her step. Maybe the pregnancy was hurting her. Or maybe the limp had always been there and he’d never noticed.

She eased herself into a chair, and he sat down opposite her. After a moment she said, “I’ve seen you like this before, Paxton.”

Right, the night his father baptized him. Rebaptized him. “I apologize,” Pax said. “I took an awful lot of vintage a while ago.”

“You were with the girls?” Her anger was clear. “Where? At your house? Tommy’s been looking all over for them.”

“They’re safe,” he said. “I found them in the woods outside Jo Lynn’s house. They ran away because Tommy was going to kidnap them.”

The reverend made a disgusted noise. “He’s not *kidnapping* them. Did the girls say that?”

“They don’t know what he’s doing. All they know is that Tommy’s going to—”

“This is not Tommy’s idea, Paxton. It’s something we all agreed to—Rhonda, Deke, and I. Rhonda called it genocide insurance.”

“Genocide? What are you talking about?”

She sighed. “We’re smuggling members of our clades out of Switchcreek, just in case the government tries to . . .” She made a vague gesture. “. . . take measures against us.”

“You think the army’s going to *kill* you all?”

"We all thought Rhonda was being paranoid when she raised the idea years ago. We never thought—*I* never thought—there'd be another quarantine, and even if there was, I didn't think we'd be threatened with that. But after Deke was killed . . ." She exhaled heavily. "We can't take the chance. We can't let the government make us disappear. If something happens at Switchcreek, the clades need to survive. So we have to get a few of us out. The first group will have two families from our clade, a handful of charlies, and two argo couples."

"But that's suicide—the roads are blocked, there are soldiers everywhere—"

"This plan existed well before the quarantine, Paxton. They'll be hiking out of Switchcreek to a rendezvous several miles away. At that point they'll be met by six vehicles, and they'll scatter—every car in a different direction."

"That's crazy! What if a helicopter—"

"We have it covered, Paxton. The National Guard will be busy with the march."

Before he could reply a little bald girl walked into the room, face scrunched against the light. She was three or four, dressed in green footy pajamas.

"Go back to bed, pumpkin, it's not time for breakfast yet."

"I'm not tired," the girl said, and started to climb into her mother's lap. Then she saw Pax. "Who's that?"

"I'm Paxton," he said. Then to the reverend he said, "Your youngest?"

"Not anymore," she said, and pushed up from the chair and took the girl's hand. "How about some Cheerios and bananas?" She led her into the kitchen.

Pax leaned forward with his elbows on his knees. He was still cold, but at least his hands weren't shaking. Yet. He could feel the vintage buzzing in his veins, adding meaning and import to everything he saw and heard. In the kitchen the reverend murmured to her daughter and he could feel her love for the girl in each note of her voice. And when the reverend returned to the room a few minutes later he felt the air shimmer with trepidation, wariness. The woman didn't know what Pax would say next, and Pax didn't know either.

Then he said, "It must have been a shock when you learned you were pregnant again."

"Pregnancy is always difficult." She stood with one hand gripping the back of her chair. "That girl in there nearly killed me—cardiomyopathy. I couldn't walk for a month after the birth."

"What did they say would happen if you got pregnant again?"

She was silent for a moment. "Doctors don't know everything," she said. "Especially about betas. I decided to take the risk."

"Decided?" he asked. "I thought you couldn't choose when to get pregnant?"

She didn't answer. Pax said, "But I suppose you could choose to *not* be pregnant." He reached into his pocket and took out the orange pill bottle. "No one would blame you if you considered other options." He showed her the label. "These have your name on them."

The reverend froze. After a moment she said, "Where did you get that?"

He rubbed a thumb across the dried mud on its side.

"I said, where did you get that?"

"I found it at Jo's house," he said. Not quite lying.

"I never took those pills."

"I guessed that," Pax said. The woman looked at least six months pregnant—bigger than Jo had been when he left. "But you thought about it."

"*Yes,* I thought about it." Her voice was almost a hiss. "But that was a moment of weakness. Fear. Once the baby started to grow . . ." She slowly shook her head. One hand rested on her stomach. "It became obvious how wrong I'd been. Crystal clear."

"The hormones kicked in," Pax said. He tried to remember what the doctor had told him. "Oxytocin, other opiates. There are chemicals that are released during pregnancy that—"

"This has nothing to do with *drugs,* it's about right and wrong. I was weak. The younger girls, they have moral clarity. I'm not so lucky. I was a human long before I was a beta. I wavered."

"The pills couldn't have been so evil if you were willing to give them to Jo," he said. "She knew you had them, and she called you the night she died. She asked you to meet her up at that clearing between her house and yours."

"I'm not going to talk about this with you. Not here."

"Yes," Pax said, "you are."

The woman did not move or change expression, but her anger rolled toward him like heat.

Pax had grown up thinking of empathy as the most Christian of feelings—loving your neighbor as yourself, indistinguishable from yourself. But it was only information, to be used or not used, for good or ill. He felt the reverend's rage and hurt, and the knowledge drew a target around her heart. As he spoke he knew exactly where his words would strike, and how deep.

"You were handing out abortion pills, Reverend," he said.

"Tell me what happened, before I have to ask every blank in this trailer park about you and Jo Lynn."

She stared at him.

"All right, fine." He stood. "I'll check back with you later."

"Please," she said. "Keep your voice down. My other daughters are sleeping."

After half a minute she said, "She called me asking for the pills. She couldn't come here, obviously, and I couldn't just drive out of the Co-op in the middle of the night—too many people would see and ask questions. So I agreed to meet her on the mountain. We'd met in that spot before, when . . . when Jo helped me think about my options when I became pregnant again."

"But I thought you were the one who ran her out of the Co-op."

"Jo's excommunication wasn't my doing," the reverend said. "I tried to keep the peace, but the white-scarf girls—"

"Right. I know how hard it is to hold on to a congregation."

"You can't begin to know until you've stood in the pulpit yourself," she said. "But Jo understood my position here, with the younger girls. We always understood each other. Even when we didn't agree, we were friends." She saw his look. "I don't care if you believe me or not."

"All right. So you went up there to help your friend. You gave her the pills. Then what?"

"Then nothing. I walked back home."

"That's it? You trotted up there and then right back down—and then a few hours later she was dead."

"It wasn't until the next morning I heard that she'd hung herself. I was shocked. She was upset that night, but she wasn't . . . I guess I didn't realize how distraught she was."

"Did she tell you she was pregnant?"

The reverend looked away. "No." Then she shook her head. "But I didn't ask. I'd been in the same situation. I hugged her, and we went our separate ways. That was the last time I saw her."

The woman was telling the truth, yet there was something measured in her words that made him think she was hiding something. What, he had no idea.

"Why didn't you tell anyone about seeing her that night, Reverend? Deke didn't mention it. And I'm sure you didn't tell the police."

"You don't know what some of these girls are like," the reverend said. "How judgmental, how *certain* they are."

"Because they're pure," Pax said. "And you're tainted." The reverend opened her mouth slightly, which Pax took to express outright shock. "I've been talking to Rainy and Sandra," he explained.

"You have no idea," the Reverend said. "If they knew I'd helped Jo—that I'd considered such a thing myself—they'd never trust me again." In the kitchen, a thunk as the girl dropped a bowl or something as big. The reverend didn't get up.

"One of them followed you up the mountain," Pax said. "Tommy. Or one of the white-scarf girls. Maybe several of them."

She shook her head. "No. Absolutely not. None of the girls—"

Outside, a car horn beeped twice.

"Somebody followed you," Pax said. "Somebody close enough to you to find out your secret. They knew you were seeing her, and then they followed you up the mountain and saw you hand over the pills."

"No."

"And after you left, they killed her."

The reverend stood up, went to the window. She pushed aside the drapes, let them fall back. "They're here," she said. He didn't know who she was referring to. "I have to get ready now."

"I'm not going anywhere until you tell me who followed you."

She turned to him. "No one followed me, Paxton. I went down the mountain the same way I went up, and no one was on the path."

"They hid from you," he said. "They hid in the trees—it's easy for them." Sandra and Rainy could swing through trees like monkeys.

"No one followed me. Now please—get out of my house."

Two beta girls about Rainy and Sandra's height came into the room. They eyed Paxton. "What's going on?"

"Nothing, girls. He's leaving now." She marched from the room. A moment later the bedroom door slammed.

Pax sat in the chair, waiting. The two girls stared at him. The littlest girl came out of the kitchen to stare as well. Her pajamas were wet where she'd dropped her cereal.

He didn't like the way they looked at him. Or maybe he didn't like what he must look like in their eyes.

"I'm not going anywhere," he said.

The oldest girl walked forward. She was a thin beta with speckled skin like an otter's. She seized his wrist. Her grip was gorilla strong and surprisingly painful.

He said, "Listen—"

She jerked him out of the chair. Then she fastened her other hand around the back of his neck and with absurd ease steered him to the front door. The other older girl ran ahead of them and opened the front door.

Outside, a dozen girls in white scarves looked up at him.

---

The reverend's daughter released him. Pax didn't move from the porch. His right hand trembled and he gripped the white railing as if it were a weapon.

A dozen yards away, four argos were stepping down out of open-topped pickups. At the end of the drive three other vehicles were coming through the front gate: a couple of sedans followed by a red-and-white four-wheel drive—Tommy Shields' Bronco.

The entire community seemed to have woken up since he'd gone inside the reverend's trailer. Beta women and a few men lined the drive, children running between them or holding on to arms or sleeping on shoulders. The older girls, the white-scarf girls, had gathered around the reverend's trailer as if they'd been preparing to storm it. Maybe they had been.

One of the argos was the young man who worked in Deke's shop—Gary? Jerry? He and the young argo woman he'd arrived with lifted enormous aluminum-frame backpacks from the bed of their truck. The argo man saw Pax and frowned, confused to see him there.

Pax looked down at the white-scarf girls. They ranged in age from perhaps fifteen years old to twenty. None of them stood much taller than Rainy and Sandra; any one of them could snap his arm.

"Which one of you?" Pax asked. "Which one of you killed her?"

They returned his gaze with eyes like black stones. He realized that he couldn't read their faces as he had the reverend's. These girls were opaque to him, inscrutable as fish.

"No takers?" Pax asked.

Tommy Shields had noticed him. A beta girl was touching his arm, pointing back at Pax. Tommy began to jog toward him.

Pax walked down the steps, and the white-scarf girls moved out of his way and fell in behind him. Tommy was running now, yelling for them to hold him. Pax strode toward him.

A young charlie couple got out of their car halfway between them. They looked at Tommy, then at Paxton. "What are you doing here, man?" the charlie man said. Pax had seen him at a few of Rhonda's paydays. He was dark haired and blockish, the girl round and pale: Mr. Square and Miss Circle, escaping together.

"Where are they?" Tommy said. "Where are the girls?"

The distance closed to a few feet—and Pax launched himself at the man. Tommy threw up his arms, but Pax tackled him and they both went down, tumbling across the sharp gravel. They clawed at each other, kicking and throwing elbows and spitting like children throwing a tantrum. Ridiculous, Pax thought, even as he surrendered to the emotion of it. Tommy hated him, he hated Tommy—it was so simple. A feedback loop of empathy.

Pax lost track of whose limbs were whose. They rolled, smacked against the wheel of a pickup. People around them shouted.

Someone gripped him by the leg and dragged him backward. Hands peeled Pax and Tommy from each other and hauled them upright. The charlie man held Paxton, and an argo had fastened a long arm around Tommy. Pax, chest heaving, tasted blood in his mouth and smiled like a madman. Tommy bled too, but not badly. All that scrabbling and they'd only scratched each other.

"Y'all fight like girls," said the charlie holding him.

"He knows where they are," Tommy said. "Sandra and Rainy. He's trying to hide them so that they can't go with us."

The argo looked at him. "Is that so?" he said in his low voice. They were surrounded by betas—white-scarf girls, young children, a smattering of males—and the charlies and argos who'd driven here for the start of the exodus.

"The girls are safe," Pax said.

"*You* can't protect them," Tommy said. "You can't even take care of them! What are you going to do with a girl in Sandra's condition? What would you do *to* her?"

Paxton stopped struggling. "What are you talking about?"

The reverend appeared between them. "Stop it. Both of you." She was dressed now in a skirt and long blouse. She turned to a pair of older beta women. "Sandra and Rainy are at Jo's house. Please take some people with you to go pick them up."

The charlie boy released his grip; Paxton was no longer fighting him anyway. The reverend watched his face, waiting to see if he finally understood.

He'd been so blind. The way Sandra had been covering herself with the blanket, the way that for all the time he'd known her she'd worn nothing but loose dresses to Rainy's tomboy clothes. The way she'd hugged him so carefully last night, touching only shoulders and arms. She couldn't have been as far along as the reverend, but she'd carefully concealed her shape from him. Rainy and Sandra had conspired to hide it.

So blind.

They didn't try to stop him from leaving. He walked between the rows of trailers, across the field. When he reached the tree line he looked back and saw Tommy's Bronco and another car rolling out the front gate. There was no way he could beat them to Jo's house, no way he could warn the girls. He wasn't sure that he would've warned them if he could. Tommy was right: Their clade could protect them, and he couldn't.

He walked into the shadow of the trees and started up the mountain.

The vintage was already dissipating from his bloodstream. A few months ago a dose of the size he'd taken would have knocked him unconscious. In August, a single taste of it had put him on the ground and left him gawking as if God were going to reach down and shake hands.

After fifteen minutes he reached the clearing. Sunlight splintered through the trees.

The bench was empty. Jo was long gone, evaporated with the vintage.

He walked across the long grass, then stopped. A figure stepped out of the trees ahead of him.

He took a step back. "There are people looking for you," he said.

"We heard the cars coming up the drive," Rainy said. "We ran." Sandra stepped out of the trees behind her, the blanket still around her shoulders.

Sandra glanced at Rainy nervously.

"You really are pregnant?" Pax asked.

"We wanted to tell you," Sandra said.

Rainy said, "We kept thinking you'd notice."

Sandra let the blanket slip to the ground. The bulge beneath her dress was hardly noticeable, but then she ran a hand down her front, smoothing out the fabric, showing the swell of her belly.

"I'm only a few months along," she said. "But I can feel her growing, every day. There may even be twins. Oh Paxton, my daughters are going to be the first children of the new generation. Do you want to feel them?"

Sandra took a step forward and he jerked back. Rainy watched him, her arms at her sides. He'd seen her use those arms to haul herself through the trees like a chimp, or carry him like a child. They could cinch shut a windpipe like a noose.

He said, "The pills weren't for your mother." He already knew the answer. He'd known it as soon as he heard that Sandra was pregnant. As soon as the reverend had looked at him, he'd understood what had happened that night—in this very spot.

"No," Rainy said.

"The night she found out—"

"She was going to kill the baby," Rainy said. "Sandra's daughter. Her own granddaughter." She shook her head. "I just couldn't understand a person who would do that. Someone had to stop her."

"But Rainy, she was your mother."

"I know who she was."

"Jesus, Rainy . . ."

"Don't look at her like that!" Sandra said. Pax had never heard her speak so sharply. The girl stepped between Paxton and her sister. "You don't know how torn up she's been. She doesn't feel *good* about what she had to do. But you said last night that sometimes good people have to do bad things."

"You were awake," Pax said.

"Mom wasn't going to stop," Sandra said. "You know how she was. Once she'd made up her mind, she wouldn't quit. We couldn't go to the Co-op, not with Hooke helping her. Rainy did what she had to do. She was protecting me. Protecting us."

"Sandra, I know how it must feel to—"

"No you don't," Sandra said. "You're not a beta. You don't get to judge."

They heard voices calling up the mountain. High tenors—beta voices. Rainy tensed as if she were about to run.

"They're not going to harm you or your baby," Pax said. "That's the last thing they'd do." He nodded toward the voices. "Tommy will protect you. And the reverend—that's over now. I don't think she understood who the pills were for."

Rainy looked down the slope, then at Paxton. "We wanted you to know," she said. "We wanted you to understand. Then maybe—"

"Maybe we could stay with you," Sandra said. "You do kinda need us, Paxton."

The voices grew louder. "You should go," Pax said. "You're worrying them."

Sandra rushed to him. She threw her arms around him, pressed her belly into his. He tried to step away, but she hugged him harder. Finally he touched the top of her smooth head.

Rainy said, "Good-bye, Pax."

"Take care of each other," he said.

Sandra released him. Rainy put the blanket over her shoulders.

He watched them until they vanished into the trees. He turned away, but then his knees felt weak, so he sat down there in the wet grass. He looked at nothing for a long time, as the sun tracked across the blue roof of the clearing.

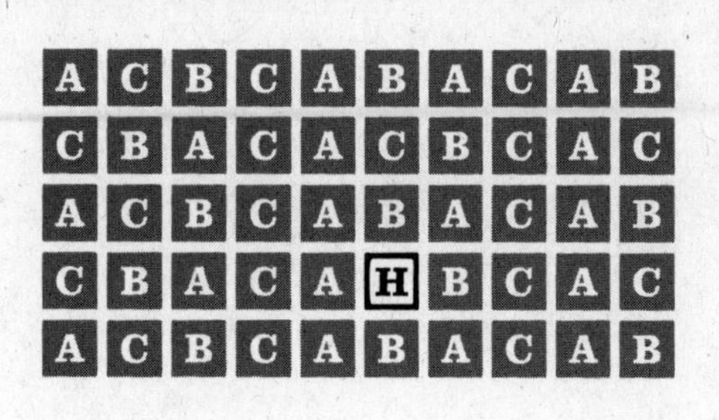
A C B C A B A C A B
C B A C A C B C A C
A C B C A B A C A B
C B A C A H B C A C
A C B C A B A C A B

# chapter 23

HE'D ALMOST FORGOTTEN the ramp.

When the van arrived, Paxton was on his stomach in the front yard, drilling through the two-by-fours into the cement foundation of the house while Amos and Paul, two argos from Alpha Furniture, held the frame steady. He'd called them yesterday in a panic. They'd built the ramp in an afternoon and delivered it this morning.

Pax got up from the cold ground, shook the dirt from the front of his jacket. It was just under forty degrees, which in Chicago would have been balmy for a December day, but here in Switchcreek felt bitterly cold. The argos stooped with their nail guns to fasten the plywood to the frame.

Dr. Fraelich had gotten out of the van, and the side door was open. His father sat in his enormous wheelchair, looking down sternly while two charlie men fussed with the chair and the winch. Finally Barron got the electric motor started, and Mr. Teestall, Paxton's old shop teacher, held the chair while it descended.

Pax said, "How you doing, Dad?"

"I told them, I can walk."

"Let's not risk it right now," Dr. Fraelich said.

"Rhonda would kill us if you broke something," Barron added.

The metal plates touched the ground. Mr. Teestall leaned into the chair and got it rolling across the yard. Barron eyed the ramp. "Will that hold him?"

Amos, the one-armed argo, said, "Of course it will. Both of us jumped on it in the shop."

"I'm going to have a concrete ramp installed eventually," Pax said.

They got Harlan through the door and across the living room. Pax had pulled up all the carpets and refinished the floors, which made the rolling a lot easier. Pax stayed back as Mr. Teestall helped Harlan move from the wheelchair to the new couch. Another Alpha creation: normal-looking on the outside, but with industrial-strength springs and a steel undercarriage cross-braced like a suspension bridge. The thing squeaked loudly as his father settled into it. He shifted his weight and it squeaked again.

"That's going to drive me crazy," Harlan said.

"I'll oil it before I go," Pax said.

"Just leave that to me," Mr. Teestall said.

Pax helped Barron ferry in supplies from the van—bandages, creams, extraction packs, cleaning solution—as well as his father's clothes and two boxes of Mr. Teestall's personal items. They finished just as Dr. Fraelich concluded her checkup of Harlan.

"You can fasten your shirt now, Mr. Martin," she said, and peeled one of the latex gloves from her hands. "As near as I can tell, you're as fit as anyone of your age, sex, and clade."

"That's an awful lot of conditions," Harlan said.

"It's the best I can do."

Pax walked the doctor out to the van, and they waited as Barron tried to cajole the winch into lifting the platform back into place.

"Your paperwork is all signed?" the doctor asked Paxton.

"It's in my suitcase." He'd been officially cleared of atypical plasmids. He'd still be required to spend two weeks in a facility in Kentucky, isolated from anyone with TDS. But after that, he'd be free to roam the world.

"Let me know if you run into any problems," she said.

"Sure, sure."

After a moment she said, "So."

He looked at her.

She pitched her voice so that Barron couldn't hear it. "How the hell did you do it?"

"Hmm?"

"You not only got Aunt Rhonda to agree to home care, but pay for it too. Not to mention biweekly visits from yours truly."

"You're not going to like it," he said.

"Indulge me."

"I traded for it," he said. He shrugged. "I gave Rhonda a gigabyte or two of data, and she gave my father the only thing he wanted—to be back in his own house." He smiled at her expression. "I told you you wouldn't like it."

"You found Jo's laptop." He didn't deny it. "And then you just *gave* it to her?"

"Well, I did keep copies—I'm not a complete idiot." The doctor still looked shocked. "Listen, I know why Jo never pulled the trigger on Rhonda. Your name's on half the documents."

The doctor flushed—it was astounding to watch the blood rush so quickly to infuse her pale skin. "I didn't know what she was doing!" she said. "Ninety percent of what I signed I thought that—" She stopped abruptly as Barron shut the van door and turned to them.

"Ready to go?" Barron asked. He saw that something unpleasant was going on.

"Just a second," Dr. Fraelich said. "Really."

Barron nodded, then walked around to the other side of the van.

Pax said, "It's okay. I don't care what you did or didn't do—everybody does business with Rhonda. Even Jo. She wasn't about to ruin your career by publishing that stuff. She was your friend."

"And what are you going to do?"

"Nothing, hopefully. Unless I'm forced to, and even then . . . I'm not sure. I'll let Rhonda worry about that."

"And me."

"I'm sorry about that. I really am. But this is the only shot I had to make Harlan happy. What choice did I have? He's my father."

"So you're doing this out of love," she said skeptically.

"Or something like it."

Barron had started the van. Pax followed her to the passenger door, and she said, "Oh, almost forgot." She reached in and handed him a manila folder. "Your DNA sample was already stored in Atlanta—everybody in Switchcreek was sampled during the Changes. I asked a friend of mine to run it through some tests."

"I thought all your friends there were fired."

"Resigned. And I still have a few left there. A couple, anyway."

He opened the folder. There were several pages. The first listed many long words he couldn't pronounce, and many long numbers he didn't understand the significance of.

He took a breath. "So, am I . . . ?"

"Bad news," Dr. Fraelich said. "For the gene sequences studied, and for the range of proteins sampled, your genetic material falls within the statistical range of only one known clade."

He stared at her.

"My condolences, Paxton. You're human."

He didn't trust himself to spend the night in the same house as his father. After supper with Harlan and Mr. Teestall he used some of his precious allotment of gasoline to drive up to Jo's house. The doors were still unlocked, the interior undisturbed. Even the heat was on. Among other things he'd learned from Jo's files was the fact that Rhonda had quietly purchased this house and many of the others left empty after the Changes. The banks had foreclosed and she'd bought them for a song. Disturbing, but not illegal—unlike many of the frankly criminal things he'd found in the files. And in a way, the real estate finagling spoke well of Rhonda. She was betting on the future of Switchcreek when almost nobody else was.

He walked around the house, looking at the things the girls had left behind, the books on Jo's shelves. He opened the Dawkins book, the thick beige one on evolution: *The Ancestor's Tale*. Jo had been looking for some trace of herself in the diagrams, some branch that ended in the betas and her daughters.

But the betas and argos and charlies weren't here. They were intrusions, pages torn from some other book and stuffed between the covers of this world. This was *his* family tree. It should have been reassuring, to be so well documented, to have a map that told him where he'd come from, with a big red dot for You Are Here.

The tree explained nothing. For years he'd been hoping for a different answer. A diagnosis that would tell him why he felt like an alien in his own skin, an outsider, an imposter. But he'd been skipped again.

He put the book back and turned to leave. Then he noticed the glint of something between the seat cushions of the couch. It was a vial he'd emptied here two months ago. His hand was inches from it when he realized what he was doing and yelled, "Fuck!"

He went to the kitchen, found a dish towel, and wrapped up the vial without touching it. Then he went to the back porch and smashed the plastic with his heel. Risking a final touch he picked up the towel and threw it like a football into the backyard among the roots of the oak tree.

He shut the door—and immediately got an image of himself sneaking out here in the middle of the night, rooting through the grass for the towel, pressing it to his face . . .

It took another five minutes to find the gas can for Jo's lawnmower. He soaked a rag and set the towel on fire. He stood back from the smoke and thought, Jesus, I got to get out of this town.

He walked back to Jo's bedroom and lay on the bed. He stared at the ceiling for a long time. Then he grew cold, so he pulled back the dusty covers and climbed inside.

I'm sorry, Jo, he thought. They killed you and I didn't tell a soul.

Even now he couldn't hate the girls. He just wanted to know that they were all right. Safe. Happy.

"Shit," he said. I think I fell in love with them, Jo.

He lay in the bed, feeling like a spy in her house—a foreign agent in deep cover. If this is what it's like to be human, he thought, no wonder the world is so fucked up.

A night in his own house had not made Reverend Martin any happier. The new bed was too stiff, the couch too big, the new paint too sloppily applied. He despised the weakness of Mr. Teestall's coffee.

"I'll talk to him about it," Pax told his father. "I'll be checking in every day."

"Don't make promises you can't keep."

"Then most days," Pax said. "Every day I possibly can." He showed Harlan again how to use the contacts list in the cell phone he'd purchased. It was a model the argos favored for its oversized buttons—good for fat charlie fingers as well. Pax had also tried to teach his father texting but had quickly given up. "And you can call me any time you want."

Harlan poked at the phone, put it down. "Rhonda won't be happy with my decreased output."

"Well, she'll have to live with that," Pax said. And so will you, Pax thought. Harlan was happier when he was producing than when he wasn't. They hoped the phone calls would trigger some production. Their theory was that there should be nothing magical about Pax's physical presence; it was the *feeling* of closeness that started the cascade. That was the theory, anyway.

Pax said, "And after the quarantine is over I'll be able to visit in person."

He saw motion outside the window and looked out. Aunt Rhonda's Cadillac was pulling into the driveway.

"Okay," Pax said. "My ride is here."

His father looked up at him. "This new job. It can't wait till after Christmas?"

"I'm sorry, Dad."

Harlan grunted. "You promise it's not doing anything illegal?"

"Uh, illegal, or immoral?"

"Paxton Abel . . ."

Pax looked out the window. Everett was outside the car now, waiting with arms crossed. "Okay, you think you can keep a secret?"

His father skewered him with a look. "Don't get smart, Son."

"I'll be setting up a safe house. They need people they can trust outside of Switchcreek. Rhonda's organizing another batch of people to leave in February."

"You could be arrested."

"Or sent back here. Same thing, right?"

"I'll start fattening the calf."

Pax stood up. He went into the kitchen and shook Mr. Teestall's hand. "Thanks again, and good luck with him. You know my number. Oh, and here are the keys to the Tempo. Drive it until it runs out of gas."

"Good luck yourself," Mr. Teestall said.

Outside, a car horn beeped.

Pax went to the guest room and grabbed his suitcase. When he got back to the living room his father had somehow pushed himself up off the couch. His face had swollen. The pores had begun to glisten.

Pax shifted his suitcase to his other hand. "I don't think I should hug you," he said.

"Ah," his father said. He looked down at himself. "'New wine in old bottles.'"

"Matthew, uh, nine?"

His father grunted. "Good boy. Nine-seventeen: 'The bottles break, and the wine runneth out.'"

Pax could smell the vintage radiating from him. "Dad, I have to go . . ."

"Go, go." He waved a hand. "Just don't forget your way back."

Everett took his suitcase and put it in the trunk. "Backseat," he said.

"But I called shotgun," Pax said.

Everett didn't bother to answer.

Pax opened the rear door to a cloud of lilac perfume. He got inside and reluctantly closed the door. "Hi, Aunt Rhonda."

The mayor sat in the front passenger seat. "It's not polite to keep a lady waiting," she said.

"Sorry about that. My dad always says that I'd be late for my own funeral."

She turned and eyed him critically. "I trust Reverend Martin is *comfortable*? Or is there some other custom treatment we can provide for him—a daily foot massage maybe?"

"He's happy," Pax said. "As happy as he can be."

They drove the western loop into town, over the single-lane bridge, past Jo's house.

Rhonda handed him a large manila envelope. "This is the address of the house we rented in Vermont, the keys, and receipts. There's a credit card and some cash in there to get you started—oh, and the prepaid phone. Use that instead of your own cell when you call Everett—and you only call Everett, never me, understand?"

"Yes, ma'am," he said.

She gave him more instructions—most of which she'd told him multiple times before.

"What about the other address?" Pax asked.

"We'll talk about that later, once you get out of detention in Louisville."

"No, we'll talk about it now. That was part of my price."

Everett gazed at him through the rearview mirror. Pax ignored him. "You know I don't have the files on me, right? My father doesn't have them either. A friend of mine outside of Switchcreek has everything—"

"Liar," Everett said.

"—and he'll release them if he doesn't hear from me on a regular basis." Actually, he and Andrew Weygand had never worked out a schedule. He hoped that if Everett killed him, Weygand would find out about it eventually. But then what? Even if he died he wasn't sure he wanted Rhonda indicted. She was the only person holding the town together. It was the threat he needed, not the execution. "In fact, there's one or two things I did not give you a copy of."

"That's it," Everett said, and hit the brakes. The car skewed and shuddered to a stop. "I'm coming back there." He opened the door and hopped out. Pax pushed to the far side of the seat and pulled on the handle—it was locked.

"Everett! Settle down, both of you!" Rhonda said. "Paxton's just trying out his big-boy muscles, aren't you, Paxton?" She looked at him over the seat back, seeming genuinely amused. "I tell you, for a second it was like having Jo Lynn back again."

She handed him an index card. "I'd appreciate it if you

memorized that and then, I don't know, eat it, burn it, whatever you'd do in that spy movie running in your head. And Everett, for goodness' sake, get back in here and close the door before you freeze me to death."

The government car was waiting for him at the Cherokee Hotel, a young soldier already at the wheel. Pax tried to show him the paperwork Dr. Fraelich had worked so hard on, but the boy waved him off. "They'll do all that at the checkpoint," he said. His voice was muffled by the mask. Pax wondered if he would keep it on all the way to Louisville.

Aunt Rhonda took Paxton's hand. "You make sure you keep eating," she said. "You're still scrawny as a barn cat."

Pax climbed into the backseat, and the soldier wheeled the car around. In a block they turned left onto the highway. They crossed the bridge, and then they were over the creek and outside of town. Piney Road went by on their left; then they passed the gravel cutoff that led to the hill behind the graveyard. In only a few minutes they were approaching the north gate, slowing as they passed two towering alabaster crosses that had been planted beside the highway.

Pax had missed the march—he'd sat in the clearing on Mount Clyburn for hours that morning—and in the weeks since he hadn't driven any farther north than Piney Road.

Pax realized the driver was saying something.

"We need your medical papers now." Another masked soldier was waiting outside the car. "And your driver's license."

"Right, right." He rolled down his window and handed the papers and the license to the man—woman?—behind the face mask. "Just a second," Pax said. He got out of the car, started walking back up the road toward the crosses. The driver yelled something at his back.

The crosses were tall as argos, twelve feet high, and white as their skin. They leaned slightly in to each other, their arms almost touching.

He reached out to one of them, pressed his fingers against the rough wood.

The soldier grabbed Paxton's arm—Pax hadn't realized he was holding on to the post. "Dude, what's the matter with you?" the man said.

"Jesus," another one said. "He's bawling like a baby."

"Sorry, sorry," Pax said. He wasn't sure who he was talking to. His legs had gone weak. He gripped the wooden post in a fierce hug.

"Are you sure you should be traveling?" the driver asked him.

"No. Yeah. I mean, I'm fine." He made his arms release the cross, then wiped the back of his hand across his eyes. "I don't know where that came from," he said.

"Get back in the car, sir," one of the soldiers said.

They guided him to the backseat, slammed the door. "I'm not usually like this," Pax said.

"Just don't do that again, okay?" the driver said. The striped crossbars were raised, and the driver hit the gas. Pax fell back against the seat, and the car carried him north.

He'd lived through twelve Chicago winters, but he'd never experienced anything like South Dakota in February. The road crossed an endless blank plain. Thuggish winds kept nudging his rental car onto the shoulder, and even with the heat on full blast, tendrils of intense cold swirled around his feet, licked at him from every seam of the car's interior. He drove hunched over the wheel, squinting through the crusted windshield, muscles tensed. The road revealed itself a few yards at a time through curtains of blowing snow.

He didn't believe the GPS when it told him he'd arrived. He saw no house, no farm, only white on white in every direction. He was a southern boy at heart, and couldn't shake the conviction that if he left the car he'd be carried away across the fields. Next June the final drift would melt to reveal his perfectly preserved corpse.

He zipped his ski jacket up to his chin and pulled on his gloves. The car door squealed as he forced it open, then cold slapped him across the face and he gasped. He walked to the front of the car and turned in place, eyes wide for lights and shapes against the twilight. Nothing.

He started to get back in the car, then had another thought. After all, it was a rental. He climbed up on the hood of the car on all fours, and then carefully stood. The sheet metal plonked beneath his boots.

A hundred yards off to his right he saw a stand of trees, the roofline of a house, and the suggestion of an off-white stripe running from the trees to intersect the road. He hopped back in the car.

The stripe turned out to be a driveway, or at least a path through the snow. He rolled past the ring of trees that guarded the house and then braked to a stop. The house was a long, one-story ranch with a marshmallow cap of snow. A low garage or workshop squatted off to the side.

Standing in front of the house was a bulky figure holding a shotgun across his or her chest.

He stepped out of the car. "Hello?" he called. "I'm looking for the DuChamp house." He walked closer, his hands away from his body—not stick-'em-up high, but enough to show respect for the gun. "My name is Paxton Martin."

The figure came closer. It was an unchanged woman, as far as he could tell, heavily bundled against the cold. "I'm Elly," she said. He'd talked to her on the phone. She was Mr. DuChamp's sister, and she'd moved out of Switchcreek years before the Changes. "Come on in, Paxton."

He jogged back to the car, switched it off, and picked up the nylon duffel from the back seat. A minute later she led him into the house to a mudroom stacked with coats. She held the shotgun and showed him where to hang his jacket and set his hiking boots. "They're in the family room," she said, and nodded toward a doorway.

He went down a short hallway and entered a large, open room. Couches and armchairs faced a huge stone fireplace.

Three faces gazed at him. If he'd never lived in Switchcreek, they might have looked identical.

Rainy jumped from her chair, took a few steps, and stopped. Sandra didn't get up from her place on the couch, but Tommy rose to his feet and stood next to Rainy.

"Merry Christmas," Pax said.

They stared at him. Then Rainy said, "Paxton, it's January."

He looked down at the duffel. "Well, I guess I could take these back." He set down the bag and held out his hand to Tommy. "Thanks for letting me come into your home, Tommy. I know that every visitor is a risk."

Tommy hesitated, and shook his hand. "You'll learn that when you set up your own house," he said. "But some visitors are worth it."

Pax walked a few steps toward the couch where Sandra lay. "How are you doing, sweetie?" he asked.

She looked up at him. The contentment on her face was unmistakable.

"Do you want to see him?" she asked.

He kneeled in front of her. She shifted the bundle in her arms, and pulled back a blanket. He was sleeping, mouth open and eyes closed. His skin was the color of merlot.

"Oh," Pax said. His eyes burned, and he blinked hard. "He's beautiful."

"Isn't he?" Sandra said.

Rainy came up behind Pax and put a hand on his shoulder. "His name's Joseph," she said. "We're calling him Joe."

"I heard." He looked up at her, then back at Tommy. "I guess you all had to scramble to come up with a boy's name."

Tommy said, "We certainly didn't have a list ready."

"What do you think it means, Paxton?" Rainy asked. "Will all of them from this generation be boys, or is he a fluke, or . . . ?"

"I don't know," Pax said. He couldn't see how a generation of males made much sense from an evolutionary point of view—but right now he didn't give a damn about the evolutionary point of view. All he knew was that the Changes weren't over—that they'd never be over. "Every generation is a mystery," he said.

He reached out and touched the boy's cheek. Joseph's lips closed, then opened with a faint smack. "I'm pretty sure, though, that a boy this beautiful is not a mistake."

## Read on for an excerpt from *Pandemonium* by Daryl Gregory

Available from Del Rey

"DEL!"

Lew, My Very Bigger Brother, bellowing from the other end of the atrium. His wife, Amra, shook her head in mock embarrassment. This was part of their shtick: Lew was loud and embarrassing, Amra was socially appropriate.

Lew met me halfway across the floor and grabbed me in a hug, his gut hitting me like a basketball. He'd always been bigger than me, but now he was six inches taller and a hundred pounds heavier. "Jesus Christ!" he said. "What took you so long? The board said your flight got in an hour ago." His beard was bushier than when I'd last seen him a year and a half ago, but it had still failed to colonize the barren patches between ear and chin.

"Sorry about that—something about four bags of heroin up my ass. Hey, Amra."

"Hello, Del."

I hugged her briefly. She smelled good as always. She'd cut her long, shiny black hair into something short and professional.

Lew grabbed the strap from my shoulder and tried to take it from me. "I got it," I said.

"Come on, you look like you haven't slept in a week." He yanked it from me. "Shit, this is heavy. How many more bags do you got?"

"That's it."

"What are you, a fuckin' hobo? Okay, we have to take a shuttle to the parking garage. Follow me." He charged ahead with the duffel on his back.

"Did you hear there was a demon in the airport?" Amra said.

"I was there. They wouldn't let us out of the terminal until he was gone. So what happened to the Cher hair?"

"Oh . . ." She made a gesture like shooing a fly. "Too much. You saw it? Which one was it—not the Kamikaze?" The news tracked them by name, like hurricanes. Most people went their whole lives without seeing one in person. I'd seen five—six, counting today's. I'm lucky that way.

"The Painter, I think. At least, it was making a picture."

Lew glanced back, gave Amra a look. He wanted her to stop talking about it. "Probably a faker," Lew said. "There's a possession conference going on downtown next week. The town'll be full of posers."

"I don't think this guy was faking," I said. That mad grin. That wink. "Afterward he was just crushed. Totally confused."

"I wonder if he even knows how to draw," Amra said.

The tram dropped us at a far parking lot, and then we shivered in the wind while Lew unlocked the car and loaded my duffel into the tiny trunk.

It was new, a bulbous silver Audi that looked futuristic and fast. I thought of my own car, crumpled like a beer can, and tried not to be jealous. The Audi was too small for Lew anyway. He enveloped the steering wheel, elbows out, like he was steering with his stomach. His seat was pushed all the way back, so I sat behind Amra. Lew flew down 294, swearing at drivers and juking between lanes. I should have been used to Lew's driving by then, but the speed and erratic turns had me gripping the back of Amra's seat. I grew up in the suburbs, but every time I came back to Chicago I experienced traffic shock. We were forty minutes from downtown, and there were four crammed lanes on each side of the road, and everyone moving at 70 mph. It was worse than Denver.

"So what have you been doing with yourself?" Lew asked. "You don't call, you don't write, you don't send flowers . . ."

"We missed you at Christmas," Amra said.

"See, Lew? From Amra, that actually means she missed me at Christmas. From you or Mom that would have meant 'How could you have let us down like that?' "

"Then she said it wrong."

They'd only been married for a year and a half, but they'd been dating on and off—mostly on—since college. "So when are you guys going to settle down and make Mom some multiracial grandbabies? The Cyclops has gotta be demanding a little baby action."

Amra groaned. "Do you have to call her that? And you're changing the subject."

"Yeah," Lew said. "Back to your faults as a son and brother. What have you been up to?"

"Well, that's a funny story."

Lew glanced at me in the rearview mirror. Amra turned in her seat to face me, frowning in concern.

"Jeez, guys." I forced a smile. "Can you at least let me segue into this?"

"What is it?" Amra said.

"It's not a big deal. I had a car accident in November, went through a guardrail in the snow, and then—"

Lew snorted in surprise. "Were you drunk?"

"Fuck you. The road was icy, and I just hit the curve too fast and lost control. I went through the rail, and then the car started flipping." My gut tightened, remembering that jolt. My vision had gone dark as I struck the rail, and I'd felt myself pitching forward, as if I were being sucked into a black well. "I ended up at the bottom of a ravine, upside down, and I couldn't get my seatbelt undone." I left out the caved-in roof, the icy water running through the car, my blind panic. "I just hung there until the cops got me out."

"Weren't you hurt?" Amra asked.

I shrugged. "My arms were scraped up, and my back was killing me, but that turned out to be just a pulled muscle. They kept me in the hospital for a day, and then they let me go. And afterward . . . well, all in all I was pretty lucky."

"Lucky?" Lew said. "Why do people say that? You get a tumor, and if it turns out that you can operate on it, people say, gee, that was lucky. No, lucky is *not* getting cancer. Lucky is not getting cancer, then finding ten bucks in your shoe."

"Are you done?" Amra said.

"He totaled his car. He's not that lucky."

Amra shook her head. "You were about to say something else, Del. What happened after the accident?"

"Yeah, afterward." I suddenly regretted bringing it up. I'd thought I could practice on Lew and Amra, get ready for the main event with Mom. Amra looked at me expectantly.

"After the accident, I had some, well, complications, and I needed to go to a different kind of hospital."

Amra frowned in concern. Lew said, "Holy shit, you mean like One-Flew-Over different?"

Amra shushed him. "Are you okay?" The tiny cabin and the

high seat between us made the space simultaneously intimate and insulating.

"I'm fine. Everything worked out."

"Fine, he says. Holy shit. Does Mom know? No, of course not, she would have told me. She would have told me, wouldn't she? Holy shit." He swept down on the rear end of a truck, and for the first time in the trip he slowed down rather than change lanes. "So what were you in for? Did you check yourself in, or did they commit you? Does Mom know?"

"I'll tell her tonight. It's not a big deal."

"You don't have to talk about this if you don't want to," Amra said. "But you should feel free to talk about this. It's not a stigma."

"Come on, it's *sort of* a stigma," Lew said.

I nodded. "There *are* a lot of crazy people in there."

Amra turned back around. "I'm trying to talk seriously. This is important."

"It's not a big deal," I said.

Lew laughed. "Every time you say that it gets more convincing." He gunned the engine, swung around a station wagon, and swerved back right across two lanes, just in time to catch our exit. I braced myself against the door as we swooped into the hard curve of the off ramp.

"So what was it?" Lew asked. He glanced left and merged onto the street. "Thought you were Napoleon? Seeing pink elephants?"

"More like hearing things."

"No shit." I'd shocked him sober.

Amra looked at Lew, back at me. "Is this about the thing that happened when you were little?"

So Lew had told her. Which I should have expected—they were married. Family. “When I was possessed, you mean.”

Amra looked so sad I made myself laugh. “Come on, I barely remember it.”

“You ask me, he was faking,” Lew said. He steered the car onto our block. Familiar trees scrolled past the windows, bare limbs raking a close, steely sky. “Del would always do anything to get Mom’s attention.”

# about the author

Daryl Gregory's short stories have appeared in *The Magazine of Fantasy & Science Fiction, Asimov's,* several year's-best anthologies, and other fine venues. In 2005 he received the *Asimov's* Readers' Award for the novelette "Second Person, Present Tense." He lives with his wife and two children in State College, Pennsylvania, where he writes both fiction and web code.